Hornblower
in the West Indies

C. S. FORESTER

Introduction by Bernard Cornwell

PENGUIN BOOKS

PENGUIN BOOKS

UK | USA | Canada | Ireland | Australia
India | New Zealand | South Africa

Penguin Books is part of the Penguin Random House group of companies
whose addresses can be found at global.penguinrandomhouse.com.

Penguin
Random House
UK

First published in Great Britain by Michael Joseph 1958
Published in Penguin Books 1990
Reissued in Penguin Books 2011, 2018
001

Set in 12.4/14.7pt Monotype Dante
By Palimpsest Book Production Limited, Falkirk, Stirlingshire
Printed in Great Britain by Clays Ltd, St Ives plc

A CIP catalogue record for this book is available from the British Library

ISBN: 978-1-405-93695-8

www.greenpenguin.co.uk

Contents

Introduction

This was the ninth Hornblower to be written and stands tenth in the chronological order of the novels. Strictly, this is not a novel but another collection of short stories, and they were published in 1957. There had been a four-year gap between *Hornblower and the Atropos* and this book, a wait resented by Forester's myriad fans, myself among them, who were impatient for a new Hornblower adventure. But Forester was a sick man. His arteriosclerosis, made worse by a heart attack, had slowed him, and it seems he was reluctant to embark on more adventures with his most famous hero.

Yet at last *Hornblower in the West Indies* appeared, and it was worth the wait. It is set in the years after Waterloo and the book includes one of his best short stories, in which Hornblower makes an official visit to New Orleans and has his curiosity aroused by the merchant ship *Daring*, which is ostensibly carrying French settlers back to France. Those settlers were veterans of Napoleon's Imperial Guard, many of whom did emigrate to Louisiana after the Emperor's defeat, but Hornblower suspects the *Daring*'s voyage has another purpose – a suspicion provoked by the presence of General Cambronne. Cambronne was made famous by his last stand at Waterloo and is a passionate Bonapartist.

Hornblower is right. The *Daring*'s mission is to free Napoleon from St Helena and carry the Emperor back to France. Hornblower must stop him but lacks the force to do it, and so must resort to ingenuity. In the end Hornblower's only weapon is his hard-won honour, and Forester's handling of the theme is masterful.

Hornblower's ingenuity is also on display in the story of the pursuit of the *Estrella del Sur*, a slaver. Hornblower conducts the pursuit aboard the frigate *Clorinda*, captained by Sir Thomas Fell, whom Hornblower dislikes, and it is typical that he therefore treats Sir Thomas with a courtesy that he denies to men he does like. That is a lovely piece of characterization and, almost more than any other book, *Hornblower in the West Indies* demonstrates how character can drive plot – and Forester, of course, had struck pure gold when he invented Hornblower.

There has been much discussion on the origins of Hornblower's character. Various models have been proposed, chief among them Admiral Sir James Gordon and Lord Cochrane. Cochrane, a madcap Scottish naval officer, was certainly extraordinarily brave and had a career that reads more strangely than most fiction. Yet I doubt Cochrane was Forester's blueprint. Forester borrowed from Cochrane's exploits, just as he did from those of Nelson and other naval officers, but Cochrane's character is almost the reverse of Hornblower's. He had a confidence Hornblower lacked and a carelessness that Hornblower would have despised. Forester himself once said that Hornblower was a composite of many real naval officers, but that a substantial part of him was based on Edward Pellew, the son of a Dover packet captain, who rose to become an admiral and the first Viscount Exmouth. Pellew's career at sea was heroic, inspirational and triumphant, but my own conviction is that the greatest part of Hornblower sprang from Forester himself. I believe he drew on his own best qualities, magnified them and salted them with his own faults. Hornblower is a self-portrait. There is no other way, I am certain, that such a series of novels could have been written.

Cecil Scott Forester was born in Egypt to British parents in 1899. His real name was Cecil Lewis Troughton Smith and he was raised in Britain, where, as a child, he was an avid reader, usually the first step in the making of a writer. In 1917, before his eighteenth birthday, he volunteered for the British army, fully expecting to fight on the Western Front, but he was rejected as medically unfit. He was a skinny, short-sighted six-footer who enjoyed sports, but the army's physical examination revealed a dangerously weak heart. So instead of serving as a soldier, Forester entered Guy's Hospital as a medical student – an experience as unhappy as it was unsuccessful – but Forester's ambitions were already fixed on writing. His first efforts failed, but he persevered and in 1924, with *Payment Deferred*, enjoyed his first success. The filming of that novel introduced Forester to Hollywood and, more crucially, California. During the Second World War he moved to the United States at the request of the British government, who wanted him to produce journalism and fiction that would encourage Americans to a favourable view of the British war effort. It was, in short, propaganda, and Forester was good at it. He also discovered he liked the United States and, though he retained British citizenship, he never lived in Britain again. Most of the Hornblower books were written in California, where, with his second wife, he remained until his death in 1966. By then he had become one of the world's most popular authors with almost sixty novels to his name and, even if he had never dreamed up Hornblower, he would be famous as the author of *The African Queen*, *The Gun*, *Brown on Resolution* and *Hunting the Bismarck*.

One theme that runs through all the Hornblower books, indeed through all naval fiction about the Napoleonic wars, is the system of prize money. It seems strange to modern sensibilities, yet it was an integral part of naval life and could make a lucky captain into a very rich man. Any captured ship could be sold, unless it was so rotten that it was good only for the shipbreakers, and the price of the ship was shared between the captain, his crew and whichever admirals were in immediate command of the victorious ship. Hornblower earns a good deal of prize money in his career, but in this book there is an interesting twist. In the peace following the Napoleonic wars the Royal Navy's chief task in the Atlantic was to stop the slave trade and for every slave freed there was a reward of five pounds 'head money'. The reward, like prize money, was instituted to encourage zeal, and while head money was unlikely to make a man rich, it was not negligible. It is typical of Forester to have discovered head money and use it in a story. In his novels we are always confident that he knows of what he speaks (not always true of historical novelists), yet it is not enough for a novelist to be a master of historical details. He has to be a storyteller above everything, and the creator of a world in which the reader wants to stay, and Forester was both those things.

Hornblower in the West Indies ends on a note of sublime happiness. One senses that Forester believed Hornblower's voyages were done, and that his hero, who has served him so well, has reached a safe and happy haven at last. Yet Forester was wrong. Though he was ill, he was to write two more Hornblower novels, *Hornblower and the Hotspur*, which precedes these Caribbean adventures, and *Hornblower and the Crisis*, which will at last see Hornblower home.

St Elizabeth of Hungary

Rear Admiral Lord Hornblower, for all his proud appointment as Commander-in-Chief of His Majesty's Ships and Vessels in the West Indies, paid his official visit to New Orleans in HM schooner *Crab* only mounting two six-pounders and with a crew of no more than sixteen men, not counting supernumeraries.

His Britannic Majesty's Consul-General at New Orleans, Mr Cloudesley Sharpe, remarked on the fact.

'I hardly expected to see Your Lordship in so diminutive a craft,' he said, looking round him. He had driven down in his carriage to the pier against which *Crab* was lying, and had sent his liveried footman to the gangway to announce him, and it had been something of an anticlimax to be received by the trilling of the only two bosun's calls that *Crab* could muster, and to find on the quarterdeck to receive him, besides the Admiral and his flag lieutenant, a mere lieutenant in command.

'The exigencies of the service, sir,' explained Hornblower. 'But if I may lead the way below I can offer you whatever hospitality this temporary flagship of mine affords.'

Mr Sharpe – surely there never was a name that accorded so ill with its possessor's figure, for he was a fat man, a mountain of puffy flesh – squeezed himself into a chair at the table in the pleasant little cabin, and replied to Hornblower's suggestion of breakfast with the statement that he had already broken his fast. He obviously had the gravest doubts as to the quality of any breakfast that could be served in this little ship. Gerard, the flag lieutenant, made himself inconspicuous in a corner of the cabin, notebook and pencil on his knee, while Hornblower reopened the conversation.

'*Phoebe* was struck by lightning off Morant Cape,' said Hornblower. 'She was the ship I had planned to come in. *Clorinda* was already in dock, refitting. And *Roebuck*'s off Curaçao, keeping an eye on the Dutchmen – there's a brisk trade in arms with Venezuela at present.'

'Well I know that,' said Sharpe.

'Those are my three frigates,' said Hornblower. 'With the arrangements all made I judged it better to come in this schooner rather than not to come at all.'

'How are the mighty fallen!' was Mr Sharpe's comment. 'Your Lordship, a commander-in-chief, with no more than three frigates and half a dozen sloops and schooners.'

'Fourteen sloops and schooners, sir,' corrected Hornblower. 'They are very desirable craft for the duties I have to perform.'

'No doubt, my lord,' said Sharpe. 'But I can remember the days when the commander-in-chief on the West India Station disposed of a squadron of ships of the line.'

'That was in time of war, sir,' explained Hornblower, recalling the verbal comments of the First Sea Lord in the interview when he had been offered this command. 'The House of Commons would sooner allow the Royal Navy to rot at its moorings than reimpose the income tax.'

'At any rate, Your Lordship has arrived,' said Sharpe.

'Your Lordship exchanged salutes with Fort St Philip?'

'Gun for gun, as your dispatch informed me had been arranged.'

'Excellent!' said Sharpe.

It had been a strange little formality; all hands on board *Crab* had lined the rail, very properly, during the salute, and the officers had stood at attention on the quarterdeck, but 'all hands' amounted to very little with four men manning the saluting gun, and one at the signal halliards and one at the helm. It had poured with rain, too; Hornblower's glittering uniform had clung damply around him.

'Your Lordship made use of the services of a steam tug?'

'Yes, by George!' exclaimed Hornblower.

'A remarkable experience for Your Lordship, apparently?'

'Indeed, yes,' said Hornblower. 'I –'

He held himself back from giving utterance to all his thoughts on that subject; they would lead to too many exciting irrelevancies. But a steam tug had brought *Crab* against the hundred miles of current from the sea to New Orleans between dawn and dusk, arriving at the very minute the tug captain had predicted. And here was New Orleans, crowded not merely with ocean-going sailing ships, but also with a fleet of long, narrow steamers, manœuvring out into the stream and against piers with a facility (thanks to their two paddle-wheels) that even *Crab* with her handy fore-and-aft rig could not attempt to emulate. And with a thresh of those paddle-wheels they would go flying upstream with a rapidity almost unbelievable.

'Steam has laid open a continent, my lord,' said Sharpe, echoing Hornblower's thoughts. 'A veritable empire. Thousands and thousands of miles of navigable waterways. The population of the Mississippi valley will be counted in millions within a few years.'

Hornblower remembered discussions at home, when he was a half-pay officer awaiting his promotion to flag rank, when the 'steam kettles' had been mentioned. Even the possibility of ocean-going ships propelled by steam had been suggested, and had been properly laughed to scorn – it would mean the ruin of good seamanship. Hornblower had not been quite so sure on either point, but he had been careful to keep his opinions to himself, having no desire to be regarded as a dangerous crank. He did not want to be drawn into any similar discussions now, not even with a mere civilian.

'What intelligence do you have for me, sir?' he asked.

'A considerable amount, my lord.'

Mr Sharpe produced a fold of papers from his tail pocket.

'Here are the latest advices from New Granada – more recent I expect than anything you have had. The insurgents –'

Mr Sharpe entered into a rapid exposition of the military and political situation in Central America. The Spanish colonies were entering into the final stage of their struggle for independence.

'It cannot be long before His Majesty's Government recognizes that independence,' said Sharpe. 'And our Minister in Washington informs me that the Government of the United States meditates a similar recognition. It remains to be seen what the Holy Alliance will have to say on that score, my lord.'

Europe under the rule of absolute monarchy would turn a jaundiced eye upon the establishment of a whole new series of republics, no doubt. But it hardly mattered what Europe had to say, as long as the Royal Navy – even the depleted peacetime navy – controlled the seas, and the two English-speaking governments continued in amity.

'Cuba shows small signs of restlessness,' went on Sharpe, 'and I have information of the issue of further letters of marque by the Spanish Government to vessels sailing from Havana –'

Letters of marque were one of the principal sources of Hornblower's troubles. They were being issued by insurgent and nationalist governments alike, to prey upon ships flying the old flags and the new, and the bearers of letters of marque turned pirates in the twinkling of an eye in the absence of legitimate prizes and efficient prize courts. Thirteen of Hornblower's fourteen small craft were scattered over the Caribbean keeping an eye on the activities of the privateers.

'I have prepared duplicates of my reports for Your Lordship's information,' concluded Sharpe. 'I have them here to give to Your Lordship, along with copies of the complaints of the master-mariners concerned.'

'Thank you, sir,' said Hornblower, while Gerard took the papers into his charge.

'Now for the slave trade, with Your Lordship's permission,' went on Sharpe, opening a fresh series of papers.

The slave trade was as acute a question as piracy,

even more acute in some ways, because the Anti-Slavery Society in England commanded a great deal of powerful and vocal support in both Houses of Parliament, and would raise an even more violent to-do about a cargo of slaves run into Havana or Rio de Janeiro than a shipping company pestered by privateers.

'At this moment, my lord,' said Sharpe, 'a raw hand newly brought from the Slave Coast is selling for eighty pounds in the Havana baracoons – and he costs no more than a pound in trade goods at Whydah. Those profits are tempting, my lord.'

'Naturally,' said Hornblower.

'I have reason to believe that ships of both British and American registry are engaged in the traffic, my lord.'

'So have I.'

The First Sea Lord had tapped ominously on the table in that interview when touching on this part of his instructions to Hornblower. Under the new law British subjects who engaged in the slave trade could be hanged, and the ships seized. But care would be necessary in dealing with ships flying American colours. If they refused to heave-to on the high seas for examination the utmost tact would have to be employed. To shoot away an American spar or to kill an American citizen would mean trouble. America had gone to war with England only nine years before over matters very similar.

'We want no trouble, my lord,' said Sharpe. He had a pair of hard, intelligent, grey eyes deep-set in his puffy face.

'I am aware of that, sir.'

'And in this connection, my lord, I must employ

special emphasis in calling Your Lordship's attention to a vessel making ready for sea here in New Orleans.'

'Which ship is this?'

'She is visible from the deck, my lord. In fact –' Sharpe struggled out of his chair and walked to the cabin window. '– yes, there she is. What do you make of her, my lord?'

Hornblower looked out from beside Sharpe. He saw a beautiful ship of eight hundred tons or more. Her fine lines, the lofty rake of her masts, the wide spread of her yards, were all clear indications of speed, for which some sacrifice of cargo-carrying capacity had been made. She was flush-decked, with six painted gun ports along each side. American shipbuilders had always evinced a tendency towards building fast ships, but this was an advanced example of the type.

'Are there guns behind those ports?' asked Hornblower.

'Twelve-pounders, my lord.'

Even in these days of peace it was not unusual for merchant vessels to carry guns, whether for voyages in the West Indies or the East, but this was a heavier armament than usual.

'She was built as a privateer,' said Hornblower.

'Quite right, my lord. She's the *Daring*; she was built during the war and made one voyage and took six prizes from us before the Treaty of Ghent. And now, my lord?'

'She could be a slaver.'

'Your Lordship is right again, of course.'

That heavy armament would be desirable in a slaver anchoring up a West African river liable to a treacherous attack; she could easily have a slave deck with that flush build; her speed would minimize deaths among the slaves during the Middle Passage; her lack of capacity for bulk cargo would be unimportant in a slaver.

'*Is* she a slaver?' asked Hornblower.

'Apparently not, my lord, despite her appearance. She is being chartered to carry a great many men, all the same.'

'I would like you to explain further, if you please, Mr Sharpe.'

'I can only tell Your Lordship the facts as disclosed to me. She is under charter to a French general, Count Cambronne.'

'Cambronne? Cambronne? The man who commanded the Imperial Guard at Waterloo?'

'That's the man, my lord.'

'The man who said, "The Old Guard dies but does not surrender"?'

'Yes, my lord, although report says he actually used a ruder expression. He was wounded and taken prisoner, but he did not die.'

'So I have heard. But what does he want with this ship?'

'It is all open and above board, apparently. After the war, Boney's Old Guard formed an organization for mutual aid. In 1816 they decided to become colonists – Your Lordship must have heard something about the project?'

'Hardly anything.'

'They came out and seized an area of land on the coast of Texas, the province of Mexico adjacent to this State of Louisiana.'

'I have heard about it, but that is the extent of my knowledge.'

'It was easy enough to start, with Mexico in the throes

of her revolt against Spain. There was no opposition to them, as you understand, my lord. But it was not so easy to continue. I cannot imagine that soldiers of the Old Guard would ever make good agriculturists. And on that pestilential coast – It is a series of dreary lagoons, with hardly an inhabitant.'

'The scheme failed?'

'As Your Lordship might expect. Half of them died of malaria and yellow fever, and half of the rest simply starved. Cambronne has come out from France to carry the survivors home, five hundred of them. The Government of the United States never liked the project, as Your Lordship can imagine, and now the insurgent government is strong enough to take exception to the presence on the shores of Mexico of a large body of trained soldiers, however peaceable their intentions. Your Lordship can see Cambronne's story could be perfectly true.'

'Yes.'

An eight-hundred-ton ship, equipped as a slaver, could pack five hundred soldiers on board and feed them during a long passage.

'Cambronne is stocking her largely with rice and water – slave rations, my lord, but the best adapted to the purpose for that very reason.'

The slave trade had had long experience of how to keep alive a close-packed body of men.

'If Cambronne is going to take them back to France I should do nothing to hinder him,' said Hornblower. 'Rather on the contrary.'

'Exactly, my lord.'

Sharpe's grey eyes met Hornblower's in an expressionless stare. The presence of five hundred trained soldiers afloat in the Gulf of Mexico was very much the concern of the British admiral commanding in chief, when the shores of the Gulf and of the Caribbean were in as much of a turmoil as at present. Bolivar and the other Spanish-American insurgents would pay a high price for their services in the present war. Or someone might be meditating the conquest of Haiti, or a piratical descent upon Havana. Any sort of filibustering expedition was possible. The actual Bourbon Government in France might be looking for a pie in which to put a finger, for that matter, a chance to snap up a colony and confront the English-speaking powers with a *fait accompli*.

'I'll keep my eye on them until they are safely out of the way,' said Hornblower.

'I have called Your Lordship's attention officially to the matter,' said Sharpe.

It would be one more drain upon Hornblower's limited resources for the policing of the Caribbean; he already was wondering which of his few craft he could detach to observe the Gulf Coast.

'And now, my lord,' said Sharpe, 'it is my duty to discuss the details of Your Lordship's stay here in New Orleans. I have arranged a programme of official calls for Your Lordship. Does Your Lordship speak French?'

'Yes,' said Hornblower, fighting down the urge to say, 'My Lordship does.'

'That is excellent, because French is commonly spoken among good society here. Your Lordship will, of course, be calling upon the naval authorities here, and upon the Governor. There is an evening reception planned for Your Lordship. My carriage is, of course, at Your Lordship's disposition.'

'That is extremely kind of you, sir.'

'No kindness at all, my lord. It is a great pleasure to me to assist in making Your Lordship's visit to New Orleans as enjoyable as possible. I have here a list of the prominent people Your Lordship will meet, along with brief notes regarding them. Perhaps it might be as well if I explain it to Your Lordship's flag lieutenant?'

'Certainly,' said Hornblower; he was able now to relax his attention a little; Gerard was a good flag lieutenant and had supported his Commander-in-Chief very satisfactorily during the ten months that Hornblower had held command. He supplied some of the social flair that Hornblower was too indifferent to acquire. The business was rapidly settled.

'Very well, then, my lord,' said Sharpe. 'Now I can take my leave. I will have the pleasure of seeing Your Lordship again at the Governor's house.'

'I am deeply obliged to you, sir.'

This city of New Orleans was an enchanting place. Hornblower was bubbling internally with excitement at the prospect of exploring it. Nor was he the only one, as appeared as soon as Sharpe had taken his leave, when Lieutenant Harcourt, captain of the *Crab*, intercepted Hornblower on the quarterdeck.

'Pardon, my lord,' he said, saluting. 'Are there any orders for me?'

There could be no doubt about what Harcourt had in mind. Forward of the mainmast most of the crew of *Crab* were congregated together looking eagerly aft – in a tiny ship like this everyone was aware of everyone else's business, and discipline ran on lines different from those in a big ship.

'Can you trust your men to be steady on shore, Mr Harcourt?' asked Hornblower.

'Yes, my lord.'

Hornblower looked forward again. The hands looked remarkably smart – they had been labouring on making new clothes for themselves all the way from Kingston, from the moment when it was announced that *Crab* would have the astonishing distinction of flying the Admiral's flag. They were wearing neat blue frock-jumpers and white ducks and shady straw hats;

Hornblower saw their self-conscious poses as he glanced towards them – they knew perfectly well what was being discussed. These were peacetime sailors, voluntarily enlisted: Hornblower had had twenty years of wartime service with pressed crews who could never be trusted not to desert, and even now he had consciously to adjust his mind to the change.

'If you could give me notice of when you intend to sail, sir – I mean my lord,' said Harcourt.

'Until dawn tomorrow in any case,' said Hornblower coming to a sudden decision; his day was full until then.

'Aye aye, my lord.'

Would the grogshops of New Orleans waterfront be any different from the grogshops of Kingston or Port of Spain?

'Now perhaps I can have my breakfast, Mr Gerard,' said Hornblower. 'Unless you have any objection?'

'Aye aye, my lord,' answered Gerard, carefully ignoring the sarcasm. He had long learned that his Admiral objected to nothing in the world as much as having to be active before breakfast.

It was after breakfast that a coloured man, trotting

bare-footed along the pier, came bearing on his head a basket of fruit which he handed in at the gangway at the moment when Hornblower was about to start off on his official round of calls.

'There's a note with it, my lord,' said Gerard. 'Shall I open it?'

'Yes.'

'It is from Mr Sharpe,' reported Gerard, after breaking the seal, and then some seconds later, 'I think you had better read this yourself, my lord.'

Hornblower took the thing impatiently.

My lord (read the note),

I have imposed upon myself the pleasure of sending some fruit to Your Lordship.

It is my duty to inform Your Lordship that I have just received information that the freight which Count Cambronne brought out here from France, and which has been lying in bond in charge of the United States Customs Services, will shortly be transferred by lighter through the agency of a bonded carrier to the 'Daring'. As Your Lordship will, of course, understand, this is an indication that the 'Daring' will be sailing soon. My information is that the amount of bonded freight is very considerable, and I am endeavouring to discover in what it consists. Perhaps Your Lordship might, from Your Lordship's coign of vantage, find an opportunity of observing the nature of this freight.

I am, with great respect,

Your Lordship's humble and obedient servant,

Cloudesley Sharpe,

HBM's Consul-General at New Orleans.

Now what could Cambronne have possibly brought from France in large amount that could be legitimately needed for the purpose he had avowed when he chartered the *Daring*? Not personal effects, certainly. Not food or liquor – he could pick those up cheaply in New Orleans. Then what? Warm-weather clothing would be a possible explanation. Those Guardsmen might well need it when returning to France from the Gulf of Mexico. It was possible. But a French general, with five hundred men of the Imperial Guard at his disposal, would bear the closest watching when the Caribbean was in such a turmoil. It would be a great help to know what kind of freight he was shipping.

'Mr Harcourt!'

'Sir – my lord!'

'I would like your company in the cabin for a moment, if you please.'

The young lieutenant stood at attention in the cabin a little apprehensively waiting to hear what his Admiral had to say.

'This isn't a reprimand, Mr Harcourt,' said Hornblower testily. 'Not even an admonition.'

'Thank you, my lord,' said Harcourt, relaxing.

Hornblower took him to the cabin window and pointed out through it, just as Sharpe had done previously.

'That's the *Daring*,' he said. 'An ex-privateer, now under charter to a French general.'

Harcourt looked his astonishment.

'That is the case,' went on Hornblower. 'And today she will be taking on some cargo out of bond. It will be brought round to her out of bond by lighter.'

'Yes, my lord.'

'I want to know as much about that cargo as possible.'

'Yes, my lord.'

'Naturally, I do not want the world to know that I am interested. I want nobody to know unnecessarily.'

'Yes, my lord. I could use a telescope from here and see a good deal, with luck.'

'Very true. You can take note of whether it is bales or boxes or bags. How many there are of each. From the tackle employed you can guess at the weights. You can do all that.'

'Aye aye, my lord.'

'Make careful note of all you see.'

'Aye aye, my lord.'

Hornblower fixed his eyes on his youthful flag captain's face, trying to estimate his discretion. He remembered so well the emphatic words of the First Sea Lord regarding the necessity for the utmost tenderness regarding American susceptibilities. Hornblower decided the young man could be trusted.

'Now, Mr Harcourt,' he said, 'pay special attention to what I have to say. The more I know about that cargo the better. But don't go at it like a bull at a gate. Should an opportunity present itself for finding out what it is, you must seize upon it. I can't imagine what that opportunity may be, but opportunities come to those who are ready for them.'

Long, long ago, Barbara had said to him that good fortune is the portion of those who merit it.

'I understand, my lord.'

'If the slightest hint of this gets out – if the Americans or the French get to know what you are doing – you will be sorry you were ever born, Mr Harcourt.'

'Yes, my lord.'

'I've no use for a dashing young officer in this connection, Mr Harcourt. I want someone with ingenuity, someone with cunning. You are sure you understand?'

'Yes, my lord.'

Hornblower at last took his eyes from Harcourt's face. He himself had been a dashing young officer once. Now he had far more sympathy than ever before with the older men who had entrusted him with enterprises. A senior officer had perforce to trust his juniors, while still carrying the ultimate responsibility. If Harcourt should blunder, if he should be guilty of some indiscretion leading to a diplomatic protest, it would certainly be true that he might wish he had never been born – Hornblower would see to that. But Hornblower would be wishing he himself had never been born, too. But there was no useful purpose to be served in pointing that out.

'That is all, then, Mr Harcourt.'

'Aye aye, sir.'

'Come on, Mr Gerard. We're late already.'

The upholstery of Mr Sharpe's carriage was of green satin, and the carriage was admirably sprung, so that although it lurched and swayed over the uneven street surfaces, it did not jolt or jerk. Yet after five minutes of lurching and swaying – the carriage had been standing for some time in the hot May sun – Hornblower felt himself turning as green as the upholstery. The Rue Royale, the Place d'Armes, the Cathedral, received hardly a glance from him. He welcomed the halts despite the fact that each halt meant a formal meeting with strangers, the kind of meeting he disliked most heartily. He stood and gulped in the humid air during the blessed moments between descending from the carriage and entering in under the ornate porticoes that stood to welcome him. It had never occurred to him before that an admiral's full dress uniform might with advantage be made of something thinner than broadcloth, and he had worn his broad red ribbon and his glittering star far too often by now to feel the slightest pleasure in displaying it.

At the Naval Headquarters he drank an excellent Madeira; the General gave him a heavy Marsala; at the Governor's mansion he was given a tall drink which had been iced (presumably with ice sent down during the winter from New England and preserved in an ice-house until nearly at midsummer it was more precious than gold) extraordinarily to the point where actual frost was visible on the tumbler. The delicious cold contents of that tumbler disappeared rapidly, and the tumbler was as rapidly refilled. He checked himself abruptly when he found himself talking a little too loudly and dogmatically regarding some point of trivial importance. He was glad to catch Gerard's eye and withdraw as gracefully as he could; he was also glad that Gerard seemed perfectly cool and sober and had charge of the card-case, dropping the necessary number of cards into the silver trays that the coloured butlers held out to receive them. By the time he reached Sharpe's house he was glad to see a friendly face – friendly even though it was only that morning that he had first set eyes on it.

'It is an hour before the guests are due to arrive, my

lord,' said Sharpe. 'Would Your Lordship care for a short rest?'

'I would indeed,' said Hornblower.

Mr Sharpe's house had a contrivance which merited much attention. It was a douche bath – Hornblower only knew the French name for it. It was in a corner of the bathroom, floored and walled with the most excellent teak; from the ceiling hung an apparatus of perforated zinc, and from this hung a bronze chain. When Hornblower stood under this apparatus and pulled the chain a deluge of delicious cold water came streaming down on him from some unseen reservoir above. It was as refreshing as ever it had been to stand under the wash-deck pump on the deck of a ship at sea, with the additional advantage of employing fresh water – and in his present condition, after his experiences of the day, it was doubly refreshing. Hornblower stood under the raining water for a long time, reviving with every second. He made a mental note to install a similar contrivance at Smallbridge House if ever he found himself at home again.

A coloured valet in livery stood by with towels to save him from the reheating exertion of drying himself, and while he was being dabbed a knock at the door heralded Gerard's entrance.

'I sent to the ship for a fresh shirt for you, my lord,' he said.

Gerard was really displaying intelligence; Hornblower put on the fresh shirt with gratitude, but it was with distaste that he tightened his stook and pulled on his heavy uniform coat again. He hung the red ribbon over his shoulder, adjusted his star, and was ready to face the next situation. The darkness of evening was descending, but it had not brought much relief from the heat; on the contrary, the drawing room of Mr Sharpe's house was brightly lit with wax candles that made it feel like an oven. Sharpe was awaiting him, wearing a black coat; his ruffled shirt made his bulky form appear larger than ever. Mrs Sharpe, sweeping in in turquoise blue, was of much the same size; she curtseyed deeply in response to Hornblower's bow when Sharpe presented him, and made him welcome to the house in a French whose soft tang rang pleasantly on Hornblower's ears.

'A little refreshment, my lord?' asked Sharpe.

'Not at present, thank you, sir,' said Hornblower hastily.

'We are expecting twenty-eight guests besides Your Lordship and Mr Gerard,' said Sharpe. 'Some of them Your Lordship already met during Your Lordship's official calls today. In addition there are –'

Hornblower did his best to keep the list of names in his mind with mental labels attached. Gerard, who came in and found himself a secluded chair, listened intently.

'And there will be Cambronne, of course,' said Sharpe.

'Indeed?'

'I could hardly give a dinner party of this magnitude without inviting the most distinguished foreign visitor, after Your Lordship, present in this city.'

'Of course not,' agreed Hornblower.

Yet six years of peace had hardly stilled the prejudices established during twenty years of war, there was something a little unnatural about the prospect of meeting a French general on friendly terms, especially the late Commander-in-Chief of Bonaparte's Imperial Guard, and the meeting might be a little strained because Bonaparte was under lock and key in St Helena and complaining bitterly about it.

'The French Consul-General will accompany him,' said Sharpe. 'And there will be the Dutch Consul-General, the Swedish –'

The list seemed interminable; there was only just time to complete it before the first of the guests was announced. Substantial citizens and their substantial wives; the naval and military officers whom he had already met, and their ladies; the diplomatic officers; soon even that vast drawing room was crowded, men bowing and women curtseying. Hornblower straightened up from a bow to find Sharpe at his elbow again.

'I have the honour of making two distinguished figures acquainted with each other,' he said, in French.

'Son Excellence Rear Admiral Milord Hornblower, Chevalier de l'Ordre Militaire du Bain. Son Excellence le Lieutenant-General le Comte de Cambronne, Grand Cordon de la Legion d'Honneur.'

Hornblower could not help being impressed, even at this moment, at the neat way in which Sharpe had evaded the thorny question of whom to introduce to whom, a French general and count and an English admiral and peer. Cambronne was an immensely tall bean-pole of a man. Across one lean cheek and the beaky nose ran a purple scar – perhaps the wound he had received at Waterloo; perhaps a wound received at Austerlitz or Jena or any other of the battles in which the French Army had overthrown nations. He was wearing a blue uniform covered with gold lace, girt about with the watered red silk ribbon of the Legion of Honour, a vast plaque of gold on his left breast.

'Enchanted to make your acquaintance, sir,' said Hornblower in his best French.

'No more enchanted than I am to make yours, milord,' replied Cambronne. He had a cold, greeny-grey eye with a twinkle in it; a grey cat's-whisker moustache adorned his upper lip.

'The Baroness de Vautour,' said Sharpe. 'The Baron de Vautour, His Most Christian Majesty's Consul-General.'

Hornblower bowed and said again that he was enchanted. His Most Christian Majesty was Louis XVIII of France, using the Papal title conferred on his house centuries earlier.

'The Count is being mischievous,' said Vautour. He indicated Cambronne's star. 'He is wearing the Grand Eagle, given him during the last régime. Officially the Grand Cordon has been substituted, as our host very properly said.'

Vautour called attention to his own star, a more modest affair. Cambronne's displayed an immense eagle of gold, the badge of the now defunct French Empire.

'I won this on the field of battle,' said Cambronne.

'Don Alphonso de Versage,' said Sharpe. 'His Most Catholic Majesty's Consul-General.'

This was the representative of Spain, then. A word or two with him regarding this pending cession of Florida might be informative, but Hornblower had hardly time to exchange formal courtesies before another presentation was being made. It was some time before Hornblower had a breathing space, and could look round the pretty scene in the candlelight, with the uniforms and the broadcloth coats, the bare arms and shoulders of the women in their bright gowns and flashing jewellery, and the two Sharpes moving unobtrusively through the throng marshalling their guests in order of precedence. The entrance of the Governor and his lady was the signal for the announcement of dinner.

The dining room was as vast as the drawing room; the table with covers for thirty-two stood comfortably in it with ample room all round for the numerous footmen. The candlelight was more subdued here, but it glittered impressively on the silver which crowded the long table. Hornblower, seated between the Governor's lady and Mrs Sharpe, reminded himself that he must be alert and careful regarding his table manners; it was the more necessary to be alert because he had to speak French on one side of him and English on the other. He looked dubiously at the six different wine glasses that stood at each place – the sherry was already being poured into the first of the glasses. He could see Cambronne seated between two pretty girls and obviously making himself pleasant to both of them. He did not look as if he had a care in the world; if he were meditating a filibustering expedition it did not weigh very heavily on his mind.

A steaming plate of turtle soup, thick with gobbets of green fat. This was to be a dinner served in the Continental fashion which had come in after Waterloo, with no hodge-podge of dishes set out on the table for the guests to help themselves. He spooned cautiously at the hot soup, and applied himself to making small talk with his dinner partners. Dish succeeded dish, and soon he had to face in the hot room the delicate question of etiquette as to whether it was more ungentlemanly to mop the sweat from his face or to leave it there, flowing and visible; his discomfort decided him in the end to mop, furtively. Now Sharpe was catching his eye, and he had to rise to his feet, striving to make his stupefied brain work while the buzz of conversation died down. He raised his glass.

'The President of the United States,' he said; he had been about to continue, idiotically, 'Long may he reign.' He checked himself with a jerk and went on, 'Long may the great nation of which he is President enjoy prosperity and the international amity of which this gathering is symbolic.'

The toast was drunk with acclaim, with nothing said about the fact that over half the continent Spaniards and Spanish-Americans were busy killing each other. He sat down and mopped again. Now Cambronne was on his feet.

'His Britannic Majesty George the Fourth, King of Great Britain and Ireland.'

The toast was drunk and now it was Hornblower's turn again, as evidenced by Sharpe's glance. He stood up, glass in hand, and began the long list.

'His Most Christian Majesty. His Most Catholic Majesty. His Most Faithful Majesty.' That disposed of France and Spain and Portugal. 'His Majesty the King of the Netherlands.'

For the life of him he could not remember who came next. But Gerard caught his despairing eye and gave a significant jerk of his thumb.

'His Majesty the King of Sweden,' gulped Hornblower. 'His Majesty the King of Prussia.'

A reassuring nod from Gerard told him that he had now included all the nations represented, and he plucked the rest of his speech out of the whirlpool of his mind.

'Long may Their Majesties reign, in increasing honour and glory.'

Well, that was over, and he could sit down again. But now the Governor was on his feet, speaking in rhetorical phrases, and it broke in upon Hornblower's dulled intelligence that his own health was the next to be drunk. He tried to listen. He was aware of keen glances shot at him from around the table when the Governor alluded to the defence of this city of New Orleans from the 'misguided hordes' who had assailed it in vain – the allusion was perhaps inevitable even though it was over six years since the battle – and he tried to force a smile. At long last the Governor reached his end.

'His Lordship Admiral Hornblower, and I couple with his name a toast to the British Navy.'

Hornblower climbed back upon his feet as the approving murmur of the company died down.

'Thank you for this unexpected honour,' he said, and gulped as he sought for further words. 'And to have my name coupled with that of the great navy in which it has been my privilege to serve so long is an additional honour for which to thank you.'

The ladies were all rising, now that he had sat down, and he stood again while they withdrew. The highly trained footmen swept the table clear of its accessories in a trice, and the men gathered to one end of the table as the decanter was put into circulation. The glasses were filled as Sharpe brought one of the merchants present into the conversation with a question about the cotton crop. It was safe ground from which to make brief and cautious sorties upon the much more debatable ground of world conditions. But only a few minutes later the butler came in and murmured something to Sharpe, who turned to convey the news he brought to the French Consul-General. Vautour rose to his feet with an expression of dismay.

'Perhaps you will accept my excuses, sir,' he said. 'I much regret the necessity.'

'No more than I regret it, Baron,' said Sharpe. 'I trust it is only a slight indisposition.'

'I trust so,' said Vautour.

'The Baroness finds herself indisposed,' explained Sharpe to the company. 'I am sure you gentlemen will all join me in hoping, as I said, that the indisposition is slight, and regretting that it involves the loss to us of the Baron's charming company.'

There was a sympathetic murmur, and Vautour turned to Cambronne.

'Shall I send back the carriage for you, Count?' he asked.

Cambronne pulled at his cat's-whisker moustache.

'Perhaps it might be better if I came with you,' he said. 'Much as I regret leaving this delightful assembly.'

The two Frenchmen took their leave, after polite farewells.

'It is a great pleasure having made your acquaintance, milord,' said Cambronne, bowing to Hornblower. The stiffness of his bow was mitigated by the twinkle in his eye.

'It has been a profound experience to meet so distinguished a soldier of the late Empire,' replied Hornblower.

The Frenchmen were escorted out of the room by Sharpe, voluble in his regrets.

'Your glasses need refilling, gentlemen,' said Sharpe on his return.

There was nothing Hornblower disliked more than drinking large glasses of port in a hot and humid room, even though he now found himself free to discuss the Florida question with the Spanish Consul-General. He was glad when Sharpe made the move to rejoin the ladies. Somewhere within earshot of the drawing room a string orchestra was playing, but luckily in a subdued manner, so that Hornblower was spared much of the irritation that he usually suffered when he was compelled to listen to music with his tone-deaf ear. He found himself sitting next to one of the pretty young women beside whom Cambronne had been sitting at dinner. In reply to her questions he was forced to admit that on this, his first day, he had seen almost nothing of the city of New Orleans, but the admission led to a discussion of other places he had visited. Two cups of coffee, poured for him by a footman passing round the drawing room, cleared his head a little; the young woman was attentive and listened well, and nodded sympathetically when the conversation revealed that Hornblower had left behind, at the call of duty, a wife and a ten-year-old son in England.

Gradually the night wore on, and at last the Governor and his lady rose to their feet and the party was over. There were the last few weary minutes of awkward conversation as the carriages were announced one by one, and then Sharpe returned to the drawing room after escorting the last of the guests to the door.

'A successful evening, I fancy. I trust Your Lordship agrees with me,' he said, and turned to his wife. 'But I must ask you, my dear, to remember to reprimand Grover about the soufflé.'

The entry of the butler with another murmured message prevented Mrs Sharpe's reply.

'Your Lordship's pardon for a moment,' said Sharpe. He wore an expression of dismay and hastened out of the room, leaving Hornblower and Gerard to begin polite words of thanks to his hostess for his pleasant evening.

'Cambronne's stolen a march on us!' exclaimed Sharpe, returning with a rapid waddle. '*Daring* left her mooring three hours ago! Cambronne must have gone on board her the moment he left here.'

He swung round on his wife.

'Was the Baroness really ill?' he demanded of her.

'She seemed decidedly faint,' replied Mrs Sharpe.

'It must have been all a plant,' said Sharpe. 'She was acting. Cambronne put the Vautours up to it because he wanted a chance to get clear away.'

'What do you think he means to do?' asked Hornblower.

'God knows. But I expect he was disconcerted by the arrival of a King's ship here. His leaving in this fashion means he's up to no good. San Domingo – Cartagena – where'll he take that Imperial Guard of his?'

'I'll get after him in any case,' said Hornblower, rising to his feet.

'You'll find it hard to overtake him,' said Sharpe –

the fact that he said 'you' and not 'Your Lordship' was a proof of his agitation. 'He has taken two tugs – the *Lightning* and the *Star* – and with the new lighthouses on the river a galloping horse wouldn't overtake him before he reaches the Pass. He'll be clear out to sea by daylight. I don't know if we can find a tug for you tonight in any case, my lord.'

'I'll start after him, all the same,' said Hornblower.

'I've ordered the carriage round, my lord,' said Sharpe. 'Forgive us, my dear, if we leave without ceremony.'

Mrs Sharpe received the hasty bows of the three men; the butler was waiting with their hats; the carriage stood at the door, and they scrambled in.

'Cambronne's bonded freight went on board at nightfall,' said Sharpe. 'My man is meeting me at your ship with his report.'

'That may help us make up our minds,' said Hornblower.

The carriage lurched in along the pitch-dark streets.

'May I make a suggestion, my lord?' asked Gerard.

'Yes. What is it?'

'Whatever scheme Cambronne has in mind, my lord, Vautour is party to it. And he is a servant of the French Government.'

'You're right. The Bourbons want a finger in every pie,' agreed Sharpe, thoughtfully. 'They take every opportunity to assert themselves. Anyone would think it was them that we beat at Waterloo, and not Boney.'

The sound of the horses' hoofs changed suddenly as the carriage reached the pier. They stopped, and Sharpe had the door open before the footman could leap down from the box, but as the three men scrambled out he stood beside the door, hat in hand, his dark face illuminated by the carriage lamps.

'Wait!' snapped Sharpe.

They almost ran along the pier to where the glimmer of a lamp revealed the gangway; the two hands of the anchor watch stood at attention in the darkness as they hastened on board.

'Mr Harcourt!' shouted Hornblower as soon as his foot touched the deck; this was no time to stand on ceremony. There was a light in the companion and Harcourt was there.

'Here, my lord.'

Hornblower pushed his way into the after cabin; a lighted lantern dangled from the deck-beam, and Gerard brought in another one.

'What's your report, Mr Harcourt?'

'The *Daring* sailed at five bells in the first watch, my lord,' said Harcourt. 'She had two tugs with her.'

'I know. What else?'

'The lighter with the freight came alongside her early in the second dogwatch. Just after dark, my lord.'

A short, dark man came unobtrusively into the cabin as he spoke, and remained in the background.

'Well?'

'This gentleman whom Mr Sharpe sent kept watch as well as me on what they took on board, my lord.'

'What was it?'

'I kept count as they swayed it up, my lord. They had lights in the mizzen-stay.'

'Well?'

Harcourt had a piece of paper in his hand, and he proceeded to read from it.

29

'There were twenty-five wooden cases, my lord.' Harcourt went on just in time to forestall an exasperated exclamation from Hornblower. 'I recognized those cases, my lord. They are the usual ones in which muskets are shipped, twenty-four stand of arms in each case.'

'Six hundred muskets and bayonets,' put in Gerard, calculating rapidly.

'I guessed as much,' said Sharpe.

'What else?' demanded Hornblower.

'There were twelve large bales, my lord. Oblong ones, and twenty other bales, long, narrow ones.'

'Couldn't you guess –'

'Would you hear the report of the hand I sent, my lord?'

'Very well.'

'Come down here, Jones,' yelled Harcourt up the companion, and then turned back to Hornblower. 'Jones is a good swimmer, my lord. I sent him and another hand off in the quarter-boat, and Jones swam to the lighter. Tell His Lordship what you found, Jones.'

Jones was a skinny, stunted young man, who came in blinking at the lights, ill at ease in this distinguished company. When he opened his mouth he spoke with the accent of Seven Dials.

'Uniforms, they was, in them big bales, sir.'

'How do you know?'

'I swum to the side of the lighter, sir. I could reach over an' feel 'em, sir.'

'Did anyone see you?' This was from Sharpe.

'No, sir. No one didn't see me at all, sir. They was all busy swayin' up the cases. Uniforms, they was, in the bales, like I said, sir. What I could feel through the sacking was buttons, sir. Not flat buttons, sir, like yours, sir. Round buttons, like bullets, sir, rows of 'em, on each coat. An' I thought I could feel hembroidery, too, gold lace, p'raps, sir. Uniforms, they was, sir, I'm sure of it.'

The dark man came forward at this moment; in his hands was a limp something that looked like a drowned black cat. Jones pointed to the object before he went on.

'I couldn't guess for the life of me what was in the other bales, sir, the long ones. So I outs with my knife –'

'You're sure no one saw you?'

'Certain sure, sir. I outs with my knife an' cuts the stitching at the end. They'll think it come apart in the handlin', sir. An' I takes the end one out an' I swims with it back to the quarter-boat, sir.'

The dark man held it forward for inspection, and Hornblower took it gingerly, a black, soggy, wet mass of hair, but his fingers encountered metal as he turned it in his hands.

'Heagles, sir,' said Jones.

There was a brass chain and a big brass badge – the same displayed eagle as he had seen that evening on Cambronne's chest. What he held in his hands was a bearskin uniform cap, soaked with its recent immersion, and adorned with the brass finery.

'Is that what the Imperial Guard wore, my lord?' suggested Gerard.

'Yes,' said Hornblower.

He had seen prints for sale often enough purporting to illustrate the last stand of the Guard at Waterloo. In London now the Guards sported bearskin caps not unlike this that he held in his hand; they had been awarded to the Guards in recognition of their overthrow of the Imperial Guard at the crisis of the battle.

'Then we know all we need to know,' said Sharpe.

'I must try and catch him,' said Hornblower. 'Call all hands, Mr Harcourt.'

'Aye aye, my lord.'

After the automatic reply Harcourt opened his mouth again to speak, but he could make no sound come from it.

'I remember,' said Hornblower, his cup of unhappiness filling to the brim. 'I said I would not need the hands before morning.'

'Yes, my lord. But they'll not be far. I'll send along the waterfront and find 'em. I'll have 'em back here in an hour.'

'Thank you, Mr Harcourt. Do your best. Mr Sharpe, we shall need to be towed as far as the Pass. Will you send and order a steam tug for us?'

Sharpe looked over at the dark man who had brought in the bearskin cap.

'Doubt if there'll be one before noon,' said the dark man. '*Daring* took two – and I know now why she did. The *President Madison*'s laid up. *Toueur*'s gone up to Baton Rouge with flat boats. *Ecrevisse* – the one that brought this ship up – went down again in the afternoon. I think *Temeraire*'s on her way up. We might be able to get her to turn round as soon as she arrives. And that's all there are.'

'Noon,' said Hornblower. 'Thirteen hours' start. *Daring*'ll be at sea before we leave here.'

'And she's one of the fastest ships built,' said Sharpe.

'She logged fifteen knots when she was being chased by *Tenedos* during the war.'

'What's the Mexican port where she'll take the soldiers on board?'

'It's only a village on a lagoon, Corpus Christi, my lord. Five hundred miles and a fair wind.'

Hornblower could picture the *Daring*, with her beautiful lines and enormous spread of canvas, booming along before the trade wind. The little *Crab* in whose cabin he stood was not intended for fast ocean runs. She had been built and rigged small and handy, to work in and out of obscure inlets, doing the police work of the West Indian archipelago. On the run to Corpus Christi *Daring* would certainly gain several hours, a day or more, perhaps, to add to the twelve hours' lead she already enjoyed. It would not take long to march or to ferry five hundred disciplined men on board, and then she would sail again. Where? Hornblower's weary brain baulked at the contemplation of the immensely complex political situation in the lands within easy run of Corpus Christi. If he could guess, he might be able to anticipate *Daring*'s arrival at the danger point; if he merely pursued her to Corpus Christi he would almost certainly arrive there to find her already gone, soldiers and all, having vanished out into the trackless sea on whatever errand of mischief she meditated.

'*Daring*'s an American ship, my lord,' said Sharpe, to add to his troubles.

That was an important point, a very important point. *Daring* had an ostensibly legal errand, and she flew the Stars and Stripes. He could think of no excuse for taking her into port for examination. His instructions had been very strict regarding his treatment of the American flag. No more than nine years ago America had gone boldly to war against the greatest maritime power in the world on account of the Royal Navy's attitude towards the American mercantile marine.

'She's armed, and she'll be full of men, my lord,' said Gerard.

That was another important point, and a very positive point at that. With her twelve-pounders and five hundred disciplined soldiers – and her large American crew as well – she could laugh at anything *Crab* could threaten with her six-pounders and her crew of sixteen. *Daring* would be within her rights to refuse to obey any signals from *Crab*, and *Crab* could do nothing to compel obedience. Shoot away a spar? Not so easy with a six-pounder, and even if no one were to be killed by accident there would be a terrible diplomatic storm if he were to fire on the Stars and Stripes. Could he shadow her, so at least to be on hand when her real purpose was revealed? No; impossible. Anywhere out at sea *Daring* had only to spread her wings to a fair wind to leave *Crab* below the horizon in an afternoon, and then *Daring* could resume her true course unpursued.

Sweating in the stifling night, Hornblower felt like a lassoed wild animal. At every moment some fresh coil was being wound about him to render him more helpless. He was tempted, like a wild animal, to lose all self control, to lapse into mad panic, to fling away all his strength in an explosion of rage. He had sometimes seen, during his long professional career, senior officers giving vent to explosions of that sort. But it would not help. He looked round at the circle of faces in the lamplight;

the faces wore the sober expressions of men who were witnessing a failure, men who were aware that they were in the presence of an Admiral who had made a woeful hash of the first important business he had encountered. That in itself could drive him insane with fury.

Pride came to help him. He would not sink to human weaknesses in the sight of these men.

'I shall sail in any case,' he said, coldly, 'as soon as I have a crew and a steam tug.'

'May I ask what Your Lordship intends to do?' asked Sharpe.

Hornblower had to think quickly to make a reasonable answer to this question; he had no idea. All he knew was that he was not going to give up without a struggle; no crisis was ever alleviated by wasting time.

'I shall employ what time I have here in the composition of orders for my squadron,' he said. 'My flag lieutenant will write them at my dictation, and I shall ask you, Mr Sharpe, to undertake the distribution of them by all the means you find available.'

'Very good, my lord.'

Hornblower remembered at that moment something he should have done already. It was not too late; this part of his duty he must still carry out. And it would at least disguise the anguish he felt.

'Mr Harcourt,' he said. 'I have to commend you greatly on the excellent way in which you executed my orders. You carried out the task of observing *Daring* in most exemplary fashion. You can be sure I shall call the attention of Their Lordships to your behaviour.'

'Thank you, my lord.'

'And this man Jones,' went on Hornblower. 'No

seaman could have acted with more intelligence. You made a good selection, Mr Harcourt, and Jones justified it. I have it in mind to reward him. I can give him an acting rating and confirm it as soon as possible.'

'Thank you, my lord. He has been rated before and disrated.'

'Drink? Is that why he was denied shore leave?'

'I'm afraid so, my lord.'

'Then what do you recommend?'

Harcourt was at a loss.

'You could say to his face what you've already said to me, my lord. You could shake his hand –'

Hornblower laughed.

'And be known through the Navy as the meanest admiral who ever flew a flag? No. A golden guinea at least. Two guineas. I'll give them to him myself, and I shall request you to give him three days' leave as soon as we see Kingston again. Let him have his debauch, if that is the only way in which we can reward him. I have to consider the feelings of the whole squadron.'

'Aye aye, my lord.'

'Now, Mr Gerard, I'll begin the writing of those orders.'

It was indeed noon before *Crab* cast off and was taken in tow by the tug *Temeraire*; it was significant of Hornblower's state of mind that he never gave a thought to the implication of that glorious name. The interval before sailing, all the long, stifling morning, was taken up by the dictation of orders, to be dispersed to every ship of his squadron. An infinity of copies was neces- sary. Sharpe would send them under seal by every British ship leaving New Orleans for the West Indies, in the hope that should one of them encounter a King's ship his orders would be passed on without the delay of being sent to Kingston and then transmitted through official channels. Every ship of the West India squadron was to keep a sharp lookout for the American ship *Daring*. Every ship was to enquire her business, and was to ascertain, if possible, whether *Daring* had troops on board; but (Hornblower sweated more feverishly than ever as he worded this) captains of HM's vessels were reminded of that passage in the Commander-in-Chief's original instructions regarding behaviour towards the American flag. If troops were not on board an effort was to be made to ascertain where they had been landed; if they were, *Daring* was to be kept in sight until they should be landed. Captains were to exercise a wide discretion regarding any interference with *Daring*'s operations.

Seeing that these orders would not leave New Orleans until tomorrow, and would travel by slow merchant ship, it was hardly likely that they would reach any ship of the squadron before *Daring* had done whatever she planned to do. Yet it was necessary to take every possible precaution.

Hornblower signed twenty copies of his orders with a sweating hand, saw them sealed, and handed them over to Sharpe. They shook hands before Sharpe went down the gangway.

'Cambronne will head for Port au Prince or Havana, in my opinion, my lord,' said Sharpe.

The two places were not more than a thousand miles apart.

'Might it not be Cartagena or La Guayra?' asked Hornblower with elaborate irony. Those places were about a thousand miles apart as well, and more than a thousand miles from Havana.

'It well might be,' said Sharpe, the irony quite wasted on him. Yet it could not be said that he was unsympathetic regarding Hornblower's difficulties, for he went on – 'The very best of good fortune, my lord, in any case. I am certain Your Lordship will command success.'

Crab cast off, and *Temeraire* had her in tow, smoke and sparks belching from her chimneys, much to Harcourt's indignation. He was afraid not only of fire but of stains on his spotless deck; he had the hands at work pumping up water from overside continuously soaking deck and rigging.

'Breakfast, my lord?' said Gerard at Hornblower's elbow.

Breakfast? It was one o'clock in the afternoon. He had not been to bed. He had drunk far too much last night, and he had had a busy morning, an anxious morning, and he was as desperately anxious at this moment. His first reaction was to say no; then he remembered how he had complained yesterday (only yesterday? It seemed more like a week ago) about his delayed breakfast. He would not allow his agitation to be so obvious.

'Of course. It could have been served more promptly, Mr Gerard,' he said, hoping he was displaying the irascibility of a man who had not broken his fast.

'Aye aye, my lord,' said Gerard. He had been Hornblower's flag lieutenant for several months now, and knew nearly as much about Hornblower's moods as a wife might have done. He knew, too, of Hornblower's kindly interior. He had received his appointment as the son of an old friend, at a moment when admiral's sons and duke's sons had yearned to serve as flag lieutenant to the fabulous Hornblower.

Hornblower forced himself to eat his fruit and his boiled eggs, to drink his coffee despite the heat. He whiled away a considerable time before he came on deck again, and during that period he had actually contrived to forget his problems – at least nearly to forget them. But they returned in full force as soon as he came on deck again. So harassing were they that he could feel no interest in this still unusual method of navigating a river, no interest in the low banks that were going by so fast alongside. This hurried departure from New Orleans was only a gesture of despair, after all. He could not hope to catch the *Daring*. She would bring off whatever coup she had in mind almost under his very nose and leave him the laughing stock of the world – of his world, at least. This would be the last command he would ever hold. Hornblower looked back over the years of half-pay he had endured since Waterloo. They had been dignified and happy years, one would think, with a seat in the Lords and a position of influence in the County, a loving wife and a growing son, but he had not been living the right life, even so. The five years after Waterloo until at last the course of nature brought his promotion to flag rank had been fretful years; he had only realized it when he knew the intense joy of his appointment to the West Indies. Now all the years to come until he went down into the grave would be as dreary as those five, more dreary, because they would be unrelieved by the hope of future employment at sea.

Here he was, pitying himself, he said to himself

bitterly, when what he should be doing was working out the problems set him. What was it Cambronne had in mind? If he could head him off, arrive triumphantly at the place where Cambronne intended to strike his blow, he could retrieve his reputation. He might be able with great good fortune to intervene decisively. But there was turmoil everywhere through Spanish America, and through the West Indies as well, save for the British colonies. One place was as likely as another; in any case it would be extremely doubtful if he would have any excuse to interfere – Cambronne probably held a commission from Bolivar or some other leader; but on the other hand the precautions Cambronne had taken seemed to imply that he would at least prefer that the Royal Navy would not have a chance to intervene. Intervene? With a crew of sixteen not counting supernumeraries, and with nothing larger than a six-pounder? Rubbish. He was a fool. But he must think, think, think.

'It will be sunset before we sight St Philip, my lord,' reported Harcourt, saluting.

'Very well, Mr Harcourt.'

There would be no salutes fired, then. He would make his departure from the United States with his tail between his legs, so to speak. There could hardly fail to be comment about the briefness of his visit. Sharpe might do his best to explain why he had left so hurriedly, but any explanation would be unsatisfactory. In every way this command for which he had yearned was turning out to be a ridiculous fiasco.

Even this visit, to which he had looked forward so eagerly, was a disappointment. He had seen almost nothing of New Orleans, of America or of the

Americans. He could take no interest in this vast Mississippi. His problems deprived him of interest in his surroundings and his surroundings distracted him from a proper attention to his problems. This fantastic method of progression, for instance – *Crab* was going through the water at a good five knots, and there was the current as well. Quite a breeze was blowing past him in consequence; it was extraordinary to be going ahead with the wind dead foul, without a heel or a pitch, with the standing rigging uttering a faint note and yet not a creak from the running rigging.

'Your dinner is served, my lord,' said Gerard, appearing on deck again.

Darkness was closing in round the *Crab* as Hornblower went below, but the cabin was hot and stuffy.

'Scotch broth, my lord,' said Giles, putting a steaming plate before him.

Hornblower dipped his spoon perfunctorily into the plate, tried to swallow a few mouthfuls, and laid his spoon down again. Giles poured him a glass of wine; he wanted neither wine nor soup, yet he must not display human weaknesses. He forced himself to take a little more of the soup, enough to preserve appearances.

'Chicken Marengo, my lord,' said Giles, putting another plate before him.

Appearances were more easily preserved with chicken; Hornblower haggled the joints apart, ate a couple of mouthfuls, and laid down his knife and fork. They would report to him from the deck if the miracle had happened, if *Daring's* two steam tugs had broken down, or if *Daring* had run aground, and they were passing her triumphantly. Absurd hope. He was a fool.

Giles cleared the table, reset it with cheese dish and cheese plate, and poured a glass of port. A sliver of cheese, a sip of port, and dinner might be considered over. Giles set out the silver spirit lamp, the silver coffee pot, the porcelain cup – Barbara's last present to him. Somehow there was comfort in coffee despite his misery; the only comfort in a black world.

On deck again it was quite dark. On the starboard bow gleamed a light, móving steadily aft to the starboard beam; that must be one of the lighthouses installed by the Americans to make the navigation of the Mississippi as convenient by night as by day. It was one more proof of the importance of this developing commerce – the fact that as many as six steam tugs were being constantly employed was a further proof.

'If you please, my lord,' said Harcourt in the darkness beside him. 'We are approaching the Pass. What orders, my lord?'

What could he do? He could only play a losing game out to the bitter end. He could only follow *Daring*, far, far astern of her, in the hope of a miracle, a fortunate accident. The odds were a hundred to one that by the time he reached Corpus Christi the bird would be flown, completely vanished. Yet perhaps the Mexican authorities, if there were any, or local gossip, if he could pick up any, might afford him some indication of the next destination of the Imperial Guard.

'As soon as we are at sea, set a course for Corpus Christi, if you please, Mr Harcourt.'

'Aye aye, my lord. Corpus Christi.'

'Study your Sailing Directions for the Gulf of Mexico, Mr Harcourt, for the pass into the lagoon there.'

'Aye aye, my lord.'

That was done, then the decision was taken. Yet he stayed up on deck, trying to wrestle with the problem in all its vague and maddening complexity.

He felt rain on his face and soon it was falling in torrents, roaring on the deck, soaking his best uniform. His cocked hat weighed on his head like lead with the accumulation of water in the brim. He was about to take shelter below when his mind began to follow an old train of thought, and he stayed. Gerard loomed up in the darkness with his sou'wester and oilskins, but he paid no attention to him. Was it possible that all this was a false alarm? That Cambronne had nothing else in mind than to take back the Guard to France? No, of course not. He would not have taken six hundred muskets on board in that case, nor bales of uniforms, and there would have been no need for a hurried and clandestine departure.

'If you please, my lord,' said Gerard, standing insistently by with his oilskins.

Hornblower remembered how, before he left England, Barbara had taken Gerard to one side and had talked to him long and earnestly. No doubt she had been telling him of the need to see he did not get wet and that he had his meals regularly.

'Too late now, Mr Gerard,' he said, with a grin. 'I'm soaked through.'

'Then please, my lord, go below and shift your clothes.'

There was genuine anxiety in Gerard's voice, a real concern. The rain was roaring on Gerard's oilskins in the darkness like the nitre-crusher of a powder-mill.

'Oh, very well,' said Hornblower.

He made his way down the little companion, Gerard following him.

'Giles!' called Gerard sharply; Hornblower's servant appeared at once. 'Put out dry clothes for His Lordship.'

Giles began to bustle round the little cabin, kneeling on the deck to fish a fresh shirt out of the chest. Half a gallon of water cascaded down beside him as Hornblower took off his hat.

'See that His Lordship's things are properly dried,' ordered Gerard.

'Aye aye, sir,' said Giles, with sufficient restrained patience in his tone to make Gerard aware that it was an unnecessary order. Hornblower knew that these men were both fond of him. So far their affection had survived his failure – for how long?

'Very well,' he said in momentary irritation. 'I can look after myself now.'

He stood alone in the cabin, stooping under the deck-beams. Unbuttoning his soaking uniform coat he realized he was still wearing his ribbon and star; the ribbon, as he passed it over his head, was soaking wet too. Ribbon and star mocked at his failure, just at the very moment when he was sneering at himself for hoping again that *Daring* might have gone aground somewhere during her passage down the river.

A tap at the door brought Gerard back into the cabin.

'I said I could look after myself,' snapped Hornblower.

'Message from Mr Harcourt, my lord,' said Gerard unabashed. 'The tug will be casting off soon. The wind is fair, a strong breeze, east by north.'

'Very well.'

A strong breeze, a fair wind, would be all in *Daring's* favour. *Crab* might have stood a chance of overhauling her in fluky, contrary airs. Fate had done everything possible to load the dice against him.

Giles had taken the opportunity to slip back into the cabin. He took the wet coat from Hornblower's hand.

'Didn't I tell you to get out?' blared Hornblower, cruelly.

'Aye aye, my lord,' replied Giles imperturbably. 'What about this – this cap, my lord?'

He had picked up the bearskin cap of the Imperial Guard which was still lying in the locker.

'Oh, take it away!' roared Hornblower.

He had kicked off his shoes and was beginning to peel off his stockings when the thought struck him; he remained stooping to consider it.

A bearskin cap – bales and bales of bearskin caps. Why? Muskets and bayonets he could understand. Uniforms, too, perhaps. But who in their sane senses would outfit a regiment for service in tropical America with bearskin caps? He straightened up slowly, and stood still again, thinking deeply. Even uniform coats with buttons and embroidery would be out of place among the ragged ranks of Bolivar's hordes; bearskin caps would be quite absurd.

'Giles!' he roared, and when Giles appeared round the door, 'Bring that cap back to me!'

He took it into his hands again; within him surged the feeling that he held in his hands the clue to the mystery. There was the heavy chain of lacquered brass, the brazen Imperial eagle. Cambronne was a fighting soldier of twenty years' experience in the field; he would never expect men wearing things like this to wage war in the pestilential swamps of Central America or the stifling canebrakes of the West Indies. Then –? The Imperial Guard in their uniforms and bearskins, already historic, would be associated in everyone's mind with the Bonapartist tradition, even now making itself felt as a political force. A Bonapartist movement? In Mexico? Impossible. In France, then?

Within his wet clothes Hornblower felt a sudden surge of warmth as his blood ran hot with the knowledge that he had guessed the solution. St Helena! Bonaparte was there, a prisoner, an exile in one of the loneliest islands in the world. Five hundred disciplined troops arriving by surprise out of a ship flying American colours would set him free. And then? There were few ships in the world faster than the *Daring*. Sailing for France she would arrive there before any warning could reach the civilized world. Bonaparte would land with his Guard – oh, the purpose of the uniforms and bearskins was quite plain. Everyone would remember the glories of the Empire. The French Army would flock to his standard as it had done once before when he returned from Elba. The Bourbons had already outworn their welcome – Sharpe had remarked how they were acting as international busybodies in the hope of dazzling the people with a successful foreign policy. Bonaparte would march again to Paris without opposition. Then the world would be in a turmoil once more. Europe would experience again the bloody cycle of defeat and victory.

After Elba a campaign of a hundred days had been

needed to overthrow Bonaparte at Waterloo, but a hundred thousand men had died during those hundred days, millions and millions of money had been expended. This time it might not even be as easy as that. Bonaparte might find allies in the disturbed state of Europe. There might be twenty more years of war, leaving Europe in ruins. Hornblower had fought through twenty years of war; he felt physically sick at the thought of their repetition. The prospect was so monstrous that he went back through the deductions he had been making, but he could not avoid reaching the same conclusion.

Cambronne was a Bonapartist; no man who had been Commander-in-Chief of the Imperial Guard could be anything else. It was even indicated by a trifle – he had worn the Bonapartist Grand Eagle of the Legion of Honour instead of the Bourbon Grand Cordon which had been substituted for it. He had done that with Vautour's knowledge and agreement. Vautour was a servant of the Bourbons, but he must be a traitorous one; the whole business of chartering the *Daring* and sending her fatal freight on board could only have been carried out with the connivance of the French author-ities – presumably France was riddled with a fresh Bonapartist conspiracy. The Baroness's behaviour was further proof.

Central America and the West Indies might be in a turmoil, but there was no particular strategic point there (as he well knew after so much pondering about it) inviting an invasion by the Imperial Guard in uniforms and bearskins. It must be St Helena, and then France. He could have no doubt about it now. Now the lives of millions, the peace of the whole world, depended on the decisions he had to make at this moment.

There was a rush of feet on the deck just above his head. He heard ropes slapping down upon it, orders being given, loud creakings. The cabin suddenly leaned over sideways with the setting of sail, catching him completely unaware, so that he staggered and dropped the bearskin cap, which lay unnoticed at his feet. *Crab* rose to an even keel again. The deck under his feet felt suddenly lively, as if the breath of life had been breathed into it. They were at sea; they were heading for Corpus Christi. With the wind east by north *Crab* would be running wing-and-wing, possibly. Now he had to think fast, with every second of value. He could not afford to run to leeward in this fashion if he were going to change his plans.

And he knew he was going to change them. He had yearned so desperately for a chance to guess whither *Daring* would head after calling at Corpus Christi. Now he could intervene. Now he had a chance to preserve the peace of the world. With his eyes, unseeing, focused upon an infinite distance, he stood in the swaying cabin calling up into his mental sight the charts of the Gulf of Mexico and the Caribbean. The North-East Trades blew across them, not quite as reliably at this time of year as during the winter, but constantly enough to be a calculable factor. A ship bound for the South Atlantic – for St Helena – from Corpus Christi would be bound to take the Yucatan Channel. Then – especially if her business were such as not to invite attention – she would head for the shoulder of South America, down the centre of the Caribbean, with scores of miles of open sea on either beam. But she would have to pass through the chain of the Antilles before breaking through into the Atlantic.

There were a hundred passages available, but only one obvious one, only one route that would be considered for a moment by a captain bound for St Helena and with the trade winds to contend with. He would round Galera Point, the northernmost extremity of Trinidad. He would give it as wide a berth as possible, but he could not give it a very wide berth because to the northward of Galera Point lay the island of Tobago, and the Tobago Channel between the two was no more than – Hornblower could not be sure exactly – certainly no more than fifty miles wide. In favourable conditions a single ship could patrol that channel and make certain that nothing passed through unsighted. It was a typical example of maritime strategy on a tiny scale. Sea power made its influence felt all over the wide oceans, but it was in the narrow seas, at the focal points, that the decisive moments occurred. The Yucatan Channel would not be nearly as suitable as the Tobago Channel, for the former was more than a hundred miles wide. *Crab* would get there first; that could be taken for granted seeing that *Daring* would have two sides of a triangle to cover, calling at Corpus Christi, and with a long beat to windward as a result. It would be best to employ the advantage so gained to hasten to the Tobago Channel. There would be just time to anticipate *Daring* there – just time – and there was a substantial chance that on the way he might meet some ship of his squadron, to take her along with him. A frigate, now. That would give him all the force he needed. He made his resolve at that moment, conscious as he did so of his quickened heartbeat.

'Giles!' shouted Hornblower.

Giles reappeared, and within the wide discretion of a spoiled servant displayed shocked disapproval at the sight of him still in his wet shirt and ducks.

'My compliments to Mr Harcourt, and I would be glad to see him here as quickly as is convenient to him.'

That was very quickly, naturally, when an admiral needed the presence of a lieutenant.

'Mr Harcourt, I have decided on a change of plan. There is no time to be lost. Kindly set a course for Cape San Antonio.'

'Cape San Antonio. Aye aye, sir.'

Harcourt was a good officer. There was neither surprise nor doubt in his voice as he heard the surprising order.

'When we are on the new course I will explain what I intend to do, if you will have the goodness to report to me with the charts, Mr Harcourt. Bring Mr Gerard with you.'

'Aye aye, sir.'

Now he could take off his wet shirt and trousers, and dab himself dry with a towel. Somehow the little cabin did not seem so oppressively hot; perhaps because they were out at sea, perhaps because he had reached a decision. He was putting on his trousers at the moment when Harcourt had the helm put down. *Crab* came round like a top, with lusty arms hauling in on the sheets. She lay far over to starboard, with the wind abeam, and Hornblower, one leg in his trousers, after a frantic hop, trying to preserve his balance, fell on his nose across his cot with his legs in the air. He struggled to his feet again; *Crab* still heeled over to starboard, farther and then less, as each roller of the beam sea passed under her, each roll taking Hornblower by surprise as he tried to put his other leg into his trousers so that he sat down twice, abruptly, on his cot before he managed it. It was as well that Harcourt and Gerard re-entered the cabin only after he had succeeded. They listened soberly while Hornblower told them of his deductions regarding *Daring*'s plans and of his intention to intercept her at the Tobago Channel; Harcourt took his dividers and measured off the distances, and nodded when he had finished.

'We can gain four days on her to San Antonio, my lord,' he said. 'That means we'll be three days ahead of her there.'

Three days should be just enough start for *Crab* in the long, long race down the length of the Caribbean.

'Could we call at Kingston on our way, my lord?' asked Gerard.

It was tempting to consider it, but Hornblower shook his head. It would be no use calling at headquarters, telling the news, possibly picking up reinforcements, if *Daring* slipped past them as they were doing so.

'It would take too long to work in,' he said. 'Even if we had the sea breeze. And there would be delay while we were there. We've nothing to spare as it is.'

'I suppose not, my lord,' agreed Gerard, grudgingly. He was playing the part of the staff officer, whose duty it was to be critical of any suggested plan. 'Then what do we do when we meet her?'

Hornblower met Gerard's eyes with a steady glance;

Gerard was asking the question that had been already asked and left unanswered.

'I am forming plans to meet that situation,' said Hornblower, and there was a rasping tone in his voice which forbade Gerard to press the matter.

'There's not more than twenty miles of navigable water in the Tobago Channel, my lord,' said Harcourt, still busy with his dividers.

'Then she can hardly pass us unobserved even by night,' said Hornblower. 'I think, gentlemen, that we are acting on the best possible plan. Perhaps the only possible plan.'

'Yes, my lord,' said Harcourt; his imagination was hard at work. 'If Boney once gets loose again –'

He could not go on. He could not face that appalling possibility.

'We have to see to it that he does not, gentlemen. And now that we have done all that we can it would be sensible if we took some rest. I don't think any one of us has had any sleep for a considerable time.'

That was true. Now that he had made up his mind upon a course of action, now that he was committed to it, for good or ill, Hornblower felt his eyelids drooping and sleep overcoming him. He lay down on his cot after his officers had left him. With the wind on the port beam and the cot against the bulkhead to starboard he could relax completely with no fear of rolling out. He closed his eyes. Already he had begun to form the answer to the question Gerard had asked. The answer was a hideous one, something horrible to contemplate. But it seemed to be inevitable. He had his duty to do, and now he could be sure that he was doing it to the best of his ability. With his conscience clear, with a reassuring certainty that he was using the best of his judgement, the inevitability of the rest of the future reinforced his need for sleep. He slept until dawn; he even dozed for a few minutes after that, before he began to think clearly enough again in the daylight for that horrible thought to begin to nag at him again.

That was how the *Crab* began her historic race to the Tobago Channel, over a distance nearly as great as the Atlantic is wide, with the brave trade wind laying her over as she thrashed along. All hands on board knew that she was engaged in a race, for in a little ship like *Crab* nothing could be kept secret; and all hands entered into the spirit of the race with the enthusiasm to be expected of them. Sympathetic eyes were turned towards the lonely figure of the Admiral standing braced on the tiny quarterdeck with the wind singing round him. Everyone knew the chances he was taking; everyone thought that he deserved to win, and no one could guess at his real torment over the certainty that was crystallizing in his mind that this was the end of his career, whether he should win the race or lose it.

No one on board begrudged the constant labour involved in getting every yard of speed out of *Crab*, the continual hauling in and letting out of the sheets as the sails were trimmed to the least variation of the wind, the lightening and urgent shortening of canvas at the last possible moment as squalls came hurtling down upon them, the instant resetting as the squalls passed on their way. All hands constituted themselves as unofficial lookouts; there was really no need for the Admiral to have offered a golden guinea to the man who should first sight *Daring* – there was always the chance of an encounter even before reaching the Tobago Channel. Nobody minded wet shirts and wet beds as the spray burst over *Crab*'s bows in dazzling rainbows and found its way below through the deck as the over-driven schooner worked her seams open in the heavy swell. The hourly casting of the log, the daily calculation of the ship's run, were eagerly anticipated by men who usually displayed all the fatalistic indifference towards these matters of the hardened sailor.

'I am shortening the water allowance, my lord,' said Harcourt to Hornblower the first morning out.

'To how much?' Hornblower asked the question trying to appear as if he were really interested in the answer, so that his misery over something else should not be apparent.

'To half a gallon, my lord.'

Two quarts of fresh water a day per man – that would be hardship for men labouring hard in the tropics.

'You are quite right, Mr Harcourt,' said Hornblower.

Every possible precaution must be taken. It was impossible to predict how long the voyage would last, nor how long they would have to remain on patrol without refilling their water casks; it would be absurd if they were driven prematurely into port as a result of thoughtless extravagance.

'I'll instruct Giles,' went on Hornblower, 'to draw the same ration for me.'

Harcourt blinked a little at that; his small experience with admirals led him to think they led a life of maximum luxury. He had not thought sufficiently far

54

into the problem to realize that if Giles had a free hand as regards drinking water for his Admiral, Giles, and perhaps all Giles's friends, would also have all the drinking water they needed. And there was no smile on Hornblower's face as he spoke; Hornblower wore the same bleak and friendless expression that he had displayed towards everyone since reaching his decision when they went to sea.

They sighted Cape San Antonio one afternoon, and knew they were through the Yucatan Channel; not only did this give them a fresh departure, but they knew that from now on it would not be extremely unlikely for them to sight *Daring* at any moment; they were pursuing very much the same course as she would be taking, from this point onwards. Two nights later they passed Grand Cayman; they did not sight it but they heard the roar of the surf on one of the outlying reefs. That was a proof of how closely Harcourt was cutting his corners; Hornblower felt that he would have given Grand Cayman a wider berth than that – it was a moment when he chafed more than usual at the convention which prohibited an admiral from interfering in the management of his flagship. The following night they picked up soundings on the Pedro Bank, and knew that Jamaica and Kingston were a scant hundred miles to windward of them. From this new departure Harcourt could set a fresh course, direct for the Tobago Channel, but he could not hold it. The trade wind took it into its head to veer round south of east, as was not surprising with midsummer approaching, and it blew dead foul. Harcourt laid *Crab* on the starboard tack – never voluntarily would any captain worth his salt yield a yard to the southward in the Caribbean – and clawed his way as close to the wind as *Crab* would lie.

'I see you've taken in the tops'ls, Mr Harcourt,' remarked Hornblower, venturing on ticklish ground.

'Yes, my lord.' In response to his Admiral's continued enquiring glance Harcourt condescended to explain further. 'A beamy schooner like this isn't intended to sail on her side, my lord. We make less leeway under moderate sail like this, my lord, as long as we're close-hauled with a strong breeze.'

'You know your own ship best, of course, Mr Harcourt,' said Hornblower, grudgingly.

It was hard to believe that *Crab* was making better progress without her magnificent square topsails spread to the breeze. He could be sure that *Daring* would have every stitch of canvas spread – perhaps a single reef. *Crab* thrashed on her way, once or twice shipping it green over her starboard bow; those were the moments when it was necessary for every man to grab and hold on. At dawn next morning there was land right ahead, a blue line on the horizon – the mountains of Haiti. Harcourt held on until noon, raising them farther and farther out of the water, and then he went about. Hornblower approved – in an hour or two the land breeze might set in and there was Beata Point to weather. It was maddening that on this tack they would actually be losing a little ground, for it was perfectly possible that *Daring*, wherever she was, might have the wind a point or two more in her favour and could be able to hold her course direct. And it was quite remarkable to see the foremast hands raising wetted fingers to test the wind, and studying the windward horizon, and criticizing the way the quartermaster at the tiller struggled to gain every yard to windward that he could.

For a day and a half the wind blew foul; in the middle of the second night Hornblower, lying sleepless in his cot, was roused by the call for all hands. He sat up and reached for his dressing gown while feet came running above his head. *Crab* was leaping madly.

'All hands shorten sail!'

'Three reefs in the mains'l!' Harcourt's voice was pealing out as Hornblower reached the deck.

The wind blew the tails of Hornblower's dressing gown and nightshirt up round him as he stood out of the way by the taffrail; darkness was roaring all round him. A midsummer squall had come hurtling at them in the night, but someone had had a weather eye lifting and had been prepared for it. Out of the southward had come the squall.

'Let her pay off!' shouted Harcourt. 'Hands to the sheets!'

Crab came round in a welter of confused water, plunged and then steadied. Now she was flying along in the darkness, belying her unlovely name. She was gaining precious distance to the northward; an invaluable squall this was, as long as it permitted them to hold this course. The roaring night was hurrying by; Hornblower's dressing gown was whipping about his legs. It was impossible not to feel exhilarated to stand thus, compelling the elements to work in their favour, cheating the wind that thought to take them by surprise.

'Well done, Mr Harcourt,' shouted Hornblower into the wind as Harcourt came and stood beside him in the darkness.

'Thank you, sir – my lord. Two hours of this is what we need.'

Fate granted them an hour and a half at any rate, before the squall died away and the trade wind pigheadedly resumed its former direction of east by south. But next morning at breakfast Giles was able to report good news.

'Wind's backing to the nor'rard, my lord,' he said – Giles was as interested as everyone else in the vessel's progress.

'Excellent,' said Hornblower; it was only some seconds later that the dull pain grew up again inside him. That wind would bear him more swiftly to his fate.

As the day wore on the trade wind displayed some of its midsummer freakishness. It died away, died away more and more, until it blew only in fitful puffs, so that there were intervals when *Crab* drifted idly over the glassy blue sea, turning her head to all points of the compass in turn, while the vertical sun blazed down upon a deck in whose seams the pitch melted. Flying fish left fleeting dark tracks upon the enamel surface of the sea. No one cared; every eye was scanning the horizon for the first hint of the next cat's-paw of wind creeping towards them. Perhaps, not too far away in this moody Caribbean, *Daring* was holding her course with all sail set and drawing. The day ended and the night went by, and still the trade wind did not blow; only occasionally would a puff send *Crab* ghosting along momentarily towards the Tobago Channel. The sun blazed down, and men limited to two quarts of water a day were thirsty, thirsty all the time.

They had seen very few sail, and the ones they saw

were of no use in furthering Hornblower's plans. An island schooner bound to Belize. A Dutchman homeward bound from Curaçao, no one with whom Hornblower could entrust a letter, and no ship of his own squadron – that was something almost beyond the bounds of possibility. Hornblower could only wait, as the days went by, in grim, bleak patience. At last the freakish wind blew again, from one point north of east, and they were able to hold their course, with topsails set again, heading steadily for the Antilles, reeling off as much as six knots hour after hour. Now as they approached the islands they saw more sails, but they were only inter-island sloops trading between the Leeward Islands and Trinidad. A square rigger seen on the horizon roused momentary excitement, but she was not the *Daring*. She flew the red and gold of Spain – a Spanish frigate heading for the Venezuelan coast, presumably to deal with the insurgents. The voyage was nearly completed; Hornblower heard the cry of land from the masthead lookout, and it was only a moment before Gerard came into the cabin.

'Grenada in sight, my lord.'

'Very well.'

Now they were entering the waters where they could really expect to meet *Daring*; now the direction of the wind was of more importance than ever. It was blowing from the north-east, now, and that was helpful. It extinguished the very faint possibility that *Daring* might pass to the northward of Tobago instead of through the Tobago Channel.

'*Daring*'s bound to make the same landfall, my lord,' said Gerard, 'and by daylight if she can.'

'We can hope for it, at least,' said Hornblower.

If *Daring* had been as long out of sight of land as had *Crab*, in the fluky winds and unpredictable currents of the Caribbean, her captain would certainly take all precautions in his approach.

'I think, Mr Harcourt,' said Hornblower, 'that we can safely hold our course for Point Galera.'

'Aye aye, my lord.'

Now was the worst period of waiting, of wondering whether the whole voyage might not prove to be a fool's errand, patrolling, beating up to within sight of Trinidad and then going about and reaching past Tobago again towards Grenada. Waiting was bad; if the voyage should not turn out to be a fool's errand it meant something that Hornblower, and Hornblower alone, knew to be worse. Gerard raised the question again.

'How do you propose to stop him, my lord?'

'There may be means,' answered Hornblower, trying to keep the harshness out of his voice that would betray his anxiety.

It was on a blue and gold, blazing day, with *Crab* ghosting along before only the faintest breeze, that the masthead lookout hailed the deck with the news of the sighting.

'Sail ho! Dead to loo'ard, sir!'

A sail might be anything, but at long intervals, as *Crab* crept closer, the successive reports made it more and more likely that the strange sail was *Daring*. Three masts – even that first supplementary report made it reasonably sure, for not many big ships plied out into the South Atlantic from the Caribbean. All sail set, even skysails, and stu'ns'ls to the royals. That did not mean quite so much.

'She looks like an American, sir!'

The skysails had already hinted strongly in the same direction. Then Harcourt went up to the mainmasthead with his own glass, and came down again with his eyes shining with excitement.

'That's *Daring*, my lord. I'm sure of it.'

Ten miles apart they lay, on the brilliant blue of the sea with the brilliant blue of the sky above them, and on the far horizon a smudge of land. *Crab* had won her race by twenty-five hours. *Daring* was 'boxing the compass,' swinging idly in all directions under her pyramids of sails in the absence of all wind; *Crab* carried her way for a while longer, and then she, too, fell motionless under the blazing sun. All eyes turned on the Admiral standing stiffly with his hands locked behind him gazing at the distant white rectangles that indicated where lay his fate. The schooner's big mainsail flapped idly, flapped again, and then the boom began to swing over.

'Hands to the sheets!' yelled Harcourt.

The air was so light that they could not even feel it on their sweating faces, but it sufficed to push the booms out, and a moment later the helmsman could feel the rudder take hold just enough to give him control. With *Crab*'s bowsprit pointed straight at *Daring* the breath of wind was coming in over the starboard quarter, almost dead astern, almost dead foul for *Daring* if ever it should reach her, but she was still becalmed. The breath of wind increased until they could feel it, until they could hear under the bows the music of the schooner's progress through the water, and then it died away abruptly, leaving *Crab* to wallow on the swell. Then it breathed again, over the port quarter this time, and then it drew further aft, so that the topsails were braced square and the foresail could be hauled over to the port side and *Crab* ran wing-and-wing for ten blessed minutes until the wind dropped again, to a dead, flaming calm. Then they could see *Daring* catch a wind, see her trim her sails, but only momentarily, only long enough to reveal her intentions before she lay once more helpless. Despite her vast sail area her greater dead weight made her less susceptible to these very faint airs.

'Thank God for that,' said Gerard, glass to his eye, as he watched her swing idly again. 'I think she aims to pass us beyond cannon shot, my lord.'

'I shouldn't be surprised at that,' agreed Hornblower.

Another breath, another slight closing of the gap, another dead calm.

'Mr Harcourt, perhaps it would be best if you let the men have their dinners now.'

'Aye aye, my lord.'

Salt beef and pease pudding under a noonday sun in the tropics – who could have any appetite for that, especially with the excitement of watching for a wind? And in the middle of dinner hands were sent again to the sheets and braces to take advantage of another breath of wind.

'At what time will you have your dinner, my lord?' asked Giles.

'Not now,' was all the answer Hornblower would give him, glass to eye.

'He's hoisted his colours, my lord,' pointed out Gerard. 'American colours.'

The Stars and Stripes, regarding which he had been expressly ordered to be particularly tender. But he could be nothing else in any case, seeing that *Daring* mounted twelve-pounders and was full of men.

Now both vessels had a wind, but *Crab* was creeping bravely along at a full two knots, and *Daring*, trying to head to the southward close-hauled, was hardly moving; now she was not moving at all, turning aimlessly in a breeze too faint to give her steerage way.

'I can see very few people on her deck, my lord,' said Harcourt; the eye with which he had been staring through his glass was watering with the glare of sun and sea.

'She'd keep 'em below out of sight,' said Gerard.

That was so likely as to be certain. Whatever *Daring*, and Cambronne, thought of *Crab*'s intentions, it would be safest to conceal the fact that she had five hundred men on board while heading for the South Atlantic.

And between her and that South Atlantic lay *Crab*, the frailest barrier imaginable. Let *Daring* once pass through the channel out into the open sea and nothing could be done to stop her. No ship could hope to overtake her. She would reach St Helena to strike her blow there, and no possible warning could be given. It was now or never, and it was Hornblower's fault that matters had reached such a pass. He had been utterly fooled in New Orleans. He had allowed Cambronne to steal a march on him. Now he had to make any sacrifice that circumstances demanded of him, any sacrifice whatever, to redeem the peace of the world. *Crab* could do nothing to stop *Daring*. It could only be done by his own personal exertions.

'Mr Harcourt,' said Hornblower, in his harsh,

expressionless monotone. 'I'll have the quarter-boat cleared away ready to lower, if you please. Have a full boat's crew told off, to double bank the oars.'

'Aye aye, my lord.'

'Who'll go in her, my lord?' asked Gerard.

'I will,' said Hornblower.

The mainsail flapped, the boom came creaking inboard, swung out again, swung in. The breeze was dying away again. For a few minutes more *Crab* held her course, and then the bowsprit began to turn away from *Daring*.

'Can't keep her on her course, sir,' reported the quartermaster.

Hornblower swept his gaze round the horizon in the blazing afternoon. There was no sign of a further breeze. The decisive moment had come, and he snapped his telescope shut.

'I'll take that boat now, Mr Harcourt.'

'Let me come too, my lord,' said Gerard, a note of protest in his voice.

'No,' said Hornblower.

In case a breeze should get up during the next half-hour, he wanted no useless weight in the boat while crossing the two-mile gap.

'Put your backs into it,' said Hornblower to the boat's crew as they shoved off. The oar-blades dipped in the blue, blue water, shining gold against the blue. The boat rounded *Crab*'s stern, with anxious eyes looking down on them; Hornblower brought the tiller over and pointed straight for *Daring*. They soared up a gentle swell, and down again, up again and down again; with each rise and fall *Crab* was perceptibly smaller and *Daring* perceptibly larger, lovely in the afternoon light, during what Hornblower told himself were the last hours of his professional life. They drew nearer and nearer to *Daring*, until at last a hail came borne by the heated air.

'Boat ahoy!'

'Coming aboard!' hailed Hornblower back again. He stood up in the sternsheets so that his gold-laced admiral's uniform was in plain sight.

'Keep off!' hailed the voice, but Hornblower held his course.

There could be no international incident made out of this, an unarmed boat's crew taking an admiral alone on board a becalmed ship. He directed the boat towards the mizzen-chains.

'Keep off!' hailed the voice, an American voice.

Hornblower swung the boat in.

'In oars!' he ordered.

With the way she carried the boat surged towards the ship; Hornblower timed his movements to the best of his ability, knowing his own clumsiness. He leaped for the chains, got one shoe full of water, but held on and dragged himself up.

'Lie off and wait for me!' he ordered the boat's crew, and then turned to swing himself over on to the deck of the ship.

The tall, thin man with a cigar in his mouth must be the American captain; the burly fellow beside him one of the mates. The guns were cast off, although not run out, and the American seamen were standing round them ready to open fire.

'Did you hear me say keep off, mister?' asked the captain.

'I must apologize for this intrusion, sir,' said Hornblower. 'I am Rear Admiral Lord Hornblower of His Britannic Majesty's Service, and I have the most urgent business with Count Cambronne.'

For a moment on the sunlit deck they stood and looked at each other, and then Hornblower saw Cambronne approaching.

'Ah, Count,' said Hornblower, and then made himself speak French. 'It is a pleasure to meet Monsieur le Comte again.'

He took off his cocked hat and held it over his breast and doubled himself in a bow which he knew to be ungainly.

'And to what do I owe this pleasure, milord?' asked Cambronne. He was standing very stiff and straight, his cat's-whisker moustache bristling out on either side.

'I have come to bring you the very worst of news, I regret to say,' said Hornblower. Through many sleepless nights he had rehearsed these speeches to himself. Now he was forcing himself to make them naturally. 'And I have come also to do you a service, Count.'

'What do you wish to say, milord?'

'Bad news.'

'Well?'

'It is with the deepest regret, Count, that I have to inform you of the death of your Emperor.'

'No!'

'The Emperor Napoleon died at St Helena last month. I offer you my sympathy, Count.'

Hornblower told the lie with every effort to appear like a man speaking the truth.

'It cannot be true!'

'I assure you that it is, Count.'

A muscle in the Count's cheek twitched restlessly beside the purple scar. His hard, slightly protruding eyes bored into Hornblower's like gimlets.

'I received the news two days back in Port of Spain,' said Hornblower. 'In consequence I cancelled the arrangements I had made for the arrest of this ship.'

Cambronne could not guess that *Crab* had not made as quick a passage as he indicated.

'I do not believe you,' said Cambronne, nevertheless. It was just the sort of tale that might be told to halt *Daring* in her passage.

'Sir!' said Hornblower, haughtily. He drew himself up even stiffer, acting as well as he could the part of the man of honour whose word was being impugned. The pose was almost successful.

'You must understand the importance of what you are saying, milord,' said Cambronne, with the faintest hint of apology in his voice. But then he said the fatal dreaded words that Hornblower had been expecting. 'Milord, do you give me your word of honour as a gentleman that what you say is true?'

'My word of honour as a gentleman,' said Hornblower.

He had anticipated this moment in misery for days and days. He was ready for it. He compelled himself to make his answer in the manner of a man of honour. He made himself say it steadily and sincerely, as if it did not break his heart to say it. He had been sure that Cambronne would ask him for his word of honour.

It was the last sacrifice he could make. In twenty years of war he had freely risked his life for his country.

He had endured danger, anxiety, hardship. He had never until now been asked to give his honour. This was the further price he had to pay. It was through his own fault that the peace of the world was in peril. It was fitting that he should pay the price. And the honour of one man was a small price to pay for the peace of the world, to save his country from the renewal of the deadly perils she had so narrowly survived for twenty years. In those happy years of the past, returning to his country after an arduous campaign, he had looked about him and he had breathed English air and he had told himself with fatuous patriotism that England was worth fighting for, was worth dying for. England was worth a man's honour, too. Oh, it was true. But it was heart-rending, it was far, far worse than death that it should be his honour that had to be sacrificed.

A little group of officers had appeared on deck and were standing grouped on either side of Cambronne listening to every word; to one side stood the American captain and his mate. Facing them, alone, his gaudy uniform flashing in the sun, stood Hornblower, waiting. The officer on Cambronne's right spoke next. He was some kind of adjutant or staff officer, clearly, of the breed that Hornblower hated. Of course, he had to repeat the question, to turn the iron in the wound.

'Your word of honour, milord?'

'My word of honour,' repeated Hornblower, still steadily, still like a man of honour.

No one could disbelieve the word of honour of a British admiral, of a man who had held His Majesty's commission for more than twenty years. He went on now with the arguments he had rehearsed.

'This exploit of yours can be forgotten now, Count,' he said. 'With the Emperor's death all hope of reconstituting the Empire is at an end. No one need know of what you had intended. You, and these gentlemen, and the Imperial Guard below decks, can remain uncompromised with the régime that rules France. You can carry them all home as you had said you would do, and on the way you can drop your warlike stores quietly overboard. It is for this reason that I have visited you like this, alone. My country, your country, do not desire any new incident to imperil the amity of the world. No one need know; this incident can remain a secret between us.'

Cambronne heard what he said, and listened to it, but the first news he had heard was of such moving importance that he could speak of nothing else.

'The Emperor is dead!' he said.

'I have already assured you of my sympathy, Count,' said Hornblower. 'I offer it to these gentlemen as well. My very deepest sympathy.'

The American captain broke into the murmurs of Cambronne's staff.

'There's a cat's-paw of wind coming towards us,' he said. 'We'll be under way again in five minutes. Are you coming with us, mister, or are you going over the side?'

'Wait,' said Cambronne; he seemingly had some English. He turned to his staff, and they plunged into debate. When they all spoke at once Hornblower's French was inadequate to follow the conversation in detail. But he could see they were all convinced. He might have been pleased, if there had been any pleasure left in the world for him. Someone walked across the deck and shouted down the hatchway, and next moment the Imperial Guard began to pour up on deck. The Old Guard, Bonaparte's Old Guard; they were all in full uniform, apparently in readiness for battle if *Crab* had been foolish enough to risk one. There were five hundred of them in their plumes and bearskins, muskets in hand. A shouted order formed them up on deck, line behind line, gaunt, whiskered men who had marched into every capital in Europe save London alone. They carried their muskets and stood at rigid attention; only a few of them did not look straight to their front, but darted curious glances at the British Admiral. The tears were running down Cambronne's scarred cheeks as he turned and spoke to them. He told them the news in broken sentences, for he could hardly speak for sorrow. They growled like beasts as he spoke. They were thinking of their Emperor dying in his island prison under the harsh treatment of his English jailers; the looks that were turned upon Hornblower now showed hatred instead of curiosity, but Cambronne caught their attention again as he went on to speak of the future. He spoke of France and peace.

'The Emperor is dead!' he said again, as if he were saying that the world had come to an end.

The ranks were ragged now; emotion had broken down even the iron discipline of the Old Guard. Cambronne drew his sword, raising the hilt to his lips in the beautiful gesture of the salute; the steel flashed in the light of the sinking sun.

'I drew this sword for the Emperor,' said Cambronne. 'I shall never draw it again.'

He took the blade in both hands close to the hilt, and

put it across his lifted knee. With a convulsive effort of his lean, powerful body he snapped the blade across, and, turning, he flung the fragments into the sea. The sound that came from the Old Guard was like a long drawn moan. One man took his musket by the muzzle, swung the butt over his head, and brought it crashing down on the deck, breaking the weapon at the small of the butt. Others followed his example. The muskets rained overside.

The American captain was regarding the scene apparently unmoved, as if nothing more would ever surprise him, but the unlit cigar in his mouth was now much shorter, and he must have chewed off the end. He approached Hornblower obviously to ask the explanation of the scene, but the French adjutant interposed.

'France,' said the adjutant. 'We go to France.'

'France?' repeated the captain. 'Not –?'

He did not say the words 'St Helena', but they were implicit in his expression.

'France,' repeated the adjutant, heavily.

Cambronne came towards them, stiffer and straighter than ever as he mastered his emotion.

'I will intrude no further on your sorrow, Count,' said Hornblower. 'Remember always you have the sympathy of an Englishman.'

Cambronne would remember those words later, when he found he had been tricked by a dishonourable Englishman, but they had to be said at this moment, all the same.

'I will remember,' said Cambronne. He was forcing himself to observe the necessary formalities. 'I must thank you, milord, for your courtesy and consideration.'

'I have done my duty towards the world,' said Hornblower.

He would not hold out his hand; Cambronne later would feel contaminated if he touched him. He came stiffly to attention and raised his hand instead in salute.

'Goodbye, Count,' he said. 'I hope we shall meet again in happier circumstances.'

'Goodbye, milord,' said Cambronne, heavily.

Hornblower climbed into the mizzen-chains and the boat pulled in to him, and he fell, rather than climbed, into the sternsheets.

'Give way,' he said. No one could feel as utterly exhausted as he felt. No one could feel as utterly unhappy.

They were waiting for him eagerly on board *Crab*, Harcourt and Gerard and the others. He still had to preserve an unmoved countenance as he went on board. He still had duties to do.

'You can let *Daring* go past, Mr Harcourt,' he said. 'It is all arranged.'

'Arranged, my lord?' This was from Gerard.

'Cambronne has given up the attempt. They are going quietly to France.'

'France? To France? My lord –?'

'You heard what I said.'

They looked across the strip of sea, purple now in the dying day; *Daring* was bracing round her yards to catch the faint breeze that was blowing.

'Your orders are to let them pass, my lord?' persisted Gerard.

'Yes, damn you,' said Hornblower, and instantly regretted the flash of rage and bad language. He turned to the other. 'Mr Harcourt, we can now proceed into

Port of Spain. I presume that even if the wind is fair you will prefer not to risk the Dragon's Mouth by night. You have my permission to wait until daylight.'

'Aye aye, my lord.'

Even then they would not leave him in peace as he turned to go below.

'Dinner, my lord?' asked Gerard. 'I'll give orders for it at once.'

Hopeless to snarl back that he wanted no dinner; the discussion that would have ensued would have been worse than going through the form of eating dinner. Even so it meant that on entering his cabin he could not do as he wanted and fall on his cot with his face in his hands and abandon himself to his misery. He had to sit up stiff and square while Giles laid and served and cleared away, while the tropical sunset flamed in the sky and black night swooped down upon the little ship on the purple sea. Only then, after Giles's last 'Goodnight, my lord' could he think again, and work back through all the horror of his thoughts.

He had ceased to be a gentleman. He was disgraced. Everything was at an end. He would have to resign his command – he would have to resign his commission. How would he ever face Barbara? When little Richard grew up and could understand what had happened how would he ever be able to meet his eyes? And Barbara's aristocratic family would sneer knowingly to each other. And never again would he walk a quarter-deck, and never again step on board with his hand to his hat and the bosun's calls shrilling in salute. Never again; his professional life was at an end – everything was at an end. He had made the sacrifice deliberately and cold-bloodedly, but that did not make it any less horrible.

His thoughts moved into the other half of the circle. He could have done nothing else. If he had turned aside to Kingston or Port of Spain *Daring* would have slipped past him, as her time of arrival off Tobago proved, and any additional strength he might have brought with him – if any, as was not likely – would have been useless. If he had stayed at Kingston and sent a dispatch to London? If he had done that he might at least have covered himself with the authorities. But it would have been unavailing. How much time would elapse between the arrival of his letter in London and the arrival of *Daring* on the coast of France with Bonaparte on board? Two weeks? Very likely less than that. The clerks at the Admiralty would have treated his dispatch at first as coming from a madman. There would be delay in its reaching the First Lord's hands, delay in its being laid before the Cabinet, delay while action was being debated, delay while the French ambassador was informed, delay while joint action was being agreed upon.

And what action, if any – if the Cabinet did not dismiss his letter as that of an unbalanced alarmist? The peacetime navy of England could never have been got to sea in time and in sufficient numbers to cover the whole coast of France so as to make it impossible for *Daring* to land her deadly cargo. And the mere inevitable leakage of the news that Bonaparte was at sea and expected to land would throw France into immediate revolution – no doubt about that, and Italy was in a turmoil too. By writing to London he would have covered himself, as he had already decided, from the censure of the Government. But it was not the measure of a man's duty to avoid blame. He had a positive duty to do, and he had done it, in the only way possible. Nothing else would have stopped Cambronne. Nothing else. He had seen where his duty lay. He had seen what the price would be, and now he was paying it. He had bought the peace of the world at the price of his own honour. He had ceased to be a gentleman – his thoughts completed the other half of the circle.

His mind plunged on, struggling desperately, like a man in utter darkness waist-deep in a slough. It would not be long before the world knew of his dishonour. Cambronne would talk, and so would the other Frenchmen. The world would hear soon of a British admiral giving his plighted word in the certain knowledge that he was telling a lie. Before then he would have left the Service, resigned his command and his commission. That must be done at once; his contaminated flag must fly no longer; he must give no further orders to gentlemen. In Port of Spain there was the Governor of Trinidad. Tomorrow he would tell him that the West India squadron no longer had a commander-in-chief. The Governor could take all the necessary official action, in circularising the squadron and informing the Government – just as if yellow fever or apoplexy had taken off the Commander-in-Chief. In this way anarchy would be reduced to a minimum, and a change of command arranged as simply as possible; that was the last service he could perform for his country, the very last. The Governor would think he was mad, of course – he might be in a strait-jacket tomorrow unless he confessed his shame. And then the

Governor would pity him; the first of the pity, the first of the contempt, he would have to face for the rest of his life. Barbara – Richard – the lost soul plunged on through the stinking slough, through the dark night.

At the end of that dark night a knock at the door brought in Gerard. The message he was bearing died on his lips as he looked at Hornblower's face, white under the tan, and at his hollow eyes.

'Are you quite well, my lord?' he asked, anxiously.

'Quite well. What is it?'

'Mr Harcourt's respects, my lord, and we are off the Dragon's Mouth. The wind is fair at nor'-nor'-east and we can make the passage as soon as day breaks, in half an hour, my lord. We'll drop anchor in Port of Spain by two bells in the forenoon watch, my lord.'

'Thank you, Mr Gerard.' The words came slowly and coldly as he forced himself to utter them. 'My compliments to Mr Harcourt and that will do very well.'

'Aye aye, my lord. This will be the first appearance of your flag in Port of Spain, and a salute will be fired.'

'Very well.'

'The Governor, by virtue of his appointment, takes precedence of you, my lord. Your Lordship must therefore pay the first call. Shall I make a signal to that effect?'

'Thank you, Mr Gerard. I would be obliged if you would.'

The horror still had to be gone through and endured. He had to make himself spick and span; he could not appear on deck unshaven and dirty and untidy. He had to shave and endure Giles' conversation.

'Fresh water, my lord,' said Giles, bringing in a

steaming can. 'Cap'n's given permission, seeing that we'll be watering today.'

There might once have been sheer sensuous pleasure in shaving in fresh water, but now there was none. There might have been pleasure in standing on deck watching *Crab* make the passage of the Dragon's Mouth, in looking about him at new lands, in entering a new port, but now there was none. There might have been pleasure once in fresh linen, even in a crisp new neckcloth, even in his ribbon and star and gold-hilted sword. There might have been pleasure in hearing the thirteen guns of his salute fired and answered, but there was none now – there was only the agony of knowing that never again would a salute be fired for him, never again would the whole ship stand at attention for him as he went over the side. He had to hold himself stiff and straight so as not to droop like a weakling in his misery. He even had to blink hard to keep the tears from overflowing down his cheeks as if he were a sentimental Frenchman. The blazing blue sky overhead might have been black for all he knew.

The Governor was a ponderous Major-General, with a red ribbon and a star, too. He went rigidly through the formalities of the reception, and then unbent as soon as they were alone together.

'Delighted to have this visit from you, my lord,' he said. 'Please sit down. I think you will find that chair comfortable. I have some sherry which I think you will find tolerable. May I pour Your Lordship a glass?'

He did not wait for an answer, but busied himself with the decanter and glasses.

'By the way, my lord, have you heard the news? Boney's dead.'

Hornblower had not sat down. He had intended to refuse the sherry; the Governor would not care to drink with a man who had lost his honour. Now he sat down with a jerk, and automatically took the glass offered him. The sound he made in reply to the Governor's news was only a croak.

'Yes,' went on the Governor. 'He died three weeks back in St Helena. They've buried him there, and that's the last of him. Well – are you quite well, my lord?'

'Quite well, thank you,' said Hornblower.

The cool twilit room was swimming round him. As he came back to sanity he thought of St Elizabeth of Hungary. She, disobeying her husband's commands, had been carrying food to the poor – an apron full of bread – when her husband saw her.

'What have you in your apron?' he demanded.

'Roses,' lied St Elizabeth.

'Show me,' said her husband.

St Elizabeth showed him – and her apron was full of roses.

Life could begin anew, thought Hornblower.

The Star of the South

Here where the trade winds blew at their freshest, just within the tropics, in the wide unbroken Atlantic, was, as Hornblower decided at that moment, the finest stretch of water for a yachting excursion to be found anywhere on the globe. This was nothing more than a yachting excursion, to his mind. Only recently he had emerged from a profound spiritual experience during which the peace of the whole world had depended on his judgement; by comparison it seemed now as if the responsibilities of being Commander-in-Chief on the West India Station were mere nothings. He stood on the quarterdeck of His Britannic Majesty's frigate *Clorinda*, balancing easily as she reached to windward under moderate sail, and allowed the morning sunshine to stream down on him and the trade wind to blow round his ears. With the pitch and the roll as *Clorinda* shouldered against the sea the shadows of the weather-rigging swooped back and forth over the deck; when she took a roll to windward, towards the nearly level morning sun, the shadows of the ratlines of the mizzen-shrouds flicked across his eyes in rapid succession, hypnotically adding to his feeling of well-being. To be a commander-in-chief, with nothing more to worry about than the suppression of the slave trade, the hunting down of piracy, and the policing of the Caribbean, was an experience more pleasant than any emperor, or even any poet, could ever know. The bare-legged seamen washing down the decks were laughing and joking; the level sun was calling up dazzling rainbows in the spray flung up by the weather bow; and he could have breakfast at any moment that he wanted it – standing here on the quarterdeck he was finding additional pleasure in anticipation and wantonly postponing that moment.

The appearance of Captain Sir Thomas Fell on the quarterdeck took something away from the feeling of well-being. Sir Thomas was a gloomy, lantern-jawed individual who would feel it his bounden duty to come and be polite to his Admiral, and who would never have the sensitivity to be aware when his presence was undesired.

'Good morning, my lord,' said the captain, touching his hat.

'Good morning, Sir Thomas,' replied Hornblower, returning the salute.

'A fine fresh morning, my lord.'

'Yes, indeed.'

Sir Thomas was looking over his ship with a captain's eye, along the decks, up aloft, and then turning aft to observe where, right astern, a smudgy line on the horizon marked the position of the hills of Puerto Rico. Hornblower suddenly realized that he wanted his breakfast more than anything on earth; and simultaneously he realized that he now could not gratify that desire as instantaneously as a commander-in-chief should be able to. There were limitations of politeness that constrained even a commander-in-chief – or that constrained him at least. He could not turn away and go below without exchanging a few more sentences with Fell.

'Maybe we'll catch something today, my lord,' said Fell; instinctively with the words the eyes of both men turned aloft to where a lookout sat perched up at the dizzy height of the maintopgallant masthead.

'Let's hope we do,' said Hornblower, and, because he had never succeeded in liking Fell, and because the last thing he wanted to do was to enter into a technical discussion before breakfast, he blundered on so as to conceal these feelings. 'It's likely enough.'

'The Spaniards will want to run every cargo they can before the convention's signed,' said Fell.

'So we decided,' agreed Hornblower. Rehashing old decisions before breakfast was not to his taste, but it was typical of Fell to do that.

'And this is the landfall they'd make,' went on Fell, remorselessly, glancing astern again at Puerto Rico on the horizon.

'Yes,' said Hornblower. Another minute or two of this pointless conversation and he would be free to escape below.

Fell took the speaking-trumpet and directed it upwards.

'Masthead, there! Keep a good lookout or I'll know the reason why!'

'Aye aye, sir!' came the reply.

'Head money, my lord,' said Fell, in apologetic explanation.

'We all find it useful,' answered Hornblower, politely.

Head money was paid by the British Government for slaves freed on the high seas, to the Royal Naval ships concerned in the capture of the slaves, and divided among the ship's company like any other prize money.

It was a small fund compared with the gigantic sums acquired during the great wars, but at five pounds a head a big capture could bring in a substantial sum to the ship making the capture. And of that substantial sum one-quarter went to the captain. On the other hand, one-eighth went to the admiral commanding, wherever he happened to be. Hornblower, with twenty ships at sea under his command, was entitled to one-eighth of all their head money. It was a system of division which explained how during the great wars the admirals commanding the Channel Fleet or in the Mediterranean became millionaires, like Lord Keith.

'No one could find it more useful than I, my lord,' said Fell.

'Maybe,' said Hornblower.

Hornblower knew vaguely that Fell was in difficulties about money. He had had many years of half-pay since Waterloo, and even now as captain of a fifth-rate his pay and allowances were less than twenty pounds a month – lucky though he was, in peacetime, to have command even of a fifth-rate. He had had experience himself of being a poor captain, of wearing cotton stockings instead of silk, and brass epaulettes instead of gold. But he had no desire whatever to discuss the Tables of Personal Pay before breakfast.

'Lady Fell, my lord,' went on Fell, persistently, 'has a position to maintain in the world.'

She was an extravagant woman, so Hornblower had heard.

'Let's hope we have some luck today, then,' said Hornblower, still thinking about breakfast.

It was a melodramatic coincidence that at that

very moment a hail came down from the masthead.

'Sail ho! Sail right to wind'ard!'

'Perhaps that's what we're waiting for, Sir Thomas,' said Hornblower.

'As likely as not, my lord. Masthead, there! How's the sail heading? Mr Sefton, bring the ship to the wind.'

Hornblower backed away to the weather-rail. He felt he could never grow used to his situation as admiral, and having to stand by and be no more than an interested spectator while the ship he was in was being handled at decisive moments. It was quite painful to be a spectator, but it would be more painful still to go below and remain in ignorance of what was going on – and much more painful than to postpone breakfast again.

'Deck, there! She's a two-master. Heading straight down for us. All sail to the royals. Captain, sir, she's a schooner! A big schooner, sir. Still running down for us.'

Young Gerard, the flag lieutenant, had come running on deck at the first hail from the masthead, to his place beside his Admiral.

'A tops'l schooner,' he said. 'A big one. She could be what we're looking for, my lord.'

'Plenty of other things she could be,' said Hornblower, doing his best to conceal his absurd excitement.

Gerard had his telescope pointing to windward.

'There she is! Coming down fast, right enough. Look at the rake of those masts! Look at the cut of those tops'ls! My lord, she's no Island schooner.'

It would not be a very remarkable coincidence if she should be a slaver; he had brought *Clorinda* here to the windward of San Juan in the full expectation that slave cargoes would be hurrying here. Spain was meditating joining in the suppression of the slave trade, and every slaver would be tempted to run cargoes and take advantage of enhanced prices before the prohibition should take effect. The main slave market for the Spanish colonies was at Havana, a thousand miles to leeward, but it could be looked upon as certain that Spanish slavers, making their passage from the Slave Coast, would touch first at Puerto Rico to refill with water if not to dispose of part of their cargo. It had only been logical to station *Clorinda* to intercept them.

Hornblower took the telescope and trained it on the fast-nearing schooner. He saw what Gerard had spoken about. Hull up now, he could see how heavily sparred she was, and how built for speed. With those fine lines it would only pay for her to carry highly perishable cargo – human cargo. As he looked he saw the rectangles of her square sails narrow vertically; the small distance between her masts widened greatly. She was wheeling away from the waiting *Clorinda* – a final proof, if any was needed, that she was what she appeared to be. Laying herself on the starboard tack, she proceeded to keep at a safe distance, and to increase that distance as fast as possible.

'Mr Sefton!' shouted Fell. 'Fill the maintops'l! After her, on the starboard tack! Set the royals!'

In an orderly and disciplined rush some of the hands hurried to the braces while others scurried aloft to set more sail. It was only a matter of moments before *Clorinda*, as close-hauled as she would lie, was thrashing to windward in pursuit. With everything braced up sharp, and carrying every inch of sail that the brisk trade wind would allow, she lay steeply over, plunging through the sea, each wave in turn bursting on her weather bow with the spray flying aft in sheets, and the taut weather-rigging shrieking in the wind. It was a remarkable transition from the quiet that had reigned not so long ago.

'Hoist the colours,' ordered Fell. 'Let's see what she says she is.'

Through the telescope Hornblower watched the schooner hoist her colours in reply – the red and yellow of Spain.

'You see, my lord?' asked Fell.

'Pardon, Cap'n,' interposed Sefton, the officer of the watch, 'I know who she is. I saw her twice last commission. She's the *Estrella*.'

'The *Australia*?' exclaimed Fell, mishearing Sefton's Spanish pronunciation.

'The *Estrella*, sir. The *Estrella del Sur* – the *Star of the South*, sir.'

'I know about her, then,' said Hornblower. 'Her captain's Gomez – runs four hundred slaves every passage, if he doesn't lose too many.'

'Four hundred!' repeated Fell.

Hornblower saw a momentary calculating look pass over Fell's face. Five pounds a head meant two thousand pounds; a quarter of that was five hundred pounds. Two years' pay at one swoop. Fell darted glances aloft and overside.

'Keep your luff, there!' he shouted at the helmsman. 'Mr Sefton! Hands to the bowlines there, for'rard.'

'She's weathering on us,' said Gerard, the glass to his eye.

It was really only to be expected that a well-designed schooner would work to windward more efficiently than even the best of square-rigged frigates.

'She's fore-reaching on us, too,' said Hornblower, gauging the distances and angles. She was not only lying closer to the wind but travelling faster through the water. Very little faster, it was true – a knot or perhaps two knots – but enough to render her safe from *Clorinda*'s pursuit.

'I'll have her yet!' said Fell. 'Mr Sefton! Call all hands! Run out the guns on the weather side. Mr James! Find Mr Noakes. Tell him to start the water. Hands to the pumps, Mr Sefton! Pump her dry.'

Hands came pouring up through the hatchways. With the gun ports opened the guns' crews flung their weight on the gun tackles, inch by inch dragging the guns on the weather side up the steep slope presented by the heeling deck. The rumble of the wooden wheels over the seams of the planking made a stirring sound; it had been the preliminary of many a desperate fight in the old days. Now the guns were merely being run out in order to keep the ship on a slightly more even keel, giving her a better grip on the water and minimizing leeway. Hornblower watched the pumps being manned; the hands threw their weight on the handles with a will, the rapid clank-clank proving how hard they were at work, pumping overside the twenty tons of drinking water which might be thought of as the life-blood of a cruising ship. But the slight reduction of draught that would result might, combined with the running out of the weather guns, add a few yards to her speed.

The call for all hands had brought Mr Erasmus Spendlove on deck, Hornblower's secretary. He looked round him at the organized confusion on deck with that air of Olympian superiority which always delighted Hornblower. Spendlove cultivated a pose of unruffled calm that exasperated some and amused others. Yet he was a most efficient secretary, and Hornblower had never once regretted acting on the recommendation of Lord Exmouth and appointing him to his position.

'You see the vulgar herd all hard at work, Mr Spendlove,' said Hornblower.

'Truly they appear to be, my lord.' He looked to windward at the *Estrella*. 'I trust their labours will not be in vain.'

Fell came bustling by, still looking up at the rigging and overside at the *Estrella*.

'Mr Sefton! Call the carpenter. I'll have the wedges of the mainmast knocked loose. More play there may give us more speed.'

Hornblower caught a change of expression on Spendlove's face, and their eyes met. Spendlove was a profound student of the theory of ship design, and Hornblower was a man with a lifetime of experience, and the glance they exchanged, brief as it was, was enough for each to know that the other thought the new plan unwise. Hornblower watched the main shrouds on the weather side taking the additional strain. It was as well that *Clorinda* was newly refitted.

'Can't say we're doing any better, my lord,' said Gerard from behind his telescope.

The *Estrella* was perceptibly farther ahead and more to windward. If she wished, she would run *Clorinda* practically out of sight by noon. Hornblower observed an odd expression on Spendlove's face. He was testing the air with his nose, sniffing curiously at the wind as it blew past him. It occurred to Hornblower that once or twice he had been aware, without drawing any conclusions from the phenomenon, that the clean trade wind had momentarily been tainted with a hint of a horrible stench. He himself tried the air again, and caught another musky whiff. He knew what it was – twenty years ago he had smelt the same stench when a Spanish galley crowded with galley slaves had passed to windward. The trade wind, blowing straight from the *Estrella* to the *Clorinda*, was bearing with it the reek from the crowded slave ship, tainting the air over the clean blue sea far to leeward of her.

'We can be sure she's carrying a full cargo,' he said.

Fell was still endeavouring to improve *Clorinda*'s sailing qualities.

'Mr Sefton! Set the hands to work carrying shot up to wind'ard.'

'She's altering course!' Half a dozen voices made the announcement at the same moment.

'Belay that order, Mr Sefton!'

Fell's telescope, like all the others, was trained on the *Estrella*. She had put her helm up a little, and was boldly turning to cross *Clorinda*'s bows.

'Damned insolence!' exclaimed Fell.

Everyone watched anxiously as the two ships proceeded headlong on converging courses.

'She'll pass us out of range,' decided Gerard; the certainty became more apparent with every second of delay.

'Hands to the braces!' roared Fell. 'Quartermaster! Starboard your helm! Handsomely! Handsomely! Steady as you go!'

'Two points off the wind,' said Hornblower. 'We stand more chance now.'

Clorinda's bows were now pointed to intercept the *Estrella* at a far distant point, several miles ahead. Moreover, lying a little off the wind as both ships now were, it seemed probable that *Estrella*'s fore-and-aft rig and fine lines might not convey so great an advantage.

'Take a bearing, Gerard,' ordered Hornblower.

Gerard went to the binnacle and read the bearing carefully.

'My impression,' said Spendlove, gazing over the blue, blue water, 'is that she's still fore-reaching on us.'

'If that's the case,' said Hornblower, 'then all we can hope for is that she carries something away.'

'We can at least hope for it, my lord,' said Spendlove. The glance he directed upwards was indicative of his fear that it would be the *Clorinda* whose gear would give way. *Clorinda* now had wind and sea very nearly abeam. She was lying over very steeply under every inch of canvas she could carry, and lifting unwillingly to the seas which came rolling in upon her, swirling in through her open gun ports. Hornblower realized that he had not a dry stitch of clothing on him, and probably no one else on board had, either.

'My lord,' said Gerard, 'you've had no breakfast as yet.'

Hornblower tried to conceal the discomfiture he felt at this reminder. He had forgotten all about breakfast, despite the cheerful anticipation with which he had once been looking forward to it.

'Quite right, Mr Gerard,' he said, jocular, but only clumsily so, thanks to being taken by surprise. 'And what of it?'

'It's my duty to remind you, my lord,' said Gerard. 'Her Ladyship –'

'Her Ladyship told you to see that I took my meals regularly,' replied Hornblower. 'I am aware of that. But Her Ladyship, owing to her inexperience, made no allowance for encounters with fast-sailing slavers just at meal-times.'

'But can't I persuade you, my lord?'

The thought of breakfast, now that it had been re-implanted in his mind, was more attractive than ever. But it was hard to go below with a pursuit being so hotly conducted.

'Take that bearing again before I decide,' he temporized.

Gerard walked to the binnacle again.

'Bearing's opening steadily, my lord,' he reported. 'She must be drawing ahead fast.'

'Clearly so,' said Spendlove, telescope trained out towards the *Estrella*. 'And it looks – it looks as if she's hauling in on her sheets. Maybe –'

Hornblower had whipped his telescope to his eye on the instant.

'She's gibing over!' he pronounced. 'See how she comes round, by George!'

Estrella must have a bold captain and a well-trained crew. They had hauled in on her sheets and had stood ready at her topsail braces. Then, with the helm hard over, she had spun round on her heel. Her whole beautiful profile was now presented to Hornblower's telescope. She was headed to cross *Clorinda*'s bows from starboard to port, and not too far ahead, either.

'Damned insolence!' said Hornblower, but full of admiration for the daring and skill displayed.

Fell was standing close by, staring at the impertinent schooner. He was rigid, even though the wind was flapping his coat-tails round him. For a few seconds it seemed as if the two vessels were heading towards a common point, where they must meet. But the impression soon passed. Even without taking a compass bearing it became apparent that *Estrella* must pass comfortably ahead of the frigate.

'Run the guns in!' bellowed Fell. 'Stand by to wear ship! Clear away the bow chasers, there!'

It might be just possible that the schooner would pass within range of the bow chasers, but to take a shot at her, at long range and on that heaving sea, would be a chancy business. Should they score a hit, it might as likely take effect in the hull, among the wretched slaves, as on the spars or rigging. Hornblower was prepared to restrain Fell from firing.

The guns were run in, and after another minute's examination of the situation Fell ordered the helm to be put a-starboard and the ship laid right before the wind. Hornblower through his telescope could see the schooner lying right over with the wind abeam, so far over that she, as she heaved, presented a streak of copper to his view, pinkish against the blue of the sea. Clearly she was drawing across the frigate's bows, as Fell tacitly acknowledged when he ordered a further turn of two points to port. Thanks to her two knots superiority in speed, and thanks also to her superior handiness and weatherliness, the *Estrella* was literally making a circle round the *Clorinda*.

'She's built for speed, my lord,' said Spendlove from behind his telescope.

So was *Clorinda*, but with a difference. *Clorinda* was a fighting ship, built to carry seventy tons of artillery, with forty tons of powder and shot in her magazines. It was no shame to her that she should be outsailed and outmanœuvred by such a vessel as the *Estrella*.

'I fancy she'll make for San Juan, Sir Thomas,' said Hornblower.

Fell's face bore an expression of helpless fury as he turned to his Admiral; it was with an obvious effort that he restrained himself from pouring out his rage, presumably in a torrent of blasphemy.

'It's – it's –' he spluttered.

'It's enough to madden a saint,' said Hornblower.

Clorinda had been ideally stationed, twenty miles to windward of San Juan; *Estrella* had run practically into her arms, so to speak, and had yet dodged neatly round her and had won for herself a clear run to the port.

'I'll see him damned, my lord!' said Fell. 'Quartermaster!'

There was now the long run ahead to San Juan, one point off the wind, in what was practically a race with an even start. Fell laid a course for San Juan; it was obvious that *Estrella*, comfortably out of range on the starboard beam, was heading for the same point. Both ships had the wind practically abeam; this long run would be a final test of the sailing qualities of the two ships, as though they were a couple of yachts completing a triangular course in a race in the Solent. Hornblower reminded himself that earlier this morning he had compared the present voyage with a yachting excursion. But the expression in Fell's face showed that his flag captain by no means looked on it in the same light. Fell was in the deadliest earnest, and not from any philanthropic feelings about slavery, either. It was the head money he wanted.

'About that breakfast, my lord?' said Gerard.

An officer was touching his hat to Fell with the request that it might be considered noon.

'Make it so,' said Fell. The welcome cry of 'Up spirits' rang through the ship.

'Breakfast, my lord?' asked Gerard again.

'Let's wait and see how we do on this course,' said Hornblower. He saw something of dismay in Gerard's face and laughed. 'It's a question of your breakfast, I fancy, as well as mine. You've had nothing this morning?'

'No, my lord.'

'I starve my young men, I see,' said Hornblower, looking from Gerard to Spendlove; but the latter's expression was peculiarly unchanging, and Hornblower remembered all he knew about him. 'I'll wager a guinea that Spendlove hasn't spent the morning fasting.'

The suggestion was answered by a wide grin.

'I am no sailor, my lord,' said Spendlove. 'But I have learned one thing while I have been at sea, and that is to snatch at any meal that makes its appearance. Fairy gold vanishes no faster than the opportunity of eating food at sea.'

'So, while your Admiral has been starving, you have been walking this deck with a full belly? Shame on you.'

'I feel that shame as deeply as the situation merits, my lord.'

Spendlove obviously had all the tact that an admiral's secretary needed to have.

'Hands to the mainbrace,' bellowed Fell.

Clorinda was hurtling along over the blue sea with the wind abeam; it was her best point of sailing, and Fell was doing all he could to get the very best out of her. Hornblower looked over at *Estrella*.

'I fancy we're falling behind,' he said.

'I think so, too, my lord,' said Gerard after a glance in the same direction. He walked over and took a bearing, and Fell glared at him with irritation before turning to Hornblower.

'I hope you will agree, my lord,' he said, 'that *Clorinda* has done all a ship can do?'

'Certainly, Sir Thomas,' said Hornblower. Fell really meant to say that no fault could be found with his handling of the ship; and Hornblower, while convinced that he himself could have handled her better, had no doubt that in any case *Estrella* would have evaded capture.

'That schooner sails like a witch,' said Fell. 'Look at her now, my lord.'

Estrella's lovely lines and magnificent sail plan were obvious even at this distance.

'She's a beautiful vessel,' agreed Hornblower.

'She's head-reaching on us for sure,' announced Gerard from the binnacle. 'And I think she's weathering on us, too.'

'And there goes five hundred pounds,' said Fell, bitterly. Assuredly he was in need of money. 'Quartermaster! Bear up a point. Hands to the braces!'

He brought *Clorinda* a little closer to the wind and studied her behaviour before turning back to Hornblower.

'I'll not give up the chase until I'm compelled, my lord,' he said.

'Quite right,' agreed Hornblower.

There was something of resignation, something of despair, in Fell's expression. It was not only the thought of the lost money that troubled him, Hornblower realized. The report that Fell had tried to capture the *Estrella*, and had failed, almost ludicrously, would reach their Lordships of the Admiralty, of course. Even if Hornblower's own report minimized the failure it would still be a failure. That meant that Fell would never be employed again after his present two years' appointment had expired. For every captain with a command in the Royal Navy now there were twenty at least hungry for commands. The slightest lapse would be seized upon as reason for ending a man's career; it could not be otherwise. Fell was now looking forward apprehensively to spending the rest of his life on half-pay. And Lady Fell was an expensive and ambitious woman. No wonder that Fell's usually red cheeks had a grey tinge.

The slight alteration of course Fell had ordered was really a final admission of defeat. *Clorinda* was retaining her windward position only at the cost of seeing *Estrella* draw more rapidly ahead.

'But I fear she'll beat us easily into San Juan,' went on Fell with admirable stoicism. Right ahead the purple smear on the horizon that marked the hills of Puerto Rico was growing loftier and more defined. 'What orders have you for me in that case, my lord?'

'What water have you left on board?' asked Hornblower in return.

'Five tons, my lord. Say six days at short allowance.'

'Six days,' repeated Hornblower, mostly to himself. It was a tiresome complication. The nearest British territory was a hundred miles to windward.

'I had to try the effect of lightening the ship, my lord,' said Fell, self-exculpatory.

'I know, I know.' Hornblower always felt testy when someone tried to excuse himself. 'Well, we'll follow *Estrella* in if we don't catch her first.'

'It will be an official visit, my lord?' asked Gerard quickly.

'It can hardly be anything else with my flag flying,' said Hornblower. He took no pleasure in official visits. 'We may as well kill two birds with one stone. It's time I called on the Spanish authorities, and we can fill up with water at the same time.'

'Aye aye, my lord.'

A visit of ceremony in a foreign port meant many calls on the activity of his staff – but not as many as on him, he told himself with irritation.

'I'll have my breakfast before anything else comes to postpone it,' he said. The perfect good humour of the morning had quite evaporated now. He would be in a bad temper now if he allowed himself to indulge in the weaknesses of humanity.

When he came on deck again the failure to intercept *Estrella* was painfully obvious. The schooner was a full three miles ahead, and had weathered upon *Clorinda* until the latter lay almost in her wake. The coast of Puerto Rico was very well defined now. *Estrella* was entering into territorial waters and was perfectly safe. All hands were hard at work in every part of the ship bringing everything into that condition of perfection – really no more perfect than invariably prevailed – which a British ship must display when entering a foreign port and submitting herself to the jealous inspection of strangers. The deck had been brought to a whiteness quite dazzling in the tropical sun; the metalwork was equally dazzling – painful when the eye received a direct reflection; gleaming cutlasses and pikes were ranged in decorative patterns on the bulkhead aft; white cotton lines were being rove everywhere, with elaborate Turk's heads.

'Very good, Sir Thomas,' said Hornblower approvingly.

'Authority in San Juan is represented by a captain-general, my lord,' said Spendlove.

'Yes. I shall have to call upon him,' agreed Hornblower. 'Sir Thomas, I shall be obliged if you will accompany me.'

'Aye aye, my lord.'

'Ribbons and stars, I fear, Sir Thomas.'

'Aye aye, my lord.'

Fell had received his knighthood of the Bath after a desperate frigate action back in 1813. It had been a tribute to his courage if not to his professional abilities.

'Schooner's taking a pilot on board!' hailed the masthead lookout.

'Very well!'

'Our turn shortly,' said Hornblower. 'Time to array ourselves for our hosts. They will be grateful, I hope, that our arrival will take place after the hour of the siesta.'

It was also the hour when the sea breeze was beginning to blow. The pilot they took on – a big, handsome quadroon – took the ship in without a moment's difficulty, although, naturally, Fell stood beside him consumed with anxiety. Hornblower, free from any such responsibility, was able to go forward to the gangway and examine the approaches to the city; it was a time of peace, but Spain had been an enemy before and might perhaps be an enemy again, and at least nothing would be lost if he knew as much as possible about the defences first-hand. It did not take very long to perceive why San Juan had never been attacked, not to speak of captured, by the numerous enemies of Spain during the long life of the city. It was ringed by a lofty wall, of stout masonry, with ditches and bastions, moats and draw-bridges. On the lofty bluff overlooking the entrance Morro Castle covered the approaches with artillery; there was another fortress – which must be San Cristobal – and battery succeeded battery along the waterfront, with heavy guns visible in the embrasures. Nothing less than a formal siege, with powerful army and a battering train, could make any impression on San Juan as long as it was defended by an adequate garrison.

The sea breeze brought them up the entrance passage; there was the usual momentary anxiety about whether the Spaniards were prepared to salute his flag, but the anxiety was speedily allayed as the guns in the Morro began to bang out their reply. Hornblower held himself stiffly to attention as the ship glided in, the fore-castle saluting carronade firing at admirably regular intervals. The hands took in the canvas with a rapidity that did them credit – Hornblower was watching unobtrusively from under the brim of his cocked hat – and then *Clorinda* rounded-to and the anchor cable rumbled through the hawse-hole. A deeply sunburned officer in a fine uniform came up the side and announced himself, in passable English, as the port medical officer, and received Fell's declaration that *Clorinda* had experienced no infectious disease during the past twenty-one days.

Now that they were in the harbour, where the sea breeze circulated with difficulty, and the ship was stationary, they were aware of the crushing heat; Hornblower felt instantly the sweat trickling down inside his shirt under his heavy uniform coat, and he turned his head uncomfortably from side to side, feeling the constriction of his starched neckcloth. A brief gesture from Gerard beside him pointed out what he had already observed – the *Estrella del Sur* in her gleaming white paint lying at the pier close beside them. It seemed as if the reek of her still reached his nostrils from her open hatchways. A file of soldiers, in blue coats with white cross-belts, was drawn up on the pier, standing somewhat negligently under command of a sergeant. From within the hold of the schooner came a most lamentable noise – prolonged and doleful wailings. As they watched they saw a string of naked Negroes come climbing with difficulty up through the hatchway. They could hardly walk – in fact some of them could not walk at all, but fell to their hands and knees and crawled in that fashion over the deck and on to the pier.

'They're landing their cargo,' said Gerard.

'Some of it at least,' replied Hornblower. In nearly a year of study he had learned much about the slave trade. The demand for slaves here in Puerto Rico was small compared with that at Havana. During the Middle Passage the slaves he saw had been confined on the slave decks, packed tight 'spoon fashion,' lying on their sides with their knees bent up into the bend of the knees of the next man. It was only to be expected that the captain of the *Estrella* would take this opportunity of giving his perishable cargo a thorough airing.

A hail from overside distracted them. A boat with the Spanish flag at the bow was approaching; sitting in the sternsheets was an officer in a brilliant gold-laced uniform that reflected back the setting sun.

'Here comes Authority,' said Hornblower.

The side was manned and the officer came aboard to the trilling of the pipes of the bosun's mates, very correctly raising his hand in salute. Hornblower walked over to join Fell in receiving him. He spoke in Spanish, and Hornblower was aware that Fell had none of that language.

'Major Mendez-Castillo,' the officer announced himself. 'First and Principal Aide-de-Camp to His Excellency the Captain-General of Puerto Rico.'

He was tall and slender, with a thin moustache that might have been put on with grease paint; he looked cautiously, without committing himself, at the two officers in their red ribbons and stars, and glittering epaulettes, who were receiving him.

'Welcome, Major,' said Hornblower. 'I am Rear Admiral Lord Hornblower, Commander-in-Chief of His Britannic Majesty's ships and vessels in West Indian waters. May I present Captain Sir Thomas Fell, commanding His Britannic Majesty's ship *Clorinda*.

Mendez-Castillo bowed to each of them, his relief at knowing which was which faintly apparent.

'Welcome to Puerto Rico, Your Excellency,' he said. 'We had, of course, heard that the famous Lord Hornblower was now commander-in-chief here, and we had long hoped for the honour of a visit from him.'

'Many thanks,' said Hornblower.

'And welcome to you and to your ship, Captain,' added Mendez-Castillo hastily, nervous in case it should be too apparent that he had been so engrossed in his meeting with the fabulous Hornblower that he had paid insufficient attention to a mere captain. Fell bowed awkwardly in reply – interpretation was unnecessary.

'I am instructed by His Excellency,' went on Mendez-Castillo, 'to enquire if there is any way in which His Excellency can be of service to Your Excellency on the notable occasion of this visit?'

In Spanish, the phrasing of the pompous sentence was even more difficult than in English. And as Mendez-Castillo spoke his glance wavered momentarily towards the *Estrella*; obviously all the details of the *Clorinda*'s attempted interception were already known – much of the unavailing pursuit must have been visible from the Morro. Something in the Major's attitude conveyed the impression that the subject of the *Estrella* was not open to discussion.

'We intend to make only a brief stay, Major. Captain Fell is anxious to renew the water supply of his ship,' said Hornblower, and Mendez-Castillo's expression softened at once.

'Of course,' he said, hastily. 'Nothing could be easier. I will give instructions to the Captain of the Port to afford Captain Fell every facility.'

'You are too kind, Major,' said Hornblower. Bows

were exchanged again, Fell joining in although unaware of what had been said.

'His Excellency has also instructed me,' said Mendez-Castillo, 'that he hopes for the honour of a visit from Your Excellency.'

'I had hoped that His Excellency would be kind enough to invite me.'

'His Excellency will be charmed to hear it. Perhaps Your Excellency would be kind enough to visit His Excellency this evening. His Excellency would be charmed to receive Your Excellency at eight o'clock, along with the members of Your Excellency's staff, at La Fortaleza, the Palace of Santa Catalina.'

'His Excellency is too good. We shall be delighted, naturally.'

'I shall inform His Excellency. Perhaps Your Excellency would find it convenient if I were to come on board at that time to escort Your Excellency and Your Excellency's party?'

'We shall be most grateful, Major.'

The Major took his leave after a final reference to the Captain of the Port and the watering of the ship. Hornblower explained briefly to Fell.

'Aye aye, my lord.'

Here came another visitor, up the port side of the ship, a squat, heavily built man in dazzling white linen, wearing a broad-brimmed hat which he took off with scrupulous politeness as he reached the quarterdeck. Hornblower watched him address himself to the midshipman of the watch, and saw the latter hesitate and look round him while trying to make up his mind as to whether he should grant the request.

'Very well, midshipman,' said Hornblower. 'What does the gentleman want?'

He could guess very easily what the gentleman wanted. This might be an opportunity of making contact with the shore other than through official channels – something always desirable, and peculiarly so at this moment. The visitor came forward; a pair of bright, quizzical blue eyes studied Hornblower closely as he did so.

'My lord?' he said. He at least could recognize an admiral's uniform when he saw it.

'Yes. I am Admiral Lord Hornblower.'

'I fear to trouble you with my business, my lord.' He spoke English like an Englishman, like a Tynesider, perhaps, but obviously as if he had not spoken it for years.

'What is it?'

'I came on board to address myself to your steward, my lord, and to the president of the wardroom mess, and to the purser. The principal ship chandler of the port. Beef cattle, my lord, chickens, eggs, fresh bread, fruits, vegetables.'

'What is your name?'

'Eduardo Stuart–Edward Stuart, my lord. Second mate of the brig *Columbine*, out of London. Captured back in 1806, my lord, and brought in here as a prisoner. I made friends here, and when the Dons changed sides in 1808 I set up as ship chandler, and here I've been ever since.'

Hornblower studied the speaker as keenly as the speaker was studying him. He could guess at much of what was left unsaid. He could guess at a fortunate marriage, and probably at a change of religion – unless Stuart had been born a Catholic, as was possible enough.

'And I am at your service, my lord,' went on Stuart, meeting his gaze without flinching.

'In a moment I'll let you speak to the purser,' said Hornblower. 'But tell me first, what impression has our arrival made here?'

Stuart's face crinkled into a grin.

'The whole town was out watching your chase of the *Estrella del Sur*, my lord.'

'I guessed as much.'

'They all rejoiced when they saw her escape you. And then when they saw you coming in they manned the batteries.'

'Indeed?'

The Royal Navy's reputation for prompt action, both daring and high-handed, must still be very much alive, if there could be even a momentary fear that a single frigate would attempt to snatch a prize from out of the shelter of a port as well guarded as San Juan.

'In ten minutes your name was being spoken in all the streets, my lord.'

Hornblower's keen glance reassured him that he was not being paid an idle compliment.

'And what is the *Estrella* going to do now?'

'She has only come in to land a few sickly slaves and renew with water, my lord. It's a poor market for slaves here. She sails for Havana at once, as soon as she can be sure of your movements, my lord.'

'At once?'

'She'll sail with the land breeze at dawn tomorrow, my lord, unless you are lying outside the port.'

'I don't expect I shall be,' said Hornblower.

'Then she'll sail without a doubt, my lord. She'll want to get her cargo landed and sold in Havana before Spain signs the Convention.'

'I understand,' said Hornblower.

Now what was this? Here were the old symptoms, as recognizable as ever, the quickened heartbeat, the feeling of warmth under the skin, the general restlessness. There was something just below the horizon of his mind, some stirring of an idea. And within a second the idea was up over the horizon, vague at present, like a hazy landfall, but as certain and as reassuring as any landfall. And beyond, still over the horizon, were other ideas, only to be guessed at. He could not help glancing over at the *Estrella*, sizing up the tactical situation, seeking further inspiration there, testing what he already had in mind.

It was all he could do to thank Stuart politely for his information, without betraying the excitement he felt, and without terminating the interview with suspicious abruptness. A word to Fell made certain that Stuart would receive the business of supplying the *Clorinda*, and Hornblower waved away Stuart's thanks. Hornblower turned away with as great an appearance of nonchalance as he could manage.

There was plenty of bustle over there by the *Estrella*, just as there was round the *Clorinda*, with preparations being made for filling the water casks. It was hard to think in the heat and the noise. It was hard to face the cluttered deck. And darkness was approaching, and then would come eight o'clock, when he would be making his call upon the Captain-General, and obviously everything must be thought out before that. And there were complications. Successive ideas were arising, one out of another, like Chinese boxes, and each one in turn had to be examined for flaws. The sun was down into the hills, leaving a flaming sky behind, when he came to his final resolution.

'Spendlove!' he snapped; excitement made him curt. 'Come below with me.'

Down in the big stern cabin it was oppressively hot. The red sky was reflected in the water of the harbour, shining up through the stern windows; the magnificent effect was dissipated with the lighting of the lamps. Hornblower threw himself into his chair; Spendlove stood looking at him keenly, as Hornblower was well aware. Spendlove could be in no doubt that his temperamental Commander-in-Chief had much on his mind. Yet even Spendlove was surprised at the scheme that was sketched out to him, and at the orders he received. He even ventured to protest.

'My lord –' he said.

'Carry out your orders, Mr Spendlove. Not another word.'

'Aye aye, my lord.'

Spendlove left the cabin, with Hornblower sitting there alone, waiting. The minutes passed slowly – precious minutes; there were few to spare – before the knock came on the door that he expected. It was Fell, entering with every appearance of nervousness.

'My lord, have you a few minutes to spare?'

'Always a pleasure to receive you, Sir Thomas.'

'But this is unusual, I fear, my lord. I have a suggestion to make – an unusual suggestion.'

'Suggestions are always welcome too, Sir Thomas.

Please sit down and tell me. We have an hour at least before we go ashore. I am most interested.'

Fell sat bolt upright in his chair, his hands clutching the arms. He swallowed twice. It gave Hornblower no pleasure to see a man who had faced steel and lead and imminent death apprehensive before him; it made him uncomfortable.

'My lord –' began Fell, and swallowed again.

'You have all my attention, Sir Thomas,' said Hornblower, gently.

'It has occurred to me,' said Fell, growing more fluent with each word until at last he spoke in a rush, 'that we still might have a chance at the *Estrella*.'

'Really, Sir Thomas? Nothing could give me greater pleasure, if it were possible. I would like to hear what you suggest.'

'Well, my lord. She'll sail tomorrow. Most likely at dawn, with the land breeze. Tonight we might – we might fix some kind of drogue to her bottom. Perhaps to her rudder. She's no more than a knot or two faster than we are. We could follow her out and catch her at sea –'

'This is brilliant, Sir Thomas. Really ingenious – but nothing more than could be expected of a seaman of your reputation, let me add.'

'You are too kind, my lord.' There was a struggle only too perceptible in Fell's expression, and he hesitated before he went on at last – 'It was your secretary, Spendlove, who put the idea in my mind, my lord.'

'Spendlove? I can hardly believe it.'

'He was too timid to make the suggestion to you, my lord, and so he came to me with it.'

'I'm sure he did no more than set the wheels of your thought turning, Sir Thomas. In any case, since you have assumed the responsibility the credit must be yours, of course, if credit is to be awarded. Let us hope there will be a great deal.'

'Thank you, my lord.'

'Now about this drogue. What do you suggest, Sir Thomas?'

'It need be no more than a large sea-anchor. A bolt of No. 1 canvas, sewn into a funnel, one end larger than the other.'

'It would have to be reinforced even so. Not even No. 1 canvas could stand the strain with *Estrella* going at twelve knots.'

'Yes, my lord, I was sure of that. Bolt-ropes sewn in in plenty. That would be easy enough, of course. We have a spare bobstay chain on board. That could be sewn round the mouth of the drogue –'

'And could be attached to the *Estrella* to take the main strain.'

'Yes, my lord. That was what I thought.'

'It would serve to keep the drogue under water out of sight as well.'

'Yes, my lord.'

Fell found Hornblower's quickness in grasping the technical points vastly encouraging. His nervousness was now replaced by enthusiasm.

'And where would you propose to attach this drogue, Sir Thomas?'

'I was thinking – Spendlove suggested, my lord – that it might be passed over one of the lower pintles of the rudder.'

'It would be likely to tear the rudder clean away when exerting its full force.'

'That would serve our purpose equally well, my lord.'

'Of course, I understand.'

Fell walked across the cabin to where the great cabin window stood open wide.

'You can't see her from here as we lie now, my lord,' he said. 'But you can hear her.'

'And smell her,' said Hornblower, standing beside him.

'Yes, my lord. They're hosing her out at present. But you can hear her, as I said.'

Over the water came very plainly to them, along with the miasma of her stench, the continued wailing of the wretched slaves; Hornblower fancied he could even hear the clanking of the leg irons.

'Sir Thomas,' said Hornblower, 'I think it would be very desirable if you would put a boat overside to row guard round the ship tonight.'

'Row guard, my lord?' Fell was not very quick in the uptake. In the peacetime Navy it was unnecessary to take elaborate precautions against desertion.

'Oh, yes, most certainly. Half these men would be overside swimming for the shore as soon as night falls. Surely you understand that, Sir Thomas. We must restrain their passion to desert from this brutal service. And in any case a guard-boat will prevent the sale of liquor through the gun ports.'

'Er – yes, I suppose so, my lord.' But Fell clearly had not grasped the implications of the suggestion, and Hornblower had to elaborate.

'Let us set a boat-rowing guard now, before nightfall.

I can explain to the authorities why it is necessary. Then when the time comes –'

'We'll have a boat ready in the water!' Enlightenment had broken in on Fell at last.

'Attracting no attention,' supplemented Hornblower.

'Of course!'

The red sunset showed Fell's face lit up with animation.

'It would be best if you gave that order soon, Sir Thomas. But meanwhile there's little time to spare. We must have this drogue in the making before we go ashore.'

'Shall I give the orders, my lord?'

'Spendlove has figures at his fingertips. He can work out the measurements. Would you be kind enough to send for him, Sir Thomas?'

The cabin was soon crowded with people as the work was put in hand. Spendlove came first; after him Gerard was sent for, and then Sefton, the first lieutenant. Next came the sailmaker, the armourer, the carpenter, and the boatswain. The sailmaker was an elderly Swede who had been forced into the British Navy twenty years ago in some conscienceless action of the press gang, and who had remained in the service ever since. His wrinkled face broke into a grin, like a shattered window, as the beauties of the scheme dawned upon him when he was told about it. He just managed to restrain himself from slapping his thigh with glee when he remembered he was in the august presence of his Admiral and his captain. Spendlove was busy sketching out with pencil and paper a drawing of the drogue, with Gerard looking over his shoulder.

'Perhaps even I might make a contribution to this scheme,' said Hornblower, and everyone turned to look at him; he met Spendlove's eye with a glassy stare that forbade Spendlove to breathe a word to the effect that the whole scheme was his original idea.

'Yes, my lord?' said Fell.

'A length of spun yarn,' said Hornblower, 'made fast to the tail of the drogue and led for'rard and the other end secured to the chain. Just a single strand, to keep it tail end forward while *Estrella* gets under way. Then when she sets all sail and the strain comes –'

'The yarn will part!' said Spendlove. 'You're right, my lord. Then the drogue will take the water –'

'And she'll be ours, let's hope,' concluded Hornblower.

'Excellent, my lord,' said Fell.

Was there perhaps a mild condescension, a tiny hint of patronage, in what he said? Hornblower felt that there was, and was momentarily nettled at it. Already Fell was quite convinced that the whole scheme was his own – despite his handsome earlier admission that Spendlove had contributed – and he was generously allowing Hornblower to add a trifling suggestion. Hornblower allayed his irritation with cynical amusement at the weaknesses of human nature.

'In this stimulating atmosphere of ideas,' he said, modestly, 'one can hardly help but be infected.'

'Y-yes, my lord,' said Gerard, eyeing him curiously. Gerard was too sharp altogether, and knew him too well. He had caught the echo of mock-modesty in Hornblower's tone, and was on the verge of guessing the truth.

'No need for you to put your oar in, Mr Gerard,'

snapped Hornblower. 'Do I have to recall you to your duty? Where's my dinner, Mr Gerard? Do I always have to starve while I'm under your care? What will Lady Barbara say when she hears you allow me to go hungry?'

'I beg pardon, my lord,' spluttered Gerard, entirely taken aback. 'I'd quite forgotten – you've been so busy, my lord –'

His embarrassment was intense; he turned this way and that in the crowded cabin as if looking about him for the missing dinner.

'No time now, Mr Gerard,' said Hornblower. Until the need for distracting Gerard's attention had arisen he had been equally forgetful of the need for dinner. 'Let's hope His Excellency will offer us some small collation.'

'I really must beg your pardon, my lord,' said Fell, equally embarrassed.

'Oh, no matter, Sir Thomas,' said Hornblower, waving the apologies aside testily. 'You and I are in the same condition. Let me see that drawing, Mr Spendlove.'

He was continually being led into playing the part of a peppery old gentleman, when he knew himself to be nothing of the sort. He was able to mellow again as they went once more through the details of the construction of the drogue, and he gave his approval.

'I believe, Sir Thomas,' he said, 'that you have decided to entrust the work to Mr Sefton during our absence ashore?'

Fell bowed his agreement.

'Mr Spendlove will remain under your orders, Mr Sefton. Mr Gerard will accompany Sir Thomas and me. I don't know what you have decided, Sir Thomas, but

I would suggest that you bring a lieutenant and a midshipman with you to His Excellency's reception.'

'Aye aye, my lord.'

'Mr Sefton, I am sure I can trust you to have this work completed by the time of our return, early in the middle watch, I fancy?'

'Yes, my lord.'

So there it was all settled, except for the dreary interval of waiting. This was just like wartime, standing by with a crisis looming in the near future.

'Dinner, my lord?' suggested Gerard, eagerly.

He wanted no dinner. He was weary now that all was settled and the tension easing.

'I'll call for Giles if I want some,' he said, looking round the crowded cabin. He wanted to dismiss the horde of people, and sought words to do so politely.

'Then I'll attend to my other duties, my lord,' said Fell, suddenly and surprisingly tactful.

'Very well, Sir Thomas, thank you.'

The cabin emptied itself rapidly; Hornblower was able by a mere look to put an end to Gerard's tendency to linger. Then he could sink back into his chair and relax, sturdily ignoring Giles when he came in with another lighted lamp for the darkening cabin. The ship was full of the sound of the business of watering, sheaves squealing in blocks, pumps clanking, hoarse orders; the noise was sufficiently distracting to prevent his thoughts maintaining any regular course. He was in half a doze when a knock on the door preceded the arrival of a midshipman.

'Cap'n's respects, my lord, and the shore boat is approaching.'

'My compliments to the captain, and I'll be on deck at once.'

The shore boat was bright with a lantern hanging over the sternsheets in the midst of the darkness of the harbour. It lit up Mendez-Castillo's resplendent uniform. Down the side they went, midshipman, lieutenants, captain, admiral, in the reversed order of naval precedence, and powerful strokes of the oars carried them over the black water towards the city, where a few lights gleamed. They passed close by the *Estrella*; there was a light hanging in her rigging, but apparently she had completed her watering, for there was no activity about her.

Nevertheless, there came a continuous faint wailing from up her open hatchways. Perhaps the slaves there were mourning the departure of those of them who had been taken from them; perhaps they were voicing their apprehension at what the future held in store for them. It occurred to Hornblower that these unfortunate people, snatched from their homes, packed into a ship whose like they had never seen before, guarded by white men (and white faces must be as extraordinary to them as emerald green ones would be to a European) could have no idea at all of what lay in store for them, any more than he himself would have if he were to be abducted to another planet.

'His Excellency,' said Mendez-Castillo beside him, 'has had pleasure in deciding to receive Your Excellency with full ceremonial.'

'That is most kind of His Excellency,' replied Hornblower, recalling himself to his present duties with an effort, and expressing himself in Spanish with even more effort.

The tiller was put over and the boat turned abruptly round a corner, revealing a brightly lit jetty, with a massive gateway beyond. The boat ran alongside and half a dozen uniformed figures stood to attention as the party climbed on shore.

'This way, Your Excellency,' murmured Mendez-Castillo.

They passed through the gateway into a courtyard lit by scores of lanterns, which shone on ranks of soldiers drawn up in two treble lines. As Hornblower emerged into the courtyard a shouted order brought the muskets to the present, and at the same moment a band burst into music. Hornblower's tone-deaf ear heard the jerky braying, and he halted at attention with his hand to the brim of his cocked hat, his fellow officers beside him, until the deafening noise – echoed and multiplied by the surrounding walls – came to an end.

'A fine military appearance, Major,' said Hornblower, looking down the rigid lines of white cross-belts.

'Your Excellency is too kind. Would Your Excellency please proceed to the door in front?'

An imposing flight of steps, lined on either side with more uniforms; beyond that an open doorway and a vast room. A prolonged whispered conference between Mendez-Castillo and an official beside the door, and then their names blared out in resounding Spanish – Hornblower had long given up hope of ever hearing his name pronounced intelligibly by a foreign tongue.

The central figure in the room rose from his chair – which was almost a throne – to receive the British Commander-in-Chief standing. He was a much younger man than Hornblower had expected, in his thirties, dark complexioned, with a thin, mobile face and a humorous expression at odds with his arrogant hooked nose. His uniform gleamed with gold lace, with the Order of the Golden Fleece on his breast.

Mendez-Castillo made the presentations; the Englishmen bowed deeply to the representative of His Most Catholic Majesty and each received a polite inclination in return. Mendez-Castillo ventured so far as to murmur their host's titles – probably a breach of etiquette, thought Hornblower, for it should be assumed that visitors were fully aware of them.

'His Excellency the Marques de Ayora, Captain-General of His Most Catholic Majesty's dominion of Puerto Rico.'

Ayora smiled in welcome.

'I know you speak Spanish, Your Excellency,' he said. 'I have already had the pleasure of hearing you do so.'

'Indeed, Your Excellency?'

'I was a major of migueletes under Claros at the time of the attack on Rosas. I had the honour of serving beside Your Excellency – I remember Your Excellency well. Your Excellency would naturally not remember me.'

It would have been too flagrant to pretend he did, and Hornblower was for once at a loss for a word, and could only bow again.

'Your Excellency,' went on Ayora, 'has changed very little since that day, if I may venture to say so. It is eleven years ago.'

'Your Excellency is too kind.' That was one of the most useful phrases in polite language.

Ayora had a word for Fell – a compliment on the

appearance of his ship – and a supplementary smile for the junior officers. Then, as if it were a moment for which he had been waiting, Mendez-Castillo turned to them.

'Perhaps you gentlemen would care to be presented to the ladies of the company?' he said; his glance passed over Hornblower and Fell and took in only the lieutenants and the midshipmen. Hornblower translated, and saw them depart a little nervously under Mendez-Castillo's escort.

Ayora, etiquette and Spanish training notwithstanding, wasted no time in coming to the point the moment he found himself alone with Hornblower and Fell.

'I watched your pursuit of the *Estrella del Sur* today through my telescope,' he said, and Hornblower once more found himself at a loss for a word; a bow and a smile also seemed out of place in this connection. He could only look blank.

'It is an anomalous situation,' said Ayora. 'Under the preliminary convention between our governments the British Navy has the right to capture on the high seas Spanish ships laden with slaves. But once within Spanish territorial waters those ships are safe. When the new convention for the suppression of the slave trade is signed then those ships will be forfeit to His Most Catholic Majesty's Government, but until that time it is my duty to give them every protection in my power.'

'Your Excellency is perfectly correct, of course,' said Hornblower. Fell was looking perfectly blank, not understanding a word of what was said, but Hornblower felt that the effort of translating was beyond him.

'And I fully intend to carry out my duty,' said Ayora, firmly.

'Naturally,' said Hornblower.

'So perhaps it would be best to come to a clear understanding regarding future events.'

'There is nothing I would like better, Your Excellency.'

'It is clearly understood, then, that I will tolerate no interference with the *Estrella del Sur* while she is in waters under my jurisdiction?'

'Of course I understand that, Your Excellency,' said Hornblower.

'The *Estrella* wishes to sail at the first light of morning tomorrow.'

'That is what I expected, Your Excellency.'

'And for the sake of the amity between our governments it would be best if your ship were to remain in this harbour until after she sails.'

Ayora's eyes met Hornblower's in a steady stare. His face was perfectly expressionless; there was no hint of a threat in that glance. But a threat was implied, the ultimate hint of superior strength was there. At Ayora's command a hundred thirty-two-pounders could sweep the waters of the harbour. Hornblower was reminded of the Roman who agreed with his Emperor because it was ill arguing with the master of thirty legions. He adopted the same pose as far as his acting ability allowed. He smiled the smile of a good loser.

'We have had our chance and lost it, Your Excellency,' he said. 'We can hardly complain.'

If Ayora felt any relief at his acquiescence it showed no more plainly than his previous hint of force.

'Your Excellency is most understanding,' he said.

'Naturally we are desirous of taking advantage of the land breeze to leave tomorrow morning,' said Hornblower, deferentially. 'Now that we have refilled with water – for the opportunity of doing so I have to thank Your Excellency – we would not like to trespass too far upon Your Excellency's hospitality.'

Hornblower did his best to maintain an appearance of innocence under Ayora's searching stare.

'Perhaps we might hear what Captain Gomez has to say,' said Ayora, turning aside to summon someone close at hand. He was a young man, strikingly handsome, dressed in plain but elegant blue clothes with a silver-hilted sword at his side.

'May I present,' said Ayora, 'Don Miguel Gomez y Gonzalez, Captain of the *Estrella del Sur?*'

Bows were exchanged.

'May I felicitate you on the sailing qualities of your ship, Captain?' said Hornblower.

'Many thanks, *señor*.'

'*Clorinda* is a fast frigate, but your ship is superior at all points of sailing.' Hornblower was not too sure about how to render that technical expression into Spanish, but apparently he contrived to make himself under-stood.

'Many thanks again, *señor*.'

'And I could even venture' – Hornblower spread his hands deprecatingly – 'to congratulate her captain on the brilliance with which he managed her.'

Captain Gomez bowed, and Hornblower suddenly checked himself. These high-flown Spanish compli-ments were all very well, but they could be overdone.

He did not want to give the impression of a man too anxious to please. But he was reassured by a glance at the expression on Gomez's face. He was actually simpering; that was the only word for it. Hornblower mentally classified him as a young man of great ability and well pleased with himself. Another compliment would not be one too many.

'I shall suggest to my government,' he went on, 'that they request permission to take off the lines of the *Star of the South*, and study the plan of her sails, in order to build a similar vessel. She would be ideal for the work of the Navy in these waters. But, of course, it would be hard to find a suitable captain.'

Gomez bowed once more. It was hard not to be self-satisfied when complimented by a seaman with the legendary reputation of Hornblower.

'His Excellency,' put in Ayora, 'is desirous of leaving the harbour tomorrow morning.'

'So we understood,' said Gomez.

Even Ayora looked a trifle disconcerted at the admission. Hornblower could see it plainly. Stuart, so helpful with his information, had not hesitated to help both sides, as Hornblower had expected he would. He had gone straight to the Spanish authorities with the intelligence Hornblower had supplied him with. But Hornblower had no desire to allow a jarring note to creep into the present conversation.

'You can understand, Captain,' he said, 'that I would be glad to leave on the same tide and with the same land breeze that takes you out. After our experiences today I fear you need be under no apprehension.'

'None at all,' said Gomez. There was something of

condescension in his smile. That agreement was all that Hornblower wanted. He was at pains to conceal his relief.

'It will be my duty to pursue you if you are still in sight when I leave,' he said, apologetically; by his glance he made it clear that the remark was addressed to the Captain-General as well as to Gomez, but it was Gomez who answered.

'I have no fear,' he said.

'In that case, Your Excellency,' said Hornblower, clinching the matter, 'I can inform Your Excellency officially that His Majesty's Ship in which my flag is being flown will leave harbour tomorrow morning as early as suits Captain Gomez's convenience.'

'That is understood,' agreed Ayora. 'I regret greatly that Your Excellency's visit should be so brief.'

'In the life of a sailor,' said Hornblower, 'duty seems invariably to interfere with inclination. But at least during this brief visit I have had the pleasure of making the acquaintance of Your Excellency, and of Captain Gomez.'

'There are numerous other gentlemen here also desirous of making Your Excellency's acquaintance,' said Ayora. 'May I be permitted to present them to Your Excellency?'

The real business of the evening had been transacted, and now it was only necessary to go through the other formalities. The rest of the reception was as dreary as Hornblower had expected and feared; the Puerto Rican magnates who were led up in turn to meet him were as dull. At midnight Hornblower caught the eye of Gerard and gathered his flock together. Ayora noted the gesture and gave, in courteous terms, the leave to depart which, as His Catholic Majesty's representative, he had to give unless his guests were to be guilty of discourtesy.

'Your Excellency has doubtless need to rest in readiness for your early start tomorrow,' he said. 'I will not attempt to detain Your Excellency in consequence, much as Your Excellency's presence here has been appreciated.'

The goodbyes were said, and Mendez-Castillo undertook to escort the party back to the *Clorinda*. It was something of a shock to Hornblower to find that the band and the guard of honour were still in the courtyard to offer the official compliments on his departure. He stood at the salute while the band played some jerky tune or other; then they went down into the waiting boat.

The harbour was pitch dark as they rowed out into it, the few lights visible doing almost nothing to alleviate the blackness. They rounded the corner and passed astern of the *Estrella* again. There was a single lantern hanging in her main rigging, and she was quiet by now – no; in the still night, at one moment, Hornblower heard the faint rattle of leg-irons as some one of the slaves in her hold indicated that he was still awake and restless. That was good. Farther along, a quiet challenge came over the inky water, issuing from a nucleus of darkness even more solid than the darkness surrounding it.

'Flag,' answered the midshipman. '*Clorinda*.'

The two brief words were all that were needed to inform the guard-boat that an admiral and a captain were approaching.

'You see, Major,' said Hornblower, 'that Captain Fell deemed it necessary to row guard round the ship during the night.'

'I understood that to be the case, Your Excellency,' answered Mendez-Castillo.

'Our seamen will go to great lengths to indulge themselves in the pleasures of the shore.'

'Naturally, Your Excellency,' said Mendez-Castillo.

The boat ran alongside the *Clorinda*; standing awkwardly in the sternsheets Hornblower said his last goodbyes, and uttered his last words of thanks, to the representative of his host before going up the side. From the entry port he watched the boat shove off again and disappear into the darkness.

'Now,' he said, 'we can make better use of our time.'

On the maindeck, just visible in the light from the lantern hanging from the mainstay, was a Thing; that was the only way to describe it, something of canvas and cordage, with a length of chain attached to it. Sefton was standing beside it.

'I see you've finished it, Mr Sefton.'

'Yes, my lord. A full hour ago. The sailmaker and his mates worked admirably.'

Hornblower turned to Fell.

'I fancy, Sir Thomas,' he said, 'that you have in mind the necessary orders to give. Perhaps you would be kind enough to tell me about them before you issue them?'

'Aye aye, my lord.'

That eternal Navy answer was the only one Fell could make in the circumstances, even if Fell had not yet given full thought to the next problems. Down in the cabin alone with his Admiral, Fell's unreadiness was a little apparent.

'I suppose,' prompted Hornblower, 'that you will tell

off the necessary personnel for the expedition. Which officer can you trust fully to exercise discretion?'

Little by little the details were settled. Powerful swimmers who could work under water; an armourer's mate who could be relied upon to put the final shackle in the chain in the darkness; the boat's crew was decided upon, summoned, and instructed in all the details of the plan. When the guard-boat came in for the relief of its crew there was another crew standing by all ready, who went down overside rapidly and quietly although encumbered with the Thing and the necessary gear.

It pushed off again into the darkness, and Hornblower stood on the quarterdeck to watch it go. There might be an international incident arising out of this, or he might be made to appear a fool in the eyes of the world, which would be just as bad. He strained his ears for any sounds in the darkness which would tell him how the work was progressing, but he could hear nothing. The land breeze had just begun to blow, gently, but strongly enough to swing *Clorinda* to her anchor; it would carry any sounds away from him, he realized – but it would also serve to obscure any suspicious noises if anyone in the *Estrella* was awake enough to hear them. She had a full counter, with, as was only to be expected, plenty of rake. A swimmer who reached her stern unobserved would be able to work at her rudder unobserved, certainly.

'My lord,' said Gerard's voice quietly beside him. 'Would not this be a suitable time to rest?'

'You are quite right, Mr Gerard. A most suitable time,' answered Hornblower, continuing to lean against the rail.

'Well, then, my lord –?'

'I have agreed with you, Mr Gerard. Surely you can be content with that?'

But Gerard's voice went on, remorseless as the voice of conscience.

'There is cold beef laid out in the cabin, my lord. Fresh bread and a bottle of Bordeaux.'

That was a different story. Hornblower suddenly realized how hungry he was; during the past thirty hours he had eaten one meagre meal, because the cold collation he had expected at the reception had failed to materialize. And he could still pretend to be superior to the weaknesses of the flesh.

'You would have made an excellent wet-nurse, Mr Gerard,' he said, 'if nature had treated you more generously. But I suppose my life will be unbearable until I yield to your importunity.'

On the way to the companion they passed Fell; he was striding up and down the quarterdeck in the darkness, and they could hear his hard breathing. It pleased Hornblower to know that even these muscular heroes could feel anxiety. It might be polite, even kind, to invite Fell to join them at this cold supper, but Hornblower dismissed the idea. He had had as much of Fell's company already as he could bear.

Down below, Spendlove was waiting in the lighted cabin.

'The vultures are gathered together,' said Hornblower. It was amusing to see Spendlove was pale and tense too. 'I hope you gentlemen will join me.'

The younger men were silent as they ate. Hornblower put his nose to his glass of wine and sipped thoughtfully.

'Six months in the tropics has done this Bordeaux no good,' he commented; it was inevitable that as host, and Admiral, and older man, his opinion should be received with deference. Spendlove broke the next silence.

'That length of spun yard, my lord,' he said. 'The breaking strain –'

'Mr Spendlove,' said Hornblower. 'All the discussion in the world won't change it now. We shall know in good time. Meanwhile, let's not spoil our dinner with technical discussions.'

'Your pardon, my lord,' said Spendlove, abashed. Was it by mere coincidence or through telepathy that Hornblower had been thinking at that very moment about the breaking strain of that length of spun yarn in the drogue; but he would not dream of admitting that he had been thinking about it. The dinner continued.

'Well,' said Hornblower, raising his glass, 'we can admit the existence of mundane affairs long enough to allow of a toast. Here's to head money.'

As they drank they heard unmistakable sounds on deck and overside. The guard-boat had returned from its mission. Spendlove and Gerard exchanged glances, and poised themselves ready to stand up. Hornblower forced himself to lean back and shake his head sadly, his glass still in his hand.

'Too bad about this Bordeaux, gentlemen,' he said.

Then came the knock on the door and the expected message.

'Cap'n's respects, my lord, and the boat has returned.'

'My compliments to the captain, and I'll be glad to see him and the lieutenant here as soon as is convenient.'

One glance at Fell as he entered the cabin was

sufficient to indicate that the expedition had been successful, so far, at least.

'All well, my lord,' he said, his florid face suffused with excitement.

'Excellent.' The lieutenant was a grizzled veteran older than Hornblower; and Hornblower could not help but think to himself that had he not enjoyed great good fortune on several occasions he would be only a lieutenant, too. 'Will you sit down, gentlemen? A glass of wine? Mr Gerard, order fresh glasses, if you please. Sir Thomas, would you mind if I hear Mr Field's story from his own lips?'

Field had no fluency of speech. His story had to be drawn from him by questions. Everything had gone well. Two strong swimmers, their faces blackened, had slipped overside from the guard-boat and had swum unseen to the *Estrella*. Working with their knives, they had been able to prise off the copper from the second rudder-brace below the waterline. With an auger they had made a space large enough to pass a line through. The most ticklish part of the work had been approaching near enough in the guard-boat and putting the drogue overside after it had been attached to the line, but Field reported that no hail had come from the *Estrella*. The chain had followed the line and had been securely shackled. Now the drogue hung at *Estrella*'s stern, safely out of sight below the surface, ready to exert its full force on her rudder when – and if – the spun yarn which held the drogue reversed should part.

'Excellent,' said Hornblower again, when Field's last halting sentence was uttered. 'You've done very well, Mr Field, thank you.'

'Thank you, my lord.'

When Field had left, Hornblower could address himself to Fell.

'Your plan has worked out admirably, Sir Thomas. Now it only remains to catch the *Estrella*. I would strongly recommend you to make all preparations for getting under way at daylight. The sooner we leave after the *Estrella* has sailed the better, don't you think?'

'Aye aye, my lord.'

The ship's bell overhead anticipated the next question Hornblower was about to ask.

'Three hours to daylight,' he said. 'I'll say goodnight to you gentlemen, then.'

It had been a busy day, of ceaseless activity, mental if not physical, since dawn. After a long, hot evening it seemed to Hornblower that his feet had swollen to twice their ordinary size and that his gold-buckled shoes had made no allowance for this expansion – he could hardly pry them off. He took off ribbon and star and gold-laced coat, and reluctantly reminded himself that he would have to put them on again for his ceremonial departure in three hours' time. He sponged himself down with water from his wash-basin, and sank down sighing with relief on his cot in the night cabin.

He woke automatically when the watch was called; the cabin was still quite dark and he was at a loss, for a couple of seconds, about why there should be this feeling of urgency within him. Then he remembered, and was wide awake at once, shouting to the sentry at the door to pass the word for Giles. He shaved by lamplight in feverish haste, and then, once more in the hated full-dress uniform, he sped up the ladder to the quarterdeck.

It was still pitch dark; no, perhaps there was the slightest glimmering of daylight. Perhaps the sky was the smallest trifle brighter over the Morro. Perhaps. The quarterdeck was crowded with shadowy figures, more even than would be found there with the ship's company at stations for getting under way. At sight of them he nearly turned back, having no wish to reveal that he shared the same weaknesses as the rest of them, but Fell had caught sight of him.

'Good morning, my lord.'

'Morning, Sir Thomas.'

'Land breeze blowing full, my lord.'

No doubt about that; Hornblower could feel it breathing round him, delightful after the sweltering stuffiness of the cabin. In these midsummer tropics it would be of short duration; it would be cut off short as soon as the sun, lifting over the horizon, should get to work in its brassy strength upon the land.

'*Estrella*'s making ready for sea, my lord.'

There was no doubt about that either; the sounds of it made their way over the water through the twilight.

'I don't have to ask if you are ready, Sir Thomas.'

'All ready, my lord. Hands standing by at the capstan.'

'Very well.'

Undoubtedly it was lighter already; the figures on the quarterdeck – now much more clearly defined – had all moved over to the starboard side, lining the rail. Half a dozen telescopes were being extended and pointed towards the *Estrella*.

'Sir Thomas, put an end to that, if you please. Send that crowd below.'

'They're anxious to see –'

'I know what they want to see. Send them below immediately.'

'Aye aye, my lord.'

Everyone, of course, was desperately anxious to see if anything was visible at the *Estrella's* waterline aft, which might reveal what had been done at night. But there could be no surer way of calling the attention of the *Estrella's* captain to something suspicious under his stern than by pointing telescopes at it.

'Officer of the watch!'

'My lord?'

'See to it that no one points a telescope for one moment towards the *Estrella*.'

'Aye aye, my lord.'

'When there's enough light to see clearly, you can sweep round the harbour as you might be expected to do. Not more than five seconds for the *Estrella*, but make sure you see all there is to see.'

'Aye aye, my lord.'

The eastern sky was now displaying faint greens and yellows, against which the Morro silhouetted itself magnificently though faintly, but in its shadow all was still dark. Even before breakfast it was a romantic moment. It occurred to Hornblower that the presence of an admiral in full dress on the quarterdeck so early might itself be a suspicious circumstance.

'I'm going below, Sir Thomas. Please keep me informed.'

'Aye aye, my lord.'

In the day cabin Gerard and Spendlove sprang to their feet as he entered; presumably they had been among those driven below by Fell's order.

'Mr Spendlove, I am profiting by your admirable example of yesterday. I shall make sure of my breakfast while I may. Would you please order breakfast, Mr Gerard? I presume you gentlemen will favour me with your company.'

He threw himself negligently into a chair and watched the preparations. Halfway through them a knock at the door brought in Fell himself.

'*Estrella*'s clearly in sight now, my lord. And there's nothing visible under her stern.'

'Thank you, Sir Thomas.'

A cup of coffee was welcome at this time in the morning. Hornblower did not have to pretend eagerness to drink it. Daylight was creeping in through the cabin windows, making the lamplight garish and unnecessary. Another knock brought in a midshipman.

'Cap'n's respects, my lord, and *Estrella*'s casting off.'

'Very well.'

Soon she would be under way, and their device would be put to the test. Hornblower made himself bite and masticate another mouthful of toast.

'Can't you young men sit still for even a moment?' he snapped. 'Pour me some more coffee, Gerard.'

'*Estrella*'s warping out into the channel, my lord,' reported the midshipman again.

'Very well,' said Hornblower, sipping fastidiously at his coffee, and hoping that no one could guess how much his pulse rate had accelerated. The minutes dragged by.

'*Estrella*'s preparing to make sail, my lord.'

'Very well.' Hornblower put down his coffee cup, slowly, and as slowly as he could manage it rose from his chair, the eyes of the two young men never leaving him.

'I think,' he said, dragging out his words, 'we might now go on deck.'

Pacing as slowly as when he had been a mourner at Nelson's funeral he walked out past the sentry and up the ladder; behind him the young men had to curb their impatience. It was dazzling bright on deck; the sun was just over the Morro. In the centre of the fairway at less than a cable's length distance lay the *Estrella*, gleaming in her white paint. As Hornblower's eyes rested on her her jib extended itself upwards, to catch the wind and swing her round. Next moment her mainsail took the wind, and she steadied herself, gathering way; in a few seconds she was moving forward past the *Clorinda*. This was the moment. Fell was standing staring at her and muttering to himself; he was blaspheming in his excitement. *Estrella* dipped her colours; on her deck Hornblower was able to recognize the figure of Gomez, standing directing the handling of the schooner. Gomez caught sight of him at the same moment, and bowed, holding his hat across his chest, and Hornblower returned the compliment.

'She's not making two knots through the water,' said Hornblower.

'Thank God for that,' said Fell.

Estrella glided on towards the entrance, preparatory to making the dog-legged turn out to sea; Gomez was handling her beautifully under her very easy sail.

'Shall I follow her now, my lord?'

'I think it's time, Sir Thomas.'

'Hands to the capstan, there! Headsail sheets, Mr Field!'

Even at two knots there would be some strain on that length of spun yarn. It must not part – it must not – before *Estrella* was well out to sea. Lusty arms and sturdy backs were heaving *Clorinda*'s cable short.

'Clear away the saluting carronade, there!'

Estrella had made the turn; the last of her mainsail was vanishing round the corner. Fell was giving his orders to get *Clorinda* under way steadily and clearly, despite his excitement. Hornblower was watching him narrowly; this was not a bad test of how he would behave in action, of how he would take his ship down into the smoke and fury of a battle.

'Maintops'l braces!'

Fell was bringing the big frigate round in as neat a fashion as Gomez had handled *Estrella*. *Clorinda* steadied herself and gathered way, moving down the channel.

'Man the rail!'

Whatever was going on round the corner, whatever was happening to the *Estrella* out of sight, the compliments must be paid. Nine-tenths of *Clorinda*'s crew on deck could be spared for the purpose; with the ship creeping forward before the land breeze the other one-tenth sufficed to keep her under control. Hornblower drew himself up and faced the Spanish flag flying over the Morro, his hand to his hat brim, Fell beside him, the other officers in rank behind, while the salute banged out and was returned, the flags dipping respectfully.

'Carry on!'

They were approaching the turn. It was possible that at any moment one of those grinning cannons up there would pitch a warning shot at them – a shot warning them that a hundred other guns were ready to pound them into a wreck; that would be if the drogue had begun to take obvious effect on the *Estrella*.

'Maintops'l braces!' came Fell's order again.

Already the big Atlantic rollers were making their effect felt; Hornblower could feel *Clorinda's* bows lift momentarily to a dying surge.

'Hard a-starboard!' *Clorinda* turned steadily. 'Meet her! Steady as you go.'

She had hardly settled on her new course when *Estrella* came in sight again a mile farther out to sea, her bows pointed in almost the opposite direction; she was still under very easy canvas, thank God, steadying herself for the final turn from the channel out into the ocean. *Clorinda's* maintopsail shivered briefly as the Morro height intercepted the land breeze, but drew again instantly. *Estrella* was turning again now. She was hardly within cannon shot of the Morro.

'Port!' came Fell's order. 'Steady!'

The land breeze was right aft now, but dying away, partly with their increased distance from land and partly with the growing heat of the sun.

'Set the mains'l.'

Fell was quite right; there was need to hasten, lest the ship be delayed in the belt of doldrums between the land breeze and the trade wind. The enormous sail area of the main course carried *Clorinda* forward boldly, and once more the sound of the ship's way through the water became audible. *Estrella* was clear of the channel now; Hornblower, watching anxiously, saw her set foresail and staysails and jibs, all her fore-and-aft canvas in fact. She was holding her course northward, close-hauled, directly away from the land; she must have caught the trade wind and was making northing, very sensibly, because she would have to weather Haiti before next morning on her course to the Old Bahama Channel and Havana. They were far enough from the Morro now, and from *Estrella*, to incur no suspicion by staring through telescopes at her. Hornblower looked long and carefully. He could detect nothing unusual about her appearance. It suddenly occurred to him that perhaps Gomez had detected the drogue under his stern and had removed it. He might even now be exploding with laughter, along with his officers, looking back at the British frigate hopefully following them.

'Port!' came Fell's order again, and *Clorinda* took the final turn.

'Leading marks in line, sir!' reported the master, looking aft at the land with his telescope to his eye.

'Very well. Steady as you go.'

Now the waves they were encountering were true Atlantic rollers, heaving up *Clorinda*'s starboard bow, and passing aft as the bows dipped to heave up the port quarter. *Estrella* right ahead was still close-hauled on a northerly course under fore-and-aft canvas.

'She'll be making six knots,' estimated Gerard, standing with Spendlove a yard from Hornblower.

'That spun yarn should hold at six knots,' said Spendlove, meditatively.

'No bottom with this line!' reported the leadsman in the chains.

'All hands make sail!'

The order was being piped through the ship. Topgallants and royals were being spread; it was not long before *Clorinda* had every stitch of canvas set.

Yet the land breeze was dying fast. *Clorinda* was hardly making steerage way. Once, twice, the sails flapped like thunder, but she still held her course, creeping forward over the blue and white sea, with the sun blazing down upon her from a blue sky with hardly a fleck of cloud.

'Can't keep her on her course, sir,' reported the quartermaster.

Clorinda was yawing sluggishly as the rollers came at her. Far ahead the *Estrella* was almost hull down. Now came a breath of a different air, the tiniest breath; Hornblower felt it, nearly imperceptible, on his sweating face long before *Clorinda* made response. It was a different air indeed, not the heated air of the land breeze, but the fresher air of the trade wind, clean with its passage over three thousand miles of ocean. The sails flapped and shivered; *Clorinda* swung more meaningly.

'Here it comes!' exclaimed Fell. 'Full and by!'

A stronger puff came, so that the rudder could bite. A lull, another puff, another lull, another puff, yet each puff was stronger yet. The next puff did not die away. It endured, heeling *Clorinda* over. A roller burst against her starboard bow in a dazzling rainbow. Now they had caught the trade wind; now they could thrust their way northwards close-hauled in the trail of the *Estrella*. With the clean, fresh wind blowing, and the sensation of successful striving with it, a new animation came over the ship. There were smiles to be seen.

'She hasn't set her tops'ls yet, my lord,' said Gerard, his telescope still to his eye.

'I doubt if she will while she makes her northing,' replied Hornblower.

'On a wind she can weather and head-reach on us,' said Spendlove. 'Just as she did yesterday.'

Yesterday? Was it only yesterday? It could have been a month ago, so much had happened since yesterday's chase.

'Do you think that drogue ought to have any effect?' asked Fell, approaching them.

'None, sir, practically speaking,' answered Spendlove. 'Not while that spun yarn keeps it tail forward.'

Fell had one huge hand clasped in the other, grinding his knuckles into his palm.

'For me,' said Hornblower, and every eye turned to him, 'I am going to say farewell to gold lace. A cooler coat and a looser neckcloth.'

Let Fell display worry and nervousness; he himself was going below as if he had no interest whatever in the outcome of the affair. Down in the hot cabin it was a relief to throw off his full-dress uniform – ten pounds of broadcloth and gold – and to have Giles get out a clean shirt and white duck trousers.

'I'll take my bath,' said Hornblower, meditatively.

He knew perfectly well that Fell thought it undignified and dangerous to discipline that an admiral should disport himself under the wash-deck pump, hosed down by grinning seamen, and he neither agreed nor cared. No miserable sponging down could take the place of his bath. The seamen pumped vigorously, and Hornblower pranced with middle-aged abandon under the stinging impact of the water. Now the clean shirt and trousers were doubly delightful; he felt a new man as he came on deck again, and his unconcern was not all pretence when Fell nervously approached him.

'She's running clean away from us again, my lord,' he said.

'We know she can, Sir Thomas. We can only wait until she puts her helm up and sets her tops'ls.'

'As long as we can keep her in sight –' said Fell.

Clorinda was lying right over, fighting her way to the northward.

'I can see that we're doing all we can, Sir Thomas,' said Hornblower, soothingly.

The morning was wearing on. 'Up spirits!' was piped, and Fell agreed with the sailing master that it was noon, and the hands were sent to dinner. Now it was only when *Clorinda* lifted to a wave that a telescope, trained over the starboard bow from the quarterdeck, could detect the gleam of *Estrella's* sails over the horizon. She still had no topsails set; Gomez was acting on the knowledge that close-hauled his schooner behaved better without her square sails – unless he was merely playing with his pursuers. The hills of Puerto Rico had sunk out of sight below the horizon far, far astern. And the roast beef at dinner, roast fresh beef, had been most disappointing, tough and stringy and without any taste whatever.

'Stuart said he'd send me the best sirloin the island could produce, my lord,' said Gerard, in answer to Hornblower's expostulations.

'I wish I had him here,' said Hornblower. 'I'd make him eat it, every bit, without salt. Sir Thomas, please accept my apologies.'

'Er – yes, my lord,' said Fell, who had been invited to his Admiral's table and who had been recalled from his own private thoughts by Hornblower's apologies. 'That drogue –'

Having said those words – that special word, rather – he was unable to say more. He looked across the table at Hornblower. His lantern-jawed face – the brick-red cheeks always looked odd in that conformation – showed his anxiety, which was accentuated by the look in his eyes.

'If we don't know all about it today,' said Hornblower, 'we'll hear all about it at some later date.'

It was the truth, even though it was not the kindest thing to say.

'We'll be the laughing-stock of the Islands,' said Fell.

No one in the world could look more miserable than he did at that moment. Hornblower himself was inclined to give up hope, but the sight of that despair roused his contrary nature.

'There's all the difference in the world between six knots, which she's making now close-hauled, and twelve knots, which she'll make when she puts up her helm,' he said. 'Mr Spendlove here will tell you that the water resistance is a function of the square of the speed. Isn't that so, Mr Spendlove?'

'Perhaps a function of the cube or even one of the higher powers, my lord.'

'So we can still hope, Sir Thomas. That spun yarn will have eight times the pull upon it when she alters course.'

'It'll be chafing now, as well, my lord,' added Spendlove.

'If they didn't see the thing last night and cast it off,' said Fell, still gloomy.

When they reached the deck again the sun was inclining towards the west.

'Masthead, there!' hailed Fell. 'Is the chase still in sight?'

'Yes, sir. Hull down from here, sir, but plain in sight. Two points or thereabouts on the weather bow.'

'She's made all the northing she needs,' grumbled Fell. 'Why doesn't she alter course?'

There was nothing to do except wait, to try and extract some pleasure from the clean wind and the blue and white sea; but the pleasure was only faint now, the sea did not seem so blue. Nothing to do except wait, with the minutes dragging like hours. Then it happened.

'Deck, there! Chase is altering course to port. She's running right before the wind.'

'Very well.'

Fell looked round at all the faces of the crowd on the quarterdeck. His own was as tense as anyone else's.

'Mr Sefton, alter course four points to port.'

He was going to play the game out to the bitter end, even though yesterday's experience, closely parallel to the present, had shown that *Clorinda* stood no chance in normal circumstances of intercepting.

'Deck, there! She's settin' her tops'ls. T'garns'ls, too, sir!'

'Very well.'

'We'll soon know now,' said Spendlove. 'With the drogue in action she *must* lose speed. She *must*.'

'Deck, there! Cap'n, sir!' The lookout's voice had risen to a scream of excitement. 'She's flown up into the wind! She's all aback! Foretopmast's gone, sir!'

'So have her rudder pintles,' said Hornblower, grimly.

Fell was leaping on the deck, actually dancing with

joy, his face radiant. But he recollected himself with all speed.

'Come two points to starboard,' he ordered. 'Mr James, get aloft with you and tell me how she bears.'

'She's taking in her mains'l!' shouted the lookout.

'Trying to get before the wind again,' commented Gerard.

'Cap'n, sir!' This was James' voice from the masthead. 'You're heading a point to loo'ard of her.'

'Very well.'

'She's coming before the wind – no, she's all aback again, sir!'

The Thing still had her by the tail, then; her struggles would be as unavailing as those of a deer in the claws of a lion.

'Steer small, you –' said Fell, using a horrible word to the helmsman.

Everyone was excited, everyone seemed to be obsessed with the fear that *Estrella* would clear away the wreck and make her escape after all.

'With her rudder gone she'll never be able to hold a course,' said Hornblower. 'And she's lost her foretopmast, too.'

Another wait, but of a very different nature now. *Clorinda*, thrashing along, seemed to have caught the excitement and to have put on a spurt as she hurled herself at her quarry, racing forward to triumph.

'There she is!' said Gerard, telescope trained forward. 'All aback still.'

As the next wave lifted *Clorinda* they all caught sight of her; they were approaching her fast. A sorry, pitiful sight she looked, her foretopmast broken off clean at the cap, her sails shivering in the wind.

'Clear away the bow chaser,' ordered Fell. 'Fire a shot across her bow.'

The shot was fired. Something rose to the schooner's main peak, and broke out into the red and gold of Spain. It hung there for a moment and then came slowly down again.

'Congratulations on the success of your plans, Sir Thomas,' said Hornblower.

'Thank you, my lord,' answered Fell. He was beaming with pleasure. 'I could have done nothing without Your Lordship's acceptance of my suggestions.'

'That is very good of you, Sir Thomas,' said Hornblower, turning back to look at the prize.

The *Estrella* was a pitiful sight, the more pitiful as they approached her, and could see more clearly the raffle of wreckage dangling forward, and the rudder torn loose aft. The sudden tug of the drogue when it took effect, using enormous force and leverage, had broken or pulled straight the stout bronze pintles on which the rudder had hung suspended. The drogue itself, weighted by its chain, still hung out of sight below the dangling rudder. Gomez, brought triumphantly aboard, had still no idea of the cause of the disaster, and had not guessed at the reason for the loss of his rudder. He had been young and handsome and dignified in the face of undeserved misfortune when he arrived on *Clorinda*'s deck. There was no pleasure in observing the change in him when he was told the truth. No pleasure at all. The sight even took away the feeling of pleasure over a professional triumph, to see him wilting under the eyes of his captors. But still, more than three hundred slaves had been set free.

Hornblower was dictating his dispatch to Their Lordships, and Spendlove, who numbered this newfangled shorthand among his surprising accomplishments, was slashing down the letter at a speed that made light of Hornblower's stumbling sentences – Hornblower had not yet acquired the art of dictation.

'In conclusion,' said Hornblower, 'it gives me particular pleasure to call Their Lordships' attention to the ingenuity and activity of Captain Sir Thomas Fell, which made this exemplary capture possible.'

Spendlove looked up from his pad and stared at him. Spendlove knew the truth; but the unblinking stare which answered him defied him to utter a word.

'Add the usual official ending,' said Hornblower.

It was not for him to explain his motives to his secretary. Nor could he have explained them if he had tried. He liked Fell no better now than before.

'Now a letter to my agent,' said Hornblower.

'Aye aye, my lord,' said Spendlove, turning a page.

Hornblower began to assemble in his mind the sentences composing this next letter. He wanted to say that because the capture was due to Sir Thomas's suggestions he did not wish to apply for his share of head money for himself. It was his desire that the share of the Flag should be allocated to Sir Thomas.

'No,' said Hornblower. 'Belay that. I won't write after all.'

'Aye aye, my lord,' said Spendlove.

It was possible to pass on to another man distinction

and honour, but one could not pass on money. There was something obvious, something suspicious, about that. Sir Thomas might guess, and Sir Thomas' feelings might be hurt, and he would not risk it. But he wished he liked Sir Thomas better, all the same.

The Bewildered Pirates

Oh, the dames of France are fo-ond a-and free
And Flemish li-ips a-are willing.

That was young Spendlove singing lustily only two rooms away from Hornblower's at Admiralty House, and he might as well be in the same room, as all the windows were open to let in the Jamaican sea breeze.

And sweet the maids of I-Ita-aly –

That was Gerard joining in.

'My compliments to Mr Gerard and Mr Spendlove,' growled Hornblower to Giles, who was helping him dress, 'and that caterwauling is to stop. Repeat that to make sure you have the words right.'

'His Lordship's compliments, gentlemen, and that caterwauling is to stop,' repeated Giles, dutifully.

'Very well, run and say it.'

Giles ran, and Hornblower was gratified to hear the noise cease abruptly. The fact that those two young men were singing – and still more the fact that they had forgotten he was within earshot – was proof that they were feeling light-hearted, as might be expected, seeing they were dressing for a ball. Yet it was no excuse, for they knew well enough that their tone-deaf Commander-in-Chief detested music, and they should also have realized that he would be more testy than usual, on account of that very ball, because it meant that he would be forced to spend a long evening listening to those dreary sounds, cloying and irritating at the same moment. There would certainly be a table or two of whist – Mr Hough would be aware of his principal guest's tastes – but it was too much to hope for that all sound of music would be excluded from the card-room. The prospect of a ball was by no means as exhilarating to Hornblower as to his flag lieutenant and to his secretary.

Hornblower tied his white neckcloth and painfully adjusted it to geometrical symmetry, and Giles helped him into his black dress coat. Hornblower regarded the result in the mirror, by the light of the candles round its frame. At least tolerable, he said to himself. The growing peacetime convention whereby naval and military men appeared in civilian clothes had a good deal to recommend it; so had the other increasing fad for men to wear black dress coats. Barbara had helped him select this one, and had supervised its fitting by the tailor. The cut was excellent, Hornblower decided, turning back and forth before the mirror, and black and white suited him. 'Only gentlemen can wear black and white,' Barbara had said, and that was very gratifying.

Giles handed him his tall hat and he studied the additional effect. Then he took up his white gloves, remembered to remove his hat again, and stepped out through the door which Giles opened for him and entered the corridor where Gerard and Spendlove, in their best uniforms, were waiting for him.

'I must apologize on behalf of Spendlove and myself for the singing, my lord,' said Gerard.

The softening effect of the black dress coat was evident when Hornblower refrained from a rasping reprimand.

'What would Miss Lucy say, Spendlove, if she heard you singing about the dames of France?' he asked.

Spendlove's answering grin was very attractive.

'I must ask Your Lordship's further indulgence not to tell her about it,' he said.

'I'll make that conditional upon your further good behaviour,' said Hornblower.

The open carriage was waiting outside the front door of Admiralty House; four seamen stood by with lanterns to add to the light thrown by the lamps on the porch. Hornblower climbed in and seated himself. Etiquette was different here on land; Hornblower missed the shrilling of the pipes that he felt should accompany this ceremonial, as it would if it were a boat he was entering, and in a carriage the senior officer entered first, so that after he was seated Spendlove and Gerard had to run round and enter by the other door. Gerard sat beside him and Spendlove sat opposite, his back to the horses. As the door shut the carriage moved forward, between the lanterns at the gate, and out to the pitch dark Jamaican night. Hornblower breathed the warm, tropical air and grudgingly admitted to himself that after all it was no great hardship to attend a ball.

'Perhaps you have a rich marriage in mind, Spendlove?' he asked. 'I understand Miss Lucy will inherit it all. But I advise you to make certain before committing yourself that there are no nephews on the father's side.'

'A rich marriage might be desirable, my lord,' replied

Spendlove's voice out of the darkness, 'but I must remind you that in affairs of the heart I have been handicapped from birth – or at least from my baptism.'

'From your baptism?' repeated Hornblower, puzzled.

'Yes, my lord. You remember my name, perhaps?'

'Erasmus,' said Hornblower.

'Exactly, my lord. It is not adapted to endearments. Could any woman fall in love with an Erasmus? Could any woman bring herself to breathe the words "Razzy, darling"?'

'I fancy it could happen,' said Hornblower.

'May I live long enough to hear it,' said Spendlove.

It was remarkably agreeable to be driving thus through the Jamaican night behind two good horses and with two pleasant young men; especially, as he told himself smugly, because he had done work satisfactory enough to justify relaxation. His command was in good order, the policing of the Caribbean was proceeding satisfactorily, and smuggling and piracy were being reduced to small proportions. Tonight he had no responsibilities. He was in no danger at all, not any. Danger was far away, over the horizons both of time and space. He could lean back, relaxed, against the leather cushions of the carriage, taking only moderate care not to crease his black dress coat or crumple the careful pleats of his shirt.

Naturally, his reception at the Hough's house was somewhat overpowering. There was a good deal of 'My lord' and 'His Lordship.' Hough was a substantial planter, a man of considerable wealth, with enough of dislike for English winters not to be the usual West Indian absentee landlord. Yet for all his wealth he was greatly impressed by the fact that he was entertaining, in one and the same person, a Peer and an Admiral and a Commander-in-Chief – and someone whose influence might at any moment be of great importance to him. The warmth of his greeting, and of Mrs Hough's, was so great that it even overflowed round Gerard and Spendlove as well. Perhaps the Houghs felt that if they wished to be sure of standing well with the Commander-in-Chief it might be as well to cultivate good relations with his flag lieutenant and secretary, too.

Lucy Hough was a pretty enough girl of some seventeen or eighteen years of age whom Hornblower had already met on a few occasions. Hornblower told himself he could feel no interest in a child straight from the schoolroom – almost straight from the nursery – however pretty. He smiled at her and she dropped her eyes, looked up at him again, and once more looked away. It was interesting that she was not nearly so timid when she met the glances and acknowledged the bows of the young men who were far more likely to be of interest to her.

'Your Lordship does not dance, I understand?' said Hough.

'It is painful to be reminded of what I am missing in the presence of so much beauty,' replied Hornblower with another smile at Mrs Hough and at Lucy.

'Perhaps a rubber of whist, then, my lord?' suggested Hough.

'The Goddess of Chance instead of the Muse of Music,' said Hornblower – he always tried to talk about music as if it meant something to him – 'I will woo the one instead of the other.'

'From what I know about Your Lordship's skill at whist,' said Hough, 'I would say that as regards Your Lordship the Goddess of Chance has but small need for wooing.'

The ball had been in progress, apparently, for some time before Hornblower's arrival. There were two score young people on the floor of the great room, a dozen dowagers on chairs round the wall, an orchestra in the corner. Hough led the way to another room; Hornblower dismissed his two young men with a nod, and settled down to whist with Hough and a couple of formidable old ladies. The closing of the heavy door shut out, luckily, nearly all the exasperating din of the orchestra; the old ladies played a sound game, and a pleasant hour enough went by. It was terminated by the entrance of Mrs Hough.

'It is time for the Polonaise before supper,' she announced. 'I really must beg you to leave your cards and come and witness it.'

'Would Your Lordship –?' asked Hough apologetically.

'Mrs Hough's wish is my command,' said Hornblower.

The ballroom was, of course, stifling hot. Faces were flushed and shiny, but there was no lack of energy apparent as the double line formed up for the Polonaise while the orchestra grated out its mysterious noises to encourage the young people. Spendlove was leading Lucy by the hand and they were exchanging happy glances. Hornblower, from the weary age of forty-six, could look with condescension at these young men and women in their immature teens and twenties, tolerant of their youth and enthusiasm. The noises the orchestra made became more jerky and confusing, but the young people could find some sense in them. They capered round the room, skirts swaying and coat-tails flapping, everyone smiling and light-hearted; the double lines became rings, melted into lines again, turned and reformed, until in the end with a final hideous crash from the orchestra the women sank low in curtsies and the men bent themselves double before them – a pretty sight once the music had ceased. There was a burst of laughter and applause before the lines broke up. The women, with sidelong looks at each other, gathered into groups which edged out of the room. They were retiring to repair the damages sustained in the heat of action.

Hornblower met Lucy's eyes again, and once more she looked away and then back at him. Shy? Eager? It was hard to tell with these mere children; but it was not the sort of glance she had bestowed on Spendlove.

'Ten minutes at least before the supper march, my lord,' said Hough. 'Your Lordship will be kind enough to take in Mrs Hough?'

'Delighted, of course,' replied Hornblower.

Spendlove approached. He was mopping his face with his handkerchief.

'I would enjoy a breath of cooler air, my lord,' he said. 'Perhaps –'

'I'll come with you,' said Hornblower, not sorry to have an excuse to be rid of Hough's ponderous company.

They stepped out into the dark garden; so bright had been the candles in the ballroom that they had to tread cautiously at first.

'I trust you are enjoying yourself,' said Hornblower.

'Very much indeed, thank you, my lord.'

'And your suit is making progress?'

'Of that I am not so sure, my lord.'

'You have my best wishes in any case.'

'Thank you, my lord.'

Hornblower's eyes were more accustomed now to the darkness. He could see the stars now when he looked up. Sirius was visible, resuming once more his eternal chase of Orion across the night sky. The air was warm and still with the cessation of the sea breeze.

Then it happened. Hornblower heard a movement behind him, a rustling of foliage, but before he could pay attention to it hands gripped his arms, a hand came over his mouth. He began to struggle. A sharp, burning pain under his right shoulder blade made him jump.

'Quiet,' said a voice, a thick, heavy voice. 'Or this.'

He felt the pain again. It was a knife point in his back, and he held himself still. The unseen hands began to hustle him away; there were at least three men round him. His nose told him they were sweating – with excitement, perhaps.

'Spendlove?' he said.

'Quiet,' said the voice again.

He was being hustled down the long garden. A momentary sharp cry, instantly stifled, presumably came from Spendlove behind him. Hornblower had difficulty in preserving his balance as he was hurried along, but the arms that held him sustained him; when he stumbled he could feel the pressure of the knife point against his back sharpen into pain as it pierced his clothes. At the far end of the garden they emerged into a narrow path where a darkness loomed up in the night.

Hornblower bumped into something that snorted and moved – a mule, apparently.

'Get on,' said the voice beside him.

Hornblower hesitated, and felt the knife against his ribs.

'Get on,' said the voice; someone else was wheeling the mule round again for him to mount.

There were neither stirrups nor saddle. Hornblower put his hands on the withers and hauled himself up astride the mule. He could find no reins, although he heard the chink of a bit. He buried his fingers in the scanty mane. All round him he could hear a bustle as the other mules were mounted. His own mule started with something of a jerk that made him cling wildly to the mane. Someone had mounted the mule ahead and was riding forward with a leading rein attached to his mule. There seemed to be four mules altogether, and some eight men. The mules began to trot, and Hornblower felt himself tossed about precariously on the slippery back of the mule, but there was a man running on each side of him helping to keep him on his perch. A second or two later they slowed down again as the leading mule turned a difficult corner.

'Who are you?' demanded Hornblower, with the first breath that the motion had not shaken out of his body.

The man by his right knee waved something at him, something bright enough to shine in the starlight. It was a cutlass – the machete of the West Indies.

'Quiet,' he said, 'or I cut off your leg.'

The next moment the mule broke into a trot again, and Hornblower could have said no more even if he were inclined to do so. Mules and men hurried along a path between great fields of cane, with Hornblower bounding about on the mule's back. He tried to look up at the stars to see which way they were going, but it was difficult, and they altered course repeatedly, winding about over the countryside. They left the cane behind, and seemed to emerge into open savannah. Then there were trees; then they slowed down for a sharp ascent, broke into a trot again down the other side – the men on foot running tirelessly beside the mules – and climbed again, the mules slipping and plunging on what appeared to be an insecure surface. Twice Hornblower nearly fell off, to be heaved back again by the man beside him. Soon he was atrociously saddle-sore – if the word could be considered appropriate when he was riding bareback – and the ridge of the mule's spine caused him agony. He was drenched with sweat, his mouth was parched, and he was desperately weary. He grew stupefied with misery, despite the pain he suffered. More than once they splashed across small streams roaring down from the mountains; again they made their way through a belt of trees. Several times they seemed to be threading narrow passes.

Hornblower had no idea how long they had been travelling when they found themselves beside a small river, seemingly placid as it reflected the stars. On the far side faint in the darkness towered a lofty cliff. Here the party halted, and the man beside him tugged at his knee in an obvious invitation to dismount. Hornblower slid down the mule's side – he had to lean against the animal for a moment when his legs refused to hold him up. When he was able to stand upright and look about him he saw a white face among the dark ones that surrounded him. He could just make out Spendlove, his knees sagging and his head lolling as he stood supported on either side.

'Spendlove!' he said.

There was an agonizing moment of waiting before the drooping figure said, 'My lord?' The voice was thick and unnatural.

'Spendlove! Are you wounded?'

'I'm – well – my lord.'

Someone pushed Hornblower in the back.

'Come. Swim,' said a voice.

'Spendlove!'

Several hands turned Hornblower away and thrust him stumbling down to the water's edge. It was hopeless to resist; Hornblower could only guess that Spendlove had been stunned by a blow and was only now recovering, his unconscious body having been carried so far by mule.

'Swim,' said the voice, and a hand pressed him forward to the water.

'No!' croaked Hornblower.

The water seemed immeasurably wide and dark. Even while Hornblower struggled at the water's edge he had a horrible realization of the indignity he was undergoing, as a commander-in-chief, acting like a child in the hands of these people. Somebody led a mule slowly down into the water beside him.

'Hold his tail,' said the voice, and there was the knife in his back again.

He took hold of the mule's tail and despairingly let himself flop into the water, spreadeagled. For a moment the mule floundered and then struck out; the water, as it closed round Hornblower, seemed hardly colder than the warm air. It was no more than a moment, it seemed, before the mule was plunging up the other bank, and Hornblower found the bottom under his feet and waded out after him, the water streaming from his clothes, the rest of the gang and the animals splashing after him. The hand was back on his shoulder, turning him to one side and urging him along. He heard an odd creaking in front of him and a swaying object struck him on the chest. His hands felt smooth bamboo and some sort of creeper, liana, knotted to it – it was a makeshift rope ladder dangling in front of him.

'Up!' said the voice. 'Up!'

He could not – he would not – and there was the knife point at his back again. He stretched his arms up and grasped a rung, feeling desperately with his feet for another.

'Up!'

He began the climb, with the ladder writhing under his feet in the animal fashion rope ladders always display. It was horrible in the darkness, feeling with his feet for each elusive rung in turn, clutching desperately with his hands. His sodden shoes tended to slip on the smooth bamboo. Nor did his hands feel secure on the creeper. Someone else was climbing close after him, and the ladder twined about unpredictably. He knew himself to be swaying pendulum-fashion in the darkness. Up he went, one rung at a time, his hands gripping so convulsively that it was only by a conscious effort that he was able to make each one unclasp in turn and seek a fresh hold. Then the gyrations and swinging grew less. His upward-stretching hand touched earth, or rock. The next moment was not easy; he was unsure of his handhold and he hesitated. He knew himself to be a prodigious height up in the air. Just below him on the ladder he heard a sharp command issued by the man following him, and then a hand above him grasped his wrist and pulled. His feet found the next rung, and there he was, lying gasping on his belly on solid earth. The hand dragged at him again and he crawled on all fours forward to make room for the man behind him. He was almost sobbing; there was no trace left now of the haughty and self-satisfied human who had admired himself in the mirror not so many hours ago.

Other people trod past him.

'My lord! My lord!'

That was Spendlove asking for him.

'Spendlove!' he answered, sitting up.

'Are you all right, my lord?' asked Spendlove, stooping over him.

Was it sense of humour or sense of the ridiculous, was it natural pride or force of habit, which made him take a grip on himself?

'As right as I might expect to be, thank you, after these rather remarkable experiences,' he said. 'But you – what happened to you?'

'They hit me on the head,' replied Spendlove, simply.

'Don't stand there. Sit down,' said Hornblower, and Spendlove collapsed beside him.

'Do you know where we are, my lord?' he asked.

'Somewhere at the top of a cliff, as far as I can estimate,' said Hornblower.

'But where, my lord?'

'Somewhere in His Majesty's loyal colony of Jamaica. More than that I can't say.'

'It will be dawn soon, I suppose,' said Spendlove, weakly.

'Soon enough.'

Nobody about them was paying them any attention. There was a great deal of chatter going on, in marked contrast with the silence – the almost disciplined silence – which had been preserved during their dash across country. The chatter mingled with the sound of a small waterfall, which he realized he had been hearing ever since his climb. The conversations were in a thick English which Hornblower could hardly understand, but he could be sure that their captors were expressing exultation. He could hear women's voices, too, while figures paced about, too excited to sit down despite the fatigues of the night.

'I doubt if we're at the top of the cliff, my lord, if you'll pardon me,' said Spendlove.

He pointed upwards. The sky was growing pale, and the stars were fading; vertically over their heads they could see the cliff above them, overhanging them. Looking up, Hornblower could see foliage silhouetted against the sky.

'Strange,' he said. 'We must be on some sort of shelf.'

On his right hand the sky was showing a hint of light, of the palest pink, even while on his left it was still dark.

'Facing north-nor'west,' said Spendlove.

The light increased perceptibly; when Hornblower looked to the east again the pink had turned to orange, and there was a hint of green. They seemed immeasurably high up; almost at their feet, it seemed, as they sat, the shelf ended abruptly, and far down below them the shadowy world was taking form, concealed at the moment by a light mist. Hornblower was suddenly conscious of his wet clothes, and shivered.

'That might be the sea,' said Spendlove, pointing.

The sea it was, blue and lovely in the far distance; a broad belt of land, some miles across, extended between the cliff on which they were perched and the edge of the sea; the mist still obscured it. Hornblower rose to his feet, took a step forward, leaning over a low, crude parapet of piled rock; he shrank back before nerving himself to look again. Under his feet there was nothing. They were indeed on a shelf in the face of the cliff. About the height of a frigate's mainyard, sixty feet or so; vertically below them he could see the small stream he had crossed holding the mule's tail; the rope ladder still hung down from where he stood to the water's edge; when, with an effort of will, he forced himself to lean out and look over he could see the mules standing dispiritedly below him in the narrow area between the river and the foot of the cliff; the overhang must be considerable. They were on a shelf in a cliff, undercut through the ages by the river below when in spate. Nothing could reach them from above, and nothing from below if the ladder were to be drawn up. The shelf was perhaps ten yards wide at its widest, and perhaps a hundred yards long. At one end the waterfall he had heard tumbled down the cliff face in a groove it had cut for itself; it splashed against a cluster of gleaming rocks and then leaped out again. The sight of it told him how thirsty he was, and he walked along to it. It was a giddy thing to do, to stand there with the cliff face at one elbow and a vertical drop under the other, with the spray bursting round him, but he could fill his cupped hands with water and drink, and drink again,

159

before splashing his face and head refreshingly. He drew back to find Spendlove waiting for him to finish. Matted in Spendlove's thick hair and behind his left ear and down his neck was a black clot of blood. Spendlove knelt to drink and to wash, and rose again touching his scalp cautiously.

'They spared me nothing,' he said.

His uniform was spattered with blood, too. At his waist dangled an empty scabbard; his sword was missing, and as they turned back from the waterfall they could see it – it was in the hand of one of their captors, who was standing waiting for them. He was short and square and heavily built, not entirely Negro, possibly as much as half white. He wore a dirty white shirt and loose, ragged blue trousers, with dilapidated buckled shoes on his splay feet.

'Now, lord,' he said.

He spoke with the Island intonation, with a thickening of the vowels and a slurring of the consonants.

'What do you want?' demanded Hornblower, putting all the rasp into his voice that he could manage.

'Write us a letter,' said the man with the sword.

'A letter? To whom?'

'To the Governor.'

'Asking him to come and hang you?' asked Hornblower.

The man shook his big head.

'No. I want a paper, a paper with a seal on it. A pardon. For us all. With a seal on it.'

'Who are you?'

'Ned Johnson.' The name meant nothing to Hornblower, nor, as a glance showed, did it mean anything to the omniscient Spendlove.

'I sailed with Harkness,' said Johnson.

'Ah!'

That meant something to both the British officers. Harkness was one of the last of the petty pirates. Hardly more than a week ago his sloop, *Blossom*, had been cut off by the *Clorinda* off Savannalamar, and her escape to leeward intercepted. Under long-range fire from the frigate she had despairingly run herself aground at the mouth of the Sweet River, and her crew had escaped into the marshes and mangrove swamps of that section of coast, all except her captain, whose body had been found on her deck almost cut in two by a round shot from *Clorinda*. This was her crew, left leaderless – unless Johnson could be called their leader – and to hunt them down the Governor had called out two battalions of troops as soon as *Clorinda* beat back to Kingston with the news. It was to cut off their escape by sea that the Governor, at Hornblower's suggestion, had posted guards at every fishing beach in the whole big island – otherwise the cycle they had already probably followed would be renewed, with the theft of a fishing-boat, the capture of a larger craft, and so on until they were a pest again.

'There's no pardon for pirates,' said Hornblower.

'Yes,' said Johnson. 'Write us a letter, and the Governor will give us one.'

He turned aside and from the foot of the cliff at the back of the shelf he picked up something. It was a leather-bound book – the second volume of *Waverley*, Hornblower saw when it was put in his hands – and Johnson produced a stub of pencil and gave him that as well.

'Write to the Governor,' he said; he opened the book at the beginning and indicated the flyleaf as the place to write on.

'What do you think I would write?' asked Hornblower.

'Ask him for a pardon for us. With his seal on it.'

Apparently Johnson must have heard somewhere, in talk with fellow pirates, of 'a pardon under the Great Seal', and the memory had lingered.

'The Governor would never do that.'

'Then I send him your ears. Then I send him your nose,' said Johnson.

That was a horrible thing to hear. Hornblower glanced at Spendlove, who had turned white at the words.

'You, the Admiral,' continued Johnson. 'You, the Lord. The Governor will do that.'

'I doubt if he would,' said Hornblower.

He conjured up in his mind the picture of fussy old General Sir Augustus Hooper, and tried to imagine the reaction produced by Johnson's demand. His Excellency would come near to bursting a blood vessel at the thought of granting pardons to two dozen pirates. The home government, when it heard the news, would be intensely annoyed, and without doubt most of the annoyance would be directed at the man whose idiocy in allowing himself to be kidnapped had put everyone in this absurd position. That suggested a question.

'How did you come to be in the garden?' he asked.

'We was waiting for you to go home, but you came out first.'

If they had been intending –

'Stand back!' yelled Johnson.

He leaped backwards with astonishing agility for his bulk, bracing himself, knees bent, body tense, on guard with the sword. Hornblower looked round in astonishment, in time to see Spendlove relax; he had been poising himself for a spring. With that sword in his hand and its point against Johnson's throat, the position would have been reversed. Some of the others came running up at the cry; one of them had a staff in his hand – a headless pike stave apparently – and thrust it cruelly into Spendlove's face. Spendlove staggered back, and the staff was whirled up to strike him down. Hornblower leaped in front of him.

'No!' he yelled, and they all stood looking at each other, the drama of the situation ebbing away. Then one of the men came sidling towards Hornblower, cutlass in hand.

'Cut off his ear?' he asked over his shoulder to Johnson.

'No. Not yet. Sit down, you two.' When they hesitated Johnson's voice rose to a roar. 'Sit down!'

Under the menace of the cutlass there was nothing to do but sit down, and they were helpless.

'You write that letter?' asked Johnson.

'Wait a little,' said Hornblower wearily; he could think of nothing else to say in that situation. He was playing for time, hopelessly, like a child at bedtime confronted by stern guardians.

'Let's have some breakfast,' said Spendlove.

At the far end of the shelf a small fire had been lighted, its smoke clinging in the still dawn in a thin thread to the sloping overhang of the cliff. An iron pot hung from a chain attached to a tripod over the fire, and two women were crouching over it attending to it. Packed against the back wall of the shelf were chests and kegs and barrels. Muskets were ranged in a rack. It occurred to Hornblower that he was in the situation common in popular romances; he was in the pirates' lair. Perhaps those chests contained untold treasures of pearls and gold. Pirates, like any other seafarers, needed a land base, and these pirates had established one here instead of on some lonely cay. His brig *Clement* had cleaned out one of those last year.

'You write that letter, lord,' said Johnson. He poked at Hornblower's breast with the sword, and the point pierced the thin shirtfront to prick him over the breastbone.

'What is it you want?' asked Hornblower.

'A pardon. With a seal.'

Hornblower studied the swarthy features in front of him. The jig was up for piracy in the Caribbean, he knew. American ships-of-war in the north, French ships-of-war working from the Lesser Antilles, and his own busy squadron based on Jamaica had made the business both unprofitable and dangerous. And this particular band of pirates, the remains of the Harkness gang, were in a more precarious position than any, with the loss of their ship, and with their escape to sea cut off by his precautions. It had been a bold plan, and well executed, to save their necks by kidnapping him. Presumably the plan had been made and executed by this rather stupid-seeming fellow, almost bewildered in appearance, before him. Appearances might be deceitful, or else the desperate need of the situation had stimulated that dull mind into unusual activity.

'You hear me?' said Johnson, offering another prick with the sword, and breaking in upon Hornblower's train of thought.

'Say you will, my lord,' muttered Spendlove close to Hornblower's ear. 'Gain time.'

Johnson turned on him, sword pointed at his face.

'Shut that mouth,' he said. Another idea occurred to him, and he glanced round at Hornblower. 'You write. Or I prick his eye.'

'I'll write,' said Hornblower.

Now he sat with the volume of *Waverley* open at the flyleaf, and the stub of pencil in his hand, while Johnson withdrew for a couple of paces, presumably to allow free play for inspiration. What was he to write? 'Dear Sir Augustus'? 'Your Excellency'? That was better. 'I am held to ransom here along with Spendlove by the survivors of the Harkness gang. Perhaps the bearer of this will explain the conditions. They demand a free pardon in exchange for –' Hornblower held the pencil poised over the paper debating the next words. 'Our lives'? He shook his head to himself and wrote 'our freedom.' He wanted no melodrama. 'Your Excellency will, of course, be a better judge of the situation than I am. Your ob'd't servant.' Hornblower hesitated again, and then he dashed off the 'Hornblower' of his signature.

'There you are,' he said, holding out the volume to Johnson, who took it and looked at it curiously, and turned back to the group of a dozen or so of his followers who had been squatting on the ground behind him silently watching the proceedings.

They peered at the writing over Johnson's shoulder;

others came to look as well, and they fell into a chattering debate.

'Not one of them can read, my lord,' commented Spendlove.

'So it appears.'

The pirates were looking from the writing over to their prisoners and back again; the argument grew more intense. Johnson seemed to be expostulating, or exhorting, and some of the men he addressed drew back shaking their heads.

'It's a question of who shall carry that note to Kingston,' said Hornblower. 'Who shall beard the lion.'

'That fellow has no command over his men,' commented Spendlove. 'Harkness would have shot a couple of them by now.'

Johnson returned to them, pointing a dark, stubby finger at the writing.

'What you say here?' he asked.

Hornblower read the note aloud; it did not matter whether he spoke the truth or not, seeing they had no way of knowing. Johnson stared at him, studying his face; Johnson's own face betrayed more of the bewilderment Hornblower had noticed before. The pirate was facing a situation too complex for him; he was trying to carry out a plan which he had not thought out in all its details beforehand. No one of the pirates was willing to venture into the grip of justice bearing a message of unknown content. Nor, for that matter, would the pirates trust one of their number to go off on such a mission; he might well desert, throwing away the precious message, to try and make his escape on his own. The poor, ragged, shiftless devils and their slatternly women were in a quandary, with no master mind to find a way out for them. Hornblower could have laughed at their predicament, and almost did, until he thought of what this unstable mob could do in a fit of passion to the prisoners in their power. The debate went on furiously, with a solution apparently no nearer.

'Do you think we could get to the ladder, my lord?' asked Spendlove, and then answered his own question. 'No. They'd catch us before we could get away. A pity.'

'We can bear the possibility in mind,' said Hornblower.

One of the women cooking over the fire called out at this moment in a loud, raucous voice, interrupting the debate. Food was being ladled out into wooden bowls. A young mulatto woman, hardly more than a child, in a ragged gown that had once been magnificent, brought a bowl over to them – one bowl, no spoon or fork. They stared at each other, unable to keep from smiling. Then Spendlove produced a penknife from his breeches pocket, and tendered it to his superior after opening it.

'Perhaps it may serve, my lord,' he said, apologetically, adding, after a glance at the contents of the bowl, 'not such a good meal as the supper we missed at the Houghs's, my lord.'

Boiled yams and a trifle of boiled salt pork, the former presumably stolen from some slave garden and the latter from one of the hogsheads stored here on the cliff. They ate with difficulty, Hornblower insisting on their using the penknife turn about, juggling with the hot food for which both of them discovered a raging appetite. The pirates and the women were mostly squatting on their heels as they ate. After their first mouthfuls they were beginning to argue again over the use to be made of their prisoners.

Hornblower looked out again from the shelf at the view extended before them.

'That must be the Cockpit Country,' he said.

'No doubt of it, my lord.'

The Cockpit Country was territory unknown to any white man, an independent republic in the north-west of Jamaica. At the conquest of the island from the Spaniards, a century and a half earlier, the British had found this area already populated by runaway slaves and the survivors of the Indian population. Several attempts to subdue the area had failed disastrously – yellow fever and the appalling difficulty of the country allying themselves with the desperate valour of the defenders – and a treaty had finally been concluded granting independence to the Cockpit Country on the sole condition that the inhabitants should not harbour runaway slaves in future. That treaty had already endured fifty years and seemed likely to endure far longer. The pirates' lair was on the edge of this area, with the mountains at the back of it.

'And that's Montego Bay, my lord,' said Spendlove, pointing.

Hornblower had visited the place in *Clorinda* last year – a lonely roadstead providing fair anchorage, and shelter for a few fishing-boats. He gazed over to the distant blue water with longing. He tried to think of ways of escape, of some method of coming to honourable terms with the pirates, but a night entirely without sleep made his brain sluggish, and now that he had eaten it was more sluggish still. He caught himself nodding and pulled himself up with a jerk. Now that he was in his middle-forties the loss of a night's sleep was a serious matter, especially when the night had been filled with violent and unaccustomed exertion.

Spendlove had seen him nod.

'I think you could sleep, my lord,' he said, gently.

'Perhaps I could.'

He let his body sink to the hard ground. He was pillowless and uncomfortable.

'Here, my lord,' said Spendlove.

Two hands on his shoulders eased him round, and now he was pillowed on Spendlove's thigh. The world whirled round him for a moment. There was the whisper of a breeze; the loud debate of the pirates and their women was monotonous in pitch; the waterfall was splashing and gurgling; then he was asleep.

He awoke some time later, with Spendlove touching his shoulder.

'My lord, my lord.'

He lifted his head, a little surprised to find where it had been resting; it took him several seconds to recall where he was and how he had come there. Johnson and one or two other pirates were standing before him; in the background one of the women was looking on, in an attitude that conveyed the impression that she had contributed to the conclusion that had evidently been reached.

'We send you to the Governor, lord,' said Johnson.

Hornblower blinked up at him; although the sun had moved round behind the cliff the sky above was dazzling.

'*You*,' said Johnson. '*You* go. We keep *him*.'

Johnson indicated Spendlove by a gesture.

'What do you mean?' asked Hornblower.

'*You* go to the Governor and get our pardon,' said Johnson. 'You can ask him, and he will give it. *He* stays here. We can cut off his nose, we can dig out his eyes.'

'Good God Almighty,' said Hornblower.

Johnson, or his advisers – perhaps that woman over there – were people of considerable insight after all. They had some conception of honour, of gentlemanly obligations. They had perceived something of the relationship between Hornblower and Spendlove – they may have been guided by the sight of Hornblower sleeping with his head pillowed on Spendlove's thigh. They knew that Hornblower could never abandon Spendlove to the mercy of his captors, that he would do everything possible to obtain his freedom. Even perhaps – Hornblower's imagination surged in a great wave over the barrier of his sleepiness – even perhaps to the extent of coming back to share Spendlove's captivity and fate in the event of not being able to obtain the necessary pardons.

'We send you, lord,' said Johnson.

The woman in the background said something in a loud voice.

'We send you now,' said Johnson. 'Get up.'

Hornblower rose slowly; he would have taken his time in any case in an effort to preserve what dignity was left to him, but he could not have risen swiftly if he had wanted to. His joints were stiff – he could almost hear them crack as he moved. His body ached horribly.

'These two men take you,' said Johnson.

Spendlove had risen to his feet too.

'Are you all right, my lord?' he asked, anxiously.

'Only stiff and rheumaticy,' replied Hornblower. 'But what about you?'

'Oh, I'm all right, my lord. Please don't give another thought to me, my lord.'

That was a very straight glance that Spendlove gave him, a glance that tried to convey a message.

'Not another thought, my lord,' repeated Spendlove.

He was trying to tell his chief that he should be abandoned, that nothing should be done to ransom him, that he was willing to suffer whatever tortures might be inflicted on him so long as his chief came well out of the business.

'I'll be thinking about you all the time,' said Hornblower, giving back glance for glance.

'Hurry,' said Johnson.

The rope ladder still dangled down from the lip of the shelf. It was a tricky business to lower himself with his creaking joints over the edge and to find foothold on the slippery bamboo rungs. The ladder swung away under the thrust of his feet as if it was a live thing determined to cast him down; he clung with frantic hands, back downward, forcing himself, against his instincts, to straighten up and allow the ladder to swing back again. Gingerly his feet found foothold again, and he continued his descent. Just as he grew accustomed to the motion of the ladder his rhythm was disturbed by the first of his escort lowering himself upon the ladder above him; he had to cling and wait again before he resumed his downward progress. His feet had hardly gratefully touched ground than first one and then the other of his escorts dropped beside him.

'Goodbye, my lord. Good luck!'

That was Spendlove calling from above. Hornblower, standing on the very edge of the river, his face towards the cliff, had to bend far backwards to see Spendlove's head over the parapet and his waving hand, sixty feet above. He waved back as his escorts led the mules to the water's edge.

Once more it was necessary to swim the river. It was no more than thirty feet across; he could have swum it last night without assistance had he been sure about that in the darkness. Now he let himself flop into the water, clothes and all – alas for that beautiful black dress coat – and, turning on his back, kicked out with his legs. But his clothes were already wet and were a ponderous burden to him, and he knew a moment of worry before his already weary limbs carried him to the rocky bank. He crawled out, the water streaming from his clothes, unwilling to move even while the mules came plunging up out of the water beside him. Spendlove up above, still leaning over the parapet, waved to him again.

Now it was a question of mounting a mule again. His wet clothes weighed upon him like lead. He had to struggle up – the animal's wet hide was slippery – and as soon as he settled himself astride he realized that he was horribly saddle-sore from the night before, and the raw surfaces caused him agony. He had to brace himself to endure it; it was dreadfully painful as his mount plunged about making his way over the irregular surface. From the river they made an abrupt ascent into the mountains. They were retracing the path they had taken the night before; hardly a path, hardly a track. They picked their way up a steep gully, down the other side, up again. They splashed across little torrents, and wound their way among trees. Hornblower was numb both in body and mind by now; his mule was weary and by no means as sure of foot as a mule should be; stumbling more than once so that only by frantic efforts could he retain his seat. The sun was sinking towards the west as they jolted on, downhill at last. Passage through a final belt of trees brought them into open country upon which the sun blazed in tropical glory. This was savannah country, hardly rocky at all; there were cattle to be seen in the distance, and, beyond, a great sea of green – the vast sugar-cane fields of Jamaica stretching as far as the eye could see. Half a mile farther they reached a well-defined track, and there his escorts checked their mounts.

'Now you can go on,' said one of them, pointing along the path winding towards the distant cane.

It was a second or two before Hornblower's stupefied brain could grasp the fact that they were turning him loose.

'That way?' he asked, unnecessarily.

'Yes,' said his escort.

The two men turned their mules; Hornblower had to struggle with his, who disliked the separation. One of the escorts struck the brute on the rump, sending him down the path in a jerky trot acutely painful to Hornblower as he sought to retain his seat. Soon the mule eased to a leg-weary walk, and Hornblower was content to sit idly as it crawled along down the path; the sun was now clouded over and it was not long before, heralded by a brisk wind, a blinding rain began to fall, blotting out the landscape and slowing the mule even more on the slippery surface. Hornblower sat exhausted on the sharp spine of the animal; so heavy was the rain that he found it difficult to breathe as it poured upon his face.

Gradually the roaring rain ceased; the sky, while it remained overcast above him, opened to the west and admitted a gleam of the setting sun, so that the landscape on his left was made glorious with a rainbow which Hornblower hardly noted. Here was the first cane-field; the track he was following became here a rough and narrow roadway through the cane, deeply rutted by cartwheels. The mule plodded on, eternally, through the cane. Now the road crossed another, and the mule pulled up at the crossroads. Before Hornblower could rouse himself to urge the mule onwards he heard a shout to his right. Far down the road he saw a group of horsemen illuminated against the sunset. With an urgent drumming of hoofs they came galloping towards him, and reined up at his side – a white man followed by two coloured men.

'It's Lord Hornblower, isn't it?' asked the white man – a young fellow; Hornblower noticed dully that, although mounted, he was still in full-dress clothes with his ruffled neckcloth all awry and bedraggled.

'Yes,' said Hornblower.

'Thank God you're safe, sir,' said the young man. 'Are you hurt? Are you wounded, my lord?'

'No,' said Hornblower, swaying with fatigue on the back of the mule.

The young man turned to one of his coloured companions and issued rapid orders, and the coloured man wheeled his horse round and went galloping full pelt down the road.

'The whole island has been turned out to seek for you, my lord,' said the young man. 'What happened to you? We have searched for you all day.'

It would never do for an admiral, a commander-in-chief, to betray unmanly weakness. Hornblower made himself stiffen his spine.

'I was kidnapped by pirates,' he said. He tried to speak nonchalantly, as if that was something that could happen to anyone any day, but it was difficult. His voice was only a hoarse croak. 'I must go at once to the Governor. Where is His Excellency?'

'He must be at Government House, I fancy,' said the young man. 'No more than thirty miles away.'

Thirty miles! Hornblower felt as if he could not ride another thirty yards.

'Very well,' he said, stiffly. 'I must go there.'

'The Hough house is only two miles down the road here, my lord,' said the young man. 'Your carriage is still there, I believe. I have already sent a messenger.'

'We'll go there first, then,' said Hornblower, as indifferently as he could manage.

A word from the white man brought the other coloured man from his horse, and Hornblower slid ungracefully from the mule. It was an enormous effort to get his foot up into the stirrup; the coloured man had to help him heave his right leg over. He had hardly gathered the reins in his hands – he had not yet discovered which was which – when the white man put his horse into a trot and Hornblower's mount followed him. It was torture to bump about in the saddle.

'My name is Colston,' said the white man, checking his horse so that Hornblower came up alongside him.

'I had the honour of being presented to Your Lordship at the ball last night.'

'Of course,' said Hornblower. 'Tell me what happened there.'

'You were missed, my lord, after the supper march had been kept waiting for you to head it with Mrs Hough. You and your secretary, Mr – Mr –'

'Spendlove,' said Hornblower.

'Yes, my lord. At first it was thought that some urgent business was demanding your attention. It was not for an hour or two, I suppose, that your flag lieutenant and Mr Hough could agree that you had been spirited away. There was great distress among the company, my lord.'

'Yes?'

'Then the alarm was given. All the gentlemen present rode out in search for you. The militia was called out at dawn. The whole countryside is being patrolled. I expect the Highland Regiment is in full march for here at this moment.'

'Indeed?' said Hornblower. A thousand infantrymen were making a forced march of thirty miles on his account; a thousand horsemen were scouring the island.

Hoofbeats sounded in front of them. Two horsemen approached in the gathering darkness; Hornblower could just recognize Hough and the messenger.

'Thank God, my lord,' said Hough. 'What happened?'

Hornblower was tempted to answer, 'Mr Colston will tell you,' but he made himself make a more sensible reply. Hough uttered the expected platitudes.

'I must go on to the Governor at once,' said Hornblower. 'There is Spendlove to think of.'

'Spendlove, my lord? Oh, yes, of course, your secretary.'

'He is still in the hands of the pirates,' said Hornblower.

'Indeed, my lord?' replied Hough.

No one seemed to have a care about Spendlove, except Lucy Hough, presumably.

Here was the house and the courtyard; lights were gleaming in every window.

'Please come in, my lord,' said Hough. 'Your Lordship must be in need of refreshment.'

He had eaten yams and salt pork some time that morning; he felt no hunger now.

'I must go on to Government House,' he said. 'I can waste no time.'

'If Your Lordship insists –'

'Yes,' said Hornblower.

'I will go and have the horses put to, then, my lord.'

Hornblower found himself alone in the brightly lit sitting room. He felt that if he threw himself into one of the vast chairs there he would never get up again.

'My lord! My lord!'

It was Lucy Hough fluttering into the room, her skirts flying with her haste. He would have to tell her about Spendlove.

'Oh, you're safe! You're safe!'

What was this? The girl had flung herself on her knees before him. She had one of his hands in both hers, and was kissing it frantically. He drew back, he tried to snatch his hand away, but she clung on to it, and followed him on her knees, still kissing it.

'Miss Lucy!'

'I care for nothing as long as you're safe!' she said, looking up at him and still clasping his hand; tears were streaming down her cheeks. 'I've been through torment today. You're not hurt? Tell me! Speak to me!'

This was horrible. She was pressing her lips, her cheek, against his hand again.

'Miss Lucy! Please! Compose yourself!'

How could a girl of seventeen act like this towards a man of forty-five? Was she not enamoured of Spendlove? But perhaps that was the person she was thinking about.

'I will see that Mr Spendlove is safe,' he said.

'Mr Spendlove? I hope he's safe. But it's you – you – you –'

'Miss Lucy! You must not say these things! Stand up, please, I beg you!'

Somehow he got her to her feet.

'I couldn't bear it!' she said. 'I've loved you since the moment I saw you!'

'There, there!' said Hornblower, as soothingly as he knew how.

'The carriage will be ready in two minutes, my lord,' said Hough's voice from the door. 'A glass of wine and a bite before you start?'

Hough came in with a smile.

'Thank you, sir,' said Hornblower, struggling with embarrassment.

'This child has been in a rare way since this morning,' said Hough, indulgently. 'These young people – She was the only person in the island, I fancy, who gave a thought to the secretary as well as to the Commander-in-Chief.'

'Er – yes. These young people,' said Hornblower.

The butler entered with a tray at that moment.

'Pour His Lordship a glass of wine, Lucy, my dear,'

said Hough, and then to Hornblower, 'Mrs Hough has been considerably prostrated, but she will be down in a moment.'

'Please do not discommode her, I beg of you,' said Hornblower. His hand was shaking as he reached for the glass. Hough took up carving knife and fork and set about carving the cold chicken.

'Excuse me, please,' said Lucy.

She turned and ran from the room as quickly as she had entered it, sobbing wildly.

'I had no idea the attachment was so strong,' said Hough.

'Nor had I,' said Hornblower. He had gulped down the whole glass of wine in his agitation. He addressed himself to the cold chicken with all the calm he could muster.

'The carriage is at the door, sir,' announced the butler.

'I'll take these with me,' said Hornblower, a slice of bread in one hand and a chicken wing in the other. 'Would it be troubling you too much to ask you to send a messenger ahead of me to warn His Excellency of my coming?'

'That has already been done, my lord,' answered Hough. 'And I have sent out messengers to inform the patrols that you are safe.'

Hornblower sank into the cushioned ease of the carriage. The incident with Lucy had at least had the effect of temporarily driving all thought of fatigue from his mind. Now he could lean back and relax; it was five minutes before he remembered the bread and chicken in his hands and set himself wearily to eat them. The long drive was not particularly restful, for there were continual interruptions. Patrols who had not heard that he was safe stopped the carriage. Ten miles down the road they encountered the Highland battalion encamped at the roadside and the colonel insisted on coming and paying his respects to the Naval Commander-in-Chief and congratulating him. Farther on a galloping horse reined up beside the carriage; it was Gerard. The light of the carriage lamp revealed that he had ridden his horse into a lather. Hornblower had to listen to him say 'Thank God, you are safe, my lord' – everyone used those same words – and explain to him what had happened. Gerard abandoned his horse at the first opportunity and got into the carriage beside Hornblower. He was full of self-reproach at having allowed this to happen to his chief – Hornblower rather resented the implication that he was incapable of looking after himself even though the event seemed to prove it – and at not having rescued him.

'We tried to use the bloodhounds they track runaway slaves with, my lord, but they were of no use.'

'Naturally, since I was on mule-back,' said Hornblower. 'In any case, the scent must have been several hours old. Now forget the past and let me think about the future.'

'We'll have those pirates dangling on ropes before two days are up, my lord.'

'Indeed? And what about Spendlove?'

'Oh – er. Yes, of course, my lord.'

Spendlove was very much of an afterthought with everyone, even with Gerard who was his friend. But to Gerard must be given the credit at least for appreciating Hornblower's difficulty the moment it was pointed out to him.

'We can't let anything happen to him, of course, my lord.'

'And how do we prevent it? Do we grant those pardons – do we persuade His Excellency to grant them?'

'Well, my lord –'

'There's nothing I would not do to set Spendlove free,' said Hornblower. 'Do you understand that? Nothing!'

Hornblower caught himself setting his jaw in grim determination; his ineradicable tendency to self-analysis revealed him to himself. He was cynically surprised at his own flow of emotion. Ferocity and tenderness intermingled; let those pirates touch one hair of Spendlove's head and – but how was he to prevent it? How to free Spendlove from men who knew that their lives, their actual lives and not merely their fortunes, depended on keeping him prisoner? How could he ever live with himself if anything were to happen to Spendlove? If the worst came to the worst he would have to go back to the pirates and yield himself up to them, as that Roman – Regulus – returned to death at the hands of the Carthaginians; and the worst seemed likely to come to the worst.

'Government House, my lord,' said Gerard, breaking in upon this train of nightmare thoughts.

Sentries at the gates, sentries at the door. A brightly lit entrance hall, where aides-de-camp looked at him curiously, curse them. So did Gerard. He was ushered through into an inner room, where after only a moment another door opened to admit His Excellency, and the escorting aide-de-camp discreetly retired. His Excellency was an angry man, angry as a man can only be who had been badly scared.

'Now, what is all this, my lord?'

There was none of the usual deference displayed towards the man who had attained a peerage, the man of legendary fame. Hooper was a full general, far above a mere rear admiral; moreover, as Governor he was absolute ruler throughout this island. His red face and bulging blue eyes – as well as the rage he was displaying – seemed to confirm the rumour that he was a grandson of the royal blood. Hornblower explained briefly and quietly what had happened; his fatigue – if not his common sense – prevented an angry reply.

'Do you realize the cost of all this, my lord?' blared Hooper. 'Every white man who can sit a horse is out. My last reserve – the Highlanders – are bivouacked at the roadside. What that will mean in malaria and yellow fever I do not dare guess. For two weeks every man of the garrison except for them has been out guarding fishing-boats and watching beaches at your request. The sick-lists are enormous. And now this!'

'My instructions, and I believe Your Excellency's as well, laid the greatest stress on the suppression of piracy, sir.'

'I don't need any whipper-snapper jumped-up Rear Admiral to interpret my instructions,' roared Hooper. 'What sort of bargain did you make with these pirates of yours?'

There it was. It was not an easy thing to explain to a man in this mood.

'I made no actual bargain, Your Excellency.'

'Hard to believe you had that much sense.'

'But my honour is pledged.'

'Your honour pledged? To whom? The pirates?'

'No, Your Excellency. To my secretary, Spendlove.'

'What was the pledge?'

'He was retained as a hostage when I was set free.'

'What did you promise him?'

What? He had said something about thinking about him.

'I made no verbal promise, Your Excellency. But one was implied, undoubtedly.'

'What was implied?'

'That I should set him free.'

'And how did you think you could do that?'

Nothing for it but to take the bull by the horns.

'I was released in order that I might solicit from Your Excellency pardons under seal for the pirates.'

'Pardons! Par –' Hooper could not even finish the word a second time. He could only gobble like a turkey for several seconds before with a gulp he was able to continue. 'Are you insane, my lord?'

'That was why I was released. And that is why Spendlove is still retained.'

'Then this Spendlove must take his chance.'

'Your Excellency!'

'Do you think I could grant pardons to a gang of pirates? What d'ye mean? So that they can live like lords on their booty? Rolling in coaches round the island? A fine way that would be of suppressing piracy! D'ye want the whole West Indies in a turmoil? Have you lost your senses?'

The effect of this speech was in no way modified by

the fact that Hornblower had guessed long before, that Hooper would argue exactly along this line.

'I fully see the difficulty of the situation, Your Excellency.'

'I'm glad you do. You know the hiding-place of these pirates?'

'Yes, Your Excellency. It is a very secure place.'

'No matter. It can be reduced, of course. A few hangings will quiet this island down again.'

What in the world was there that he could do or could say? The sentence he framed in his mind was patently absurd to him even before he uttered it.

'I shall have to go back there before you take any steps, Your Excellency.'

'Go back there?' Hooper's eyes almost came out of their sockets as the implications of what Hornblower was saying dawned upon him. 'What new foolery do you have in mind?'

'I must go back and join Spendlove if Your Excellency does not see fit to grant the pardons.'

'Rubbish! I can grant no pardons. I cannot. I will not.'

'Then I have no alternative, Your Excellency.'

'Rubbish, I said. Rubbish! You made no promise. You said yourself that you gave no pledge.'

'I am the judge of that, Your Excellency.'

'You're in no condition to judge anything at present, if ever you were. Can you imagine for one moment I'll let you tie my hands like this?'

'No one regrets the necessity more than I do, my lord.'

'Necessity? Are you dictating to me? I'll have you know that I'm your superior officer as well as Governor of this island. One more word and you'll be under arrest, my lord. Let's hear no more of this nonsense.'

'Your Excellency –'

'Not one more word, I said. This Spendlove is one of the King's servants. He must run the risks of his position, even though he is only a secretary.'

'But –'

'I order you to keep silence, my lord. You have fair warning. Tomorrow when you're rested we can plan to smoke out this wasps' nest.'

Hornblower himself checked the protest that still rose to his lips. Hooper meant what he said when he threatened arrest. The massive discipline that permeated the armed forces of the Crown had Hornblower in its grip as surely as if he were the least seaman. To disobey an order was hopeless from the start. The irresistible force of his own conscience might be driving him forward, but here he was up against the immovable barrier of discipline. Tomorrow? Tomorrow was another day.

'Very well, Your Excellency.'

'A night's rest will do you all the good in the world, my lord. Perhaps it would be best if you slept here. I will give the necessary orders. If you instruct your flag lieutenant as to the fresh clothes you will need I will send to Admiralty House for them to be ready for you in the morning.'

Clothes? Hornblower looked down at himself. He had forgotten entirely that he was wearing his black full-dress. One glance was enough to tell him that never again could he wear that suit. Now he could guess about the rest of his appearance. He knew that his haggard cheeks must be sprouting a bristly beard, his neckcloth in wild disorder. No wonder that people had looked at him curiously in the anteroom.

'Your Excellency is very kind,' he said.

There was no harm in being formally polite in the face of the temporarily inevitable. There had been that in Hooper's tone which told him that the invitation might as well have been an order, that he was as much a prisoner in Government House as if Hooper had actually carried out his threat of putting him under arrest. It was best to yield gracefully since he had to yield for the moment at least. Tomorrow was another day.

'Allow me to conduct you to your room, my lord,' said Hooper.

The mirror in the bedroom confirmed his worst fears regarding his appearance. The bed, with its enormous mosquito net, was wide and inviting. His aching joints clamoured that he should allow himself to fall across that bed and repose himself; his weary brain demanded that he should sink into oblivion, forget his troubles in sleep as a drunkard might forget them in liquor. It was a relaxation to soap himself in a tepid bath, despite the smarting protests of the raw places on his body. And yet, bathed and relaxed, with one of His Excellency's nightshirts flapping round his knees, he could not give way to his weaknesses. His innermost ego refused to recognize them. He found himself hobbling bare-footed about the room. He had no quarterdeck to pace; the candle-heated tropical air of the bedroom was not as conducive to inspiration as was a fresh sea breeze; mosquitoes buzzed about him, stinging his neck and his bare legs and distracting him. It was one of those dreadful nights; sometimes he relaxed so far as to sit on a chair, but within a few seconds a new train of thought brought him to his feet again, to limp up and down.

It was maddening that he could not keep his thoughts concentrated on the problem of Spendlove. He felt a contempt for himself that he should find his mind deserting his devoted secretary; there was a rival train of thought which was frequently successful in holding his attention. He knew, before the night was over, just how he would deal with the pirates' lair if his hands were free; he even knew satisfaction in recapitulating his plans, only to find the satisfaction replaced by sick despair at the thought of Spendlove in the pirates' hands. There were moments when his stomach turned over as he remembered Johnson's threat to dig out Spendlove's eyes.

Weariness took him by surprise in the end; he had sat down and rested his head on his hand, and then awakened with a start as he fell forward in his chair. The awakening was not complete enough; unconscious of what he was doing he settled himself back in his chair and slept in that fashion, the vast, comfortable bed untenanted, until a knocking at his door roused him to blink about him wondering where he was before bracing himself to make it seem as if it were the most ordinary thing in the world to sleep in a chair when a bed was available.

It was Giles who came in, bearing clean linen and a uniform and razors; the business of shaving and of dressing carefully served to steady him and kept him from thinking too furiously about the problem he would have to solve in the next few minutes.

'His Excellency would be glad if His Lordship would take breakfast with him.'

That was a message conveyed through the door to Giles; the invitation must be accepted, of course, as it was the equivalent of a royal command. Hooper, apparently, was partial to a steak for breakfast; a silver dish of steak and onions was brought in almost as soon as Hornblower had uttered his formal good morning. Hooper looked at Hornblower oddly when he answered the butler's enquiry with a request for papaya and a boiled egg – that was a bad start, for it confirmed Hooper in his opinions of Hornblower's eccentricity that he should have these outlandish Frenchified notions about breakfast. Years of living on shore had not yet dulled the appetite for fresh eggs in their shells which Hornblower had acquired during decades at sea. Hooper daubed mustard on his steak and set about it with appetite.

'Did you sleep well?'

'Well enough, thank you, Your Excellency.'

Hooper's abandonment of the formal 'my lord' was a not too subtle indication that he was willing to forget last night's discussion and to act magnanimously as if Hornblower was a normal person with only a temporary lapse on his record.

'We'll leave business until we've eaten.'

'As you wish, Your Excellency.'

But not even a Governor can be sure of his future. There was a bustle at the door, and a whole group of people came hurrying in, not merely the butler but two aides-de-camp and Gerard and – and – who was that? Pale and ragged and weary, almost unable to stand on tottering legs.

'Spendlove!' said Hornblower, his spoon clattering to the floor as he rose and hurried to him.

Hornblower clasped his hand, grinning with delight. Perhaps there had never been a moment in his life which had held so much sheer pleasure for him.

'Spendlove!' He could only repeat the name at first.

'Is this the return of the prodigal?' asked Hooper from the table.

Hornblower remembered his manners.

'Your Excellency,' he said, 'may I take it upon myself to present my secretary, Mr Erasmus Spendlove?'

'Glad to see you, young man. Take a seat at the table. Bring Mr Spendlove some food! He looks as if a glass of wine would not come amiss. Bring the decanter and a glass.'

'You're not wounded?' asked Hornblower. 'You're not hurt?'

'No, my lord,' said Spendlove, extending his legs cautiously under the table. 'It is only that seventy miles on horseback have stiffened my unaccustomed limbs.'

'Seventy miles?' asked Hooper. 'From where?'

'Montego Bay, Your Excellency.'

'Then you must have escaped in the night?'

'At nightfall, Your Excellency.'

'But what did you do, man?' demanded Hornblower. 'How did you get away?'

'I jumped, my lord. Into the water.'

'Into the water?'

'Yes, my lord. There was eight feet of water in the river at the foot of the cliff; enough to break my fall from any height.'

'So there was. But – but – in the dark?'

'That was easy, my lord. I looked over the parapet during the day. I did when I said goodbye to Your Lordship. I marked the spot and I measured the distance with my eye.'

'And then?'

'And then I jumped when it was fully dark, and raining hard.'

'What were the pirates doing?' asked Hooper.

'They were taking shelter, Your Excellency. They were paying no attention to me, thinking I was safe enough there, with the ladder pulled up.'

'And so –?'

'So I took a run, Your Excellency, and jumped the parapet, as I said, and came down feet first into the water.'

'Unhurt?'

'Unhurt, Your Excellency.'

Hornblower's vivid imagination conjured up everything about the feat, the half-dozen strides through the dark and the roaring rain, the leap, the endless fall. He felt the hair at the back of his neck lifting.

'A most commendable deed,' commented Hooper.

'Nothing for a desperate man, Your Excellency.'

'Perhaps not. And then? After you were in the water? Were you pursued?'

'As far as I can tell, Your Excellency, I was not. Perhaps it was some time before they noticed my absence. Even then they would have to let down the ladder and climb down it. I heard nothing as I made off.'

'Which way did you go?' asked Hornblower.

'I kept to the river, my lord, making my way downstream. It reaches the sea at Montego Bay, as we decided, if you remember, my lord, when we were making our first observations.'

'Was it an easy journey?' asked Hornblower. Something was stirring in his mind, demanding his attention despite the strong emotions he was experiencing.

'Not easy in the dark, my lord. There were rapids in places, and the boulders were slippery. I fancy the main pass is narrow, although I could not see it.'

'And at Montego Bay?' asked Hooper.

'There was the guard over the fishing-boats, a half-company of the West Indian Regiment, Your Excellency. I had their officer awakened, and he found me a horse, and I took the road through Cambridge and Ipswich.'

'You got yourself remounts on the way?'

'I claimed I was on a mission of the greatest importance, Your Excellency.'

'You made good time, even then.'

'The patrol at Mandeville told me His Lordship was on his way to Your Excellency, and so I rode straight to Government House.'

'Very sensible.'

To the picture in Hornblower's mind of the leap in the darkness were now added others, of a nightmare journey down the river, falling over slippery boulders, tumbling into unexpected pools, struggling along invisible banks; then the endless, weary ride.

'I shall represent your conduct to the Lords Commissioners, Mr Spendlove,' he said, formally.

'I must thank Your Lordship.'

'And I shall represent it to the Secretary of State,' added Hooper.

'Your Excellency is too kind.'

To Hornblower it was not the least of Spendlove's achievements (guessed at from a glance at his plate) that Spendlove had contrived somehow to gulp down a whole plateful of steak and onions while making his report. The man must have learned to dispense with chewing.

'Enough of compliments,' said Hooper, mopping up his gravy with a piece of bread. 'Now we have to destroy these pirates. This lair of theirs – you say it is strong?'

Hornblower let Spendlove answer.

'Impregnable to direct assault, Your Excellency.'

'M'm. D'ye think they'll make a stand there?'

For the past several minutes Hornblower had been debating this point with himself. Those leaderless men, dazed now by the complete failure of their scheme – what would they do?

'They could scatter all over the island, Your Excellency,' said Spendlove.

'So they could. Then I'll have to hunt them down. Patrols on every road, movable columns in the mountains. And the sick-list is high already.'

Troops exposed to the weather and the night air for long in the West Indies died like flies, and it might well take weeks to run the outlaws down.

'Maybe they'll scatter,' said Hornblower, and then he committed himself, 'but in my opinion, Your Excellency, they will not.'

Hooper looked at him sharply.

'You think not?'

'I think not, Your Excellency.'

That gang had been despairing as well as desperate

when he had been among them. There was something childlike about them, leaderless as they were. On the cliff they had shelter, food – they had a home, if the expression could be tolerated. They would not readily leave it.

'And you say this place is impregnable? It would mean a long siege?'

'I might reduce them quickly with a naval force, Your Excellency, if Your Excellency would give me leave to try.'

'Your Lordship is welcome to try anything that will save lives.'

Hooper was looking at him curiously.

'Then I'll make my arrangements,' said Hornblower.

'You'll go round to Montego Bay by sea?'

'Yes.'

Hornblower restrained himself from saying 'of course.' Soldiers always found it hard to realize the convenience of the sea for rapid and secret movements.

'I'll maintain my patrols in case they bolt while you smoke out the nest,' said Hooper.

'I think Your Excellency would be taking a wise precaution in doing so. I trust my plan will not take long in execution. With Your Excellency's leave –'

Hornblower rose from the table.

'You're going now?'

'Every hour is of importance, Your Excellency.'

Hooper was looking at him more inquisitively than ever.

'The Navy displays its notorious reserve,' he said. 'Oh, very well then. Order His Lordship's carriage. You have my leave to try, my lord. Report to me by courier.'

There they were, in the warm morning air, sitting,

the three of them, Hornblower, Spendlove, and Gerard, in the carriage.

'The dockyard,' ordered Hornblower briefly. He turned to Spendlove. 'From the dockyard you will go on board *Clorinda* and convey my order to Captain Fell to make ready for sea. I shall be hoisting my flag within an hour. Then it is my order to you that you get yourself some rest.'

'Aye aye, my lord.'

At the dockyard the Captain-Superintendent did his best not to appear surprised at an unheralded visit from his Admiral who by the last news had been kidnapped.

'I want a boat mortar, Holmes,' said Hornblower, brushing aside the expressions of pleased surprise.

'A boat mortar, my lord? Y-yes, my lord. There's one in store, I know.'

'It's to go on board *Clorinda* at once. Now, there are shells for it?'

'Yes, my lord. Uncharged, of course.'

'I'll have *Clorinda*'s gunner charge 'em while we're under way. Twenty pounds apiece, I believe. Send two hundred, with the fuses.'

'Aye aye, my lord.'

'And I want a punt. Two punts. I've seen your hands using 'em for caulking and breaming. Twenty-foot, are they?'

'Twenty-two-foot, my lord,' answered Holmes; he was glad that he could answer this question while his Admiral had not insisted on an answer regarding so obscure a matter as the weight of boat-mortar shells.

'I'll have two, as I said. Send them round to be hove on deck.'

'Aye aye, my lord.'

Captain Sir Thomas Fell had his best uniform on to greet his Admiral.

'I received your order, my lord,' he said, as the twittering of the pipes died away in a last wail.

'Very well, Sir Thomas. I want to be under way the moment the stores I have ordered are on board. You can warp your ship out. We are going to Montego Bay to deal with pirates.'

'Aye aye, my lord.'

Fell did his best not to look askance at the two filthy punts that he was expected to heave on to his spotless deck – they were only the floating stages used in the dockyard for work on ships' sides – and the two tons of greasy mortar shells for which he had to find space were no better. He was not too pleased when he was ordered to tell off the greater part of his ship's company – two hundred and forty men – and all his marine detachment for a landing party. The hands were naturally delighted with the prospect of a change of routine and the possibility of action. The fact that the gunner was weighing out gunpowder and putting two pounds apiece in the shells, a glimpse of the armourer going round with the Admiral on an inspection of the boarding-pikes, the sight of the boat mortar, squat and ugly, crouching on its bed at the break of the forecastle, all excited them. It was a pleasure to thrash along to the westward, under every stitch of canvas, leaving Portland Point abeam, rounding Negril Point at sunset, catching some fortunate puffs of the sea breeze which enabled them to cheat the trade wind, ghosting along in the tropical darkness with the lead at work in the chains, and anchoring with the dawn among the shoals of Montego Bay, the green mountains of Jamaica all fiery with the rising sun.

Hornblower was on deck to see it; he had been awake since midnight, having slept since sunset – two almost sleepless nights had disordered his habits – and he was already pacing the quarterdeck as the excited men were formed up in the waist. He kept a sharp eye on the preparations. That boat mortar weighed no more than four hundred pounds, a mere trifle for the yardarm tackle to lower down into the punt alongside. The musketmen were put through an inspection of their equipment; it was puzzling to the crew that there were pikemen, axemen, and even malletmen and crow-barmen as well. As the sun climbed higher and blazed down hotter the men began to file down into the boats.

'Gig's alongside, my lord,' said Gerard.

'Very well.'

On shore Hornblower returned the salute of the astonished subaltern commanding the detachment of the West Indian Regiment on guard over the boats – he had turned out his men apparently expecting nothing less than a French invasion – and dismissed him. Then he ran a final glance over the rigid lines of the marine detachment, scarlet tunics and white cross-belts and all. They would not be nearly as tidy by the end of the day.

'You can make a start, captain,' he said. 'Keep me informed, Mr Spendlove, if you please.'

'Aye aye, my lord.'

With Spendlove as guide the marines marched forward; they were the advanced guard to secure the main body from surprise. It was time to give orders to *Clorinda*'s first lieutenant.

'Now, Mr Sefton, we can move.'

The little river had a little bar at its mouth, but the two punts carrying the mortar and the ammunition had been floated in round it. For a mile there was even a track beside the water, and progress was rapid as they dragged the punts along, while the vegetation closed in round them. The shade was gratifying when they first entered into it, but they found it breathless, damp, stifling, as they progressed farther in. Mosquitoes stung with venomous determination. Men slipped and fell on the treacherous mud-banks, splashing prodigiously. Then they reached the first stretch of shallows, where the river came bubbling down a long perceptible slope between steep banks under the light filtering in through the trees.

At least they had saved a mile and more by water carriage even this far. Hornblower studied the grounded punts, the soil and the trees. This was what he had been thinking about; it was worth making the experiment before putting the men to the toil of carrying the mortar up by brute force.

'We'll try a dam here, Mr Sefton, if you please.'

'Aye aye, my lord. Axemen! Pikemen! Malletmen!'

The men were still in high spirits; it called for exertion on the part of the petty officers to restrain their exuberance. A line of pikes driven head downward where the soil was soft enough to receive them formed the first framework of the dam. Axemen felled small trees with a childish delight in destruction. Crowbarmen levered at stumps and rocks. A small avalanche came tumbling down into the river bed. The water swirled about the trash; already there was sufficient obstruction to hold it. Hornblower saw the level rise before his very eyes.

'More rocks here!' roared Sefton.

'Keep your eye on those punts, Mr Sefton,' said Hornblower – the clumsy craft were already afloat again.

Felled trees and rocks extended, heightened, and strengthened the dam. There was water spouting through the interstices, but not as much as was being held back.

'Get the punts upstream,' ordered Hornblower.

Four hundred willing hands had achieved much; the water was banked up sufficient to float the punts two-thirds of the way up the shallows.

'Another dam, I think, Mr Sefton, if you please.'

Already they had learned much about the construction of temporary dams. The stream bed was choked in a twinkling, it seemed. Splashing knee-deep in water the men dragged the punts higher still. They grounded momentarily, but a final heave ran them over the last of the shallows into a reach where they floated with ease.

'Excellent, Mr Sefton.'

That was a clear gain of a quarter of a mile before the next shallows.

As they were preparing to work on the next dam the flat report of a musket shot came echoing back to them in the heated air, followed by half a dozen more; it was several minutes before they heard the explanation, brought back by a breathless messenger.

'Captain Seymour reports, sir. We was fired on by someone up there, sir. Saw 'im in the trees, sir, but 'e got away.'

'Very well.'

So the pirates had posted a lookout downstream. Now they knew that a force was advancing against them. Only time would show what they would do next; meanwhile the punts were afloat again and it was time to push on. The river curved back and forth, washing at the foot of vertical banks, preserving, for a time, miraculously, enough depth of water to float the punts at the expense of occasionally dragging them up slight rapids. Now it began to seem to Hornblower as if he had spent days on this labour, in the blinding patches of sunlight and the dark stretches of shade, with the river swirling round his knees, and his feet slipping on the rocks. At the next dam he was tempted to sit and allow the sweat to stream down him. He had hardly done so when another messenger arrived from the advanced guard.

'Captain Seymour reporting, sir. 'E says to say the pirates 'ave gorn to ground, sir. They're in a cave, sir, right up in the cliff.'

'How far ahead of here?'

'Oh, not so very fur, sir.'

Hornblower could have expected no better answer, he realized.

'They was shooting at us, sir,' supplemented the messenger.

That defined the distance better, for they had heard no firing for a long time; the pirates' lair must be farther than the sound could carry.

'Very well. Mr Sefton, carry on, if you please. I'm going ahead. Come along, Gerard.'

He set himself to climb and scramble along the river bank. On his left hand as he progressed he noticed the bank was growing steeper and loftier. Now it was really a cliff. Another stretch of rapids at a corner, and then he opened up a fresh vista. There it was, just as he remembered it, the lofty, overhanging cliff with the waterfall tumbling down it to join the river at its foot, and the long horizontal seam halfway up the cliff; open grassland with a few trees on his right, and even the little group of mules on the narrow stretch of grass between the cliff and the river. Red-coated marines were strung out over the grassland, in a wide semicircle whose centre was the cave.

Hornblower forgot his sweating fatigue and strode hastily forward to where he would see Seymour standing among his men gazing up at the cliff, Spendlove at his side. They came to meet him and saluted.

'There they are, my lord,' said Seymour. 'They took a few shots at us when we arrived.'

'Thank you, captain. How do you like the look of the place now, Spendlove?'

'As much as before, my lord, but no more.'

'Spendlove's Leap,' said Hornblower.

He was pressing forward along the river bank towards the cave, staring upwards.

'Have a care, my lord,' said Spendlove, urgently.

A moment after he had spoken something whistled sharply just above Hornblower's head; a puff of smoke appeared over the parapet of the cave, and a sharp ringing report came echoing from the cliff face. Then, made tiny by the distance, doll-like figures appeared over the parapet, waving their arms in defiance, and the yells they were uttering came faintly to their ears.

'Someone has a rifle up there, my lord,' said Seymour.

'Indeed? Perhaps then it would be best to withdraw out of range before he can reload.'

The incident had made little impression on Hornblower until that moment. Now he suddenly realized that the almost legendary career of the great Lord Hornblower might have been terminated then and there, that his future biographer might have had to deplore the ironic chance which, after so many pitched battles, brought him death at the hands of an obscure criminal in an unknown corner of a West Indian island. He turned and walked away, the others at his side. He found he was holding his neck rigid, his muscles tense; it had been a long time since his life was last in danger. He strove to appear natural.

'Sefton will be up with the mortar before long,' he said, after casting about in his mind for something natural to say; and he hoped it did not sound as unnatural to the others as it did to him.

'Yes, my lord.'

'Where shall we site it?' He swung round and looked about him, measuring ranges with his eye. 'It had better be out of range of that rifle.'

His interest in what he was doing immediately erased the memory of his danger. Another puff of smoke from the parapet; another echoing report.

'Did anyone hear that bullet? No? Then we can assume we're out of rifle shot here.'

'If you please, my lord,' asked Spendlove. 'What range can you expect with a boat mortar?'

'The encyclopedic Spendlove displaying ignorance! Seven hundred yards with a one-pound charge of powder, and a time of flight of fifteen seconds. But here we have to burst the shell sixty feet above the firing-point. A nice problem in ballistics.' Hornblower spoke with perfect indifference, confident that no one knew that at one o'clock that morning he had been studying those figures in the manual. 'Those trees there will be useful when we come to sway the mortar up. And there's level ground within twenty feet of them. Excellent.'

'Here they come, my lord.'

The first of the main body appeared round the distant corner of the cliff, hurrying along the river bank. As they took in the situation they broke into a yell and a run, leaping and scrambling over the broken ground; Hornblower was reminded of hounds rushing up clamouring at sight of their quarry at bay.

'Silence, there!' he roared. 'You midshipman, there, can't you keep your men under control? Mark their names for punishment, and I'll mention yours to Mr Sefton.'

Abashed, the seamen formed up quietly. Here came the punts, gliding like fate along the silent pool, towed by working parties scrambling along the bank.

'Orders, my lord?' asked Sefton.

Hornblower glanced finally round the terrain before issuing them. The sun was long past its zenith as eager men clambered up the trees to fix the tackles; soon the mortar hung dangling from a stout limb while the mortar bed was hoisted out and settled in a smooth spot, the gunner fussing over it with a spirit level to make sure it was horizontal. Then, with violent manual labour, the mortar was swung over and finally heaved up into position, and the gunner drove the keys through the eye-bolts.

'Shall I open fire, my lord?' asked Sefton.

Hornblower looked over at the distant seam in the face of the cliff across the river. The pirates there would be watching them. Had they recognized this squat object, inconsiderable in size, undistinguished in shape, which meant death to them? They might well not know what it was; they were probably peering over the parapet trying to make out what it was that had occupied the attention of so considerable a body of men.

'What's your elevation, gunner?'

'Sixty degrees, sir – my lord.'

'Try a shot with a fifteen-second fuse.'

The gunner went carefully through the processes of loading, measuring the powder charge and wadding it down into the chamber, clearing the touch-hole with the priming iron and then filling it with fine-grain powder from the horn. He took his bradawl and drove it carefully into the wooden stem of the fuse at the selected point – these were very newfangled fuses, graduated with ink lines to mark the time of burning – and screwed it into the shell. He lowered the shell down upon the wad.

'Linstocks,' he said.

Someone had been chipping away with flint and steel to catch a spark upon the slow match. He transferred the glow to a second linstock which he handed to the gunner. The gunner, stooping, checked the pointing of the weapon.

'Fuse!' he said. His assistant touched his linstock down, and the fuse spluttered. Then the gunner thrust his glowing match upon the touch-hole. A roar and a billow of powder smoke.

Standing far back from the mortar Hornblower already had his face turned to the sky to track the shell in its flight. Against that light blue there was nothing to be seen – no, there at the height of the trajectory there was a brief black streak, instantly invisible again. A further wait; an inevitable thought that the fuse had failed, and then a distant explosion and a fountain of smoke, down at the base of the cliff somewhat to the right of the cave. There was a groan from the watching seamen.

'Silence, there!' bellowed Sefton.

'Try again, gunner,' said Hornblower.

The mortar was trained round a trifle on its bed. Its bore was sponged out and when the charge had been put in the gunner took a gill measure from his pocket and added a measure of powder to the charge. He pierced the fuse again, lowered the shell into the bore, gave his final order, and fired. A wait; and then a bold puff of smoke hung in the air, seemingly right in line with the seam in the cliff. The wretched people there were watching their fate creeping up on them.

'Fuse a little short,' said Hornblower.

'Range short, I fancy, my lord,' said the gunner.

At the next shot there was a cloud of dust and a small avalanche from the cliff face high above the seam, and instantly afterwards the burst of the shell on the ground at the near edge of the river where it had fallen.

'Better,' said Hornblower. He had seen the principles of ranging with a mortar – a huge thirteen-inch one – at the siege of Riga nearly twenty years before.

Two more shots, both wasted – the shells exploded at the top of their trajectory, high, high up. Apparently those newfangled fuses were not quite reliable. Fountains spouted momentarily from the river surface as fragments rained into it. But the pirates must by now be fully aware of what the mortar implied.

'Give me that telescope, Gerard.'

He trained the instrument on the seam in the face of the cliff. He could see every detail now, the rough stone parapet, the waterfall at one end, but he could see no sign of the garrison. They were at the back of the cave or crouching behind the parapet.

'Fire another shot.'

Fifteen long seconds after the report. Then he saw fragments flying from under the overhang.

'Good shot!' he called, still watching. The shell must have fallen right into the cave. But as he uttered the words a dark figure appeared at the parapet, the arms swinging together. He saw the tiny black disc of the shell against the background of rock curving downwards and then a burst of smoke. Someone had seized the hot shell in his two hands and slung it over the parapet in the nick of time. A desperate deed.

'Pitch another shell there with a second's less fuse and it will be all over,' he said, and then – 'Wait.'

Surely those helpless people must surrender, and not stay to be massacred. What must he do to persuade them? He knew perfectly well.

'Send a white flag forward, my lord?' asked Spendlove, voicing his thoughts.

'I was thinking about it,' said Hornblower.

It would be a dangerous mission. If the pirates were determined not to surrender they would not respect a flag of truce, and would fire on the bearer of it. There were a score of muskets and at least one rifle up there. Hornblower wanted neither to order someone forward nor to ask for a volunteer.

'I'll do it, my lord,' said Spendlove. 'They know me.'

This was the price he had to pay, thought Hornblower, for his lofty position, for being an admiral. He had to order his friends to their death. Yet on the other hand –

'Very well,' said Hornblower.

'Let's have your shirt and your pike, my man,' said Spendlove.

A white shirt tied by the sleeves to a pikestaff made a fair white flag. As Spendlove went forward with it, through the cordon of red-coated marines, Hornblower was tempted to call him back. It was only unconditional surrender that could be offered, after all. He went as far as to open his mouth, but closed it again without saying the words he had in mind. Spendlove walked towards the river bank, stopping every few seconds to wave the flag. Through the telescope Hornblower could see nothing up in the cave. Then he saw a flash of metal, and a line of heads and shoulders over the parapet. A dozen muskets were taking aim at Spendlove. But Spendlove saw them too, and halted, with a wave of his flag. There were long seconds of tension, and then Spendlove turned his back upon the muskets and began to retrace his steps. As he did so there was a puff of smoke from the parapet; the rifleman had fired as soon as he had seen there was no chance of luring Spendlove within musket shot. Spendlove came walking back, trailing the pike and the shirt.

'He missed me, my lord,' he said.

'Thank God,' said Hornblower. 'Gunner, fire.'

The wind may have shifted a little, or the powder was not consistent. The shell burst in the air just below the level of the cave – so that the fuse must have been efficient – but some considerable distance from the cliff.

'Fire again,' said Hornblower.

There it was. A burst of smoke, a fountain of fragments, right in the cave. Horrible to think of what was happening there.

'Fire again.'

Another burst right in the cave.

'Fire again – No! Wait.'

Figures were appearing on the parapet – there had been some survivors, then, from those two bursts. Two figures – tiny dolls in the field of the telescope – seemed to hang in the air as they leaped. The telescope followed them down. One struck water in a fountain of spray. The other fell on the rocky shore, broken and horrible. He raised the telescope again. There was the ladder being thrown over from the parapet. There was a figure – and another figure – climbing down. Hornblower shut the telescope with a snap.

'Captain Seymour! Send a party forward to secure the prisoners.'

He did not have to see the horrors of the cave, the mutilated dead and the screaming wounded. He could see them in his mind's eye when Seymour made his report of what he found when he ascended the ladder. It was done, finished. The wounded could be bandaged and carried down to the beach on litters to the death that awaited them, the unwounded driven along with them with their wrists bound. A courier could be sent off to the Governor to say that the pirate horde had been wiped out, so that the patrols could be called in and the militia sent home. He did not have to set eyes on the wretched people he had conquered. The excitement of the hunt was over. He had set himself a task to do, a problem to solve, just as he might work out a longitude from lunar observations, and he had achieved success. But the measure of that success could be expressed in hangings, in dead and in wounded, in that shattered, broken-backed figure lying on the rocks, and he had undertaken the task merely on a point of pride, to re-establish his self-esteem after the indignity of being kidnapped. It was no comfort to argue with himself – as he did – that what he had done would otherwise have been done by others, at great cost in disease and in economic disturbance. That only made him sneer at himself as a hair-splitting casuist. There were few occasions when Hornblower could do what was right in Hornblower's eyes.

Yet there was some cynical pleasure to be derived from his lofty rank, to be able to leave all this after curt orders to Sefton and Seymour to bring the landing party back to the shore with the least delay and the shortest exposure to the night air, to go back on board and eat a comfortable dinner – even if it meant Fell's rather boring company – and to sleep in a comfortable bed. And it was pleasant to find that Fell had already dined, so that he could eat his dinner merely in the company of his flag lieutenant and his secretary. Nevertheless, there was one more unexpected crumpled petal in his roseleaf bed, and he discovered it, contrariwise, as a result of what he intended to be a kindly action.

'I shall have to add a further line to my remarks about you to Their Lordships, Spendlove,' he said. 'It was a brave deed to go forward with that flag of truce.'

'Thank you, my lord,' said Spendlove, who bent his gaze down on the tablecloth and drummed with his fingers before continuing, eyes still lowered in unusual nervousness. 'Then perhaps Your Lordship will not be averse to putting in a word for me in another quarter?'

'Of course I will,' replied Hornblower in all innocence. 'Where?'

'Thank you, my lord. It was with this in mind that I did the little you have been kind enough to approve of. I would be deeply grateful if Your Lordship would go to the trouble of speaking well of me to Miss Lucy.'

Lucy! Hornblower had forgotten all about the girl. He quite failed to conceal his surprise, which was clearly apparent to Spendlove when he lifted his glance from the tablecloth.

'We jested about a wealthy marriage, my lord,' said Spendlove. The elaborate care with which he was choosing his words proved how deep were his emotions. 'I would not care if Miss Lucy had not a penny. My lord, my affections are deeply engaged.'

'She is a very charming young woman,' said Hornblower, temporizing desperately.

'My lord, I love her,' burst out Spendlove, casting aside all restraint. 'I love her dearly. At the ball I tried to interest her in myself, and I failed.'

'I'm sorry to hear that,' said Hornblower.

'I could not but be aware of her admiration for you, my lord. She spoke of Your Lordship repeatedly. I realized even then that one word from you would carry more weight than a long speech from me. If you would say that word, my lord –'

'I'm sure you overestimate my influence,' said Hornblower, choosing his words as carefully as Spendlove had done, but, he hoped, not as obviously. 'But of course I will do all I can.'

'There is no need for me to reiterate my gratitude, my lord,' said Spendlove.

This pleading creature, this poor love-lorn fellow, was the Spendlove whose cool daring had risked a leap in the darkness down a sixty-foot precipice. Hornblower remembered Lucy's lips on his hands, remembered how she had followed him on her knees across the floor. The less he had to do with any of this the better, he decided. But the passion of a child hardly out of the schoolroom for a man of mature years was likely to be fleeting, transient, and the memory of her lost dignity would later be as painful to her as it was to him. She would find need to assert herself, to show him that he was not the only man in the world – and how could she demonstrate that more plainly than by marrying someone else? To use a vulgar phrase, there was quite a chance that Spendlove might catch her on the rebound.

'If good wishes can help,' he said, 'you have all mine, Spendlove.'

Even an admiral had to choose his words with care. Two days later he was announcing his immediate departure to the Governor.

'I'm taking my squadron to sea in the morning, Your Excellency,' he said.

'Aren't you going to stay for the hangings?' asked Hooper in surprise.

'I fear not,' answered Hornblower, and added an unnecessary explanation. 'Hangings don't agree with me, Your Excellency.'

It was not merely an unnecessary explanation; it was a foolish one, as he knew as soon as he saw the open astonishment in Hooper's face. Hooper could hardly have been more surprised at hearing that hangings did not agree with Hornblower than he would have been if he had heard that Hornblower did not agree with hangings – and that was very nearly as correct.

The Guns of Carabobo

She was exactly like a British ship of war; naturally, perhaps, since she had been one most of her life until she was sold out of the Service. Now, as she came up into the harbour, she could pass without question for a man-o'-war brig except that she flew the Royal Yacht Squadron burgee instead of a commission pendant. Hornblower put down the telescope through which he had been watching, curiously, her progress into Kingston harbour, and referrred again to Barbara's letter, two months old now, which had arrived a fortnight ago.

My dearest husband, (wrote Barbara. She sometimes misused her superlatives; that 'dearest,' strictly, implied that she had at least three husbands, even though it also implied that Hornblower rated highest of the three.)

You are shortly going to have a visitor, a Mr Charles Ramsbottom, a millionaire, who has purchased an old ship of the Navy to use as a yacht, which he has named the 'Bride of Abydos', and in which he proposes to visit the West Indies. He has only lately made his appearance in society, having inherited his father's fortune – Bradford wool and army clothing contracts! Yet despite this obscure origin he has succeeded in entering into society, perhaps because he is very young, very charming, unmarried, mildly eccentric, and, as I said, a millionaire. I have met

him frequently of late, in very good houses, and I
recommend him to you, dearest, if for no other reason
than that he has won some small portion of my heart by a
delightful mixture of deference and interest which I might
have found irresistible were I not married to the most
irresistible man in the world. He has, indeed, won golden
opinions in society, both on the Government side and with
the Opposition, and he might become an important factor
in politics should he decide to enter into them. I have no
doubt that he will bring you introductions from personages
even more influential than your loving wife . . .

Hornblower had to read the letter through to the end, although it contained no further reference to Mr Charles Ramsbottom, but he returned again to the opening paragraph. It was the first time he had ever seen this new word 'millionaire', which occurred twice. He disliked it on sight. It was inconceivable that a man should have a million pounds, and presumably not in broad estates but in factories and in stocks and shares, probably with a huge holding in Consols and an immense balance at the bank as well. The existence of millionaires, whether in society or not, was something as distasteful as the word itself now called into existence. And this one had been charming to Barbara – he was not too sure if that really constituted a recommendation. He picked up the telescope again and watched the brig come to an anchor. The rapidity with which she took in sail showed that she carried a large crew. Hornblower, as a commander-in-chief of a squadron and accountable to the niggardly Lords of the Admiralty for every penny expended, knew perfectly well what this sort of thing cost. This Mr

Ramsbottom, to indulge himself in his naval toy, was expending enough money to maintain a thousand families in bread and beer and bacon.

The brig rounded-to and anchored very neatly indeed; if she had been a vessel included in his command he would have grunted with grudging satisfaction. As it was he grunted with a mixture of envy and derision and turned away to await the inevitable call in the seclusion of Admiralty House.

When it came he fingered the visiting card with its plain 'Mr Charles Ramsbottom' and found some small satisfaction in deciding that he had at last come across a name more unlovely than his own. But the owner of the name, when he was ushered in, made a better impression. In his very early twenties, he was small and slight and – for what it was worth – strikingly handsome, with black hair and eyes and what could only be described as 'chiselled features' deeply tanned after weeks at sea; not at all what might be expected of a Bradford wool manufacturer, while his dark-green coat and formal white breeches were in quiet good taste.

'My wife wrote to me about you, Mr Ramsbottom,' said Hornblower.

'That was very kind of Lady Hornblower. But of course she is kindness personified. May I present my letters of introduction from Lord Liverpool and Bishop Wilberforce, my lord?'

Barbara was perfectly right, then, in predicting that Ramsbottom would win favour with both political parties – here were letters from the Prime Minister himself and a prominent member of the Opposition. Hornblower glanced through them, and was conscious of an undernote of cordiality despite their formal wording.

'Excellent, Mr Ramsbottom,' said Hornblower. He tried to adopt the tone which he presumed would be adopted by a man who had just read a letter of introduction from the Prime Minister. 'Is there any way in which I can be of service to you?'

'None that I am aware of at present, my lord. I must complete with water and stores, naturally, but my purser is a capable man. I intend to continue my voyage through these charming islands.'

'Of course,' said Hornblower, soothingly. He could not imagine why anyone should voluntarily spend any time in these waters where piracy was still smouldering, nor why anyone should wish to visit countries where malaria and yellow fever were endemic, and where civil war, revolution and massacre claimed even heavier toll.

'You find the *Bride of Abydos* a comfortable ship?' asked Hornblower.

Those eighteen-gun brigs of the Royal Navy were notoriously unpleasant craft, crowded and crank.

'Comfortable enough, my lord, thank you,' answered Ramsbottom. 'I lightened her by changing the armament; she mounts only twelve guns now – two long sixes and ten carronades, twenty-four-pounders instead of thirty-two-pounders.'

'So you could still deal with a pirate?'

'Oh, yes indeed, my lord. And with the reduction in weight on deck – a full ten tons – and modifications in her sail plan I have made a seaworthy craft of her, I believe and hope.'

'I'm sure you have, Mr Ramsbottom,' said Hornblower. It was likely enough; the brigs-of-war were naturally crammed with guns and warlike stores to the limit of stability and human endurance, so that a moderate reduction in dead weight might have profound results in comfort and handiness.

'It would give me the greatest pleasure,' went on Mr Ramsbottom, 'if I could induce Your Lordship to visit me on board. It would indeed be an honour, and would gratify my crew. Perhaps I could even persuade Your Lordship to dine on board?'

'We can discuss that after you have dined with me, Mr Ramsbottom,' replied Hornblower, remembering his manners and his obligation to invite to dinner any bearer of a reasonable introduction.

'You are most kind, my lord,' said Mr Ramsbottom. 'I must, of course, present my introductions to His Excellency at the earliest opportunity.'

There was something quite winning about Mr Ramsbottom's smile as he said this, an awareness and a tolerance of the rules of social etiquette. A visitor to Jamaica would normally be bound to pay his respects first to the Governor, but Ramsbottom was no ordinary visitor; as captain of a ship his first call was due to the Naval authorities, to Hornblower, in fact. A trivial point, as his smile implied, but, etiquette being etiquette, trivial points demanded strict attention.

By the time Ramsbottom took his leave he had made a very good impression on the reluctant Hornblower. He had talked sensibly about ships and the sea, he was easy and natural in his manner, and not in the least like Lord Byron, who was probably more responsible than anyone else for the growing fad for yachting among the wealthy. Hornblower was even prepared to forgive him for having 'won some small portion' of Barbara's heart. And in the course of his several days' stay in Jamaica Hornblower really came to like the young man, especially after having lost two pounds to him in a desperate tussle at whist and then winning ten pounds back in another tussle where admittedly Ramsbottom encountered a run of bad luck. Jamaican society gave Ramsbottom a warm welcome; even the Governor looked on him with approval, and the Governor's wife, Lady Hooper, was loud in her praises of his excellent manners and considerate ways.

'I wouldn't have expected it of a Bradford manufacturer's son,' said Hooper, grudgingly.

'Are you dining on board the *Bride of Abydos*, sir?' asked Hornblower.

'I am going there to dinner,' answered Hooper, who enjoyed food, 'but seeing that it is only a yacht I have little hope of dining.'

Hornblower arrived on board early, at Ramsbottom's suggestion, so as to have time to inspect the vessel. He was received in Navy fashion with sideboys attending the side and a long flourish on boatswain's pipes as he stepped on board. He looked keenly about him even while he shook Ramsbottom's hand. He could not have said he was not in a King's ship, as his eye took in the gleaming white deck, the ropes coiled in perfect symmetry, the gleaming trophy of pikes and cutlasses against the bulkhead, the brass winking in the sunshine, the disciplined orderly crew in blue jumpers and white trousers.

'May I present my officers, my lord?' asked Ramsbottom.

They were two half-pay lieutenants, hardbitten men; as Hornblower shook their hands he told himself that if it had not been for a dozen strokes of luck he himself might still be a lieutenant, perhaps eking out his half-pay by serving in a rich man's yacht. As Ramsbottom led him forward he recognized one of the hands standing at attention by a gun.

'You were with me in the *Renown*, out here in 1800,' he said.

'Yes, sir, my lord, so I was, sir.' The man grinned with uneasy pleasure as he shyly took Hornblower's outstretched hand. 'And Charlie Kemp, sir, my lord, over there, sir, 'e was with you in the Baltic. And Bill Cummings, up on the fo'c'sle, 'e was foretopman in the *Lydia* round the Horn with you, sir, my lord.'

'Glad to see you again,' said Hornblower. That was true, but he was equally glad that he had not been under the necessity of remembering names. He moved on.

'You seem to have a Navy crew, Mr Ramsbottom,' he remarked.

'Yes, my lord. They are nearly all man-o'-wars men.'

In these years of peace and depression it would be easy enough to recruit a crew, thought Hornblower. Ramsbottom might be considered to be doing a public service in providing easy employment for these men who had deserved well of their country. Listening to the sharp orders given as the crew was put through their paces Hornblower could not suppress a smile. It was a harmless enough fad, he supposed, for Ramsbottom to indulge himself in playing at commanding a ship of war.

'You have a most efficient ship and a well-trained crew, Mr Ramsbottom,' he said.

'It is a pleasure to hear Your Lordship say so.'

'You have seen no service yourself?'

'None, my lord.'

There was a certain degree of surprise still to be found in the fact that in this year of 1821 there were to be found grown men, even heads of families, who nevertheless had been too young to see service in the wars that had devastated the world for a whole generation. It made Hornblower feel like a centenarian.

'Here come further guests, my lord, if you will pardon me.'

Two planters – Hough and Doggart – and then the Chief Justice of the island. So the arrival of the Governor would make a dinner party of six, three officials and three men in private life. They gathered under the awning, which, stretched across the main boom, shaded the quarterdeck, and watched the reception of His Excellency.

'Do you think the dinner will come up to the ceremonial?' asked Doggart.

'Ramsbottom's purser bought two tons of ice yesterday,' said Hough.

'At sixpence a pound that bids fair,' commented Doggart.

Jamaica was the centre of a small trade in ice, brought down from New England in fast schooners. Cut and stored away in deep places during the winter, it was hurried to the Caribbean insulated in a packing of sawdust. At the height of summer it commanded fantastic prices. Hornblower was interested; he was more interested still in the sight of a seaman down in the waist steadily turning a crank. It did not seem a very hard labour, although unremitting. He could not for the life of him think of what function that crank could play in the life of the ship. The guests made their bows to His Excellency, and at his suggestion seated themselves in the comfortable chairs. A steward appeared at once passing round glasses of sherry.

'Excellent, by George!' exclaimed the Governor after his first cautious sip. 'None of your Olorosos, none of your sweet sticky dark sherries.'

The Governor by virtue of his reputed royal blood as well as in consequence of his position could make remarks that well might appear rude in another man. But the sherry was indeed delightful; pale, dry, infinitely delicate in flavour and bouquet, cool but not chilled. A new sound struck on Hornblower's ear, and he turned and looked forward. At the foot of the mainmast a small orchestra had struck up, of various stringed instruments whose names he had never bothered to learn except for the fiddle. If it were not for the intrusion of this horrible music there could be nothing more delightful than to sit under an awning on the deck of a well-found ship with the sea breeze just beginning to come in, drinking this excellent sherry. The Governor made a small gesture which brought a fresh glass promptly to him.

'Ah!' said the Governor. 'You keep a good orchestra, Mr Ramsbottom.'

It was well known that the royal family inherited a taste for music.

'I must thank Your Excellency,' said Ramsbottom, and the glasses went round again before he turned an ear to the murmured words of the steward. 'Your Excellency, my lord, gentlemen, dinner is served.'

They filed down the companion; apparently every bulkhead had been taken down in the after-part of the ship to make a cabin spacious though low. The carronades on either side struck a subdued warlike note in a scene of luxury, for there were flowers everywhere; the dining table stood in the centre concealed under a glittering linen cloth. Wind scoops at the scuttles helped to deflect the trade wind into the cabin, which, under the double shade of the awning and the deck, was pleasantly cool, but Hornblower's eye at once caught sight of a couple of strange objects, like small wheels, set in two scuttles and ceaselessly whirling round. Then he knew why the seaman was turning that crank in the waist; he was driving these two wheels, which by some ingenious mechanism propelled currents of air from outside into the cabin, acting like windmill vanes but in the opposite sense.

Seated at the table in accordance with the courteous indications of their host, the guests awaited the serving of the dinner. The first course made its appearance – two ample dishes set in dishes even more ample filled with cracked ice. The inner dishes held a grey granular substance.

'Caviare!' exclaimed His Excellency, helping himself liberally after his first astonished stare.

'I hope it is to your taste, sir,' said Ramsbottom. 'And I hope you will accompany it with some of the vodka here. It is the same as is served at the Russian Imperial table.'

Conversation regarding caviare and vodka occupied

the attention of all during the first course. The last time Hornblower had tasted the combination was during the defence of Riga in 1812; the experience enabled him to add his quota to the conversation. The next course made its appearance.

'You gentlemen are accustomed to this dish,' said Ramsbottom, 'but I need not apologize for it. It is, I believe, one of the delicacies of the Islands.'

It was flying fish.

'Certainly no need to apologize when it is served like this,' commented His Excellency. 'Your *chef de cuisine* must be a man of genius.'

The sauce that came with it had the merest hint of mustard.

"Ock or champagne, my lord?' murmured a voice in Hornblower's ear. Hornblower had already heard the Governor answer the same question with 'I'll try the hock first.' The champagne was dry and insidiously delicate, an ideal companion for the food. The great eaters of antiquity, Nero or Vitellius or Lucullus, had never known what it was like to partake of champagne and flying fish.

'You'll be living differently from this soon, Hornblower,' said His Excellency.

'No doubt about that, sir.'

Ramsbottom, between them, looked a polite inquiry.

'Your Lordship's going to sea?'

'Next week,' replied Hornblower. 'I take my squadron to sea for exercises before the coming of the hurricane season.'

'Of course that would be necessary to maintain efficiency,' agreed Ramsbottom. 'The exercises will last for long?'

'A couple of weeks or more,' said Hornblower. 'I have to keep my men accustomed to hard tack and salt pork and water from the cask.'

'And yourself too,' chuckled the Governor.

'Myself too,' agreed Hornblower ruefully.

'And you take your whole squadron, my lord?' asked Ramsbottom.

'All I can. I work 'em hard and try to make no exceptions.'

'A good rule, I should think,' said Ramsbottom.

The soup that followed the flying fish was a fiery mulligatawny, well adapted to West Indian palates.

'Good!' was the Governor's brief comment after his first spoonful. The champagne went round again and conversation became livelier and livelier, and Ramsbottom deftly kept it going.

'What news from the mainland, sir?' he asked the Governor. 'This fellow Bolivar – is he making any progress?'

'He fights on,' answered the Governor. 'But Spain hurries out reinforcements whenever her own troubles permit. The government at Caracas is looking for the arrival of more at this moment, I believe. Then they may be able to conquer the plains and drive him out again. You know he was a refugee here in this very island a few years ago?'

'Indeed, sir?'

All the guests at the table were interested in the desperate civil war that was being fought on the mainland. Massacre and murder, blind heroism and devoted self-sacrifice, loyalty to the King and thirst for independence – all these were to be found in Venezuela; war and pestilence were laying waste the fertile plains and depopulating the crowded cities.

'How will the Spaniards stand now that Maracaibo has revolted, Hornblower?' asked the Governor.

'It's not a serious loss, sir. As long as they have the use of La Guaira their sea communications remain open – the roads are so bad that Caracas has always made use of La Guaira to preserve contact with the outside world; it's only an open roadstead but it provides good anchorage.'

'Has Maracaibo revolted, Your Excellency?' asked Ramsbottom mildly.

'The news came this morning. A feather in Bolivar's cap after his recent defeats. His army must have been growing disheartened.'

'His army, sir?' This was the Chief Justice speaking. 'Half his men are British infantry.'

Hornblower knew that to be true. British veterans formed the backbone of Bolivar's army. The *Ilaneros* – the men of the Venezuelan plains – supplied him with a brilliant cavalry, but not with the material for permanent conquest.

'Even British infantry could grow disheartened in a hopeless cause,' said the Governor, solemnly. 'The Spaniards control most of the coast – ask the Admiral here.'

'That's so,' agreed Hornblower. 'They've made it hard for Bolivar's privateers.'

'I hope you're not going to venture into that turmoil, Mr Ramsbottom,' said the Governor.

'They'll make short work of you if you do,' added the Chief Justice. 'The Dons will tolerate no interference. They'll snatch you up and you'll languish in a Spanish prison for years before we can extricate you from King Ferdinand's clutches. Unless jail fever carries you off first. Or they hang you as a pirate.'

'I have certainly no intention of venturing near the mainland,' said Ramsbottom. 'At least not while this war continues. It is a pity, because Venezuela was my mother's country, and it would give me pleasure to visit it.'

'Your mother's country, Mr Ramsbottom?' asked the Governor.

'Yes, sir. My mother was a Venezuelan lady. There I would be Carlos Ramsbottom y Santona.'

'Most interesting,' remarked the Governor.

And more grotesque than Horatio Hornblower. It was significant of the worldwide interests of British commerce that a Bradford woollen manufacturer should have a Venezuelan mother. At any rate it accounted for Ramsbottom's dark, almost swarthy, good looks.

'I can very well wait until peace is settled one way or the other,' said Ramsbottom off-handedly. 'There will be other voyages to make. Meanwhile, sir, let me call your attention to this dish here.'

The main course had now arrived on the table, roast chickens and a leg of pork as well as the dish that Ramsbottom indicated. What lay in it was concealed by poached eggs covering the surface.

'A made dish?' asked the Governor, doubtfully. His tone indicated that at this stage of the dinner he looked rather for a substantial roast.

'Please try it, sir,' said Ramsbottom coaxingly.

The Governor helped himself and tasted cautiously.

'Pleasant enough,' he decided. 'What is it?'

'A ragout of preserved beef,' answered Ramsbottom. 'Can I persuade you gentlemen to try it? My lord?'

At least it was something new; it was like nothing Hornblower had ever tasted before – certainly not in the least like the beef preserved in brine which he had eaten for twenty years.

'Extremely good,' said Hornblower. 'How is it preserved?'

Ramsbottom made a gesture to the waiting steward, who laid a square box, apparently of iron, upon the table. It weighed heavy in Hornblower's hand.

'Glass serves equally well,' explained Ramsbottom, 'but it is not as convenient on shipboard.'

The steward was now at work upon the iron box with a stout knife. He cut it open and prized back the top and offered it for inspection.

'A tinned box,' went on Ramsbottom, 'sealed at a high temperature. I venture to suggest that this new method will make a noticeable difference to the food supply on shipboard. This beef can be eaten cold on removal from the box, or it can be hashed as you have it here.'

'And the poached egg?' asked the Governor.

'That was the inspiration of my cook, sir.'

Discussion of this new invention – and of the excellent burgundy served with this course – distracted attention from the troubles of Venezuela, and even from Ramsbottom's Venezuelan mother. Conversation became general, and somewhat disjointed, as the wine flowed. Hornblower had drunk as much as he desired, and, with his habitual dislike of excess, contrived to avoid drinking more. It was noticeable that Ramsbottom remained sober as well, cool and quiet-voiced, while the other faces grew redder and redder, and the cabin echoed to the roaring toasts and the bursts of inconsequential song. Hornblower guessed that his host was now finding the evening as tedious as he himself found it. He was glad when at last His Excellency rose, supporting himself by the table, to take his leave.

'A damned good dinner,' he said. 'And you're a damned good host, Ramsbottom. Wish there were more like you.'

Hornblower shook hands.

'It was very good of you to come, my lord,' said Ramsbottom. 'I regret that I must take this opportunity to say goodbye to Your Lordship.'

'You are sailing soon?'

'In a couple of days, I expect, my lord. I trust you will find your squadron exercises satisfactory.'

'Thank you very much. Where will you head for now?'

'I shall beat back through the Windward Channel, my lord. Perhaps I shall see something of the Bahamas.'

'Be careful of your navigation there. I must wish you good luck and a pleasant voyage. I shall write to my wife and tell her of your visit.'

'Please give Lady Hornblower my best wishes and respects, my lord.'

Ramsbottom's good manners persisted to the end; he remembered to send round his cards *'Pour prendre congé'* before he left, and mothers of unmarried daughters much regretted his leaving. Hornblower saw the *Bride of Abydos* in the early dawn reaching to the eastward to round Morant Point with the land breeze, and then forgot about her in the bustle of taking his squadron to sea for exercises.

It never failed to raise a wry smile on his face when he looked about him at 'His Majesty's ships and vessels in the West Indies' under his command. In wartime he would have had a powerful fleet; now he had three small frigates and a motley collection of brigs and schooners. But they would serve his purpose; in his scheme the frigates became three-deckers and the brigs seventy-fours and the schooners frigates. He had a van, a centre, and a rear; he cruised in formation ready to meet the enemy, with rasping reprimands soaring up his signal halliards when any ship failed to keep station; he cleared for action and he turned by divisions into fighting line ahead; he tacked to double on the imaginary enemy's line. In pitch darkness he would burn blue lights with the signal 'Enemy in sight', so that a score of captains and a thousand seamen came tumbling from their beds to deal with the non-existent foe.

Without warning he would hang out a signal putting the most junior lieutenants in command of their respective ships, and then he would plunge into intricate manœuvres calculated to turn the anxious substantive captains, looking helplessly on, grey with anxiety – but those junior lieutenants might some day be commanding ships of the line in a battle on which the destiny of England might depend, and it was necessary to steel their nerves and accustom them to handle ships in dangerous situations. In the middle of sail drill he would signal 'Flagship on fire. All boats away.' He called for landing parties to storm non-existent batteries on some harmless, uninhabited cay, and he inspected those landing parties once they were on shore, to the last flint in the last pistol, with a rigid disregard for excuses that made men grind their teeth in exasperation. He set his captains to plan and execute cutting-out expeditions, and he commented mordantly on the arrangements for defence and the methods of attack. He paired off his ships to fight single-ship duels, sighting each other on the horizon and approaching ready to fire the vital opening broadside; he took advantage of calms to set his men to work towing and sweeping in desperate attempts to overtake the ship ahead. He worked his crews until they were ready to drop, and then he devised further tasks for them to prove to them that they still had one more effort left in them, so that it was doubtful whether 'Old Horny' was mentioned more often with curses or with admiration.

It was a toughened squadron that Hornblower led back to Kingston; but while *Clorinda* was still working up into the harbour a shore boat came pulling out to her, with on board an aide-de-camp of the Governor's with a note for Hornblower.

'Sir Thomas, would you have the kindness to call away my barge?' asked Hornblower.

There was much apparent need for haste, for the note from Government House said, briefly:

My lord,
    It is necessary that Your Lordship should attend here at the earliest possible moment to offer an explanation regarding the situation in Venezuela. Your Lordship is therefore requested and required to report to me immediately.
    Augustus Hooper, Governor.

Hornblower naturally had no idea of what had happened in Venezuela for the last two weeks and more. He made no guess while the carriage took him up to Government House at its best pace, and in any case if he had tried he would never have succeeded in coming near to the truth.

'What is all this, Hornblower?' were the Governor's opening words to him. 'What authority have you for blockading the Venezuelan coast? Why was I not informed?'

'I've done nothing of the sort,' replied Hornblower, indignantly.

'But – Damn it, man, I've the proof here. I've Dutchmen and Spaniards and half the nations of the earth here all protesting about it.'

'I assure you, sir, I have taken no action on the Venezuelan coast. I have not been within five hundred miles of it.'

'Then what does this mean?' shouted the Governor. 'Look here at this!'

He held some papers up with one hand and slapped wildly at them with the other, so that Hornblower had some difficulty in taking them from him. Hornblower was bewildered already; he was more bewildered still as he read. One paper was an official dispatch in French, from the Dutch Governor of Curaçao; the other was larger and clearer, and he read it first. It was a big sheet of paper with bold writing.

Whereas – it began – notice has been received by the Lords Commissioners for executing the office of the Lord High Admiral from the Right Honourable Viscount Castlereagh, one of His Britannic Majesty's Principal Secretaries of State, concerning the need to establish a Blockade of the Coast of His Most Catholic Majesty's Dominion of Venezuela, and of the Islands pertaining to the Dominion of His Majesty the King of the Netherlands, namely and to wit Curaçao, Aruba, and Bonaire.

Therefore I, Horatio Lord Hornblower, Knight Grand Cross of the Most Honourable Order of the Bath, Rear Admiral of the White Squadron, Commanding His Britannic Majesty's Ships and Vessels in West Indian Waters,

Hereby Proclaim that

The Coast of the Continent of South America from Cartagena to the Dragon's Mouth and

The Dutch Islands aforesaid of Curaçao, Aruba, and Bonaire

Are now in a state of blockade, and that

Any vessel of whatever description, whether carrying materials of war or not, found attempting to enter any port harbour or roadstead within the Territory so defined, or

Hovering with the intent to enter any such port harbour or roadstead

Will be boarded and sent in for adjudication under His Britannic Majesty's High Court of Admiralty and

Will be condemned and seized without compensation to owners, freight owners, charterers, captain, or crew.

Given under my hand this First Day of June 1821,
Hornblower, Rear Admiral

Having read this document Hornblower was able to spare a second glance at the other. It was a vigorous protest from the Dutch Governor at Curaçao demanding explanations, apologies, the immediate withdrawal of the blockade, and exemplary compensation. Hornblower stared at Hooper in astonishment.

'This is in legal form,' he said, indicating the proclamation, 'but I never signed it. This is not my signature.'

'Then –?' spluttered Hooper. 'I thought you might be acting under secret orders from London.'

'Of course not, sir.' Hornblower stared at Hooper for another long second before the explanation came to him. 'Ramsbottom!'

'What do you mean?'

'He's been posing as me, or as one of my officers at least. Is the Dutch officer who brought this available?'

'He's waiting in the next room. There's a Spaniard there, too, sent over in a fishing-boat by Morillo from La Guaira.'

'Can we have them in, sir?'

The Dutchman and the Spaniard were men full of indignation, which was not abated in the least by their presentation to the Admiral responsible, in their minds, for this trouble. The Dutchman spoke fluent English, and it was to him that Hornblower first addressed himself.

'How was this proclamation delivered?' he asked.

'By one of your ships. By one of your officers.'

'What ship?'

'The brig-of-war *Desperate*.'

'I have no such ship. There's none in the Navy List. Who brought it?'

'The captain.'

'Who was he? What was he like?'

'He was an officer. A commander, with epaulettes.'

'In uniform?'

'In full uniform.'

'Young? Old?'

'Very young.'

'Small? Slender? Handsome?'

'Yes.'

Hornblower exchanged a glance with Hooper.

'And this brig, the *Desperate*. About a hundred and seventy tons, bowsprit steved nearly level, mainmast stepped rather far aft?'

'Yes.'

'That settles it, sir,' said Hornblower to Hooper, and, to the Dutchman, 'You've been fooled, I'm sorry to say. This man was an impostor. This proclamation is a forgery.'

The Dutchman stamped with annoyance. He was unable to find words to express himself in a foreign tongue for some moments. Finally from his splutterings emerged a name, which he repeated until it was understandable.

'The *Helmond*! The *Helmond*!'

'What is the *Helmond*, sir?' asked Hornblower.

'One of our ships. Your ship – this *Desperate* – captured her.'

'A valuable ship?'

'She had on board the guns for the Spanish Army. Two batteries of field artillery, guns, limbers, ammunition, everything.'

'Piracy!' exclaimed Hooper.

'It sounds like it,' said Hornblower.

The Spanish officer had been standing by impatiently, apparently only half understanding the English conversation. Hornblower turned to him, and, after desperately trying to recapture his half-forgotten Spanish, entered upon a limping explanation. The Spaniard replied volubly, so volubly that more than once Hornblower had to ask him to speak more slowly. Ramsbottom had come sailing into La Guaira and had brought his precious proclamation with him. At the merest hint that the British Navy was instituting a blockade no ship had dared to stir on the South American coast, except for the *Helmond*. She had been badly needed. Bolivar was marching on Caracas; a battle was imminent on which depended the entire Spanish control of Venezuela. Morillo and the Spanish Army were in need of artillery. Now not only were they left destitute, but with this news it could be taken as certain that those guns, those two batteries of field artillery, were in Bolivar's hands. The Spanish officer wrung his hands in despair.

Hornblower translated briefly for the Governor's benefit, and Hooper shook his head in sympathy.

'Bolivar has those guns. No doubt about it. Gentlemen, I much regret this occurrence. But I must impress upon you that His Majesty's Government assumes no responsibility for it. If your chiefs took no steps to detect this impostor –'

That touched off a new explosion. The British Government should make sure that no impostor wore its uniform or posed as an officer in its service. It called for all Hooper's elephantine tact to quiet down the angry officers.

'If you will permit me to consult with the Admiral, gentlemen, we may reach some satisfactory conclusion.'

Alone with the Governor again Hornblower struggled with a smile; he had never outgrown his tendency to laugh during a crisis. There was something amusing in the thought that a cocked hat and a pair of epaulettes should change the course of a war; it was a tribute to the power of the Navy that a single tiny ship should exert such enormous pressure.

'Ramsbottom and his Venezuelan mother!' said Hooper. 'It's not merely piracy, it's high treason. We shall have to hang him.'

'M'm,' said Hornblower. 'He probably holds a privateering commission from Bolivar.'

'But masquerading as a British officer? Forging official documents?'

'That was a ruse of war. An American officer deceived the Portuguese authorities in Brazil in much the same way in 1812.'

'I've heard some things about you, too,' added Hooper with a grin.

'No doubt, sir. In war a belligerent who believes what he's told is a fool.'

'But we're not belligerents.'

'No, sir. And we've suffered no loss. The Dutch and the Spaniards have only themselves to blame.'

'But Ramsbottom's a subject of His Majesty.'

'Quite true, sir. But if he holds Bolivar's commission he can do things as an officer of the revolutionary forces which he could not do as a private person.'

'D'ye mean to suggest we ought to allow him to continue this blockade of his? Nonsense, man.'

'Of course not, sir. I'll arrest him, and I'll send his ship in for adjudication, at the first opportunity. But a friendly Power has asked you, sir, the representative of His Majesty, if you have instituted a blockade. You must do everything in your power to demonstrate the truth.'

'Now for once you're talking like a sensible man. We must send word at once to Curaçao and Caracas. That will be your immediate duty. You'd better go in person.'

'Yes, sir. I'll sail with the land breeze. Have you any further instructions for me, sir?'

'None whatever. What goes on on the high seas is your affair, not mine. You're answerable to the Cabinet through the Admiralty. I don't envy you, frankly.'

'No doubt I'll survive, sir. I'll sail for La Guaira, and send another vessel to Curaçao. Perhaps if Your Excellency were to write official replies to the enquiries addressed to you they would be ready by the time I sail?'

'I'll draft 'em now.' The Governor could not repress one further outburst. 'This Ramsbottom – and his corned beef and caviare!'

'He used a sprat to catch a mackerel, Your Excellency,' said Hornblower.

So it came about that the crew of HMS *Clorinda* did not spend that night in the debauchery of Kingston as they had expected. Instead they worked until dawn completing with stores and water, so hard that they had no breath to spare to curse the Admiral who did these things to them. In the very first light of morning they warped their ship out with the aid of the faint puffs of the land breeze, and *Clorinda*, her Admiral's flag flying at the mizzen, headed close-hauled to the south-eastward on her thousand-mile voyage to La Guaira. She had on board Brigadier-General Don Manuel Ruiz, Morillo's representative, to whom Hornblower had offered a passage back to his headquarters. The man was in a fever to return and put an end to Ramsbottom's blockade; it was clear that the royal forces in Venezuela were hard pressed. He had no thought for anything else during that voyage. The lovely sunsets meant to him merely that another day had gone by without his reaching his destination. The gallant way in which *Clorinda* held her course, close-hauled, shouldering the long rollers aside in showers of spray, held no fascination for him, for she was not flying before the wind at her best speed. At noon each day, when the ship's position was pricked off on the chart, he would look long and despairingly, estimating by eye the further distance to be traversed. He had not had sufficient experience at sea to acquire the knack of resigning himself to the influence of forces beyond human control. When the wind drew southerly and foul, as it did for two days consecutively, he was clearly on the verge of accusing Hornblower of being in league with his enemies, and made no attempt to understand Hornblower's soothing explanation that on the starboard tack on which *Clorinda* was compelled to lie they were making easting which might be invaluable in possible later eventualities. He resented the caution of Captain Fell which led to *Clorinda*'s shortening sail as they entered the dangerous proximity of Grand Cay, and at dawn next day he was climbing the foremast shrouds as high as he dared, looking out for the first sight of the mountains of Venezuela – and even then he did not recognize as land the blue streak which he saw.

A shore boat came out to them before ever they dropped anchor, and there was an urgent conference on *Clorinda*'s quarterdeck between Ruiz and the officer it brought out.

'My General is in Carabobo,' said Ruiz to Hornblower. 'A battle is going to be fought. Bolivar is marching on Puerto Cabello, and my General has taken the army to meet him.'

'Where is Ramsbottom and his ship?'

Ruiz looked to the arrival for the information.

'Near Puerto Cabello.'

That was, of course, the likeliest place, a hundred miles or less to the westward, a roadstead where supplies might possibly be landed, and an ideal situation for intercepting all communications between Curaçao and La Guaira.

'Then I shall head for Puerto Cabello,' said Hornblower. 'You can accompany me if you wish, Don Manuel. The wind is fair and I'll land you there quicker than a horse would carry you.'

Ruiz hesitated for a moment; he knew all about horses and he was suspicious about ships. But the advantage was so obvious that he accepted.

'Very well, then,' said Hornblower. 'Sir Thomas, we'll hoist that anchor again, if you would be so kind. Set a course for Puerto Cabello.'

Now *Clorinda* had the lusty trade wind on her quarter, her best point of sailing; she had her studding sails out and every possible stitch of canvas out, and she flew along. A horse at full gallop might go faster, but no horse could do as *Clorinda* was doing and maintain full speed for hour after hour, nor could any horse ever attain full speed on the mountain tracks of the Maritime Andes. Naturally, no amount of speed could satisfy Ruiz. With telescope to his eye he watched the distant coast go by until his weary eye was almost blind, and then he paced about the quarterdeck, trickles of sweat running down his forehead and cheeks as the sun, climbing to its noontide height, blazed vertically down on him. He turned a suspicious eye on Hornblower when the crew of *Clorinda* poured aloft to take in sail.

'We are going in to shore now, General,' explained Hornblower soothingly.

The leadsmen were in the chains as *Clorinda* headed in towards the roadstead. In the middle of their chant Ruiz suddenly turned to Hornblower and stood rigid, listening to another, more distant, sound.

'Cannons!' he said.

Hornblower strained his ears. The faintest, almost imperceptible noise, and then silence, save for the sound of the ship through the water and the bustle of preparing to come to an anchor.

'Order the "still" for a moment, if you please, Sir Thomas.'

Now the leadsmen ceased their chant, and every man in *Clorinda* stood silent, even though the wind still played through the rigging and the sea chattered alongside. A very distant, flat detonation. Another. Two more.

'Thank you, Sir Thomas. You may carry on now.'

'Cannons!' repeated Ruiz, glaring at Hornblower. 'They are fighting the battle.'

Somewhere on the outskirts of Puerto Cabello Royalists and Republicans were locked in combat. And those guns that they had heard? They might well be those that the *Helmond* had carried, now in the hands of the insurgents and firing upon their legal owners. The fact that artillery was being employed indicated a pitched battle, no petty skirmish. Over there the fate of Venezuela was being decided. Ruiz was pounding his fist into his open palm.

'Sir Thomas, kindly have a boat ready to land the General without delay.'

As the gig pulled away from *Clorinda*'s side Hornblower looked up at the sun, called up before his mind's eye the chart of the Venezuelan coast, and reached a further decision. As always in the Service, a long, dull interval had heralded a period of activity. As the gig came skimming back again he was ready with his next order.

'Will you be so good as to make sail again, Sir Thomas? We can continue to search to the westward for Ramsbottom while daylight lasts.'

It was desirable to obtain the earliest possible news of the result of the battle, but it was also, or more, desirable to lay hands on Ramsbottom as quickly as might be. They had not sighted him between La Guaira and Puerto Cabello; he could not be much farther along the coast. The sun was descending now, dazzling the lookouts as they peered towards it while *Clorinda* continued her course along the shores of the province of Carabobo. Not so far ahead the land trended abruptly northward to San Juan Point – a lee shore. It was curious that Ramsbottom should have gone even this far to leeward; unless he had put up his helm and headed clear away, guessing that his period of grace was at an end.

'Deck, there!' The lookout at the foretopgallant masthead was hailing. 'There's summat on the port bow, just in sight. Right in the eye of the sun. But it may be a ship, sir. A ship's masts an' yards, sir, with no sail set.'

It would be incredible that Ramsbottom had anchored here on this dangerous lee shore. But incredible things have to be done in war. *Clorinda* had long ago taken in her studding sails. Now after a sharp order from Fell, and five minutes' activity on the part of her crew, she was gliding along under topsails and headsails alone. The sun sank into a bank of cloud, suffusing it with scarlet.

'Deck, there!' Two ships, sir. At anchor. One of 'em's a brig, sir.'

A brig! Ramsbottom almost for certain. Now with the sun behind the cloud it was possible to train a telescope in the direction indicated. There they were, sharp and clear against the sunset, silhouetted in black against the scarlet cloud, the masts and yards of a ship and a brig at anchor. Sir Thomas was looking to Hornblower for orders.

'Approach as close as you consider advisable, if you please, Sir Thomas. And a boarding party ready to take possession.'

'An armed boarding party, my lord?'

'As you please. He'll never dare to oppose us by force.'

The guns of the brig were not run out, there were no boarding-nettings rigged. In any case the little brig stood no chance in an unsheltered anchorage against a frigate.

'I'll anchor if I may, my lord.'

'Certainly.'

That was the *Bride of Abydos*, without a doubt. No mistaking her at all. And the other one? Most likely the *Helmond*. With the revolt of Maracaibo this part of the coast had fallen into the power of the insurgents. The batteries of field artillery that she had carried could be rafted ashore here – there was a beach in that little cove where it would be possible – and delivered to the insurgent army gathering for its march on Puerto Cabello. Ramsbottom, his task completed, would presumably be prepared to brazen it out, pleading – as

Hornblower had already guessed – some privateering commission from Bolivar.

'I'll go with the boarding party, Sir Thomas.'

Fell shot a questioning glance. Admirals had no business boarding strange craft from small boats, not only when bullets might fly, but when one of the infinite variety of accidents possible in small boats might lead to an elderly and not so active senior officer being dropped overside and never coming up again, with endless trouble later for the captain. Hornblower could follow Fell's train of thought, but he was not going to wait quiescent on *Clorinda*'s quarterdeck until a report came back from the *Bride of Abydos* – not when a word would give him the power of finding out several minutes earlier.

'I'll get your sword and pistols, my lord,' said Gerard.

'Nonsense!' said Hornblower. 'Look there!'

He had kept his telescope trained on the anchored ships, and had detected a significant activity around them. Boats were pulling hastily away from both of them and heading for the shore. Ramsbottom seemed to be absconding.

'Come along!' said Hornblower.

He ran to the ship's side and leaped for the boat's falls; sliding down, clumsily, cost him some of the skin from his soft palms.

'Cast off! Pull!' he ordered as Gerard tumbled in beside him. 'Pull!'

The boat swung away from the ship's side, soared giddily up a swell and down again, the men throwing their weight on the oars. But the boat that was leaving the *Bride of Abydos* was not being handled in the man-o'-

war fashion one would have expected of Ramsbottom. The oars were being plied without any coordination; the boat swung round on the swell, and then as somebody caught a crab swung round again. In next to no time Hornblower found himself alongside the struggling craft. The men at the oars were not the spruce seamen he had seen on board the *Bride of Abydos*. They were swarthy men clothed in rags. Nor was that Ramsbottom in the sternsheets. Instead, it was someone with a heavy black moustache wearing some vestiges of a blue and silver uniform. The reddening sunset glared down upon him.

'Who are you?' demanded Hornblower, and then repeated the question in Spanish.

The boat had ceased its struggles and was lying on its oars, rising and falling on the swell.

'Lieutenant Perez of the First Regiment of Infantry of the Army of Greater Colombia.'

Greater Colombia. That was what Bolivar called the republic he was trying to establish by his rebellion against Spain.

'Where is Mr Ramsbottom?'

'The Admiral has been on shore for the last week.'

'The Admiral?'

'Don Carlos Ramsbottom y Santona, Admiral of the Navy of Greater Colombia.' An admiral; no less.

'What were you doing on board that ship?'

'I was taking care of her until Your Excellency came.'

'Is there nobody on board, then?'

'Nobody.'

The boats soared up a swell and sank down again. It was a sickly thing to do, not conducive to logical thought. He had been prepared to arrest Ramsbottom, but it would be another matter to arrest a lieutenant of infantry, in territorial waters.

'Where is the crew of the ship?'

'On shore with the Admiral. With the army.'

Fighting for Bolivar, presumably. And presumably as artillerymen serving the stolen guns.

'Very well. You may go.'

It was sufficient to make sure of the *Bride of Abydos*; there was no purpose in laying hands on men of Bolivar's army who had only been obeying the orders of their superiors.

'Lay me alongside the brig.'

In the fading light the deck of the *Bride of Abydos* was not in too great disorder. The departing crew had apparently left everything shipshape, and the caretaking party of South American soldiers had not disturbed anything – although below deck it would probably be a different story. But what would have happened if a gale had blown up in this perilous anchorage on a lee shore would not bear thinking about. Presumably Ramsbottom had not cared what happened to his little ship once he had brought off his coup.

'Ahoy! Ahoy!'

Someone was hailing through a speaking-trumpet from the other ship. Hornblower took the speaking-trumpet from its becket by the wheel and hailed back.

'I am Admiral Lord Hornblower of His Britannic Majesty's Service. I am coming aboard.'

It was almost dark when he mounted to the deck of the *Helmond*, to be welcomed by the light of a couple of lanterns. The captain who greeted him was a thick-set man speaking excellent English with a marked accent, Dutch, presumably.

'You have not arrived too soon, sir,' was his uncompromising beginning, not the way to address any officer of the Royal Navy, certainly not an Admiral and a Peer.

'I'll thank you to be civil,' snapped Hornblower, his temper frayed.

Two angry men faced each other in the wavering light, and then the Dutchman realized that it would be better to restrain his ill-temper in dealing with someone who, after all, had the power on this lonely coast to enforce any orders he might issue.

'Please come below, sir,' he said. 'Perhaps a glass of schnapps –?'

It was a comfortable, well-furnished cabin in which Hornblower was offered a seat and a glass.

'I was glad when I saw your topsails, sir,' said the Dutch captain. 'For ten days I have been through misery. My ship – my cargo – this shore –'

The disjointed words conveyed the anxieties of finding himself in the hands of the insurgents, and of being compelled to anchor off a lee shore with an armed guard on board.

'What happened?' asked Hornblower.

'That damned little brig fired a shot across my bows with Bonaire still in sight. They boarded me when I hove-to. Put an armed party on board. I thought she was one of yours, a ship-of-war. They brought me here and anchored, and the army came out to us. That was when I knew she was not a ship-of-war, not British.'

'Then they took your cargo?'

'They did. Twelve nine-pounder field guns, with limbers and caissons and horse harness. One ammunition waggon. One repair cart with tools. Two thousand rounds of ammunition. One ton of gunpowder in kegs. Everything.' The Dutchman was obviously quoting verbatim from his bill of lading.

'How did they get it ashore?'

'On rafts. Those Britishers worked like madmen. And there were seamen among them.'

It was a handsome admission, hardly grudging. Presumably keg-pontoons had been employed; Hornblower told himself that he would have tackled the problem of getting the cargo on to the beach in that way, at least. Presumably a good deal of unskilled labour had been provided on shore by the insurgent forces, but that hardly detracted from the achievement.

'And then every single man went off with the guns?' asked Hornblower.

'Every man. Not too many for twelve guns.'

Not too many. The *Bride of Abydos* carried a crew of some seventy-five men – hardly sufficient, in fact, to man two batteries in action.

'And they left a Venezuelan guard on board?'

'Yes. You saw them go when you came. They kept me here, at anchor on a lee shore.'

That, of course, was to prevent the Dutchman spreading the news of the fraud that had been practised.

'Those – those brigands knew nothing about ships.' The Dutchman was continuing his tale of tribulation. 'The *Desperate* started dragging her anchor once. I had to send my own men –'

'You were lucky they didn't burn your ship,' said

246

Hornblower. 'Luckier still they didn't plunder it. You're lucky not to be in some prison on shore.'

'That may be so, but –'

'As it is, sir,' said Hornblower, rising, 'you are free. You can use the land breeze to make an offing. Tomorrow night you can anchor in Willemstadt.'

'But my cargo, sir? I have been detained. I have been in danger. My country's flag –?'

'Your owners can take action as they please. I understand that Ramsbottom is a wealthy man. He can be sued for damages.'

'But – but –' The Dutchman could find no words that would express adequately his feelings regarding both his recent treatment and Hornblower's scant sympathy.

'Your Government can address protests, of course. To the Government of Greater Colombia, or to King Ferdinand.' Hornblower kept his face expressionless as he made the ridiculous suggestion. 'I must congratulate you, sir, on your escape from very serious dangers. I trust you will have a prosperous voyage home.'

He had freed the *Helmond*, and he had laid hands on the *Bride of Abydos*. That much he had accomplished so far, said Hornblower to himself as the boat took him back to *Clorinda*. The Governments at home could squabble over the legal details, if they cared to go to the trouble. What the Cabinet and the Admiralty would think about his actions he could not imagine; he was conscious of a slight chill of apprehension when his mind dwelt upon that side of the situation. But an Admiral could not show apprehension to anyone, certainly not to a captain as stupid as Sir Thomas Fell.

'I'll be obliged, Sir Thomas,' he said, when he

regained *Clorinda*'s deck, 'if you will send a prize-crew on board the brig. Would you please be good enough to instruct the officer whom you put in command to keep company with us? We shall sail for Puerto Cabello again as soon as it is convenient to you.'

Fell might be stupid, but he was a capable seaman. Hornblower could leave to him the anxious business of making his way back along the coast at night; the land breeze, fluky and unpredictable though it might be, afforded an opportunity which must not be missed of regaining the precious miles that had been squandered to leeward. Hornblower could go down into his stifling cabin and compose himself to sleep. It had been a busy day, and he was physically weary. He lay on his cot with the sweat trickling irritatingly over his ribs, trying to persuade his mind to cease from debating the situation. The British public was turning a kindly eye on the struggle for liberty that was being waged in every corner of the world. British volunteers were playing their part – Richard Church had been leading the Greek rebellion against the Turks for years now; Cochrane was at this very moment fighting in the Pacific for South American independence. For that matter, as he knew, thousands of British soldiers were serving in the ranks of Bolivar's army just over there on the mainland. Private fortunes in England had been lavished in the cause of liberty, just as Ramsbottom had been lavishing his.

But none of this was any indication as to how the British Cabinet would react; national policy might well be at odds with national opinion. And the Lords of the Admiralty could be counted upon to be as unpredictable as ever. And that was equally true of His Majesty King

George IV; Hornblower suspected that the First Gentleman of Europe had long ago forsaken his half-hearted liberalism. The near future might hold a severe reprimand for His Majesty's Commander-in-Chief in the West Indies; it might even hold disavowal and recall.

Hornblower's mind had now attained the comforting certainty that the future was uncertain, and that nothing he could do during the next few hours could change it. With that, he might well have gone to sleep; he was, in fact, on the point of dozing off when he brushed what he thought was a trickle of sweat from his bare ribs. It was not sweat. A flurry against his fingers told him it was a cockroach crawling over his skin, and he started up in disgust. The Caribbean was notorious for its cockroaches, but he had never grown to tolerate them. He walked across in the darkness and opened the door to the after cabin, admitting light from the lamp that swung there, and this revealed a dozen of the disgusting creatures scuttling about.

'My lord?' It was the faithful Gerard hurrying out of bed as soon as he heard his Admiral stirring.

'Go back to bed,' said Hornblower.

He put on the silk nightshirt with the elaborate smocking down the front which had been laid out for him, and went on deck. The moon had risen now, and *Clorinda* was creeping steadily along with the land breeze now blowing fresh abeam. Cockroaches had driven away all thought of his troubles; he could lean against the rail and contemplate the beauties of the beautiful night with placidity. It fell calm at dawn, but half an hour later a fortunate slant of wind enabled *Clorinda*, and the *Bride of Abydos* a mile astern, to hold their course for Puerto Cabello; the town on its peninsula was already in sight through the telescope and *Clorinda* approached rapidly. There were fishing-boats setting out from the town, small craft which were using oars to enable them to get to seaward despite the unfavourable wind. Something about them appeared strange in the telescope, and as *Clorinda* drew up to them it became apparent that they were crowded with people, ridiculously overloaded. But they plied their oars unceasingly, and boldly rounded the peninsula into the open sea, turning eastward towards La Guaira.

'I think General Morillo has lost his battle,' said Hornblower.

'Indeed, my lord?' said Fell, deferentially.

'And I think there are plenty of people in Puerto Cabello who have no desire to be found there when El Liberador comes marching in,' added Hornblower.

He had heard that the war of independence was being waged with Spanish ferocity, that even Bolivar's reputation had been clouded by executions and massacres. Here was a proof of it. But those crowded boats were also a proof that Puerto Cabello was expected to fall to Bolivar. He had won his battle of Carabobo; a victory in the open field so close to Caracas meant the certain collapse of the royal cause. Carabobo would be the Yorktown of the South American war of independence; no doubt about that. Presumably Ramsbottom would consider the loss of the *Bride of Abydos* as a small thing compared with the freeing of a continent.

It was necessary that all this should be confirmed without doubt, however. The Cabinet would be anxious for early and first-hand information regarding the situation in Venezuela.

'Sir Thomas,' said Hornblower, 'I shall go ashore.'

'You'll have an armed guard, my lord?'

'As you will,' said Hornblower. A dozen seamen with muskets would hardly save him from the clutches of a conquering army, but agreement saved him from argument and reproachful looks.

By the time Hornblower set foot on the pier in the blinding sunlight the little harbour was deserted. Not a fishing-boat was left, nor was there a human being in sight. He pressed on, his guard tramping behind him and Gerard at his side. The long, winding street was not quite deserted; there were a few women, a few old men, a few children to be seen, peering out of the houses. Then away to his right he heard a brief rattle of musketry, the reports sounding flat in the heavy, damp air. Now here came a ghastly column of sick and wounded, half-naked, hobbling along the road; some fell down to struggle to their feet again, and some, under Hornblower's very eyes, fell, not to rise again, and of these some managed to roll to the side of the road while others lay still while their staggering comrades stumbled over them. Wounded, half-naked, bare-footed, crazy with fever or bending double with abdominal pains, they came reeling along the road, while behind them the rattle of musketry came nearer and nearer. At the heels of the last of the wounded came the first of the rearguard, soldiers whose rags were faintly reminiscent of the blue and white of the Spanish Royal Army. Hornblower made a mental note that the royal forces still could provide a disciplined rearguard, and so were not in total rout, but the rearguard was woefully small, a couple of hundred men, perhaps; they were not keeping good order, but they were fighting a steady fight, biting open their cartridges, ramming home their charges, spitting their bullets into their musket barrels, and waiting in ones and two behind cover to get a fair shot at their pursuers. A dozen officers, their drawn swords flashing in the sun, were among them. The mounted officer-in-command caught sight of Hornblower and his party and reined round his horse in astonishment.

'Who are you?' he shouted.

'English,' replied Hornblower.

But before another word could be exchanged the firing in the rear increased in intensity; not only that, but suddenly from out of a side lane level with the rearguard appeared a dozen horsemen, lancers, their spear-points reflecting the sun, and the rearguard broke in disorder, running wildly down the road to escape being cut off. Hornblower saw a lance-point enter between the shoulders of a running man, saw him fall on his face, sliding over the surface of the road for a yard before the lance-point tore its way out again, leaving him struggling like a broken-backed animal. Over him swept the skirmishers of the insurgent advanced guard, a swarm of men of every shade of colour, running, loading, and firing. There was a moment when the air was full of bullets.

'My lord –' expostulated Gerard.

'That's all right. It's all over now,' said Hornblower.

The fight had swept past them up the road; no one had paid them any attention save for the single question of the mounted Spanish officer. The small column of infantry marching in regular order behind the skirmishers saw them, however, saw the glittering gold, the epaulettes and the cocked hats. Again a mounted officer wheeled towards them with the same question, to receive the same answer from Hornblower.

'Ingleses?' repeated the officer. 'English? Why – you're a British admiral!'

'Commanding the British Squadron in West Indian waters,' said Hornblower.

'A pleasure to see you, sir. William Jones, late Captain, Twenty-Third Foot, now Major commanding a battalion in the Army of Greater Colombia.'

'Delighted to make your acquaintance, Major.'

'Pardon me, but I must attend to my duties,' said Jones, wheeling his horse again.

'Hooray for England!' yelled someone in the marching ranks, and he was answered by a thin cheer; half of these ragged scarecrows must have been British, mingled indiscriminately with Negroes and South Americans. The cavalry followed them, regiment after regiment, a flood of men and horses filling the road like a river brimming its banks. Lancers and light horse, sore-backed horses and lame horses; most of the men had coiled ropes at their saddle bows, and they were all ragged and drooping in their saddles with fatigue; from the appearance of both men and beasts they had marched far and fought hard, and now they were pressing on to the limit of their strength after their defeated foe. A thousand men had passed, estimated Hornblower, judging the column as well as he could, when a new sound came to his ears through the monotonous trampling of the horses' hoofs. A thumping and a jingling, loud and irregular. Here came the guns, dragged along by weary horses; at the heads of the horses walked men, ragged and bearded – they were wearing the remains of blue jumpers and white trousers. It was the crew of the *Bride of Abydos*. One of them lifted his weary head and recognized the party at the roadside.

'Good old Horny!' he shouted; his voice was thin with fatigue and sounded like an old man's.

In the mounted officer riding alongside Hornblower recognized one of Ramsbottom's lieutenants; he sat his plodding horse like a sailor, and raised his arm in a weary salute. One gun clattered by, and another followed it. The guns of Carabobo, which had won the independence of a continent.

Hornblower realized that he had not yet seen Ramsbottom, whom he would have expected to be at the head of the artillery column, but as the realization came to him he saw something now beside the second gun. It was a horse litter, extemporized from two poles and some sheets of canvas. It was slung from two horses, one fore and one aft; the bight of canvas between the poles was shaded by an awning spread above it, and lying in the trough was a man, a smallish man, black-bearded, lying feebly against pillows behind his back. A seaman walked at the head of each horse, and with the plodding step of the animals the litter lurched and rolled, and the black-bearded man lurched and rolled at the same time. Yet he was able to take note of the group by the roadside, and he made an effort to sit up, and he called an order to the seamen leading the horses which caused them to turn out of the road and stop by Hornblower.

'Good morning, my lord,' he said; he spoke shrilly, like someone hysterical.

Hornblower had to look twice and more to recognize him. The black beard, the feverish eyes, the shocking dead pallor upon which the tan looked like some unnatural coating, all made identification difficult.

'Ramsbottom!' exclaimed Hornblower.

'The very same but a little different,' said Ramsbottom, with a cackling laugh.

'Are you wounded?' asked Hornblower; at the moment the words passed his lips he perceived that Ramsbottom's left arm was concealed in a roll of rags – Hornblower had been looking so intently at the face that the arm had escaped his notice until then.

'I have made my sacrifice in the cause of liberty,' said Ramsbottom, with the same laugh – it might have been a laugh of derision or a laugh of mere hysteria.

'What happened?'

'My left hand lies on the field of Carabobo,' cackled Ramsbottom. 'I doubt if it has received Christian burial.'

'Good God!'

'Do you see my guns? My beautiful guns. They tore the Dons apart at Carabobo.'

'But you – what treatment have you received?'

'Field surgery, of course. Boiling pitch for the stump. Have you ever felt boiling pitch, my lord?'

'My frigate is anchored in the roadstead. The surgeon is on board –'

'No – oh no. I must go on with my guns. I must clear El Liberador's path to Caracas.'

The same laugh. It was not derision – it was something the opposite. A man on the edge of delirium keeping a desperate hold on his sanity so as not to be diverted from his aim. Nor was it a case of a man laughing lest he weep. He was laughing lest he should indulge in heroics.

'Oh, you can't –'

'Sir! Sir! My lord!'

Hornblower swung round. Here was a midshipman from the frigate touching his hat, agitated by the urgency of his message.

'What is it?'

'Message from the cap'n, my lord. Ships-of-war in sight in the offing. A Spanish frigate an' what looks like a Dutch frigate, my lord. Bearing down on us.'

Desperate news indeed. He must have his flag flying in *Clorinda* to meet these strangers, but it was a maddening moment in which to be told about it. He turned back to Ramsbottom and back again to the midshipman, his customary quickness of thought not as apparent as usual.

'Very well,' he rasped. 'Tell the captain I'm coming immediately.'

'Aye aye, my lord.' He turned again to Ramsbottom.

'I must go,' he said. 'I must –'

'My lord,' said Ramsbottom. Some of his feverish vitality had left him. He was leaning back again on his pillows, and it took him a second or two to gather his strength to speak again, and when he did the words lagged as he uttered them. 'Did you capture the *Bride*, my lord?'

'Yes.' He must end this; he must get back to his ship.

'My bonny *Bride*. My lord, there's another keg of caviare in the after-lazarette. Please enjoy it, my lord.'

The cackling laugh again. Ramsbottom was still laughing as he lay back with his eyes closed, not hearing the hurried 'goodbye' which Hornblower uttered as he turned away. It seemed to Hornblower as if that laugh followed him while he hastened to the pier and down into the boat.

'Shove off! Put your backs into it!'

There lay *Clorinda* at anchor, with the *Bride of Abydos* close to her. And there, undoubtedly, were the topsails of two frigates heading in towards them. He scrambled up the ship's side with hardly a moment to spare for the compliments with which he was received. He was too busy taking in the tactical situation, the trend of the shore, the position of the *Bride of Abydos*, the approach of the strangers.

'Hoist my flag,' he ordered, curtly, and then, recovering his poise, with the customary elaborate politeness, 'Sir Thomas, I'd be obliged if you'd get springs on the cable, out of the after-ports on both sides.'

'Springs, my lord? Aye aye, my lord.'

Cables passed through the after-ports to the anchor cable; by hauling in on one or the other with the capstan he could turn the ship to bring her guns to bear in any direction. It was only one of the many exercises Hornblower had put his crews through during the recent manœuvres. It called for heavy, closely coordinated labour on the part of the hands. Orders were bellowed; warrant and petty officers ran at the heads of their different parties to rouse out the cables and drag them aft.

'Sir Thomas, please order the brig to kedge closer in. I want her inshore of us.'

'Aye aye, my lord.'

Now it became apparent that there was some time in hand. The approaching frigates, hull up now when a glass was trained on them from the quarterdeck, were shortening sail, and then, even while Hornblower held them in the field of his telescope, he saw their main-topsails suddenly broaden as they were swung round. They were heaving-to, and a moment later he saw a boat lowered from the Dutch frigate and pull to the Spanish one. That would mean a consultation, presumably. Thanks to the difference of language they could hardly be expected to agree on a course of action by signal nor even by speaking-trumpet.

'The Spaniard's wearing a commodore's broad pendant, Sir Thomas. Will you please be ready to salute it as soon as he salutes my flag?'

'Aye aye, my lord.'

The consultation took some little time, the second half of one sand-glass and the beginning of the next. A monstrous creaking down below, and a clanking of the capstan, told that the springs were being tested. *Clorinda* swung a trifle to starboard, and then a trifle to port.

'Springs are tested and ready, my lord.'

'Thank you, Sir Thomas. Now will you be good enough to send the hands to quarters and clear for action?'

'Clear for action? Aye aye, my lord.'

It was a detestable nuisance to take this precaution. It meant that his bedding and books and personal equipment down below would be swept away in a horrible muddle that might take days to straighten. But on the other hand, if those frigates came down determined to fight, his reputation would never survive being unready for them. It would be chaos to try to clear away the guns and bring up cartridges while actually under fire;

the battle – if there were to be a battle – would be lost before it was begun. And there was something of the old thrill about these preparations; the pealing of the whistles, the hoarse cries of the petty officers, the orderly rush of the men to the guns, the tramp of the marines to the quarterdeck and the sharp order of their officer as they dressed into a rigid line.

'Ship cleared for action, my lord.'

'Thank you, Sir Thomas. Stand by, if you please.'

There would have been just time even if the strangers had come instantly down and gone into action without parley. By a rapid use of his springs he would rake the first-comer thoroughly enough to have made her captain wish he had never been born. Now he must wait, and the ship's company, standing by their guns, must wait with him, the matches smouldering in their tubs, the fire parties standing by with their buckets, the powder boys, cartridge carriers in hand, waiting to start their race from powder magazine to guns and back again.

'Here they come, my lord!'

Those topsails were narrowing again; those masts were coming into line. Now the frigates' bows were pointed straight at *Clorinda* as they came towards her. Hornblower held them steady in his telescope; no guns were run out, he could see, but it was impossible to tell if they were cleared for action. Nearer and nearer; now they were almost within extreme random cannon shot. At that moment where was a puff of smoke from the Spaniard's starboard bow, and for the life of him Hornblower could not check a gulp of excitement. The breeze blew the puff away, and then the puff was replaced by another; as the second appeared, the heavy thud of the first discharge came to Hornblower's ears. There was a momentary temptation to plunge into the luxury of mental arithmetic, involving the speed of sound conveyed over water, and the five seconds' interval between saluting guns, and the distance between the ships, but it had to be foregone.

'You may return the salute to the broad pendant, Sir Thomas.'

'Aye aye, my lord.'

Thirteen guns for a rear admiral's flag; eleven for a commodore; twenty-four guns, one hundred and twenty seconds, exactly two minutes; those ships, approaching at four miles in the hour would be a cable's length closer at the end of the salutes, within distant gunshot.

'Sir Thomas, I would be glad if you would take several turns upon the starboard spring.'

'Aye aye, my lord.'

The violent creaking made itself heard again, and *Clorinda* turned herself to present her broadside towards the newcomers. No harm whatever in letting them know that a hot reception was awaiting them if they intended mischief; it might save much trouble later.

'They're taking in sail, my lord!'

So he could see for himself, but there was nothing to be gained by saying so. The two ships obviously had heavy crews, judging by the rapidity with which sail was got in. Now round they went, up into the wind. Hornblower believed he could hear the roar of the cables as they anchored. It seemed like a decisive moment, and Hornblower was about to mark it by shutting up his telescope with a snap when he saw a boat lowering from the Spaniard.

'I fancy we'll be having a visitor shortly,' said Hornblower.

The boat seemed to fly over the glittering water; the men at the oars were pulling like madmen – presumably the eternal desire of the men of one navy to show another navy what they could do.

'Boat ahoy!' hailed the officer of the watch.

The Spanish officer in the sternsheets, conspicuous by his epaulettes, hailed back; Hornblower could not be sure of what he said, but the letter that was waved at the same time told the story.

'Receive him on board, if you please, Sir Thomas.'

The Spanish lieutenant looked sharply round him as he came over the ship's side; no harm in his seeing the men at quarters and the preparations made. He picked out Hornblower at once, and with a salute and a bow presented his letter.

'*Su excellencia el Almirante Sir Hornblower*,' said the superscription.

Hornblower broke the seal; he could read the Spanish of the letter easily enough.

The Brigadier, Don Luiz Argote, would be honoured if His Excellency Sir Hornblower would accord him the opportunity of an interview. The Brigadier would be delighted if he could visit His Excellency's ship and would be equally delighted if His Excellency would visit His Most Catholic Majesty's ship.

In Spanish naval usage, Hornblower knew, 'Brigadier' was equivalent to 'Commodore'.

'I'll write a reply,' said Hornblower. 'Sir Thomas,

please make this gentleman welcome. Come with me, Gerard.'

Down below, with the ship cleared for action, it was a nuisance to hunt up writing paper and ink; it was even more of a nuisance to have to compose a letter in Spanish, for in writing misspellings and bad grammar would be far more evident than in speech. Luckily the Brigadier's letter itself supplied most of the spelling and the tricky conditional form.

Rear Admiral Lord Hornblower would be delighted to receive the Brigadier Don Luiz Argote in his flagship whenever the Brigadier wishes.

Sealing wax and seal and candle had to be discovered; it would never do to appear careless about these formalities.

'Very well,' said Hornblower, giving grudging approval of the second impression after the failure of the first attempt. 'Take a boat to the *Bride of Abydos* as quick as lightning and see if there's any of that sherry left which Ramsbottom served at his dinner party.'

The Brigadier, when he came up *Clorinda*'s side, to be received with the appropriate compliments, was followed by another figure in cocked hat and epaulettes. Hornblower bowed and saluted and introduced himself.

'I took the liberty of asking Captain Van der Maesen, of the Royal Netherlands Navy, to accompany me,' said the Brigadier.

'It is with much pleasure that I welcome Captain Van der Maesen on board,' said Hornblower. 'Perhaps you gentlemen will accompany me below. I regret very much that we will not be very comfortable, but, as you see, I have been exercising my crew in their duties.'

A screen had been hurriedly run across the after-part of the frigate, and the table and chairs replaced. The Brigadier sipped with increasing and astonished appreciation at the glass of wine offered him. Inevitably several minutes passed in desultory conversation – Spanish was the one language the three had in common – before the Brigadier began to discuss business.

'You have a beautiful ship here, milord,' he said. 'I regret much to find you in company with a pirate.'

'You mean the *Bride of Abydos, señor*?'

'Naturally, milord.'

Hornblower saw a trap opening before him.

'You call her a pirate, *señor*?'

'What do you call her, milord?'

'I am waiting to hear your opinion, *señor*.' It was important not to commit himself.

'Her actions call for explanation, milord. She has captured and plundered a Dutch ship. That can be interpreted as an act of piracy. On the other hand it might be said she is operating under a so-called commission issued by the rebels in Venezuela. In the one case Captain Van der Maesen will seize her as a pirate. On the other, if she is a privateer, I will seize her as an enemy of my country.'

'In neither case, *señor*, has a court of law determined her status. In the meanwhile, gentlemen, she is in my possession.'

Hats were in the ring now. Hornblower met the eyes of the others with the least expression he could manage. Of one thing he was certain, that whatever might be eventually decided regarding the *Bride of Abydos* neither the British Government nor the British public would approve of his tamely allowing her to be taken out of his hands.

'Milord, I have assured Captain Van der Maesen of my support in any action he may decide to take, and he has given me the same assurance.'

The Dutch captain confirmed this with a nod and a half-intelligible sentence. Two to one, in other words; odds that *Clorinda* could not hope to face.

'Then I hope, gentlemen, I hope very sincerely indeed, that you decide upon approving of my course of action.'

It was the politest way of defying them that he could think of.

'I find it very hard to believe, milord, that you extend the protection of His Britannic Majesty's Navy to pirates, or to privateers in a war in which His Majesty is neutral.'

'You may have noticed, *señor*, that the *Bride of Abydos* is flying His Britannic Majesty's flag. Of course, you understand that as a naval officer I cannot permit that flag to be hauled down.'

There it was, the ultimate defiance. Ten minutes from now and the guns might be firing. Ten minutes from now and this deck might be littered with dead and wounded. He might be dead himself. The Spaniard looked at the Dutchman and back to Hornblower.

'We would much regret taking strong action, milord.'

'I am delighted to hear that, *señor*. That confirms me in my decision. We can part the best of friends.'

'But –'

The Brigadier had not intended his last sentence to

be interpreted as a sign of yielding. He had been uttering, he thought, a further threat. Hornblower's interpretation of it left him speechless for a moment.

'I am overjoyed to find that we are in agreement, gentlemen. Perhaps we can drink the healths of our sovereigns in another glass of this wine, *señor* – and may I take this opportunity of acknowledging the debt the rest of the world owes to your country for such an exquisite production?'

By taking their withdrawal for granted he was giving them a chance of withdrawing gracefully. The bitter moment of admitting that they had been outfaced had come and gone before they had realized it. Once more the Spaniard and the Dutchman exchanged unavailing glances, and Hornblower seized the opportunity to pour more wine.

'To His Most Catholic Majesty, *señor*. To His Majesty the King of the Netherlands.'

He held his glass high. They could not refuse that toast, even though the Brigadier's mouth still opened and shut as he struggled to find words for his emotions. Common politeness forced the Brigadier to complete the toast, as Hornblower waited, glass in hand.

'To His Britannic Majesty.'

They drank together.

'This has been a delightful visit, gentlemen,' said Hornblower. 'Another glass? No? It cannot be that you are leaving so soon? But I expect you have many duties calling for your attention.'

As the sideboys, white-gloved, formed up at the entry port, and the bosun's mates pealed upon their whistles, and the ship's company, still at their guns, stood to attention, in compliment to the departing visitors, Hornblower could spare a moment to glance round. Those sideboys and bosun's mates and gun's crews might be facing imminent death at this moment if that interview had taken a more stormy course. He deserved their gratitude, but of course he would never receive it. Shaking hands with the Brigadier he made the final clarification of the situation.

'A prosperous voyage, *señor*. I hope I shall have the pleasure of meeting you again. I shall be sailing for Kingston as soon as the land breeze serves.'

One of Barbara's regular letters, received months later, helped to round off the incident.

My dearest husband, (wrote Barbara as usual, and, as usual Hornblower read those words with a smile. There were several sheets to the letter, and the first sheet contained much of interest to Hornblower, but it was not until the second sheet that Barbara began her usual society and professional gossip.)

Last night the Lord Chancellor was my left-hand partner at dinner, and he had much to say about the 'Bride of Abydos,' and in consequence, to my great pleasure, much to say about my dear husband. The Spanish and Dutch Governments, through their ambassador and minister, have naturally lodged protests with the Foreign Secretary, who has only been able to acknowledge receipt of the notes and to promise a further reply when the legal aspects of the case are made clear. And, in all the history of Admiralty law, said the Lord Chancellor, there never was a case as complicated as this one. The insurers plead negligence on the part of the assured (I hope that I have these technical terms right, my very dearest) because the captain of the 'Helmond' took no steps to verify the bona fides of the 'Bride of Abydos', and they further plead negligence on the part of the Dutch Government because the capture took place within Dutch territorial waters off Bonaire, and the Dutchmen deny hotly both that they were negligent and that the capture was really within their territorial waters. Further, the actual plundering and detention took place in Spanish territorial waters. And there seem to be untold complications arising from the fact that you found the 'Bride of Abydos' abandoned by her crew – did you know, dearest, that it seems a matter of great legal importance as to whether her anchor was actually touching bottom or not? In any case, there has been no legal action in any court so far because no one seems to be able to decide which court has jurisdiction in the matter (I hope, dearest, you will give your wife all credit for listening attentively and taking note of these difficult expressions). Taking one thing with another, and allowing four months on the average for each necessary round trip to the West Indies to take evidence on commission, and taking into account demurrers and rebuttals and sur-rebuttals, the Lord Chancellor thinks that it will be thirty-seven years before any case reaches the House of Lords, and he went on to say, cackling into his soup, that our interest in the case will be greatly diminished by then.

This is by no means all the news, dearest. There is something further which would greatly distress me if it were not for the fact that I know my husband the Admiral will be delighted. Taking tea today with Lady Exmouth (I know how your dear eyes will open wide with horror at women being in possession of such secrets) I heard that

*Their Lordships take a most favourable view of your
attitude towards the Spanish and Dutch naval authorities –
dearest, I am so delighted, even though I could never doubt
it. It has already been decided to extend your command for
the extra year, and my pleasure in knowing how pleased
you will be at this compliment almost – quite – allays my
sorrow at the thought of our further separation. Dearest,
there is no woman who could love you – there is no woman
on earth who could love any man as much as I love you,
the truest, the bravest, the boldest, the cleverest – I must
not write like this because there is still further news to add.*

*This is that the Government has always, apparently,
looked with favour at the attempt of the Spanish colonies to
attain their independence, and with the greatest disfavour
upon the decision of the Spanish Government to attempt
their reconquest with troops went out from Europe. There
have been hints that the other Powers, uneasy at the
movement towards liberty, have been meditating giving
military assistance to Spain in Spanish America. The
victory at Carabobo, where poor Mr Ramsbottom and his
guns played such a part, has made this intervention more
unlikely. It is a great State secret, so great that over the
teacups it is mentioned only in whispers, that the British
Government meditates making a declaration that it will not
permit military intervention in Spanish America. And it
appears that our Government is in accord with the
Americans over this, for it is believed that President Monroe
is planning to issue a declaration regarding a similar
doctrine, and discussions regarding it are taking place. So
that my dearest husband finds himself at the centre of
world affairs, as he has always been at the centre of his
wife's fondest affections.*

The Hurricane

Hornblower came walking into his office at Admiralty House at half-past five o'clock in the morning exactly. Now that the summer was come there was just enough daylight at that time to transact business and it was a fairly cool moment as well. Gerard and Spendlove, his flag lieutenant and secretary, were waiting for him there – it would have gone hard with them if they had not been – and they pulled themselves erect, without any clicking of heels (for in three years they had found that their chief discountenanced the practice) and they said 'Good morning, my lord,' 'Good morning, my lord' as if they were the two barrels of a shotgun.

'Morning,' said Hornblower. He had not had his breakfast coffee yet; otherwise he would have put 'good' in front of 'morning'.

He sat down at his desk, and Spendlove came to hover over his shoulder with a sheaf of papers while Gerard made the dawn report.

'Weather conditions normal, my lord. High water today at eleven-thirty. No arrivals during the night, and nothing in sight this morning from the signal station. No news of the packet, my lord, and no news of *Triton*.'

'A negative report if ever there was one,' said Hornblower. The negatives in the last two phrases balanced each other; HMS *Triton* was bringing out his successor to relieve him of his command at the end of his three years' appointment, and Hornblower was not happy over the prospect of ceasing to be Commander-in-Chief in the West Indies; but the West India packet was bringing out his wife, whom he had not seen during all this time, and to whose arrival he was eagerly looking forward. She was coming out so as to make the return voyage to England with him.

'The packet's due any day, my lord,' said Gerard, soothingly.

'Your business is to tell me things I don't know, Mr Gerard,' snapped Hornblower. It annoyed him to be soothed like a child, and it annoyed him still more that his personal staff should think him human enough to be anxious to see his wife. He looked over his shoulder at his secretary. 'What do you have there, Spendlove?'

Spendlove made a hasty rearrangement of the papers in his hand. Hornblower's morning coffee was due at any moment, and Spendlove had something he did not want to show his chief until it had come and was half drunk at least.

'Here are the dockyard returns to the thirty-first ultimo, my lord,' he said.

'Can't you say "to the end of last month"?' demanded Hornblower, taking them from him.

'Aye aye, my lord,' said Spendlove, passionately hoping the coffee would come soon.

'Anything in these?' asked Hornblower, glancing over them.

'Nothing for your special attention, my lord.'

'Then why trouble me with them? Next?'

'The warrants for the new gunner in *Clorinda*, my lord, and for the dockyard cooper.'

'Your coffee, my lord,' said Gerard at this moment, the relief in his voice perfectly apparent.

'Better late than never,' snapped Hornblower. 'And for God's sake don't fuss round me. I'll pour it for myself.'

Spendlove and Gerard were busily making room on his desk for the tray to be put down, and Spendlove hastily withdrew his hand from the coffee-pot handle.

'Too damned hot,' said Hornblower, taking a sip. 'It's always too damned hot.'

Last week the new system had been begun, whereby coffee was brought in to him after his arrival in his office, instead of awaiting him there, because he had complained then that it was always too cold, but neither Spendlove nor Gerard saw fit to remind him of this.

'I'll sign those warrants,' said Hornblower. 'Not that I think that cooper's worth his salt. His barrels open up into birdcages.'

Spendlove scattered sand from the caster over the wet ink of Hornblower's signatures, and put the warrants aside. Hornblower took another sip of coffee.

'Here's your refusal of the Crichtons' invitation, my lord. In the third person, so your signature isn't necessary.'

If that had been said to him a little while before, Hornblower would have demanded why in that case he was being bothered with it, forgetful of his own standing order that nothing was to go out in his name without his seeing it. But even two sips of coffee had done their work.

'Very well,' he said, glancing over it, and taking up his cup again.

Spendlove watched the level of the liquid sink in the

cup, and judged the moment to be more propitious now. He laid a letter on the desk.

'From Sir Thomas, my lord.'

Hornblower uttered a small groan as he picked it up; Captain Sir Thomas Fell of HMS *Clorinda* was a fussy individual, and a communication from him usually meant trouble – unnecessary trouble, and therefore to be grudged. Not in this case, though. Hornblower read the official document and then craned over his shoulder at Spendlove.

'What's all this about?' he demanded.

'It's rather a curious case, I hear, my lord,' answered Spendlove.

It was a 'circumstantial letter', a formal request from Captain Fell for a court martial to be held on Bandsman Hudnutt of the Royal Marines, for 'wilful and persistent disobedience to orders'. Such a charge if substantiated meant death, or else such a flogging that death would be preferable. Spendlove was perfectly well aware that his Admiral detested hangings and floggings.

'The charges are preferred by the Drum-Major,' commented Hornblower to himself.

He knew the Drum-Major, Cobb, perfectly well, or at least as well as the peculiar circumstances permitted. As Admiral and Commander-in-Chief Hornblower had his own band, which was under the command of Cobb, holding warrant rank. Previous to all official occasions where music had to be provided Cobb reported to Hornblower for orders and instructions, and Hornblower would go through the farce of agreeing with the suggestions put forward. He had never publicly admitted that he could not tell one note from another; he could actually distinguish one tune from another by the jigginess or otherwise of the time. He was a little uneasy in case all this was more common knowledge than he hoped.

'What d'you mean by "a curious case", Spendlove?' he asked.

'I believe an artistic conscience is involved, my lord,' replied Spendlove, cautiously. Hornblower was pouring, and tasting, his second cup of coffee; that might have a bearing on the breaking of Bandsman Hudnutt's neck, thought Spendlove. At the same time Hornblower was feeling the inevitable irritation resulting from having to listen to gossip. An admiral in his splendid isolation never – or only rarely – knew as much about what was going on as his most junior subordinate.

'An artistic conscience?' he repeated. 'I'll see the Drum-Major this morning. Send for him now.'

'Aye aye, my lord.'

He had received the one necessary clue, and need not demean himself by prying further unless the interview with Cobb should prove unfruitful.

'Now let's have that draught report until he comes.'

Drum-Major Cobb did not arrive for some time, and his resplendent uniform when he did arrive hinted that he had taken care about his appearance; tunic and pantaloons were freshly ironed, his buttons glittered, his sash was exactly draped, his sword-hilt shone like silver. He was an enormous man with an enormous moustache, and he made an enormous entrance into the room, striding over the resounding floor as if he were twice as heavy as he actually was, clashing his boot-heels together as he halted before the desk and swept his hand upward in the salute fashionable at the moment among the Royal Marines.

'Good morning, Mr Cobb,' said Hornblower, mildly; the 'Mr', like the sword, was an indication that Cobb was a gentleman by virtue of his warrant even though he had risen from the ranks.

'Good morning, my lord.' There was as much flourish in the phrase as there had been in the salute.

'I want to hear about these charges against this bandsman – Hudnutt.'

'Well, my lord –' A sideways glance from Cobb gave Hornblower a hint.

'Get out of here,' said Hornblower to his staff. 'Leave Mr Cobb alone with me.'

When the door was shut Hornblower was all good manners.

'Please sit down, Mr Cobb. Then you can tell me at your ease what really happened.'

'Thank you, my lord.'

'Well, now?'

'That young 'Udnutt, my lord, 'e's a fool if ever there was one. I'm sorry this 'as 'appened, my lord, but 'e deserves all 'e's going to get.'

'Yes? He's a fool, you say?'

''E's a downright fool, my lord. I'm not saying 'e isn't a good musician, 'cause 'e is. There ain't no one 'oo can play the cornet the way 'e does. That's the truth, my lord. 'E's a boy wonder at it. The cornet's a newfangled instrument, my lord. We ain't 'ad it in our bands for more'n a year. Blow it like a trumpet, you do, you 'ave to 'ave a lip for it, although it 'as keys as well, my lord. An' 'e's a marvel at it, or 'e was, my lord.'

That change to the past tense indicated that in Cobb's positive opinion Hudnutt, through death or disablement, would never play the cornet again.

'He's young?'

'Nineteen, my lord.'

'And what did he do?'

'It was mutiny, my lord, flat mutiny, although I've only charged him with disobedience to orders.'

Mutiny meant death by the Articles of War; disobedience to orders meant 'death or such less penalty –'

'How did it happen?'

'Well, my lord, it was like this. We was rehearsing the new march that come out in the last packet. *Dondello*, it's called, my lord. Just the cornet an' the drums. An' it sounded different, an' I had 'Udnutt play it again. I could 'ear what 'e was doin', my lord. There's a lot of B flat accidentals in that march, an' 'e wasn't flatting them. I asked 'im what 'e meant by it, an' he said it sounded too sweet. That's what 'e said, my lord. An' it's written on the music. *Dolce*, it says, and *dolce* means sweet, my lord.'

'I know,' lied Hornblower.

'So I says, "You play that again and you flat those Bs." An' 'e says, "I can't." An' I says, "You mean you won't?" An' then I says, "I'll give you one more chance" – although by rights I shouldn't 'ave, my lord – an' I says, "This is an order, remember," 'an I gives 'em the beat an' they starts off and there was the B naturals. So I says, "You 'eard me give you an order?" an' 'e says, "Yes." So there wasn't nothing I could do after that, my lord. I calls the guard an' I 'ad 'im marched to the guard-'ouse. An' then I 'ad to prefer charges, my lord.'

'This happened with the band present?'

'Yes, my lord. The 'ole band, sixteen of 'em.'

Wilful disobedience to an order, before sixteen witnesses. It hardly mattered if there were six or sixteen or sixty; the point was that everyone in Hornblower's command knew by now that discipline had been defied, an order deliberately disobeyed. The man must die, or he must be flogged into a crippled wreck, lest other men defy orders. Hornblower knew he had his command well in hand, but he knew, too, of the turbulence that lay below the surface. And yet – if the order that had been disobeyed had been something different, if there had been a refusal to lay out along a yard, say, however perilous the conditions, Hornblower would not have given all this thought to the matter, despite his detestation of physical cruelty. That sort of order must be instantly obeyed. 'Artistic conscience,' Spendlove had said. Hornblower had no idea of any difference between B and B flat, but he could dimly understand that it might be important to some people. A man might be tempted to refuse to do something that offended his artistic sensibilities.

'I suppose the man was sober?' he demanded suddenly.

'As sober as you and me, my lord.'

Another idea crossed Hornblower's mind.

'What's the chances of a misprint in the music?' he asked; he was struggling with things he did not understand.

'Well, my lord, there *is* such things. But it's for me to say if there's a misprint or not. An' although he can read music I don't know if 'e can read print, my lord, an' if 'e can I don't expect 'e can read Eyetalian, but there it says *dolce*, it says, on the official music, my lord.'

In Cobb's eyes this aggravated the offence, if aggravation were possible. Not only had his order been disobeyed, but Hudnutt had not respected the written instructions sent by whoever was responsible in London for sending out music to marine bands. Cobb was a marine first and a musician second; Hudnutt might be a musician first and a marine second. But – Hornblower pulled himself up sharply – that made Hudnutt's condemnation all the more necessary. A marine had to be a marine, first, foremost, and all the time. If marines started to choose whether they could be marines or not, the Royal Regiment would cease to be a military body, and it was his duty to maintain it as a military body.

Hornblower studied Cobb's expression intently. The man was speaking the truth, at least as far as the truth was apparent to him. He was not wilfully distorting facts because of personal prejudice or as a result of some old feud. If his action, and his report on it, had been influenced by jealousy or natural cruelty, he was unaware of it. A court martial would be impressed by his reliability as a witness. And he remained unperturbed under Hornblower's steady stare.

'Thank you, Mr Cobb,' said Hornblower at last. 'I am glad to have had such a clear statement of the facts. That will be all for the present.'

'Thank you, my lord,' answered Cobb, shooting his great bulk up out of the chair with an astonishing mixture of agility and military rigidity. His heels clashed as his hand swept up in the salute; he turned about with parade precision, and marched out of the room with resounding steps as precise as if timed by his own metronome.

Gerard and Spendlove came back into the room to find Hornblower staring at nothing, but Hornblower shook off his preoccupation instantly. It would never do for his subordinates to guess that he was moved by human feelings over a mere administrative matter.

'Draft an answer to Sir Thomas for my signature, if you please, Mr Spendlove. It can be a mere acknowledgement, but then add that there is no possibility of immediate action, because I cannot assemble the necessary number of captains at present with so many ships detached.'

Except in emergency a court where sentence of death might be passed could not be convened unless there were seven captains and commanders at least available as judges. That gave him time to consider what action he should take.

'This man's in the dockyard prison, I suppose,' went on Hornblower. 'Remind me to take a look at him on my way through the dockyard today.'

'Aye aye, my lord,' said Gerard, careful to betray no surprise at an admiral allotting time to visit a mutinous marine.

Yet it was not far out of Hornblower's way. When the time came he strolled slowly down through the beautiful garden of Admiralty House, and Evans, the disabled sailor who was head gardener, came in a jerky hurry to open the wicket gate in the fifteen-foot palisade that protected the dockyard from thieves, in this portion of its course dividing the Admiralty garden from the dockyard. Evans took off his hat and stood bobbing by the gate, his pigtail bobbing at his back, and his swarthy face split by a beaming smile.

'Thank you, Evans,' said Hornblower, passing through.

The prison stood isolated at the edge of the dock-yard, a small cubical building of mahogany logs, set diagonally in a curious fashion, possibly – probably – more than one layer. It was roofed with palm thatch a yard or more thick, which might at least help to keep it cool under the glaring sun. Gerard had run on ahead from the gate – with Hornblower grinning at the thought of the healthful sweat the exercise would produce – to find the officer-in-charge and obtain the key to the prison, and Hornblower stood by while the padlock was unfastened and he could look into the darkness within. Hudnutt had risen to his feet at the sound of the key, and when he stepped forward into the light he was revealed as a painfully young man, his cheeks hardly showing a trace of his one-day's beard. He was naked except for a waistcloth, and the officer-in-charge clucked with annoyance.

'Get some clothes on and be decent,' he growled, but Hornblower checked him.

'No matter. I've very little time. I want this man to tell me why he is under charges. You others keep out of earshot.'

Hudnutt had been taken by surprise by this sudden visit, but he was a bewildered person in any case, obviously. He blinked big blue eyes in the sunlight and wriggled his gangling form with embarrassment.

'What happened? Tell me,' said Hornblower.

'Well, sir –'

Hornblower had to coax the story out of him, but bit by bit it confirmed all that Cobb had said.

'I couldn't play that music, sir, not for nothing.'

The blue eyes looked over Hornblower's head at infinity; perhaps at some vision invisible to the rest of the world.

'You were a fool to disobey an order.'

'Yes, sir. Mebbe so, sir.'

The broad Yorkshire which Hudnutt spoke sounded odd in this tropical setting.

'How did you come to enlist?'

'For the music, sir.'

It called for more questions to extract the story. A boy in a Yorkshire village, not infrequently hungry. A cavalry regiment billeted there, in the last years of the war. The music of its band was like a miracle to this child, who had heard no music save that of wandering pipers in the ten years of his life. It made him conscious of – it did not create for it already existed – a frightful, overwhelming need. All the children of the village hung round the band (Hudnutt smiled disarmingly as he said this) but none so persistently as he. The trumpeters noticed him soon enough, laughed at his infantile comments about music, but laughed with sympathy as time went on; they let him try to blow their instruments, showed him how to cultivate a lip, and were impressed by the eventual result. The regiment returned after Waterloo, and for two more years the boy went on learning, even though those were the hungry years following the peace, when he should have been bird-scaring and stone-picking from dawn to dark.

And then the regiment was transferred and the hungry years went on, and the boy labourer began to handle the plough still yearning for music, while a trumpet cost more than a year's full wages for a man.

Then an interlude of pure bliss – the disarming smile again – when he joined a wandering theatrical troupe, as odd-job boy and musician; that was how he came to be able to read music although he could not read the printed word. His belly was empty as often as before; a stable yard meant a luxurious bed to him; those months were months of flea-bitten nights and foot-sore days, and they ended in his being left behind sick. That happened in Portsmouth, and then it was inevitable that, hungry and weak, he should be picked up by a marine recruiting-sergeant marching through the streets with a band. His enlistment coincided with the introduction of the *cornet à pistons* into military music, and the next thing that happened to him was that he was shipped off to the West Indies to take his place in the Commander-in-Chief's band under the direction of Drum-Major Cobb.

'I see,' said Hornblower; and indeed he could dimly see.

Six months with a travelling theatrical troupe would be poor preparation for the discipline of the Royal Marines; that was obvious, but he could guess at the rest, at this sensitiveness about music which was the real cause of the trouble. He eyed the boy again, seeking for ideas regarding how to deal with this situation.

'My lord! My lord!' This was Gerard hastening up to him. 'The packet's signalled, my lord. You can see the flag at the lookout-station masthead!'

The packet? Barbara would be on board. It was three years since he had seen her last, and for three weeks now he had been awaiting her from minute to minute.

'Call away my barge. I'm coming,' he said.

A wave of excitement swept away his concern

regarding the Hudnutt affair. He was about to hurry after Gerard, and then hesitated. What could he say in two seconds to a man awaiting trial for his life? What could he say when he himself was bubbling with happiness, to this man caged like an animal, like an ox helplessly awaiting the butcher?

'Goodbye, Hudnutt.' That was all he could say, leaving him standing dumbly there – he could hear the clash of keys and padlock as he hastened after Gerard.

Eight oars bit into the blue water, but no speed that they could give the dancing barge could be fast enough to satisfy him. There was the brig, her sails trimmed to catch the first hesitant puffs of the sea breeze. There was a white dot at her side, a white figure – Barbara waving her handkerchief. The barge surged alongside and Hornblower swung himself up into the main-chains, and there was Barbara in his arms; there were her lips against his, and then her grey eyes smiling at him, and then her lips against his again, and the afternoon sun blazing down on them both. Then they could stand at arm's length and look at each other, and Barbara could raise her hands and twitch his neckcloth straight, so that he could be sure they were really together, for Barbara's first gesture was always to straighten his neckcloth.

'You look well, my dear,' she said.

'So do you!'

Her cheeks were golden with sunburn after a month at sea; Barbara never strove after the fashionable creaminess that distinguished the lady of leisure from the milkmaid or the goose-girl. And they laughed in each other's faces out of sheer happiness before they kissed again and then eventually drew apart.

'Dear, this is Captain Knyvett, who has looked after me so kindly on the voyage.'

'Welcome aboard, my lord.' Knyvett was short and stocky and grizzled. 'But I fancy you'll not be staying with us long today.'

'We'll both be your passengers when you sail again,' said Barbara.

'If my relief has come,' said Hornblower, adding to Barbara, '*Triton* hasn't arrived yet.'

''Twill be two full weeks before we're ready to sail again, my lord,' said Knyvett. 'I trust we shall have the pleasure of your company and Her Ladyship's.'

'I sincerely hope so,' said Hornblower. 'Meanwhile we'll leave you for now – I hope you'll dine at Admiralty House as soon as you have leisure. Can you get down into the barge, my dear?'

'Of course,' said Barbara.

'Gerard, you'll stay on board and look after Her Ladyship's baggage.'

'Aye aye, my lord.'

'No time even to say how d'ye do to you, Mr Gerard,' said Barbara, as Hornblower led her away to the main-chains.

Barbara had no hoops in her skirts; she knew enough about shipboard breezes to dispense with those. Hornblower dropped down into the sternsheets of the barge, and a growl from the coxswain at the tiller turned the eyes of the boat's crew to seaward so that they would see nothing they should not see, while Knyvett and Gerard swung Barbara down into Hornblower's arms in a flurry of petticoats.

'Give way!'

The barge surged away from the ship's side, over the blue water, towards the Admiralty House pier, with Barbara and Hornblower hand in hand in the sternsheets.

'Delightful, dear,' said Barbara, looking about her when she landed. 'A commander-in-chief's life is spent in pleasant places.'

Pleasant enough, thought Hornblower, except for yellow fever and pirates and international crises and temperamental marines awaiting trial, but this was not the time to mention such things. Evans, hobbling on his wooden leg, was at the pier to greet them, and Hornblower could see that he was Barbara's slave from the first moment that he was presented to her.

'You must take me round the gardens the first moment I'm free,' said Barbara.

'Yes, Your Ladyship. Of course, Your Ladyship.'

They walked slowly up to the house; here it was a delicate business to show Barbara round and to present the staff to her, for Admiralty House was run along lines laid down at the Admiralty; to alter a stick of furniture or to change the status of any of the naval ratings working there was something Barbara would not be able to do. She was only a tolerated visitor there, and barely tolerated at that. She would certainly itch to change the furniture about and to reorganize the staff, but she was doomed to frustration.

'It seems to be as well, darling,' said Barbara with a twinkle, 'that my stay here is to be short. How short?'

'Until Ransome arrives in *Triton*,' answered Hornblower. 'You should know that, dear, considering how much gossip you picked up from Lady Exmouth and the others.'

'Yes, but it's still confusing to me. When does your appointment end?'

'It ended yesterday, legally. But my command continues until I am legally relieved of it by Ransome when he comes. *Triton* has made a long passage.'

'And when Ransome comes?'

'He takes over from me, and, of course, moves into this house. His Excellency has invited us to be his guests at Government House until we sail for home, dear.'

'I see. And if Ransome is so late that we miss the packet?'

'Then we wait for the next. I hope not. It would be uncomfortable.'

'Is Government House as bad as that?'

'It's tolerable, dear. But I was thinking of Ransome. No new commander-in-chief wants to have his predecessor staying on.'

'Criticizing all his actions, of course. Is that what you'd do, dear?'

'I wouldn't be human if I did not.'

'And I know so well you're human, dear,' said Barbara, putting out her hands to him. They were in the bedroom now, out of sight of servants and staff, and they could be human for a few precious moments until a thunderous knock at the door heralded the arrival of Gerard and the baggage, and on his heels came Spendlove with a note for Barbara.

'A note of welcome from Her Excellency, dear,' explained Barbara when she had read it. 'We are commanded to dinner *en famille*.'

'No more than I expected,' said Hornblower, and

then, looking round to see that Spendlove had withdrawn, 'no more than I feared.'

Barbara smiled into his eyes conspiratorially.

'A time will come,' she said.

There was so much to talk about, so much news to be exchanged; the long, long letters that had passed between them during their three years' separation needed amplification and explanation, and in any case, Barbara had been five weeks at sea without news. Late on the second day, while they were dining alone together, a mention of Hudnutt came into the conversation. Hornblower explained the situation briefly.

'You're going to court martial him?' asked Barbara.

'Likely enough, when I can convene a court.'

'And what will the verdict be?'

'Guilty, of course. There's no doubt about it.'

'I don't mean the verdict. I mean the sentence. What will that be?' Barbara was entitled to ask questions like this, and even to express an opinion regarding her husband's performance of his official duties, now that he had let slip a mention of the subject to her.

Hornblower quoted from the Articles of War which had regulated his official life for nearly thirty years.

'Every person so offending, being convicted thereof by the sentence of the court martial, shall suffer death, or such less punishment as from the nature and degree of the offence the court martial shall deem him to deserve.'

'You don't mean that, dear?' Barbara's grey eyes opened wide across the little table from him. 'Death? But you said "such less punishment". What could that be?'

'Flogging round the fleet. Five hundred lashes.'

'Five hundred lashes? For playing B natural instead of B flat?'

That was exactly what one might expect a woman to say.

'Dear, that's not the charge. The charge is wilful disobedience to orders.'

'But it's such a trifling matter.'

'Dear, disobedience to orders can never be a trifling matter.'

'Would you flog a man to death because he won't play a B flat? What a bloodthirsty way to balance the account!'

'There's no thought of balancing accounts, dear. Punishment is inflicted to deter other men from disobeying orders. It's not revenge.'

But womanlike Barbara clung to her position, however much her flank might be turned by cold logic.

'But if you hang him – or if you flog him, I expect – he'll never play another B natural again. What good does that do?'

'It's the good of the Service, dear –'

Hornblower, on his part, was holding a position which he knew to be not quite tenable, but Barbara's vehemence was causing him to grow heated in defence of his beloved Service.

'They'll hear about this in England,' said Barbara, and then a new thought struck her. 'He can appeal, of course – can he?'

'In home waters he could. But I am a commander-in-chief in a foreign station, and from my decision there is no appeal.'

It was a sobering speech. Barbara gazed across the table at this man, changed suddenly from her tender, loving, sensitive husband into a potentate who held the power of life and death. And she knew that she could not, she must not, exploit her privileged position as wife to influence his decision. Not because of the good of the Service, but for the sake of their married happiness.

'And the trial will be soon?' she asked; the change in her was apparent in her tone.

'The moment I can convene a court. Delay in matters of discipline defeats its own object. If a man were to mutiny on Monday he should be tried on Tuesday and hanged on Wednesday. But there are not enough captains available. *Triton*'s captain, when Ransome arrives, would give the necessary number, but then I shall be relieved of command and the matter will be out of my hands. But if *Flora* should come in before that – I detached her to the Gulf Coast – I shall be responsible.'

'I see, dear,' said Barbara, not taking her eyes from his face. Even before he spoke again she was aware that there was something which would modify the harshness of what he had said so far.

'Naturally, I have not made up my mind yet, dear,' he said. 'But there is a further possibility which I'm considering.'

'Yes?' She could hardly breathe the word.

'The confirmation of the finding and the sentence would be the last act of my command. That would present an excuse – a reason. I could commute the sentence as an act of clemency in recognition of the good behaviour of the squadron during the period I have commanded it.'

'I see, dear. And if Ransome arrives before *Flora*?'

'I can do nothing, except –'

'Except –?'

'I could suggest to Ransome that he might begin his command with an act of clemency.'

'And would he?'

'I know very little about Ransome, dear. I simply cannot say.'

Barbara opened her mouth to speak. She was going to say, 'Will he think a B flat more important than a man's life?' but she changed her speech in the nick of time. Instead she said the other thing that had also, and longer, been hovering on her lips.

'I love you, darling,' she said.

Again their eyes met across the table, and Hornblower felt his passion flooding to meet hers like a union of two rushing rivers. He knew perfectly well that all he had said about discipline and examples had been of no effect in changing Barbara's mind; a woman (even more than a man) convinced against her will was of the same opinion still. But Barbara had not said so; she had said something else – and something (as always) more appropriate to the occasion. And not by one single variation of tone, not by a hair's-breadth raising of an eyebrow, had she brought into the conversation the fact that he was tone deaf. A lesser woman would have used that as if it were a relevant argument in this matter. She knew of his tone deafness, and he knew she knew, and she knew that he knew; and so on *ad infinitum*, but there had never been any need for him to admit the defect or for her to admit her knowledge, and he loved her.

Next morning he had to tell himself that the

Commander-in-Chief in the West Indies, even if he were awaiting his relief, still had duties to do; even if his wife had newly joined him. But it was delightful to have Barbara walk down with him through the Admiralty House gardens to see him on his way as far as the wicket gate in the lofty dockyard palisade. It was a little unfortunate that at the moment when Evans was unlocking the gate Hudnutt should appear on the other side of the palisade taking his exercise. He was marching up and down between a file of marines under command of a corporal, the guard in parade uniform with bayonets fixed, Hudnutt hatless, as a prisoner under charges had to be.

'Pris'ner an' escort – halt!' bellowed the corporal at sight of his Admiral. 'Escort, present – arms!'

Hornblower formally acknowledged the salute before turning to say goodbye to his wife.

'Escort, sl-o-o-ope arms!' bellowed the corporal, in marine fashion, as if the escort had been at the other side of the dockyard instead of two yards from him.

'Is that the bandsman – Hudnutt, dear?' asked Barbara.

'Yes,' said Hornblower.

'Pris'ner an' escort, by the right, quick – march!' bellowed the corporal, and the little group marched off. Barbara watched it go; she could look now that Hudnutt had his back to her and was unaware of it. Previously she had refrained from staring at the man who would soon be on trial for his life. The trim marine uniform could not conceal the gangling, undeveloped body; and the sun shone on the fair hair.

'He's nothing more than a boy,' said Barbara.

That could be another irrelevant fact if she wanted to argue with her husband regarding his duty. Seventeen or seventy, a man under orders must obey orders.

'He's not very old, dear,' agreed Hornblower.

Then he kissed the cheek that Barbara held up to him – he was not at all sure if an admiral in uniform should kiss his wife goodbye in the presence of his staff, but Barbara had no doubts about it. He left her standing there by the gate chatting to Evans, looking round her at the lovely garden on the one side of the palisade and at the businesslike dockyard through the palings.

The presence of his wife was delightful, even though it meant greatly increased activities for him. The next two or three days involved considerable entertaining; island society wished to make the most of the fleeting presence of an admiral's wife, a peeress, and of the bluest of blood in her own right. To Hornblower, regretfully contemplating the immediate end of his period in command, it was a little like the aristocrats during the French Revolution dancing before the summons to the guillotine, but Barbara seemed to enjoy it all, perhaps because she had just endured five very dull weeks at sea and was facing the prospect of five more.

'You danced a good deal with young Bonner, dear,' he remarked to her when they were home again after the Governor's party.

'He's a very good dancer,' said Barbara.

'He's something of a villain, I believe,' countered Hornblower. 'There's never been anything proved, but much suspected – smuggling, slave running, and all the rest of it.'

'He's invited to Government House,' said Barbara.

'Nothing proved, as I said. But in my official capacity I've often been interested in the activities of those fishing-boats of his. You may find you've been dancing with a jailbird one of these days, dear.'

'Jailbirds are more amusing than military secretaries,' smiled Barbara.

Barbara's activity was astonishing. Even after a night's gaiety she went riding during the day, and Hornblower was content that she should, as long as there were young men available eager to act as Lady Hornblower's escort, seeing that he had his duties to attend to and disliked horses in any case. It was even amusing to observe the transparent adoration which she received from everyone, from His Excellency, from the young men who rode with her, from Evans the gardener, from everyone she had anything to do with.

Barbara was out riding one morning, before the heat of the day, when a messenger was brought in to Hornblower at Admiralty House.

'Message from the cap'n, my lord. *Triton's* signalled. She's heading in with a fair wind.'

Hornblower stared for a moment; although this was a message that might have come at any time during the last month he was not ready for its full impact.

'Very well. My compliments to the captain, and I'll come down.'

So this was the end of his three years as Commander-in-Chief. Ransome would take over command, possibly today, but certainly tomorrow, and he himself would be on half-pay and due to go home. A queer mixture of thoughts went through his mind as he made himself ready to meet Ransome; young Richard about to enter

Eton; the thought of a freezing winter in Smallbridge; the auditing of his final accounts; it was not until he was on his way to his barge that he remembered that now he would be relieved of the necessity to come to a decision in the Hudnutt case.

Triton wore no admiral's flag, for Ransome legally held no command until he had taken over; the salutes at the moment merely acknowledged *Triton's* joining the West Indian command. Ransome was a burly man with the heavy, fashionable side-whiskers, more grey than black. He wore a small decoration of Companion of the Bath, insignificant compared with Hornblower's magnificent Grand Cross. Presumably if he survived this appointment without any great blunder he might hope for knighthood. He presented his captain, Coleman, with whom Hornblower was quite unacquainted, and then turned an attentive ear to Hornblower's explanation of the arrangements made so far and of future plans.

'I'll assume command tomorrow,' decided Ransome.

'That will allow time to arrange the full ceremonial,' agreed Hornblower. 'In that case, sir, would you care to spend tonight at Government House? I understand a command there awaits you if you think it convenient.'

'No need to move twice,' said Ransome. 'I'll spend tonight on board here.'

'Admiralty House will be ready for you tomorrow, of course, sir. Perhaps you might like to give us the honour of your company at dinner today? There might perhaps be information that I could give you regarding the situation here.'

Ransome shot a glance at Hornblower charged with

a certain amount of suspicion; he did not wish to have any ready-made policies thrust upon him by his predecessor. Yet the suggestion was obviously sensible.

'It would be a great pleasure. I must thank you, my lord.'

Hornblower took a tactful step to allay that suspicion.

'The packet in which my wife and I are taking passage to England is making ready for sea at present, sir. We sail in her, in a matter of a few days only.'

'Very well, my lord,' said Ransome.

'Then, having repeated my welcome, sir, I shall take my leave. Shall we expect you at four o'clock? Or would some other time be convenient?'

'Four o'clock will suit me well,' said Ransome.

The king is dead, long live the king, thought Hornblower, on his way back. Tomorrow he would be supplanted, and would become a mere half-pay officer. The splendour and dignity of a commander-in-chief would be transferred from him to Ransome. And he found the thought a little irksome; he had found his polite pose of deference to Ransome more than a little irksome; and he really thought Ransome could have been more polite in return. He gave vent to a good deal of this feeling as he told Barbara about the interview, and he checked himself at sight of Barbara's amused twinkle and raised eyebrow.

'You are the sweetest simpleton, my very dearest,' said Barbara. 'Have you no idea at all of any possible explanation?'

'None, I'm afraid,' said Hornblower.

Barbara came up close to him and looked into his face.

'No wonder that I love you,' she said. 'Don't you understand that no man could find it easy to replace Hornblower? Your period of command has been overwhelmingly successful. You've set a standard Ransome will find it hard to live up to. One might say he's jealous, envious – and he showed it.'

'I can't really believe that,' said Hornblower.

'And I love you because you can't believe it,' said Barbara. 'I could tell you so in a hundred ways, if I did not have to go and put on my finest gown to win Admiral Ransome's heart.'

Ransome was a man of fine presence, bulk and sidewhiskers and all; Hornblower had not really appreciated the fact at their first meeting. His manner was somewhat more cordial in Barbara's presence, which might have been the effect of Barbara's personality, but might also have been, as Hornblower realized, the result of Ransome's knowing that Lady Hornblower was a person of much influence in political circles. Hornblower did his best to exploit Ransome's faint cordiality. He passed the wine, he let slip as casually as possible bits of useful information regarding West Indian conditions – casually, so that Ransome could not suspect him of trying to bring influence to bear on him regarding his future policy, and yet useful information that Ransome could snap up and treasure with a smile at Hornblower's carelessness. Yet all the same, dinner was not a tremendous success. There was still a certain tenseness.

And as dinner was approaching its end Hornblower was conscious of a glance darted at him by Barbara; it was only one glance, and of the most fleeting nature. Ransome could not have been conscious of it, but

Hornblower understood. Barbara was jogging his memory regarding a matter that was important to her. He awaited a suitable turn in the conversation before mentioning the subject.

'Oh, yes,' he said, 'there's a court martial pending. A marine bandsman –'

He went on to tell Ransome the circumstances of the case, treating it lightly. He was aware, even if Ransome was not, of the closeness with which Barbara was studying Ransome's expression as the narrative continued.

'"Repeated and deliberate disobedience to a lawful order,"' Ransome was repeating to himself Hornblower's own words. 'It could have been mutiny.'

'So it could,' agreed Hornblower. 'But it's rather a curious case. I'm glad you have the decision to make regarding it, and not I.'

'It seems to me as if the evidence will be quite incontrovertible.'

'No doubt.' Hornblower made himself smile, telepathically conscious of the intensity of Barbara's interest. 'But the circumstances are a little unusual.'

The stony expression on Ransome's face was most discouraging. Hornblower knew the situation to be hopeless. He would have abandoned any further effort if Barbara had not been there, but as it was he went on, uselessly.

'If the trial had been held during the period of my command I might have – naturally I had not made up my mind – commuted the sentence to mark my appreciation of the good behaviour of the squadron.'

'Yes?' said Ransome; no monosyllable could have

expressed greater disinterest, but Hornblower plunged on.

'It had occurred to me that you might find this a favourable opportunity to display clemency as your first official act.'

'That will be a matter for my own decision.'

'Of course,' agreed Hornblower.

'And I cannot imagine my taking any action of that sort, naturally. I cannot have the squadron believing that I shall be lenient as regards discipline. I cannot have my command unsettled at the start.'

'Of course,' said Hornblower again. He could see the uselessness of further argument, and he might as well be graceful about it. 'You are the best judge of all the circumstances, as well as the only judge.'

'Now I shall leave you gentlemen to your wine,' said Barbara, suddenly. Hornblower looked at her just in time to see her frozen expression melt into the smile he knew so well. 'I shall say goodnight to you, Admiral. I shall make every effort – as far as the rules of the Navy allow – to see that this house is in good condition for you to take over tomorrow, and I hope you will be comfortable in it.'

'Thank you,' said Ransome; the two men were on their feet now.

'Goodnight, dear,' said Barbara to Hornblower. The latter was aware that the smile she gave him was not quite real, and he knew her to be acutely upset.

She left them, and Hornblower passed the port, and settled down again to what proved to be a long evening. Ransome, having asserted himself, and having made it perfectly clear that he would remain uninfluenced by any suggestion Hornblower might put forward, was by no means averse to acquiring any information that might come his way. Nor to finishing the bottle of port and starting on another.

So that it was very late before he went to bed, and he used no light for fear of disturbing Barbara. He crept about the room as silently as he could. In the darkness the glances that he directed at the other bed (naval establishments made small allowance for wives, and that allowance did not include double beds) under its mosquito net revealed nothing to him, and he was glad. If Barbara had been awake they could hardly have avoided discussing the Hudnutt case.

Nor was there any time next morning, for the moment Hornblower was called he had to hurry into the dressing room and array himself in his best uniform with his ribbon and star and hasten away to the ceremony of the change of command. As the officer to be relieved he was first upon the quarterdeck of the *Clorinda*, and stationed himself on the starboard side, his staff behind him. Captain Sir Thomas Fell had received him, and next busied himself with receiving the other captains as they came on board. The marine band – without Hudnutt – played selections on the poop; the pipes of the bosun's mates twittered unceasingly to welcome the continuous arrivals; the sun blazed down as if this were just some ordinary day. Then came a pause, intense in its drama. Then the band burst into a march again, there were ruffles of drums and flourishes of bugles as Ransome came up the side with his staff behind him, to take up his station on the port side. Fell came forward to Hornblower with his hand at his hat brim.

'Ship's company fallen in, my lord.'

'Thank you, Sir Thomas.' Spendlove pressed a paper into Hornblower's hand; Hornblower stepped forward. 'Orders from the Lords Commissioners for the execution of the office of Lord High Admiral, to me, Horatio Lord Hornblower, Knight Grand Cross of the Most Honourable Order of the Bath, Rear Admiral of the Red Squadron –'

He really had trouble in preventing his voice from trembling, forcing himself to read in a harsh and matter-of-fact tone. He folded the paper and gave his last order.

'Sir Thomas, please have the goodness to haul down my flag.'

'Aye aye, my lord.'

The first of the thirteen saluting guns went off as the red ensign came slowly down from the mizzen-peak. A long, long, descent; sixty seconds for thirteen guns, and when the flag completed its descent Hornblower was the poorer by forty-nine pounds three shillings and seven pence a month command pay. A moment later Ransome came forward, paper in hand, to read the orders of the Lords Commissioners to him, Henry Ransome, Companion of the Most Honourable Order of the Bath, Rear Admiral of the Blue Squadron.

'Hoist my flag, Sir Thomas.'

'Aye aye, sir.'

Up to the mizzen-peak rose the Blue Ensign; until it broke at the peak the ship was silent, but then it unfolded itself in the breeze and the salute roared out and the band played. When the last gun fired Ransome was legally Commander-in-Chief of His Majesty's Ships and Vessels in West Indian waters. More blaring from the band, and in the midst of it Hornblower stepped forward raising his hand in salute to the new Commander-in-Chief.

'Permission to leave the ship, sir?'

'Permission granted.'

Ruffles of drums, bugle calls, pipes, and he went down the ship's side. He might have been sentimental; he might have felt agony of regret, but there was instant distraction awaiting him.

'My lord,' said Spendlove beside him in the stern-sheets.

'Well?'

'That prisoner – Hudnutt, the marine bandsman –'

'What about him?'

'He's escaped, my lord. He broke prison during the night.'

That settled Hudnutt's fate beyond all doubt. Nothing could save him. He was as good as dead; or soon perhaps he would be worse than dead. No deserter, no escaped prisoner, ever succeeded in evading recapture in Jamaica. It was an island, and not too large an island. And there was a standing reward of ten pounds sterling for information resulting in the apprehension of a deserter, and in Jamaica, far more than in England, ten pounds was a fortune. A journeyman's wages for a year or more; more money than any slave could hope to see in a lifetime. No deserter stood a chance; his white face, to say nothing of his uniform, would call attention to him wherever he might be in the island, and the standing reward made it certain that he would be betrayed. Hudnutt was doomed to recapture. And he was doomed beyond that. There would be additional charges at his court martial. Prison breaking. Desertion. Damage to government property. Damage to his uniform. He would probably be hanged. The only other chance was that he would be flogged round the fleet to die for certain under the lash. Hudnutt was a dead man, and this was the end of his talent for music.

It was a sombre enough thought to occupy his mind all the way to the pier, and it kept him silent as he climbed into the Governor's carriage to be driven to Government House – he had no Commander-in-Chief's carriage now. He was still silent as they drove away.

But they had hardly gone a mile when they met a lively cavalcade clattering down on horseback towards them. First Hornblower saw Barbara – he would have picked her out in any crowd even if she had not been conspicuous on a white horse. His Excellency rode on one side of her and Lady Hooper on the other, chattering eagerly. Behind them came a mixed party, of aides-de-camp and civilians; at the rear rode the Assistant Provost-Marshal and two troopers of his guard.

'Ha, Hornblower!' called the Governor, reining up. 'Your ceremonial seems to have finished earlier than I expected.'

'Good morning, sir,' said Hornblower. 'Your servant, ma'am.'

Then he smiled at Barbara – he could always smile at the sight of her despite any depression. In her hunting veil the smile she gave him in return was hardly apparent.

'You can join us in our hunt. One of my aides-de-camp will give you his horse,' said Hooper, and then, peering into the carriage, 'No, perhaps not, in those silk stockings. You can follow us in the carriage, like a lady with certain expectations. Like the Queen of France, by Gad! Turn that carriage, coachman.'

'What are you hunting, sir?' asked Hornblower, a little bewildered.

'That deserter of yours. He might show us some sport,' answered Hooper.

They were hunting man, the biggest game of all – but Hudnutt, dreamy, scatterbrained Hudnutt, would be poor game. Two coloured servants rode in the party, each holding a leash of bloodhounds, tawny and black; grim, horrible creatures. He wanted to have nothing to do with this hunt, nothing whatever. He wanted to order the carriage to turn back again. This was a nightmare, and it was beyond his power to awaken himself from it. It was horrible to see Barbara taking part in it. At the dockyard gate, at the high palisade, the cortège halted.

'That's the prison,' said the Assistant Provost-Marshal, pointing. 'You can see the hole in the roof, sir.'

An area of thatch had been torn away. Probably that prison was not very strongly built; to escape from it meant that the fifteen-foot palisade had to be scaled next – and even then certain recapture somewhere in the island awaited the man to achieve that feat.

'Come on,' said the Assistant Provost-Marshal, and he and his guard and the men with the bloodhounds trotted into the dockyard to the prison and dismounted. They took the bloodhounds into the prison, where presumably the hounds smelt at the prisoner's bedding. Then they reappeared at the door, smelling at the ground below the hole in the roof. Instantly they caught the scent, throwing themselves against their leashes so that the coloured servants had a difficult task to remount, and then they came pelting across the dock-yard again. They threw themselves against the palisade, leaping up at it, slavering with excitement.

'Bring 'em round to this side!' shouted the Governor, and then, turning to Hornblower, 'Your man's a marine, isn't he? Even a sailor would find it hard to scale that palisade.'

Hudnutt might have done it in some exalted mood, thought Hornblower – those dreamers were like madmen sometimes.

The bloodhounds were brought round through the dockyard gate again and led to the corresponding point on the outside of the palisade. They caught the scent again in a flash, throwing themselves against their leashes and galloping down the road.

'Gone away!' yelled the Governor, spurring his horse after them.

Hudnutt had climbed that fifteen-foot palisade, then. He must have been insane. The cavalcade had all gone on ahead; the coachman was urging the carriage horses along as fast as their dignity and the inequalities of the road would permit; the carriage lurched and leaped, throwing Hornblower against Gerard beside him and sometimes even against Spendlove opposite. Straight up the road they went, heading for the open country and the Blue Mountains beyond. The horsemen ahead reined back into a trot, and the coachman followed their example, so that the progress of the carriage became more sedate.

'A hot enough scent, my lord,' said Gerard, peering

forward at the bloodhounds still straining at their leashes.

'And yet this road must have been well travelled since he went along it,' said Spendlove.

'Ah!' said Gerard, still peering forward. 'They're leaving the road.'

As the carriage reached the corner they saw that the horsemen had turned up a broad lane through fields of cane; the coachman, nothing daunted, swung up into the lane after them, but after two more miles of rapid progress he pulled his horses to a halt.

'A check here, Hornblower,' said the Governor. 'This lane fords the Hope River here.'

The halted cavalcade was breathing the horses; Barbara waved her gloved hand to him.

'No scent the other side,' explained the Governor, and then, calling to the men with the bloodhounds. 'Cast upstream as well as down. And on both sides.'

The Assistant Provost-Marshal acknowledged the order with a salute.

'Your man knew we'd have bloodhounds after him,' said the Governor. 'He waded along the river. But he has to come out sooner or later, and we'll pick up the scent again there.'

Barbara guided her horse to the side of the carriage, and raised her veil to speak to him.

'Good morning, dear,' she said.

'Good morning,' said Hornblower.

It was hard to say more, when the events of the last hour or two, and all their implications, were allowed for. And Barbara was hardly flushed with the heat and the exercise. She looked drawn and tired; her smile was positively wan. It occurred to Hornblower that she was participating in this hunt as unwillingly as he was. And it seemed likely that she had allowed the move from Admiralty House to Government House this morning to trouble her; womanlike she would not have been able to allow the Navy to execute the task without her supervision even though the Navy had made similar moves by the hundred thousand. She had tried to order it all and was weary in consequence.

'Come and sit in the carriage, dear,' he said. 'Gerard will take your horse.'

'Mr Gerard is wearing silk stockings the same as you are, dear,' replied Barbara, smiling through her weariness, 'and I have too much respect for his dignity to set him on a side-saddle in any case.'

'My groom will lead your horse, Lady Hornblower,' interposed the Governor. 'This hunt looks as if it's going to turn out badly.'

Hornblower scrambled down from the carriage to help Barbara from the side-saddle and up into the carriage. Gerard and Spendlove, who had followed him out, followed them back after a moment's hesitation and sat with their backs to the horses.

'We should have heard something from the blood-hounds by now,' said the Governor. The four bloodhounds had now cast up and down both banks for a considerable distance. 'Can he have climbed a tree?'

A man could be more resourceful than any fox, Hornblower knew. But it was an unexpected aspect of Hudnutt's character.

'Not a trace of scent, Your Excellency,' said the Assistant Provost-Marshal trotting up. 'Nothing at all.'

'Oh, well then, we'll go home again. A poor day's sport after all. We'll precede you, Lady Hornblower, with your permission.'

'We'll see you at the house, dear Lady Hornblower,' echoed Lady Hooper.

The carriage turned again and followed the horsemen down the lane.

'You've had a busy morning, I fear, my dear,' said Hornblower; with his staff sitting across the carriage from them he had to retain a certain formality of tone.

'Not busy at all,' answered Barbara, turning her head to meet his glance. 'A very pleasant morning, thank you, dear. And you – your ceremonial went off without a hitch, I hope?'

'Well enough, thank you. Ransome –' he changed what he was going to say abruptly. What he would say about Ransome to Barbara's private ear was not the same as what he would say in the hearing of his staff.

The carriage trotted on, and conversation proceeded only fitfully in the heat. It was long before they swung through the gates of Government House, with Hornblower acknowledging the salute of the sentry, and drew up at the door. Aides-de-camp and butlers and maids awaited them; but Barbara had already dealt with the move, and in the vast, cavernous bedroom and dressing room allotted to principal guests Hornblower's things were already disposed along with hers.

'At last alone,' smiled Barbara. 'Now we can look forward to Smallbridge.'

Indeed that was so; this was the beginning of one of those periods of transition which Hornblower knew so well, as did every sailor, the strange days, or weeks, between one life and the next. He had ceased to be a commander-in-chief; now he had to endure existence until he would at least be master in his own house. The urgent need at the moment was for a bath; his shirt was sticking to his ribs under his heavy uniform coat. Perhaps never again, never in all his life, would he take a bath under a wash-deck pump somewhere out with the trade winds blowing upon him. On the other hand, he would not, at least while he was in Jamaica, have to wear a uniform again.

It was later in the day that Barbara made her request to him.

'Dear, would you please give me some money?'

'Of course,' said Hornblower.

He felt a delicacy about this which most men would laugh at. Barbara had brought a good deal of money to their marriage, which, of course, was now his property, and he felt an absurd guilt that she should have to ask him for money. That feeling of guilt was perfectly ridiculous, of course. Women were not supposed to dispose of money in any way, except small sums for housekeeping. They could not legally sign a cheque, they could not enter into no business transaction at all, which was perfectly right and proper seeing how incapable women were. Except perhaps Barbara. It was the husband's business to keep all moneys under his own hand and dole out under his own supervision what was needed.

'How much would you like, dear?' he asked.

'Two hundred pounds,' said Barbara.

Two hundred pounds? Two hundred pounds! That was something entirely different. It was a fortune. What in the world would Barbara want two hundred pounds for here in Jamaica? There could not be one single gown or pair of gloves in the whole island that Barbara could possibly want to buy. A few souvenirs, perhaps. The most elaborate tortoiseshell toilet set in Jamaica would not cost five pounds. Two hundred pounds? There would be a few maids to whom she would have to give vails on leaving, but five shillings each, half a guinea at most, would settle those.

'Two hundred pounds?' he said it aloud this time.

'Yes, dear, if you please.'

'It will be my business to tip the butler and grooms, of course,' he said, still trying to find reasons why she should think she needed this stupendous sum.

'Yes, no doubt, dear,' said Barbara, patiently. 'But I need some money for other purposes.'

'But it's a lot of money.'

'I think we can afford it, though. Please, dear –'

'Of course, of course,' said Hornblower hastily. He could not bear it that Barbara should have to plead to him. All he had was hers. It was always a pleasure to him to anticipate her wants, to forestall any request so that it never need be uttered. He felt shame that Barbara, exquisite Barbara, should ever have to abase herself so low as to ask a favour of him, unworthy as he was.

'I'll write an order on Summers,' he said. 'He's Coutts's correspondent in Kingston.'

'Thank you, dear,' said Barbara.

Yet as he handed the order over he could not refrain from further speech.

'You'll be careful, dear, won't you?' he said. 'Two hundred pounds, whether in notes or gold –'

His misgivings ceased to be voiced, died away in incoherent mumblings. He had no wish to pry. He had no wish to exert over Barbara the sort of parental authority that both law and custom gave a husband over his wife. And then he thought of a possible explanation. Lady Hooper was a keen and clever card-player. Presumably Barbara had lost heavily to her. Well, in that case he need not worry. Barbara was a good player, too, and level-headed, and cool. She would win it back. In any case she was no gambler. Perhaps on the voyage home they would have a few hands of piquet – if Barbara had any fault at all it was a tendency to discard a little thoughtlessly when playing the younger hand, and he could give a little unobtrusive advice. And there was a smug pleasure, and a tender pleasure, in the thought of Barbara not caring to admit, to a husband who notoriously won, that she had lost at cards. The deep respect that he felt for her was accompanied (as the flavour of a beef steak may be accompanied by that of mustard) by the knowledge that she was still human. Hornblower knew that there can be no love without respect – and no love without a twinkle of amusement as well.

'You are the dearest man in the world,' said Barbara, and he realized that her eyes had been fixed on his face for the last several seconds.

'It is my greatest happiness to hear you say so,' he answered, with a sincerity that no one could doubt. And then a recollection of their position in this house, as mere guests, came to them both to modify the intensity of their feelings.

'And we shall be the most unpopular people in Jamaica if we keep Their Excellencies waiting for their dinner,' said Hornblower.

They were only guests, now, mere hangers-on, their presence only tolerated by people who had their official lives still to live; that was what Hornblower thought at dinner-time when the new Commander-in-Chief sat in the place of honour. He thought of the Byzantine General, blinded and disgraced, begging in the market-place, and he nearly said, 'Spare a penny for Belisarius' when the Governor turned to include him in the conversation.

'Your marine hasn't been apprehended yet,' said Hooper.

'Not my marine any longer, sir,' laughed Hornblower. 'Admiral Ransome's marine now.'

'I understand there's no doubt that he *will* be apprehended,' said Ransome.

'We've not lost a deserter yet during the time of my appointment here,' said Hooper.

'That's very reassuring,' was Ransome's comment.

Hornblower stole a glance at Barbara across the table. She was eating her dinner with apparent composure; he had feared lest this reminder should upset her, for he knew how strongly she felt about Hudnutt's fate. A woman was liable to think that the inevitable should not be inevitable in matters in which she was interested. Barbara's mastery of her feelings was something more to admire about her.

Lady Hooper changed the subject, and conversation became general and gay. Hornblower actually began to enjoy himself, with a light-headed feeling of irresponsibility. There were no cares on his shoulders; soon – the moment the packet was ready to sail – he would be on his way to England, and he would be pleasantly settled in Smallbridge while these people here went on dealing with unrewarding problems in tropical heat. Nothing here mattered to him any more. If Barbara were happy he had not a care in the world, and Barbara was seemingly happy, chattering away to her neighbours on either hand.

It was pleasant, too, that there was not to be any heavy drinking, for after dinner there was to be a reception in honour of the new Commander-in-Chief to which all the island society not eligible for dinner had been invited. He found himself looking at life with fresh eyes and actually approving of it.

After dinner, when the men and the ladies met again in the drawing room and the first new guests were being announced, he was able to exchange a word or two with Barbara and to see that she was happy and not over-tired. Her smile was bright and her eyes sparkling. He had to turn away from her in the end to shake hands with Mr Hough, just arrived with his wife. Other guests were streaming in; a sudden influx of blue and gold and white marked the arrival of Coleman, *Triton*'s captain, and a couple of his lieutenants. Ransome himself was presenting Coleman to Barbara, and Hornblower could not help but hear the conversation close behind him.

'Captain Coleman is an old friend of mine,' said Barbara. 'You were Perfecto Coleman in those days, weren't you, Captain?'

'And you were Lady Leighton, ma'am,' said Coleman.

A harmless enough remark, but enough to shatter Hornblower's frail happiness, to darken the brightly lit room, to set the babble of conversation in the room roaring in Hornblower's ears like a torrent, through the din of which Barbara's words pierced shrill like a whistle note.

'Captain Coleman was my first husband's flag lieutenant,' said Barbara.

She had had a first husband; she had been Lady Leighton. Hornblower nearly always contrived to forget this. Rear Admiral Sir Percy Leighton had died for his country, of wounds received in the battle of Rosas Bay, thirteen full years ago. But Barbara had been Leighton's wife, Leighton's widow. She had been Leighton's wife before she had been Hornblower's. Hornblower hardly ever thought about it, but when he did he still experienced a jealousy which he knew to be insane. Any reminder not only reawoke that jealousy, but brought back to him with agonizing clarity the recollection of the despair, the envy, the black self-derision he had known in those days. He had been a desperately unhappy man then, and this made him the same desperately unhappy man now. He was no longer the successful sailor, terminating a brilliant period of command. He was the thwarted lover, despised even by his own despicable self. He knew again all the misery of limitless and yet unsatisfied desire, to blend with the jealousies of the moment.

Hough was awaiting a reply to some remark he had made. Hornblower forced himself to extemporize some casual sentence which may or may not have been relevant. Hough drifted away, and Hornblower found himself against his will looking over at Barbara. She had her ready smile for him, and he had to smile back, and he knew it to be a dreadful, lopsided, mirthless smile, like a grin on the face of a dead man. He saw a worried look come on her face; he knew how instantly she was conscious of his moods, and that made it worse than ever. She was the heartless woman who had spoken of her first husband – that jealousy of his was a mood she knew nothing of, was not susceptible to. He was a man who had stepped suddenly from firm ground into a morass of uncertainty that would engulf him.

Captain Knyvett had entered the room, bluff and grizzled, dressed in blue broadcloth with unpretentious brass buttons. As he approached Hornblower could only with an effort remember him as the captain of the Jamaica packet.

'We sail a week from today, my lord,' he said. 'The announcement for the mail will be made tomorrow.'

'Excellent,' said Hornblower.

'And I can see from all this,' went on Knyvett, with a gesture indicating Admiral Ransome's presence, 'that I shall have the pleasure of Your Lordship's company, and Her Ladyship's.'

'Yes, yes, quite so,' said Hornblower.

'You will be my only passengers,' said Knyvett.

'Excellent,' repeated Hornblower.

'I trust Your Lordship will find the *Pretty Jane* a well-found and comfortable ship.'

'I trust so,' said Hornblower.

'Her Ladyship, of course, is familiar with the deck-house that will be your accommodation. I shall ask her if she can suggest any addition that will add to your comfort, my lord.'

'Very well.'

Knyvett drifted away after this cold reception, and it was only after he had gone that Hornblower realized that Knyvett must have received an impression of a top-lofty peer with hardly bare politeness for a mere packet-captain. He regretted it, and made a desperate effort to get himself under control again. A glance at Barbara revealed her chatting animatedly with young Bonner, the fishing-boat owner and general merchant with the shady reputation, against whom Hornblower had already warned her. That could have added to his misery if it were possible.

Again he made the effort to control himself. He knew the expression on his face to be frozen and blank, and he tried to make it more pleasing as he forced himself to stroll through the crowd.

'Can we tempt you, Lord Hornblower?' asked an old lady standing by the card-table in an alcove. She was a good whist player, Hornblower remembered.

'Why certainly, with pleasure,' he made himself say.

He had something to think about now; for the first few hands it was hard to concentrate, especially as the noise of an orchestra was added to the din of the party, but old habits reasserted themselves with the necessity to remember the distribution of fifty-two cards. By sheer willpower he achieved the transformation of himself into a thinking machine, playing coldly and correctly, and then, when the rubber appeared to be lost, he was carried away despite himself. The next hand afforded an opportunity for brilliance, for that injection into his so-far mechanical play of the human quality, the flexibility, the unpredictable cunning which marked the difference between a second-class player and a first-class one. By the fourth lead he had made a fair estimate of the hands. One particular lead might enable him to clear the board, to win every trick and the rubber; with orthodox play the hand would end with his making only twelve tricks and the rubber still in doubt. It was worth trying – but it was now or never. Without hesitation he led his queen of hearts to the ace that his partner was forced to play; he took the next trick and along with it control of the situation, cleared trumps, led out his established winners, saw with satisfaction his opponents discard first the knave and then the king of hearts, and he finally laid down the three of hearts to take the last trick amid the dismay of his opponents.

'Why, that's Grand Slam,' said the old lady who was his partner, quite astonished. 'I don't understand – I don't see how – we've won the rubber after all!'

It had been a neat piece of work; there was a perceptible glow of accomplishment within him. That was a hand that he would be able to play over in his mind in future while composing himself to sleep. When the card-playing was finished and the guests beginning to leave he was able to meet Barbara's eye with a more natural expression, and Barbara with a relieved sigh was able to tell herself that her husband was coming out of his unpredictable mood.

It was as well that he was, for the next few days were bound to be difficult. There was almost nothing for him to do as the *Pretty Jane* made ready for sea. As a helpless spectator he had to stand by and watch Ransome taking over the command he had held for three years. The Spanish question was likely to be difficult with the French invasion of Spain to restore Ferdinand VII; there was the Mexican question as well as the Venezuela question; he could not help fretting over the possibility of

Ransome mishandling them. On the other hand, there was the small comfort that Hudnutt had so far succeeded in evading capture; Hornblower honestly feared that if he should be apprehended and sentenced while they were still in the island Barbara might take action herself with personal appeals to Ransome or even to the Governor. Barbara actually seemed to have forgotten about the case, which was more than Hornblower had; he was still profoundly disturbed about it, and inclined to fret himself into a fever at his complete lack of power to exert any influence in the matter. It was hard to be philosophic about it, to tell himself that no individual, not even Hornblower, could hold back the working of the inexorable machine of the Articles for the Regulating and Better Government of His Majesty's Navies. And Hudnutt was a more capable person than he had ever imagined, seeing that he had been able to maintain himself free from capture for a week now – unless perhaps he was dead. That might be best for Hudnutt.

Captain Knyvett came in person with the news that the *Pretty Jane* was almost ready for sea.

'The last of the cargo's going on board now, my lord,' he said. 'The logwood's all in and the coir is on the quay. If Your Lordship and Her Ladyship will come on board this evening we'll sail with the land breeze at dawn.'

'Thank you, Captain. I am greatly obliged to you,' said Hornblower, trying not to be fulsome to make up for his coldness at the Governor's party.

Pretty Jane was a flush-decked brig, save that amidships she carried a small but substantial deckhouse for her passengers. Barbara had inhabited it for five weeks on the outward voyage. Now they entered it together, with all the bustle of the ship's getting ready for sea going on round them.

'I used to look at that other bed, dear,' she said to Hornblower as they stood in the deckhouse, 'and I used to tell myself that soon my husband would be sleeping there. It seemed too good to be possible, dear.'

A noise outside distracted them.

'This case, ma'am?' asked the Government House servant who was bringing their baggage on board under Gerard's supervision.

'That? Oh, I've asked the captain about that already. It's to go in the steerage.'

'Yes, ma'am.'

'Delicacies in tin boxes,' explained Barbara to Hornblower. 'I brought them all the way out for you to enjoy while going home, dear.'

'You are too good to me,' said Hornblower.

A case that size and weight would be a nuisance in the deckhouse. In the steerage its contents would be readily accessible.

'What is coir?' asked Barbara, looking out to see one of the final bales going down the hatchway.

'The hairy husks of coconuts,' explained Hornblower.

'What in the world are we carrying those to England for?' asked Barbara.

'There are machines now which can weave it. They make coco-matting by the mile in England now.'

'And logwood?'

'They extract a dye from it. A bright red dye.'

'You are my unfailing source of information, dear,' said Barbara, 'as well as everything else in life for me.'

'Here's Their Excellencies coming, my lord,' warned Gerard, arriving at the deckhouse door.

That meant the final goodbyes, in the dying evening. A painful, sad moment; much shaking of hands; kisses on each cheek for Barbara from Lady Hooper; the word 'goodbye' repeated over and over again, overwhelming in its finality. Goodbye to friends and to acquaintances, goodbye to Jamaica and to the command-in-chief. Goodbye to one life, with the next still to disclose itself. Goodbye to the last shadowy figure disappearing in the darkness of the quay, and then to turn again to Barbara standing beside him, permanent in these transitions.

In the first light of next morning Hornblower could hardly be blamed for being on deck, feeling oddly awkward with the necessity for keeping out of the way, watching while Knyvett warped the *Pretty Jane* away from the quay, to catch the land breeze and head out of the harbour. Luckily Knyvett was made of sturdy stuff, and was not in the least discomposed at having to handle his ship under the eye of an admiral. The land breeze filled the sails; *Pretty Jane* gathered way. They dipped the flag to Fort Augusta, and then, with the helm hard over, came round to leave Drunken Cay and South Cay on their port side before beginning the long reach to the eastward. And Hornblower could relax and contemplate the new prospect of breakfasting with his wife on shipboard.

He surprised himself at the ease with which he accustomed himself to being a passenger. At first he was so anxious to give no indication of interference that he did not even dare to look into the binnacle to note their course. He was content to sit with Barbara in two hammock chairs in the shade of the deckhouse – there were beckets to which the chairs could be hooked to prevent them sliding down the deck to leeward as *Pretty Jane* heeled over – and think about nothing in particular, watching the flying fish furrowing the surface, and the patches of yellow Sargasso weed drift by, gold against the blue, and an occasional turtle swimming manfully along far from land. He could watch Captain Knyvett and his mate take their noon sights and assure himself that he had no interest at all in the figures they were obtaining – and in truth he was really more interested in the punctuality of meal-times. He could crack an idle joke with Barbara to the effect that *Pretty Jane* had made this run so often she could be trusted to find her way home without supervision; and his mind was lazy enough to think that funny.

It was actually his first holiday after three years of strenuous work. During much of that time he had frequently been under severe strain, and during all of it he had been busy. He sank into idleness as a man might sink into a warm bath, with the difference that he had not expected to find this relaxation and ease in idleness, and (more important, perhaps) in the cessation of responsibility. Nothing mattered during those golden days. He was the person least concerned in all the ship, as *Pretty Jane* thrashed her way northward, in the burning question as to whether the wind would hold steady to enable her to weather Point Maysi, without having to go about, and he did not care when they did not succeed. He endured philosophically the long beat to windward back towards Haiti, and he smiled patronizingly at the petty jubilation on board when they succeeded on the next tack and passed through the Windward Channel so that they might almost consider themselves out of the Caribbean. A persistent northward slant in the trades kept them from attempting the Caicos Passage, and they had to hold away to the eastward for Silver Bank Passage. Caicos or Silver Bank – or for that matter Turks Island or Mouchoir – he did not care. He did not care whether he arrived home in August or September.

Yet his instincts were only dormant. That evening, when they were truly in the Atlantic, he felt restless and disturbed for the first time since leaving Jamaica. There was something heavy in the breathing of the air, and something unusual about the swell that was rolling the *Pretty Jane* so heavily. A gale before morning, he decided. A little unusual in these latitudes at this time of year, but nothing really to worry about. He did not trouble Barbara with his notions, but he woke several times in the night to find the ship still rolling heavily. When the watch was called he noted that all hands were kept on deck to shorten sail, and he was tempted to go out to see what was happening. A clatter outside awoke Barbara.

'What's that?' she asked, sleepily.

'Only the deadlights, dear,' he answered.

Someone had slammed the deadlights against the deckhouse windows and clamped them home – Knyvett must be expecting to ship some heavy seas. Barbara went back to sleep, and Hornblower actually followed her example, but in half an hour he was awake again. The gale was unceasing, and the ship was working considerably in the swell, so that everything was groaning and creaking. He lay in the darkness to feel the ship heaving and lying-over under him, and he could both hear and actually feel the vibration of the taut standing rigging transmitted to his bunk via the deck. He would like to go out and have a look at the weather, but he did not wish to disturb Barbara.

'Awake, dear?' said a small voice the other side of the deckhouse.

'Yes,' he answered.

'It seems to be getting rough.'

'A little,' he said. 'There's nothing to worry about. Go to sleep again, dear.'

Now he could not go out because Barbara was awake and would know about it. He made himself lie still; it was pitch dark in the deckhouse with the deadlights in, and, perhaps because of the cessation of ventilation, it was now overpoweringly hot despite the gale. *Pretty Jane* was leaping about extravagantly, and every now and then lying over so far that he feared lest Barbara should be rolled out of her bunk. Then he was conscious of a change in the vessel's behaviour, of a difference in the thunderous creaking that filled the darkness. Knyvett had hove the *Pretty Jane* to; she was not lying over, but she was pitching fantastically, indicating a really heavy sea outside. He wanted so much to go out and see for himself. He had no idea even of what the time was – it was far too dark to look at his watch. At the thought that it might be dawn he could restrain himself no longer.

'Awake, dear?' he asked.

'Yes,' said Barbara.

She did not add, 'How could anyone sleep in this din?'

for Barbara lived up to the principle that no person of breeding should ever complain about things he was unable, or unwilling, to do anything to remedy.

'I shall go out on deck if you do not mind my leaving you, dear,' he said.

'Please go if you wish to, of course, dear,' answered Barbara, nor did she add that she wished she could go out too.

Hornblower groped for his trousers and his shoes, and felt his way to the door. Long experience warned him to brace himself as he unfastened it, but even he was a little surprised at the raging wind that awaited him; it was wild even though, with *Pretty Jane* hove-to, the door on the after side was in the lee of the deck-house. He stepped over the coaming and managed to slam the door. The wind was tremendous, but what was more surprising still was its warmth; it seemed to be of brick-kiln heat as it screamed round him. He balanced himself on the heaving deck in the hot, noisy darkness, and timed his rush to the wheel, and he was only just prepared for the extra violence of the wind when he emerged from the lee of the deckhouse. Out of that lee, too, the air was full of flying spray which drenched him and modified his impression of the heat of the air – he was aware of all this by the time he reached the wheel. There were shadowy figures there in the darkness; a white shirt-sleeve waved to him to acknowledge his presence, indicating that Knyvett was there. Hornblower looked into the binnacle; it was really an effort to collect his faculties and make the correct deductions from what he could see of the swinging needle. The wind was blowing from well out to the west of north. Looking up in the darkness he could just make out that the brig was hove-to under the maintopmast staysail, of which only a corner was showing. Knyvett was shouting into his ear.

'Hurricane!'

'Likely enough,' shouted Hornblower in reply. 'Worse before it's better!'

A hurricane had no business to appear at this time of year, a good two months earlier than one should be expected, but that hot breath, the indications of yesterday evening, the direction of the wind at present, all seemed to prove that that was what they were experiencing. It remained to be seen whether they were right in the path of it or only on its fringe. *Pretty Jane* shuddered and lurched drunkenly as a mass of water came in over her bow, gleaming white, almost phosphorescent, as it raced aft at them; Hornblower hung on desperately as it surged past him waist deep – a nasty warning of what might be still to come. They were in very considerable danger. *Pretty Jane* might not endure the pounding she would have to undergo, and in any case, with the considerable leeway she was making they might be cast ashore, and utterly destroyed, on San Domingo or Puerto Rico or some intervening cay. The wind shrieked at them, and a combination of wind and wave laid *Pretty Jane* over, over until the deck was almost vertical, with Hornblower hanging on as his feet could gain no hold on the planking. A wave burst against her exposed bottom clean over her, cascading round them, and then she came slowly back again. No ship would be expected to endure that sort of thing for long. A muffled bang aloft, followed by a series of sharper sounds, attracted his attention to the topmast staysail just as it blew out from its gaskets and flew into ribbons which cracked like whips while they lasted. One thundering small fragment remained, whipping from the stay, just enough to keep *Pretty Jane's* starboard bow to the sea.

Daylight was coming; there was a yellow tinge all about them, shut in by the low sky overhead. As Hornblower looked aloft he saw a hump, a bubble, appear on the mainyard, and the bubble promptly burst into fragments. The wind was tearing the sail from its gaskets. The process was repeated along the yard, as the wind with fingers of steel pried into the solid roll of the sail to tear it loose, rip it open, split it into ribbons, and then tear off the ribbons to whirl them away to leeward. It was hard to believe that a wind could have such power.

It was hard to believe, too, that waves could be so high. A glance at them explained at once the fantastic motion of the ship. They were appalling in their immensity. The one approaching the starboard bow was not as high as a mountain – Hornblower had used the expression 'mountain high' himself, and now, trying to estimate the height, had to admit to himself that it was an exaggeration – but it was as high as a lofty church steeple. It was a colossal ridge of water moving, not with the speed of a racehorse, but with the speed of a hurrying man, straight upon them. *Pretty Jane* lifted her bow to it, lurching and then climbing, rising ever more steeply as she lay upon the towering slope. Up – up – up; she seemed to be almost vertical as she reached the crest, where it was as if the end of the world awaited her. At the crest the wind, temporarily blanketed by the wave, flung itself upon her with redoubled force. Over she lay, over and over, while at the same time her stern heaved itself up as the crest passed under her. Down – down – down; the deck almost vertical, bows down, and almost vertical on her beam, and as she wallowed down the slope minor waves awaited her to burst over her. With the water surging round him waist deep, chest deep, Hornblower felt his legs carried away from under him and he had to hang on with every ounce of his strength to save himself.

Here was the ship's carpenter trying to say something to the captain – it was impossible to speak intelligently in that wind, but he held up one hand with the fingers spread. Five feet of water in the hold, then. But the carpenter repeated the gesture. Then he tried again. Two spreadings of the fingers – ten feet of water, then. It could hardly be the case, but it was true – the heavy heavings of the *Pretty Jane* showed she was water-logged. Then Hornblower remembered the cargo with which she was laden. Logwood and coir; logwood floated only sluggishly, but coir was one of the most buoyant substances known. Coconuts falling into the sea (as they often did, thanks to the palm's penchant for growing at the water's edge) floated for weeks and months, carried about by the currents, so that the wide distribution of the coconut palm was readily accounted for. It was coir that was keeping *Pretty Jane* afloat even though she was full of water. It would keep her afloat for a long time – it would outlast the *Pretty Jane*, for that matter. She would work herself to fragments before the coir allowed her to sink.

So perhaps they had another hour or two of life before them. Perhaps. Another wave, cascading green over *Pretty Jane*'s upturned side, brought a grim warning that it might not be as long as that. And amid the rumble and the roar of the bursting wave, even as he hung on desperately, he was conscious of a succession of other sounds, harder and sharper, and of a jarring of the deck under his feet. The deckhouse! It was lifting on its bolts under the impact of the water. It could not be expected to stand that battering long; it was bound to be swept away, soon. And – Hornblower's visual imagination was feverishly at work – before then its seams would be forced apart, it would fill with water. Barbara would be drowned inside it before the weight of water within tore the deckhouse from its bolts, for the waves to hurl it overside with Barbara's drowned body inside. Clinging to the binnacle Hornblower went through some seconds of mental agony, the worst he had ever known in his life. There had been times and times before when he had faced death for himself, when he had weighed chances, when he had staked his own life, but now it was Barbara's life that he was staking.

To leave her in the deckhouse meant her certain death soon. The alternative was to bring her out upon the waveswept deck. Here, tied to the mast, she would live as long as she could endure the buffeting and the exposure, until the *Pretty Jane* broke up into fragments, possibly. For himself he had played out a losing game to the bitter end more than once; now he had to brace himself to do the same for Barbara. He made the decision. On Barbara's behalf he decided to struggle on as long as was possible. Forcing himself to think logically while the stupefying wind roared round him, he made his plans. He awaited a comparatively calm moment, and then made the perilous brief journey to the foot of the mainmast. Now he worked with frantic rapidity. Two lengths of the maintopsail halliards; he had to keep his head clear to prevent his fumbling fingers from entangling them. Then two desperate journeys, first to the wheel, and then to the deckhouse. He tore open the door and stumbled in over the coaming, the lines in his hands. There were two feet of water in the deckhouse, surging about with the motion of the ship. Barbara was there; he saw her in the light from the door. She had wedged herself as well as she might in her bunk.

'Dearest!' he said. Within the deckhouse it was just possible to be heard, despite the frantic din all round.

'I'm here, dear,' she replied.

Another wave burst over the *Pretty Jane* at that moment; water came pouring in through the gaping seams of the deckhouse and he could feel the whole thing lift again on its bolts and he knew a moment of wild despair at the thought that he might already be too late, that the deckhouse was going to be swept away at this moment with them in it. But it held – the surge of the water as *Pretty Jane* lay over the other way flung Hornblower against the other bulkhead.

'I must get you out of here, dear,' said Hornblower, trying to keep his voice steady. 'You'll be safer tied to the mainmast.'

'As you wish, of course, dear,' said Barbara, calmly.

'I'm going to put these lines round you,' said Hornblower.

Barbara had managed to dress herself in his absence; at any rate she had some sort of dress or petticoat on. Hornblower made fast the lines about her while the ship rolled and swayed under their feet; she held her arms up for him to do so. He knotted the lines round her waist, below her tender bosom.

'Listen carefully,' said Hornblower, and he told her, while they were still in the comparative calm of the deckhouse, what he wanted her to do, how she had to watch her chance, rush to the wheel, and from there to the mainmast.

'I understand, dear,' said Barbara. 'Kiss me once more, my very dearest.'

He kissed her hurriedly, his lips against her dripping cheek. It was only the most perfunctory kiss. To Hornblower's subconscious mind Barbara in making her request was risking their lives for it – staking ten thousand future kisses against one immediate one. It was womanlike for her to do so, but odds of ten thousand to one had no appeal for Hornblower. And still she lingered.

'Dearest, I've always loved you,' she said; she was speaking hurriedly and yet with no proper regard for the value of time. 'I've loved no one but you in all my life. I had another husband once. I couldn't say this before because it would have been disloyal. But now – I've never loved anyone but you. Never. Only you, darling.'

'Yes, dear,' said Hornblower. He heard the words, but at that urgent moment he could not give them their rightful consideration. 'Stand here. Hold on to this. Hold on!'

It was only a lesser wave that swept by them.

'Wait for my signal!' bellowed Hornblower into Barbara's ear, and then he made the hurried dash to the binnacle. One group of men had bound themselves to the wheel.

There was a frantic moment as he looked about him. He waved, and then Barbara crossed the heaving deck as he took up on the line. He had just time to fling a bight round her and pull it tight and seize hold himself as the next crest burst over the ship. Over – over – over. Sluggishly the *Pretty Jane* wallowed up again. He had an idea that one man at least was missing from the group at the wheel, but there was no time to think about that, for there was the passage to the mainmast still to be accomplished.

At last that was done. There were four men there already, but he was able to make Barbara as secure as possible, and then himself. *Pretty Jane* lay over again, and again; it was at some time shortly after this that a fresh monstrous wave swept away the deckhouse and half the ship's rail – Hornblower saw the wreckage go off to leeward, and noted the fact, dully. He had been right in taking Barbara away from there.

It may have been the loss of the deckhouse that called his attention to the behaviour of the *Pretty Jane*. She was lying in the trough of the sea, not riding with her bows to the waves. The loss of the windage of the deckhouse, right aft, perhaps made this more noticeable. She was rolling wildly and deeply in consequence, and was being swept by the waves more thoroughly. She could not be expected to survive this for long, nor could the miserable human beings on her deck – of whom Barbara was one and he was another. The *Pretty Jane* would rack herself to pieces before long. Something was needed to keep her bows to the sea. In the normal way a small area of canvas exposed right aft would bring this about, but no canvas would stand against that wind, as had been early demonstrated. In the present circumstances the pressure of the wind against the foremast and bowsprit with their standing rigging balanced that against the mainmast, keeping her lying broadside on to wind and wave. If canvas could not be exposed aft then the windage forward must be reduced instead. The foremast should be cut away. Then the pressure on the mainmast would bring her bows on to the sea, increasing her chances, while the loss of the mast would perhaps ease the roll as well. There was no doubt about it; the mast should be cut away, instantly.

Aft there was Knyvett, bound to the wheel, no more than a few feet away; it was his decision as captain. As *Pretty Jane* wallowed to bring her deck horizontal for a moment, with water no more than knee deep over it, Hornblower waved to him. He pointed forward to the weather-foremast shrouds; he gesticulated, he thought he conveyed his meaning clearly enough, but Knyvett showed no sign of understanding. He certainly made no move to act upon the suggestion. He merely gazed stupidly and then looked away. Hornblower felt a moment of fury; the next roll and submergence made up his mind for him. The discipline of the sea might be disregarded in the face of this indifference and incompetence.

But the other men beside him at the mainmast were as indifferent as Knyvett. He could not rouse them to join him in the effort. They had a momentary safety here at the mast, and they would not leave it; probably they could not understand what he had in mind. That outrageous wind was perfectly stupefying as it screamed round them, and the constant deluges of water, and the desperate need to struggle for a footing, gave them no chance to collect their thoughts.

An axe would perhaps be best to cut those shrouds, but there was no axe. The man beside him had a knife in a sheath at his belt. Hornblower put his hand on the hilt, and made himself think reasonably again. He tested the edge, found it sharp, and then unbuckled belt and all and rebuckled it about his own waist – the man offering no objection, merely gazing stupidly at him as he did so. Again there was need to plan, to think clearly, in the howling wind and the driving spray and the solid water that surged round him. He cut himself two lengths of line from the raffle about him, and made each of them fast round his chest with an end hanging free. Then he looked over to the foremast shrouds, planning again. There would be no time to think things out when the moment for action began. A length of the rail still survived its battering there – presumably the weather shrouds had acted as some sort of breakwater to it. He eyed and measured the distance. He eased the knots that held him to the mast. He spared a glance at Barbara, forcing himself to smile. She was standing there in her bonds; the hurricane was blowing her long hair, wet though it was, straight out horizontally from her head. He put another line about her to make her secure. There was nothing else he could do. This was Bedlam, this was insanity, this was a wet, shrieking hell, and yet a hell in which he had to keep his head clear.

He watched his moment. First he almost misjudged it, and had to draw back, swallowing hard in the tense excitement, before the next wave engulfed him. As it surged away he watched *Pretty Jane*'s motion again, set his teeth, and cast off his bonds and made the rush up the steep deck – wave and deck offering him a lee which saved him from being blown away by the wind. He reached the rail with five seconds to spare – five seconds in which to secure himself, to knot himself to the shrouds as the crest burst over him, in a torrent of water which first swept his legs from under him, and next tore his grip loose so that for a second or two only the lines held him before an eddy enabled him to re-establish his grip.

Pretty Jane wallowed clear again. It was awkward to fasten the lanyard of the sheath knife to his wrist, but he had to consume precious moments in doing so; otherwise all his efforts so far would be wasted in ridiculous failure. Now he was sawing desperately at the shroud; the soaked fibres seemed like iron, but he felt them part little by little, a few fibres at a time. He was glad he had made sure the knife was sharp. He had half-severed the rope before the next deluge burst over him. The moment his shoulders were clear of the water he continued to saw at the rope; he could feel, as he cut, a slight variation of tension as the ship rolled and the shroud faintly slackened. He wondered if, when the rope parted, it would fly dangerously, and he decided that as long as the other shrouds held the reaction would not be too violent.

So it proved; the shroud simply vanished under his knife – the wind caught its fifty-foot length and whirled it away out of his world, presumably blowing it out as a streamer from the masthead. He set about the next, sawing away in the intervals of being submerged under the crashing waves. He cut and he hung on; he struggled for air in the driving spray, he choked and suffocated under the green water, but one shroud after another parted under his knife. The knife was losing its edge, and now he was faced with an additional problem; he had severed nearly every shroud – the aftermost ones – within reach and soon he would have to shift his position to reach the foremost ones. But he did not have to solve that problem after all. At the next roll and the next wave, actually while he was struggling under water, he was conscious of a series of shocks transmitted through the fabric of the ship through his clutching hands – four minor ones and then a violent one. As the wave fell away from him his swimming eyes could see what had happened. The four remaining shrouds had parted under the strain, one, two, three, four, and then the mast had snapped off; looking back over his shoulder he could see the stump standing eight feet above the deck.

The difference it made to the *Pretty Jane* was instantly apparent. The very next roll ended half-heartedly in a mere violent pitch, as the shrieking wind, acting upon her mainmast, pushed her stern round and brought her bows to the sea, while the loss of the leverage of the lofty foremast reduced the amplitude of the roll in any case. The sea that broke over Hornblower's head was almost negligible in violence and quantity. Hornblower could breathe, he could look about him. He observed something else; the foremast, still attached to the ship by the lee shrouds, was now dragging ahead of her as she made stern way through the water under the impulse of the wind. It was acting as a sea-anchor, a very slight restraint upon the extravagance of her motions; moreover, as the point of attachment was on the port side, she was slightly turned so that she met the waves a trifle on her port bow, so that she was riding at the best possible angle, with a very slight roll and a long pitch. Waterlogged though she was, she still had a chance – and Hornblower on the starboard bow was comparatively sheltered and able to contemplate his handiwork with some sort of pride.

He looked across at the pitiful groups of people, clustering bound to the mainmast and the wheel and binnacle; Barbara was out of his sight in the group at the mainmast, hidden from him by the men there, and he was consumed with a sudden anxiety lest further mishap might have befallen her. He began to cast himself loose to return to her, and it was then, with the cessation of the all-consuming preoccupation regarding the ship, that a sudden recollection struck him, so forcibly that he actually paused with his fingers on the knots. Barbara had kissed him, in the lee of the vanished deckhouse. And she had said – Hornblower remembered well what she had said; it had lain stored in his memory until this moment, awaiting his attention when there should be a lull in the need for violent action. She had not merely said that she loved him; she had said she had never loved anyone else. Hornblower, huddled on the deck of a waterlogged ship with a hurricane shrieking round him, was suddenly aware that an old hurt was healed, that he would never again feel that dull ache of jealousy of Barbara's first husband, never, as long as he lived.

That was enough to bring him back to the world of practical affairs. The remaining length of his life might well be measured in hours. He would more likely than not be dead by nightfall, or by tomorrow at latest. And so would Barbara. So would Barbara. The absurd tiny feeling of well-being that had sprung up within him was instantly destroyed and replaced by a frantic sorrow and a despair that was almost overwhelming. He had to exert all his willpower to make himself master of his drooping body again, and of his weary mind. He had to act and to think, as though he was not exhausted and as though he did not despair. The discovery that the sheath knife still dangled at his wrist awoke the self-contempt that invariably stimulated him; he untied the lanyard and secured the knife in its sheath before setting himself to study the motion of the *Pretty Jane*.

He cast himself loose and dashed for the mainmast. The tremendous wind might well have carried him clean aft and overboard, but the upheaving of the stern checked his progress sufficiently for him to swing into the lee of the group at the mainmast and to clutch one of the lines there and hang on. The men there, hanging apathetic in their lashings, spared him hardly a glance and made no move to help him. Barbara, her wet hair streaming out sideways, had a smile and a hand for him, and he forced his way into the group beside her and bound himself next to her. He took her hand in his again, and was reassured by the return of the pressure he gave it. Then there was nothing to do except to remain alive.

Part of the process of remaining alive was not to think about being thirsty, as the day wore on and the yellow daylight was replaced by black night. It was hard not to do so, once he had realized how thirsty he was, and now he had a new torment when he thought that Barbara was suffering in that way, too. There was nothing he could do about that at all, nothing, except to stand in his bonds and endure along with her. With the coming of night, however, the wind lost its brick-kiln heat and blew almost chilly, so that Hornblower found himself shivering a little. He turned in his bonds and put his arms round Barbara, holding her to him to conserve her bodily warmth. It was during the night that he was troubled by the behaviour of the man next to him, who persisted in leaning against him, more and more heavily, so that repeatedly Hornblower had to take his arms from around Barbara and thrust him fiercely away. At the third or fourth of those thrusts he felt the man fall limply away from him and guessed he was dead. That made a little more room about the mast, and he could put Barbara squarely against it, where she could lean back with her shoulders supported. Hornblower could guess that she would find that a help, judging by the agonizing cramp in his legs, and the utter weariness of every part of his body. There was a temptation, a terrible temptation, to give up, to let everything go, to let himself fall to the deck and die like the man beside him. But he would not; that was for the sake of the wife in his arms more than for himself; because of his love rather than because of his pride.

With the change in the temperature of the wind came a gradual moderation in its violence; Hornblower, during those black hours, would not allow himself to hope at first, but he became more and more convinced of it as the night wore on. At last there was no denying the fact. The wind was dying away – the hurricane was moving away from them, most likely. Some time during the night it was only a strong gale, and later on Hornblower, lifting his head, made himself admit that it was nothing more than a fresh breeze which would call for only a single reef – a topgallant breeze, in fact. The motion of the *Pretty Jane* continued to be violent, as was only to be expected; the sea would take much longer to die away than would the wind. She was still pitching and plunging wildly, heaving up and racing down, but she was not being swept by the waves to nearly such a great extent, even allowing for her improved behaviour, bows to sea. It was not great cataracts of water that came surging by them, dragging them against their bonds to lacerate their skin. The water ceased to be waist high; later on it only surged past their knees and the spray had ceased to drive past them.

With that Hornblower was able to notice something else. It was raining, raining in torrents. If he turned his face to the sky a few precious drops fell into his parched, open mouth.

'Rain!' he said into Barbara's ear.

He released himself from her arms – he did it actually roughly, so anxious was he not to waste a single second of this rainstorm. He took off his shirt – it tore into rags as he dragged it from the lines that encompassed him – and held it out in the invisible rain that lashed down on them in the darkness. He must not waste a second. The shirt was wet with seawater; he wrung it out, working over it feverishly, alternately with spreading it in the rain. He squeezed a fragment into his mouth; it was still salt. He tried again. He had never wished for anything so much as now, for the rainstorm to continue in this violence and for the sea spray not to be driving too thickly. The water he wrung from the fragment of shirt could be considered fresh now. He felt for Barbara's face with the sopping wet object, pressing it against her.

'Drink!' he croaked into her ear.

When she put up her hands to it he guessed from her movements that she understood, that she was sucking the precious liquid from the fabric. He wanted her to hurry, to drink all she could, while the rain persisted; his hands were shaking with desire. In the darkness she would not know that he was waiting so anxiously. She yielded the shirt back to him at last, and he spread it to the rain again, hardly able to endure the delay. Then he could press it to his mouth, head back, and gulp and swallow, half mad with pleasure. The difference it made to squeeze that water into his mouth was beyond measure.

He felt strength and hope returning – the strength came with the hope. Perhaps that shirt held five or six wineglassfuls of water; it was sufficient to make this vast difference. He spread the shirt again above his head, to soak it again in the torrential rain, and gave it to Barbara, and when she returned it to him in the darkness he repeated the process for himself. And when he had squeezed it almost dry he realized that while he was doing so the rain had ceased, and he felt a moment's regret. He should have saved that wet shirt as a reserve, but he ceased to chide himself. Most of the water in it would have drained out, and there was still enough spray in the air to have made the remainder undrinkable in a few minutes.

But now he could think better; he could soberly decide that the wind was moderating fast – the rainstorm itself was an indication that the hurricane had gone on its way, leaving in its wake the prodigious rains that were not unusual then. And there, over the starboard bow, was the faintest hint of pink in the sky, not the threatening yellow of the hurricane, but the dawn of a different day. He felt for the knots that held him bound, and by slow degrees he fumbled them undone. As the last one released him he staggered back with the heave of the ship, and sank back with a thump and a splash into a sitting position on the wet deck. That was a fantastic pleasure, to sit down, hip deep in the water still washing over the deck. Just to sit, and very slowly flex and straighten his knees, to feel life returning into his dead thighs; that was heaven, and it would be a seventh heaven to put his head down and allow sleep to overcome him.

That was something he must not do, all the same. Sleeplessness and physical fatigue were things that must be stoically ignored, as long as there was a chance that they would survive, and daylight increasing round them. He heaved himself up to his feet and walked back to the mast on legs that would hardly obey him. He released Barbara, and she at least could sit down, deck awash or not. He eased her until her back was to the mast and then passed a line around her again. She could sleep in that fashion; she was already so weary that she did not notice – or she gave no sign of it if she did – the doubled-up corpse that lay within a yard of her. He cut the corpse loose and dragged it with the heave of the ship out of the way, before attending to the other three there. They were already fumbling with the knots of their lashings, and as Hornblower began to cut the lines first one and then another opened their mouths and croaked at him.

'Water!' they said. 'Water!'

They were as helpless and as dependent as nestlings. It was apparent to Hornblower that not one of them had had the sense, during that roaring rainstorm in the dark, to soak his shirt; they could hardly have failed to have held up open mouths to the rain, but what they would catch then would be a trifle. He looked round the horizon. One or two distant squalls were visible there, but there was no predicting when or if they would pass over the *Pretty Jane*.

'You'll have to wait for that, my lads,' he said.

He made his way aft to the other group around the wheel and binnacle. There was a corpse here still hanging in its lashings – Knyvett. Hornblower took note of the fact, with the terse requiem that perhaps with death overpowering him there might be some excuse for his not attempting to cut away the foremast. Another corpse lay on the deck, among the feet of the six survivors here. Nine men had survived of the crew of sixteen, and apparently four had disappeared entirely, washed overboard during the night, or perhaps during the night before. Hornblower recognized the second mate and the steward; the group, even the second mate, were croaking for water just like the others, and to them Hornblower made the same grim reply.

'Get those dead men overboard,' he added.

He took stock of the situation. Looking over the side he could see that *Pretty Jane* had about three feet of freeboard remaining, as close as he could judge while she was pitching extravagantly in the still-turbulent sea. He was conscious now, as he walked about right aft, of dull thumpings under his feet corresponding to the heave and the roll. That meant floating objects battering on the underside of the deck as they were flung up against it by the water inside surging about. The wind was steady from the north-east – the trade wind had reasserted itself after the temporary interruption of the hurricane; the sky was still gloomy and overcast, but Hornblower could feel in his bones that the barometer must be rising rapidly. Somewhere down to leeward, fifty miles away, a hundred miles, two hundred perhaps, was the chain of the Antilles – he could not guess how far, or in what direction, *Pretty Jane* had drifted during the storm. There was still a chance for them, or there would be if he could solve the water problem.

He turned to the tottering crew.

'Get the hatches up,' he ordered. 'You, Mr Mate, where are the water casks stowed?'

'Amidships,' said the mate, running a dry tongue over his dry lips at the thought of water. 'Aft of the main hatchway.'

'Let's see,' said Hornblower.

Water casks constructed to keep fresh water in would also perhaps keep seawater out. But no cask was ever quite tight; every cask leaked to some extent, and only a small amount of water percolating in would make the contents unfit to drink. And casks that had been churned about for two nights and a day by the surging seawater below decks would probably be stove in, every one of them.

'It's only a faint hope,' said Hornblower, anxious to minimize the almost certain disappointment ahead of them; he looked round again to see what chance there was of a rain-squall coming.

When they looked down the open hatchway they could appreciate the difficulties. The hatchway was jammed with a couple of bales of coir; as they watched them they could see them move uneasily with the motion of the ship. The water that had invaded the ship had floated up the cargo – *Pretty Jane* was actually supported by the upward pressure of the cargo on the underside of the deck. It was a miracle that she had not broken her back. And there was not a chance of going down there. It would be certain death to venture amid those surging bales. There was a general groan of disappointment from the group round the hatchway.

But another possibility was present in Hornblower's mind, and he turned upon the steward.

'There were green coconuts for the use of the cabin,' he said. 'Were there any left?'

'Yes, sir. Four or five dozen.' The man could hardly speak, with thirst, or weakness, or excitement.

'In the lazarette?'

'Yes, sir.'

'In a sack?'

'Yes, sir.'

'Come along,' said Hornblower.

Coconuts floated as lightly as coir, and were more watertight than any cask.

They pried up the after-hatch cover, and looked down at the heaving water below. There was no cargo there; the bulkhead had stood the strain. The distance down to the surface corresponded to the three-foot freeboard remaining to *Pretty Jane*. There were things to be seen there – almost at once a wooden piggin came floating into sight, and the surface was nearly covered with fragments. Then something else floated into view – a coconut. Apparently the sack had not been fastened – Hornblower had hoped he might find a whole sackful floating there. He leaned far down and scooped it up. As he rose to his feet again with the thing in his hand there was a simultaneous wordless croak from the whole group; a dozen hands stretched out for it, and Hornblower realized that he must maintain order.

'Stand back!' he said, and when the men still advanced on him he pulled out his sheath knife.

'Stand back! I'll kill the first man to lay a hand on me!' he said. He knew himself to be snarling like a wild beast, his teeth bared with the intensity of his feeling, and he knew that he would stand no chance in fight, one against nine.

'Come now, lads,' he said. 'We'll have to make these last. We'll ration 'em out. Fair divs all round. See how many more you can find.'

The force of his personality asserted itself; so did what remained of the common sense of the crew, and they drew back. Soon three men were kneeling round the hatchway, with the others leaning precariously over them to look over their shoulders.

'There's one!' croaked a voice.

An arm went down and a coconut was scooped up.

'Give it here,' said Hornblower, and he was obeyed without question; another was already visible, and another after that. They began to pile up at Hornblower's feet, a dozen, fifteen, twenty, twenty-three of the precious things, before they ceased to appear further.

'With luck we'll find some more later,' said Hornblower. He looked round the group, and over at Barbara huddled at the foot of the mainmast. 'Eleven of us. Half a one each for today. Another half each tomorrow. And I'll go without for today.'

No one questioned his decision – partly, perhaps, because they were all too anxious to wet their lips. The first coconut was chopped open at the end, with desperate care lest a drop be spilt, and the first man took a drink. There was no chance at all of his drinking more than his half, with everyone grouped round him, and the man destined for the other half snatching it from his lips at every sip to see how far down the surface had sunk. The men forced to wait were wild with eagerness, but they had to wait all the same. Hornblower could not trust them to make a division without fighting or waste unless he was supervising. After the last man had drunk he took the remaining half over to Barbara.

'Drink this, dear,' he said, as at the touch of his hand she blinked awake from her heavy doze.

She drank eagerly before she took the nut from her lips.

'You've had some, dear?' she asked.

'Yes, dear, I've had mine,' said Hornblower steadily.

When he returned to the group they were scraping the thin jelly out from inside the nuts.

'Don't damage these shells, lads,' he said. 'We'll need 'em when we get a rain-squall. And we'll put those nuts under Her Ladyship's guard. We can trust her.'

They obeyed him again.

'We got two more up while you was away, sir,' volunteered one of the men.

Hornblower peered down the hatchway at the litter-covered water. Another idea came up into his mind, and he turned to the steward again.

'Her Ladyship sent a chest of food on board,' he said. 'Food in tin boxes. It was put aft here somewhere. Do you know where?'

'It was right aft, sir. Under the tiller ropes.'

'M'm,' said Hornblower.

As he thought about it a sudden motion of the ship tossed the water below up in a fountain through the hatchway. But it ought to be possible to reach that chest, break it open, and bring up its contents. A strong man, able to stay submerged for long periods, could do it, if he did not mind being flung about by the send of the water below.

'We'd have something better to eat than coconut jelly if we got those boxes up,' he said.

'I'll have a go, sir,' said a young seaman, and Hornblower was inexpressibly relieved. He did not want to go down there himself.

'Good lad,' he said. 'Put a line round yourself before you go down. Then we can haul you out if we have to.'

They were setting about their preparations when Hornblower checked them.

'Wait. Look for'rard!' he said.

There was a rain-squall a mile away. They could see it, a vast pillar of water to windward streaming down from the sky, well defined; the cloud was lower whence it fell, and the surface of the sea which received it was a different grey from the rest. It was moving down towards them – no, not quite. The centre was heading for a point some distance on their beam, as everyone could see after a moment's study. There was an explosion of blasphemy from the grouped hands as they watched.

'We'll get the tail of it, by God!' said the mate.

'Make the most of it when it comes,' said Hornblower.

For three long minutes they watched it approach. A cable's length away it seemed to stand still, even though they could feel the freshening breeze around them. Hornblower had run to Barbara's side.

'Rain,' he said.

Barbara turned her face to the mast, and bent down and fumbled under her skirt. A moment's struggle brought down a petticoat, and she stepped out of it and did her best to wring the salt damp out of it as they waited. Then came a few drops, and then the full deluge. Precious rain; ten shirts and a petticoat were extended to it, wrung out, re-extended, wrung out again, until the wringings tasted fresh. Everyone could drink, madly, with the rain roaring about them. After two minutes of it Hornblower was shouting to the crew to fill the empty coconut shells, and a few men had sense and public spirit enough to wring their shirts into them before returning to the ecstasy of drinking again – no one wanted to waste a single second of this precious rain. But it passed as quickly as it came; they could see the squall going away over the quarter, as far out of their reach as if it were raining in the Sahara Desert. But the young hands of the crew were laughing and joking now; there was an end to their care and their apathy. There was not one man on board except Hornblower who spared a thought for the possibility, the probability, that this might be the only rain-squall to touch the ship for the next week. There was urgent need for action, even though every joint and muscle in his body ached, even though his mind was clouded with weariness. He made himself think; he made himself rally his strength. He cut short the silly laughter, and turned on the man who had volunteered to venture down into the steerage.

'Put two men to tend your line. The steward had better be one of 'em,' he said. 'Mr Mate, come for'rard with me. We want to get sail on this ship as soon as may be.'

That was the beginning of a voyage which was destined to become legendary, just as did the hurricane which had just passed – it was called Hornblower's Hurricane, singled out not only because Hornblower was involved in it but also because its unexpected arrival caused widespread damage. Hornblower never thought that the voyage itself was particularly notable, even though it was made in a waterlogged hulk precariously balanced upon bales of coir. It was only a matter of getting the hulk before the wind; a spare jib-boom (the only spare spar surviving the storm) made a jury mast when fished to the stump of the foremast, and the sacking from coir bales provided sails. Spread on the jury foremast these enabled them to get the *Pretty Jane* before the trade wind, to creep along at a mile an hour while they set to work on extemporizing after-sails that doubled her speed.

There were no navigating instruments – even the compass had been dashed from its gimbals during the storm – and on the first two days they had no idea where they were, except that somewhere to leeward lay the chain of the Antilles, but the third day proved fine and clear and dawn had hardly broken before a hand at the mainmasthead saw the faintest, tiniest dark streak on the horizon far ahead. It was land; it might be the high mountains of San Domingo far off, or the low mountains of Puerto Rico somewhat nearer; there was no knowing at present, and even when the sun had set they were still ignorant – and they were thirsty, with small appetite for the meagre ration of corned beef that Hornblower doled out to them from the recovered stores.

And despite fatigue they could sleep that night on their coir mattresses on the deck that an occasional small wave still swept. Next morning the land was nearer still, a low profile that seemed to indicate it might be Puerto Rico, and it was in the afternoon that they saw the fishing-boat. It headed for them, puzzled at the strange vessel bearing down on them, and it was not long before it was alongside, the mulatto fishermen staring at the group of strange figures waving to them. Hornblower had to urge his dazed mind, stupid with lack of sleep and fatigue and hunger, to remember his Spanish as he hailed them. They had a breaker of water on board, and they had a jar of cold garbanzos as well; there was a can of corned beef to add to the feast. Barbara caught, even though she spoke no Spanish, two words of the excited conversation that went on.

'Puerto Rico?' she asked.

'Yes, dear,' said Hornblower. 'Not very surprising – and much more convenient for us than San Domingo. I wish I could remember the name of the Captain-General there – I had dealings with him in the affair of the *Estrella del Sur*. He was a marquis. The Marques de – de – Dearest, why don't you lie down and close your eyes? You're worn out.'

He was shocked anew at her pallor and look of distress.

'I'm well enough, thank you, dear,' replied Barbara, even though the strained tone of her voice denied her words. It was one more proof of her indomitable spirit.

It was when they were discussing what to do next that the second mate showed the first sign of any spirit. They could all desert the waterlogged hulk and sail into Puerto Rico in the fishing-boat, but he stoutly refused to do so. He knew the law about salvage, and there might be some value still in the poor hull, and certainly in its cargo. He would work the *Pretty Jane* in tomorrow himself, and he insisted on staying on board with the hands.

Hornblower faced a decision of a sort he had never yet encountered in a varied career. To leave the ship now savoured of desertion, but there was Barbara to think of. And his first reaction, that he would not dream of deserting his men, was promptly ended by his reminding himself that they were not 'his men' at all.

'You're only a passenger, my lord,' said the mate – it was odd how 'my lord' seemed to come naturally again now that they were in touch with civilization.

'That's so,' agreed Hornblower. Nor could he possibly condemn Barbara to another night on the deck of this waterlogged hulk.

So they came sailing into San Juan de Puerto Rico, two years after Hornblower had last visited the place in very different circumstances. Not unnaturally their arrival set the whole place in an uproar. Messengers sped to the Fortaleza, and it was only a few minutes later that a figure appeared on the quay which Hornblower's swimming eyes contrived to recognize, tall and thin, with a thin moustache.

'Mendez-Castillo,' he said, saving Hornblower any further trouble about remembering his name. 'It grieves me greatly to see Your Excellencies in such distress, even while I have much pleasure in welcoming Your Excellency again to Puerto Rico.'

Some sort of formalities had to be observed, even in these conditions.

'Barbara, my dear, allow me to present Señor – Major – Mendez-Castillo, aide-de-camp to His Excellency the Captain-General.' Then he continued in Spanish. 'My wife, la Baronesa Hornblower.'

Mendez-Castillo bowed deeply, his eyes still busy estimating the extent of the weakness of the new arrivals. Then he reached the very important decision.

'If Your Excellencies are agreeable, I would suggest that your formal welcome by His Excellency should be postponed until Your Excellencies are better prepared for it.'

'We are agreeable,' said Hornblower. In his exasperation he was about to burst out violently regarding Barbara's need for rest and care, but Mendez-Castillo, now that the point of etiquette was settled, was all consideration.

'Then if Your Excellencies will give yourselves the trouble of stepping down into my boat I shall have the pleasure of escorting you to make your informal entrance into the Palace of Santa Catalina. Their Excellencies will receive you, but formal etiquette need not be observed, and Your Excellencies will be able to recover from the dreadful experiences I fear Your Excellencies have undergone. Would Your Excellencies be so kind as to come this way?'

'One moment, first, if you please, *señor*. The men out there in the ship. They need food and water. They may need help.'

'I will give an order for the port authorities to send out to them what they need.'

'Thank you.'

So they went down into the boat for the brief trip across the harbour; despite his mortal fatigue Hornblower was able to note that every fishing-boat and coasting craft there was hurriedly getting to sea, presumably to examine the chances of salvaging or plundering the *Pretty Jane*; the second mate had been perfectly right in refusing to leave her. But he did not care, now. He put his arm about Barbara as she drooped beside him. Then up through the water-gate of the Palace, with attentive servants awaiting them. Here were His Excellency and a dark, beautiful woman, his wife: she took Barbara under her protection instantly. Here were cool, dark rooms, and more servants scurrying about in obedience to the orders His Excellency volleyed out. Valets and maids and body servants.

'This is Manuel, my principal valet, Your Excellency. Any orders Your Excellency may give him will be obeyed as if they came from me. My physician has been sent for and will be here at any moment. So now my wife and I will withdraw and leave Your Excellencies to rest, assuring Your Excellencies that our sincerest hope is for your rapid recovery.'

The crowd thinned away. For one more moment Hornblower had to keep his faculties alert, for the doctor came bustling in, to feel pulses and to look at tongues. He produced a case of lancets and was making preparations to draw blood from Barbara and it was only with difficulty that Hornblower stopped him, and with further difficulty prevented him from substituting leeches for venesection. He could not believe that bleeding would hasten the cure of the lacerations Barbara bore on her body. He thanked the doctor and saw him out of the room again with a sigh of relief and mental reservations regarding the medicines he promised to send in. The maids were waiting to relieve Barbara of the few rags she wore.

'Do you think you will sleep, darling? Is there anything more I can ask for?'

'I shall sleep, dearest.' Then the smile on Barbara's weary face was replaced by something more like a grin, perfectly unladylike. 'And as nobody else but us here can speak English I am free to tell you that I love you, dearest. I love you, I love you, more than any words that I know can tell you.'

Servants or no servants, he kissed her then before he left her to go into the adjoining room where the valets awaited him. His body was criss-crossed with angry welts still raw where, during the storm, the force of the waves had flung him against the ropes that held him to the mast. They were horribly painful as he was sponged with warm water. He knew that Barbara's sweet, tender body must be marked in the same fashion. But Barbara was safe; she would soon be well, and she had said that she loved him. – And – and she had said more than that. What she had told him in that deckhouse had drawn out all the pain from a mental wound far, far, deeper than the physical hurts he now bore. He was a happy man as he lay down in the silk nightshirt with the elaborate heraldic embroidery which the valet had ready for him. His sleep was at first deep and untroubled, but conscience awoke him before dawn, and he went out on to the balcony in the first light, to see the *Pretty Jane* creeping into the harbour, escorted by a dozen small craft. It irked him that he was not on board, until he thought again of the wife sleeping in the next room.

There were happy hours still to come. That balcony was deep and shaded, looking out over harbour and sea, and there he sat in his dressing gown an hour later, rocking idly in his chair, with Barbara opposite him, drinking sweet chocolate and eating sweet rolls.

'It is good to be alive,' said Hornblower; there was a potency, an inner meaning, about those words now – it was no hackneyed turn of speech.

'It is good to be with you,' said Barbara.

'*Pretty Jane* came in this morning safely,' said Hornblower.

'I peeped out at her through my window,' said Barbara.

Mendez-Castillo was announced, presumably having been warned that His Excellency's guests were awake and breakfasting. He made enquiries on behalf of His Excellency, to receive every assurance of a rapid recovery, and he announced that news of the recent events would be dispatched at once to Jamaica.

'Most kind of His Excellency,' said Hornblower. 'Now, as regards the crew of the *Pretty Jane*. Are they being looked after?'

'They have been received into the military hospital. The port authorities have stationed a guard on board the vessel.'

'That is very well indeed,' said Hornblower, telling himself that now he need feel no more responsibility.

The morning could be an idle one now, only broken by a visit from the doctor, to be dismissed, after a new feeling of pulses and looking at tongues, with grateful thanks for his untasted medicines. There was dinner at two o'clock, a vast meal served ceremoniously but only sampled. A siesta, and then supper eaten with more appetite, and a peaceful night.

Next morning was busier, for there was now the question of clothes to be dealt with. Dressmakers were sent in to Barbara by Her Excellency, so that Hornblower found all the mental exercise he needed in acting as interpreter over matters demanding a vocabulary he did not possess, and shirt-makers and tailors sent in to him by His Excellency. The tailor was somewhat disappointed on being told that Hornblower did not wish him to make a complete uniform for a British Rear Admiral, gold lace and all. As a half-pay officer, with no appointment, Hornblower did not need anything of the sort.

After the tailor came a deputation, the mate and two members of the crew of *Pretty Jane*.

'We've come to enquire after Your Lordship's health, and Her Ladyship's,' said the mate.

'Thank you. You can see Her Ladyship and I are quite recovered,' said Hornblower. 'And you? Are you being well looked after?'

'Very well, thank you.'

'You're master of the *Pretty Jane* now,' commented Hornblower.

'Yes, my lord.'

It was a strange first command for a man to have.

'What are you going to do with her?'

'I'm having her hauled out today, my lord. Maybe she can be patched up. But she'll have lost all her copper.'

'Very likely.'

'I expect I'll have to sell her for what she'll fetch, hull and cargo,' said the mate, with a note of bitterness in his voice – that was to be expected in a man who had received his first command only to face losing it instantly.

'I hope you're lucky,' said Hornblower.

'Thank you, my lord.' There was a moment's hesitation before the next words came. 'And I have to thank Your Lordship for all you did.'

'The little I did I did for my own sake and Her Ladyship's,' said Hornblower.

He could smile as he said it; already, in these blissful surroundings, the memory of the howl of the hurricane and the crash of the waves sweeping *Pretty Jane*'s deck was losing its painful acuteness. And the two seamen could grin back at him. Here in a vice-regal palace it was hard to remember how he had stood, with bared teeth and drawn knife, disputing with them possession of a single green coconut. It was pleasant that the interview could end with smiles and goodwill, so that Hornblower could lapse back into delightful idleness with Barbara beside him.

Seamstresses and tailors must have worked hard and long, for next day some of the results of their efforts were ready to be tried on.

'My Spanish grandee!' said Barbara, eyeing her husband dressed in coat and breeches of Puerto Rican cut.

'My lovely *señora*,' answered Hornblower with a bow. Barbara was wearing comb and mantilla.

'The *señoras* of Puerto Rico wear no stays, fortunately,' said Barbara. 'I could bear nothing of the sort at present.'

That was one of the few allusions Barbara made regarding the lacerations and bruises that she bore all over her body. She was of a Spartan breed, trained in a school which scorned to admit physical weakness. Even in making her mock-formal curtsey to him as she spoke she was careful to betray none of the pain the movement cost her; Hornblower could hardly guess at it.

'What am I to tell Mendez-Castillo today when he comes to make his enquiries?' asked Hornblower.

'I think, dear, that now we can safely be received by Their Excellencies,' said Barbara.

Here in little Puerto Rico was to be found all the magnificence and ceremonial of the court of Spain. The Captain-General was the representative of a king in whose veins ran the blood of Bourbons and Habsburgs, of Ferdinand and Isabella, and his person had to be surrounded by the same ritual and etiquette, lest the mystic sanctity of his master should be called into question. Even Hornblower did not come to realize, until he began to discuss the arrangements with Mendez-Castillo, the enormous condescension, the extreme strain put upon palace etiquette, involved in the backstairs visit Their Excellencies had paid to the battered castaways who had claimed their hospitality. Now that was all to be forgotten in their formal reception.

There was amusement to be found in Mendez-Castillo's apologetic and nervous mentioning of the fact that Hornblower could not expect the same formalities as had welcomed him on his last visit. Then he had been a visiting commander-in-chief; now he was only a half-pay officer, a distinguished visitor (Mendez-Castillo hastened to add) but an unofficial one. It dawned upon him that Mendez-Castillo expected him to flare out and to be offended at being told that this time he would be received only by flourishes and not by a full band, by the salutes of the sentries instead of by the turning out of the whole guard. He was able to confirm his reputation for tact by declaring quite truthfully – his candour was mistaken for the most diplomatic concealment of his own feelings – that he did not care in the least.

So it turned out. Barbara and Hornblower were smuggled unobtrusively out of the postern gate of the Palace and escorted into a boat, to be rowed round to the massive water-gate where Hornblower had made his previous entrance. There with slow and solemn step they passed in through the gate, Barbara on Hornblower's left arm. On either hand the sentries presented arms and Hornblower acknowledged the salute by taking off his hat. As they came into the courtyard beyond they were welcomed by the flourishes that Mendez-Castillo had promised. Even Hornblower's tone-deaf ear could assure him that there was no stinting of those flourishes. Long drawn out, continued until Hornblower wondered how the trumpeter's breath could last so long; and he could guess from the variation between squeakiness and dullness that the trumpeter was displaying a considerable virtuosity. Two more sentries stood at the foot of the steps beyond, presenting arms; the trumpeter stood at the top of the steps over to one side, and he put his instrument to his lips for a further series of fanfares as Hornblower removed his hat again and he and Barbara began the climb. Tremendous, those flourishes were; even though Hornblower was bracing himself to make his ceremonial entrance into the great hall he could not help but dart a glance at the trumpeter. One glance called for a second glance. Pigtailed and powdered; dressed in a glittering uniform; what was there about that figure to demand his attention? He felt Barbara on his arm stiffen and miss her step. The trumpeter took his instrument from his lips. It was – it was Hudnutt. Hornblower almost dropped his hat with surprise.

But they were over the threshold of the great door, and he must walk steadily forward with Barbara if he were not to ruin all the precious ceremonial. A voice bellowed their names. Ahead of them at the end of an avenue of halberdiers were two chairs of state backed by a semicircle of uniforms and court gowns, with Their Excellencies sitting awaiting them. On Hornblower's last visit the Captain-General had risen and taken seven steps forward to meet him, but that had been when he was a commander-in-chief; now he and Barbara were only private persons and Their Excellencies remained sitting, as he and Barbara went through the moves they had been instructed to make. He bowed to His Excellency, having already been presented to him; he waited while Barbara was presented and made her two curtsies; he bowed again as he was presented to Her Excellency; then they drew a little to one side to await Their Excellencies' words.

'A great pleasure to welcome Lord Hornblower again,' said His Excellency.

'An equally great pleasure to make the acquaintance

of Lady Hornblower,' said Her Excellency.

Hornblower went through the form of consulting with Barbara as to how he should reply.

'My wife and I are deeply appreciative of the great honour done us by our reception,' said Hornblower.

'You are our welcome guests,' said His Excellency, with a finality in his tone that indicated the end of the conversation. Hornblower bowed again, twice, and Barbara went down in two more curtsies, and then they withdrew diagonally so as to allow Their Excellencies no glimpse of their backs. Mendez-Castillo was on hand to present them to other guests, but Hornblower had first to pour out to Barbara his astonishment at the recent encounter.

'Did you see the trumpeter, dear?' he asked.

'Yes,' answered Barbara, in an expressionless tone. 'It was Hudnutt.'

'Amazing,' went on Hornblower. 'Extraordinary. I'd never have believed he was capable of it. He broke out of prison and he climbed that fence and he got himself out of Jamaica over to Puerto Rico – Quite remarkable.'

'Yes,' said Barbara.

Hornblower turned to Mendez-Castillo. 'Your – your *trompetero*,' he said; he was guessing at the Spanish word for 'trumpeter,' and he put his hand up before his mouth in a gesture that indicated what he was trying to say.

'You thought he was good?' asked Mendez-Castillo.

'Superb,' said Hornblower. 'Who is he?'

'The best of the musicians in His Excellency's orchestra,' answered Mendez-Castillo.

Hornblower looked keenly at him, but Mendez-Castillo preserved a diplomatic lack of expression.

'A fellow countryman of yours, sir?' persisted Hornblower.

Mendez-Castillo spread his hands and elevated his shoulders.

'Why should I concern myself about him, my lord?' he countered. 'In any case, art knows no frontiers.'

'No,' said Hornblower. 'I suppose not. Frontiers are elastic in these days. For instance, *señor*, I cannot remember if a convention exists between your Government and mine regarding the mutual return of deserters.'

'A strange coincidence!' said Mendez-Castillo. 'I was investigating that very question a few days ago – quite idly, I assure you, my lord. And I found that no such convention exists. There have been many occasions when, as a matter of goodwill, deserters have been handed back. But most lamentably, my lord, His Excellency has altered his views in that respect since a certain ship – the *Estrella del Sur*, whose name you may possibly recall, my lord – was seized as a slaver outside this very harbour in circumstances that His Excellency found peculiarly irritating.'

There was no hostility; nor was there any hint of glee in Mendez-Castillo's expression as he made this speech. He might as well have been discussing the weather.

'I appreciate His Excellency's kindness and hospitality even more now,' said Hornblower. He hoped he was giving no indication that he was a man who had just been hoist by his own petard.

'I will convey that information to His Excellency,' said Mendez-Castillo. 'Meanwhile there are many guests who are anxious to make Your Lordship's acquaintance and that of Her Ladyship.'

Later in the evening it was Mendez-Castillo who came to Hornblower with a message from Her Excellency, to the effect that the Marquesa quite understood that Barbara might be tired, not having fully recovered yet from her recent experiences, and suggesting that if Her Ladyship and His Lordship chose to retire informally Their Excellencies would understand; and it was Mendez-Castillo who guided them to the far end of the room and through an unobtrusive door to where a backstairs led to their suite. The maid allotted to attend to Barbara was waiting up.

'Ask the maid to go, please,' said Barbara. 'I can look after myself.'

Her tone was still flat and expressionless, and Hornblower looked at her anxiously in fear lest her fatigue should be too much for her. But he did what she asked.

'Can I help in any way, dear?' he asked as the maid withdrew.

'You can stay and talk to me, if you will,' answered Barbara.

'With pleasure, of course,' said Hornblower. There was something strange about this situation. He tried to think of some topic to relieve the tension. 'I still can hardly believe it about Hudnutt –'

'It is about Hudnutt that I wanted to speak,' said Barbara. There was something positively harsh about her voice. She was standing more stiffly and more rigidly than usual – no back could ever be straighter – and she was meeting Hornblower's eyes with a kind of fixed stare like a soldier at attention awaiting sentence of death.

'Whatever is the matter, dearest?'

361

'You are going to hate me,' said Barbara.

'Never! Never!'

'You don't know what it is I'm going to tell you.'

'Nothing you could tell me –'

'Don't say that yet! Wait until you hear. I set Hudnutt free. It was I who arranged for his escape.'

The words came like sudden forked lightning. Or it was as if in a dead calm the maintopsail yard had fallen without warning from its slings on to the deck.

'Dearest,' said Hornblower, unbelieving, 'you're tired. Why don't you –'

'Do you think I'm delirious?' asked Barbara. Her voice was still unlike anything Hornblower had ever heard; so was the brief, bitter laugh that accompanied her words. 'I could be. This is the end of all my happiness.'

'Dearest –' said Hornblower.

'Oh –' said Barbara. There was a sudden overwhelming tenderness in that single sound, and her rigid attitude relaxed, but instantly she stiffened again and snatched back the hands she had held out to him. 'Please listen. I've told you now. I set Hudnutt free – I set him free!'

There could be no doubting that she meant what she said, truth or not. And Hornblower, standing unable to move, staring at her, gradually reached the realization that it was true after all. The realization seeped through the weak places in his unbelief, and as he thought of each piece of evidence it was as if he were marking off a new height in a rising tide.

'That last night at Admiralty House!' he said.

'Yes.'

'You took him out through the wicket gate into the gardens!'

'Yes.'

'Then Evans helped you. He had the key.'

'Yes.'

'And that fellow in Kingston – Bonner – must have helped you, too.'

'You said he was something of a villain. He was ready for adventure at least.'

'But – but the scent the bloodhounds followed?'

'Someone dragged Hudnutt's shirt along the ground on a rope.'

'But – but even so –?' She did not need to tell him; as he said those words he made the next deduction. 'That two hundred pounds!'

'The money I asked you for,' said Barbara, sparing herself nothing. A ten-pound reward would not avail if someone were willing to spend two hundred pounds to help a prisoner escape.

Hornblower knew all about it now. His wife had flouted the law. She had set at naught the authority of the Navy. She had – the rising tide reached suddenly up to a new level.

'It's a felony!' he said. 'You could be transported for life – you could be sent to Botany Bay!'

'Do I care?' exclaimed Barbara. 'Botany Bay! Does that matter now that you know? Now that you'll never love me?'

'Dearest!' Those last words were so fantastically untrue that he had nothing else to say in reply. His mind was hard at work thinking about the effect of all this on Barbara. 'That fellow Bonner – he could blackmail you.'

'He's as guilty as I am,' said Barbara. The unnatural harshness of her voice reached its climax there, and a sudden softness came back into her voice with her next words, an overwhelming tenderness, which she could not help as she smiled her old quizzical smile at this husband of hers. 'You're only thinking about me!'

'Of course,' said Hornblower, surprised.

'But you must think about yourself. I've deceived you. I've cheated you. I took advantage of your kindness, of your generosity – oh!'

The smile changed to tears. It was horrible to see Barbara's face distort itself. She was still standing like a soldier at attention. She would not allow her hands to cover her face; she stood with the tears streaming down and her features working, sparing herself nothing of her shame. He would have taken her into his arms at that moment except that he was still immobilized by astonishment, and Barbara's last words had set a fresh torrent of thought pouring through his mind to hold him paralysed. If any of this were to come out the consequences would be without limit. Half the world would believe that Hornblower, the legendary Hornblower, had connived at the escape and desertion of a petty criminal. Nobody would believe the truth – but if the truth did find credence half the world would laugh at Hornblower being outwitted by his wife. There was a horrible gaping chasm opening right beside him. But there was already this other chasm – this awful distress that Barbara was suffering.

'I was going to tell you,' said Barbara, still erect, blinded by her tears so that she could see nothing. 'When we reached home I was going to tell you. That's what I thought before the hurricane. And there in the deckhouse I was going to tell you, after – after I told you the other. But there wasn't time – you had to leave me. I had to tell you I loved you, first. I told you that, and I should have told you this instead. I should have.'

She was advancing no excuse for herself; she would not plead; she would face the consequences of her act. And there in the deckhouse she had told him she loved him, that she had never loved any other man. The last realization came upon him. Now he could shake off the astonishment, the bewilderment, that had held him helpless up to that moment. Nothing counted in the world except Barbara. Now he could move. Two steps forward and she was in his arms. Her tears wetted his lips.

'My love! My darling!' he said, for, unbelieving and blinded, she had not responded.

And then she knew, in the darkness that surrounded her, and her arms went about him, and there was no such happiness in all the world. There had never been such perfection of harmony. Hornblower found himself smiling. He could laugh out loud out of sheer happiness. That was an old weakness of his, to laugh – to giggle – in moments of crisis. He could laugh now, if he allowed himself – he could laugh at the whole ridiculous incident; he could laugh and laugh. But his judgement told him that laughter might be misunderstood at this moment. He could not help smiling, though, smiling as he kissed.